Praise for
An Unfortunate Prairi

"Harrison takes her time resolving these criminal matters, allowing us to linger in Blue Deer long enough to learn its history, drink in the scenery and laugh at the kinks and quirks of its idiosyncratic residents. No wonder the world-weary Jules came running back home the first chance he got—the place is heaven."
—Marilyn Stasio, *The New York Times Book Review*

"Harrison writes with humor, intelligence and heart."
—*Publishers Weekly*

"Harrison can really write. *An Unfortunate Prairie Occurrence* is so full of pithy and thoughtful language that almost every page has at least one memorable line." —*The Seattle Times*

ALSO BY JAMIE HARRISON

The River View
The Center of Everything
The Widow Nash
Blue Deer Thaw
Going Local
The Edge of the Crazies

AN UNFORTUNATE *PRAIRIE* OCCURRENCE

A Jules Clement Novel

JAMIE HARRISON

COUNTERPOINT
CALIFORNIA

AN UNFORTUNATE PRAIRIE OCCURRENCE

This is a work of fiction. All of the characters, organizations, and events portrayed in this novel are either products of the author's imagination or are used fictitiously.

Library of Congress Cataloging-in-Publication Data
Names: Harrison, Jamie, 1960- author.
Title: An unfortunate prairie occurrence : a Jules Clement mystery / Jamie Harrison.
Description: First Counterpoint edition. | California : Counterpoint, 2024.
Identifiers: LCCN 2024010032 | ISBN 9781640092983 (trade paperback) | ISBN 9781640092990 (ebook)
Subjects: LCSH: Clement, Jules (Fictitious character)—Fiction. | Blue Deer (Mont. : Imaginary place)—Fiction. | Sheriffs—Fiction. | LCGFT: Detective and mystery fiction. | Novels.
Classification: LCC PS3558.A6712 U54 2024 | DDC 813/.54—dc23/eng/20240301
LC record available at https://lccn.loc.gov/2024010032

Series design by Jaya Miceli
Cover design by Victoria Maxfield
Book design by Laura Berry

COUNTERPOINT
Los Angeles and San Francisco, CA
www.counterpointpress.com

Printed in the United States of America

10 9 8 7 6 5 4 3 2 1

*To my parents, who aren't a bit
like any of the parents in this book,
with love*

Oh, let it go.

—THE DYING EMMANUEL LEWIS
WHEN ASKED, WHILE IN THE
PRESENCE OF HIS ASSAILANTS,
WHO HAD SHOT HIM

CONTENTS

1	Bones	3
2	Names	8
3	The Ladies	34
4	The Elements	65
5	Dancing	80
6	Cactus	108
7	On Safari	130
8	A Leg	161
9	Snakes	186
10	Wind	218
11	A Night on the Town	241
12	All Souls	265
13	The Poor Man's Gun	283
14	Collectors	300
15	The Tall Boy	331
16	Picture This	349
17	The Mummy	372
18	More Adventures in the Out-of-Doors	393
19	The Oldest Sin	416
20	Family	430

1 *Bones*

BLUE DEER BULLETIN
SHERIFF'S REPORT, WEEK OF OCTOBER 10–16

October 10—A woman complained about trash blowing out of a neighbor's yard and into hers. An officer talked to the neighbor.

October 11—An officer responded to a child custody dispute at the Small Planet Daycare. Peace was achieved.

October 12—A woman reported neighbors were dumping refuse in her garbage cans, then making rude gestures and denying they had done so when she complained. An officer talked to the neighbors.

A citizen reported youths smoking a suspicious substance on Magpie Island. An officer warned the youths and took them home.

October 13—A man was reported shooting at phone and electric poles on Seventh Street. The man was apprehended.

October 14—A man reported that a bear was breaking the branches of his apple tree. He was advised to leave the bear alone.

A woman reported that her dog had been stolen, as well as a dog bowl and a sack of toys.

October 15—An abandoned van with mirror windows was reported on Barney Road. The caller worried someone might be inside.

October 16—A man reported that a group of hunters shot a deer within fifty feet of his house, hitting one of his cars, and left without making restitution. Officers are investigating.

THE WOODS WERE FILLED WITH IDIOTS, THE PLAINS with relatively intelligent local boys. The idiots struggled up mountain trails and lingered in dense, sterile stands of lodgepole pine, aiming at stray mice and wind shadows, marching into town every afternoon to drink whiskey and schnapps. The local boys lurked on the river bottoms, keeping their beer cold and safe in cottonwood roots, or simply stopped on dirt two-tracks and sighted in a promising specimen over their car hood.

Big game season had only begun at dawn on Sunday, and as an opening salvo that temperate, misty Monday morning, an antelope hunter from Cleveland blew off his best friend's hand. They were only twenty yards from their truck in a wooded campground parking lot, and the "something" the shooter had seen flitting through the early-morning murk proved to have been an old copy of the *Blue Deer Bulletin*, left behind at a campsite.

Several other unfortunate things happened in Absaroka County, Montana, that October 17:

A woman named Mary McLinchey walked into the sheriff's office in Blue Deer at 8:30 a.m. holding a year-old baby and reported that she had been raped. Grace Marble, the dispatcher, gave her an extra sweater, a cup of coffee and a doughnut, and after one of the deputies, Caroline

Fair, took a preliminary report, McLinchey was driven to the hospital.

In a valley ten miles south of Blue Deer, a small woman named Edie Linders screamed in rage and threw a peanut butter sandwich at a tall man named Jules Clement. Jules happened to be the sheriff of Absaroka County, and he was late for work.

A former county native named Wayne Contway, now residing in the maximum-security wing at Deer Lodge, the state penitentiary, gave an interview in which he did an about-face on a decade of noisy innocence and admitted that not only had he killed his neighbor's wife, he could show the authorities where to find her body in the alpine backcountry.

A Maryland hotel cook, in the fourth hour of a beer-drinking tour with his area hosts, suddenly demanded they stop the car on a particularly scenic bridge over the Yellowstone River south of Blue Deer. He climbed out, stripped off his shirt, dove into the river, and did not reappear.

At three that afternoon, an elderly obstetrician-gynecologist, Hans Craitson, shot arrows through his own picture window and inadvertently put one into the ear of a neighbor's Jack Russell. He confided to Sheriff Clement that the dog was a nasty piece of shit but his real target had been the tires of his son's Plymouth. The son demanded the father be arrested. Jules settled for confiscating the bow.

A couple from Pennsylvania set up camp on the tip of Magpie Island, which lay just southwest of town in the middle of the Yellowstone River. Once the tent was up, the man wandered off into the maze of willow saplings to answer the long-delayed call of nature, and pried up a large rock to make a hole. Underneath the rock he discovered the perfectly articulated bones of a human foot.

Jules, who'd begun to hate his profession for intellectual as well as visceral reasons, took everything personally that day. Being the town thug (this is how he saw the job lately; all its interesting moral ambiguity had been swamped by banality) filled him with self-pity and boredom. Most of his constituents filled him with annoyance and dread. The victims he dealt with filled him with pity and horror. That Monday's flurry of activity only promised to give Jules less time to think, or at least less time to stop thinking over a drink.

Late that evening he sat at his desk, alone in the station but for the night dispatcher, hunkered down over a staff schedule in the yellow light of a desk lamp. He'd spent most of the afternoon searching the Yellowstone for the Maryland swan diver. The diver's hysterical friends, who had said repeatedly that he was the kind of guy who just wanted to have fun, thought that maybe he was pulling their legs, hiding in some willows downriver and giggling. Jules had answered that people didn't usually joke around after a thirty-foot dive into three feet of water; he said their friend had turned into a turtle.

They'd looked for the turtle until dusk, then tarped a hundred square feet of Magpie Island in the last light of the day. Jules, peering down at the foot and part of an ankle with a flashlight, wasn't sure if the evident age of the bones would be a blessing or a curse. The other old body would have to wait even longer. Wayne Contway, a former hunting guide, claimed to have buried her eight miles from a trailhead in the Absaroka-Beartooth Wilderness, somewhere in the middle of two thousand square miles of grizzlies that were slow to hibernate in a bad berry year. That trip, probably a two-nighter, would have to wait until later in the week, and Jules would have to bring the asshole along for directions. Maybe Contway had confessed for the sake of some fresh air.

Both Cleveland hunters would survive, though a great friendship had probably ended. Mary McLinchey, the woman who'd been raped, claimed to be fine, but she had more of Jules's sympathy than the other wounded or the dead. The man who had raped her was his biggest problem: Mary was the third woman to be attacked since summer.

Jules worked until eleven, then walked to the Blue Bat Tavern. There were a dozen men and women scattered around the dark room, and he knew almost all of them because he'd been born in Blue Deer, and he liked bars. Delly Bane, the owner, recognized potential entertainment and bought him a whiskey. That afternoon's *Bulletin* had been a hot commodity, and Jules's fellow drinkers were frankly curious, torn between the idiotic hunting accident, a tourist who'd misjudged the river, and a local who'd finally confessed. No one mentioned the rape, and the island bones had been discovered after the paper went to press. At midnight Jules headed home to his own house, to sleep alone. He had no intention of apologizing to Edie.

2 Names

JULES CLEMENT WAS BROWN-HAIRED, TALL AND angular. He was thirty-five and essentially solitary, currently locked into an unhappy phase in an at best intermittent love life. He had a fairly good sense of humor, but it had been beaten down of late by work. He was good at his job, despite a lack of self-confidence or despotic practicality. Jules was that final anomaly, a liberal officer of the law.

Whatever else could be said about Jules, no one had ever claimed he looked like a cop when out of uniform. A bartender, maybe, a carpenter or even a ski bum in his healthier moments. This morning, waiting in a corner of the Honorable Miles Birdland's office to have an arrest warrant signed, he looked a bit like a fishing guide: he was wet to the knees from a dawn search for the missing Maryland diver. Four boats, twenty other searchers on the banks, all of it a massive waste of time undertaken largely to save a fisherman a nasty sight a week down the line.

Jules paged through the judge's magazines and politely avoided looking directly at the other people in the room.

Neil Amundsen, the judge's grandson and a deputy county attorney, was arguing, and he sounded reasonable enough until the gist of the conversation sank in.

"Mr. Jump had custody for September; Mrs. Jump had

custody for October. It's spelled out in their agreement, alternate months."

Birdland's voice was querulous, dangerous. "He wanted to take the dog hunting, right?"

"Yes sir," said Peter Johansen, the defense attorney. "Their agreement cites that right, for the dog's own welfare. This is petty stuff."

"The mention is vague, and any hunting was to depend on Mrs. Jump's assent," Neil began. "Instead of asking her, Mr. Jump kidnapped the dog—"

"Spare me," said Miles Birdland. "You keep your mouth shut as well for a moment, Mr. Johansen." He shuffled through his papers, a thin, tall man, quick and graceful in his mid-seventies, with a border of dark hair and a bald spot that managed to look distinguished. He tended to listen intently while blinking slowly, at regular intervals Jules had timed during dozens of tedious testimonies. Sometimes Birdland seemed to simply fix on a face and unleash poetic venom, the way a shark might fix on a particular pair of thrashing legs at a crowded beach and bite. The man had a nose for assholes.

"This is a clear case of custodial interference," said Neil. "He came onto her property, broke her window to open her door—"

"If you'd like to push for burglary or property damage, be my guest. Waste county money. But I am not going to allow you to bring criminal charges against a man for taking his dog from his ex-wife—"

"Your Honor, you're showing bias by saying 'his' dog."

There was an ominous silence. Jules lifted his eyes and met Peter's. Peter gave a tiny, desperate shake of the head and stayed poker-faced. He'd gone back to being an attorney a few months earlier, after playing hooky as a reporter for several years, and since he'd taken on county defense work he'd had time to fish exactly twice. Jules, who'd only fished three times in the same span, lacked the guts to inquire if the income boost had been worth the pain.

The judge tapped his pen violently on a pile of paperwork. "Neil, do you think I'm blessed with an abundance of time?"

Neil, only in his late twenties, had a surly look on his face that tamped down the handsome features and made them small and mean. "No sir."

"What do you imagine I'd rather be doing?"

Jules feigned interest in a *National Geographic* article on mining in Indonesia. Peter stared at the ceiling. "Taking a walk?" asked Neil with just an edge of the smart-ass.

"Sitting with your dying grandmother!" screamed Birdland. "Now either go for a b-and-e or leave it to civil court!"

Meetings with Birdland often ended in this fashion. He'd been district judge for thirty years and tended toward brutal efficiency during court time, though his written opinions were Gothic and dense. You couldn't count on his sympathies, which his defenders took as proof of a lack of bias, and which nonfans, including Peter Johansen, put down to everything from indigestion to reactionary politics to simple, old-fashioned meanness. Miles Birdland didn't have a predictable knee-jerk reaction to certain types, had no special blood lust for teenage dropouts, drinking mothers, child support shirkers, pot smokers versus drinkers versus pill poppers.

"Why are you here?" he asked Jules abruptly.

"Alston Hantz blew his parole twice over the weekend, and I need a warrant signed."

"Jesus," said the judge. The top of his head was still pink with rage. "Enough is enough."

"You would think," said Jules. "But Alston doesn't think."

"Did he at least try to be sneaky?"

"Showed up drunk as a monkey for happy hour at the Blue Bat on Friday, then hit the Bucket Sunday afternoon."

"I won't feel much compunction about sending him out of the county," said Birdland, handing Jules the warrant and moving on to the rest of his pile.

As if he ever felt compunction, Jules thought. He started to edge out the door, but the judge spoke again. "There's a rumor going 'round that you found a body on the island," he said, signing papers as fast as his secretary could hand them to him.

"Yes sir," said Jules. "Yesterday afternoon."

"Old or new?" The judge didn't look up.

"Old," said Jules. "Maybe several decades, unless there's something funny in the soil. I won't know more until I get out of here."

Birdland looked up and Jules kept his face unreadable, not a difficult task as his left jaw was crooked from a horse kick. That corner of his mouth tended to curl up in a gentle and often unfelt smile.

"Sorry to keep you from more important tasks," said Birdland with great sarcasm.

"That's, of course, not how I meant the comment," said Jules evenly.

The judge had missed a page, and when his secretary murmured a mild corrective he snatched it from her hand. "Well, good," he said finally. "I was wondering if we'd have another mess on our hands, if I should simply retire now, let Axel age himself."

Miles Birdland was not given to humor; in the words of his tenacious secretary, now staring fixedly at the diplomas on the wall, the man was too dry to spit. Axel Scotti was the county attorney, Neil's boss, and he wanted Birdland's job, though probably not enough to run against an institution in the next election.

"No mess," said Jules. "I'm only worried about the rapist."

"I'd be surprised if you catch that man before I retire. I knew someone like him once, a man who kept his evil invisible in the daytime. This person could be the town's finest teacher, saving up pain for the night."

Encouraging words. Jules felt a glimmer of pity for Neil, who crawled in to apologize to his grandfather as Jules was walking out. It wasn't always easy, everyone being related to everyone else. Hardly any of the first settlers in Absaroka County had stuck it out, but in a town of new blood, virtually none had oozed through the courthouse walls. Until Axel Scotti had pushed the county's lenient standards of nepotism that spring by hiring a twenty-six-year-old with only one year of experience, no one in town had seemed to mind that Scotti was married to Jules's cousin Jetta, or that Jules and Peter had been roommates in college, or that Birdland's daughter and Scotti's wife had been inseparable since kindergarten. Now Jules found himself minding; it was part of the reason he'd hired two out-of-towners as deputies that summer.

"What are you smiling at?" snapped Neil.

"Life's infinite variety," said Jules.

He walked down the hall toward the sheriff's department, past a procession of flanking photographs, black-and-white images of Absaroka County's increasingly inbred legal system. The most recent photos came last: Jules himself, looking fettered in a tie; Axel Scotti, fifty, vain and charcoal-haired; and Miles Birdland, who'd looked every bit as poisonous twenty years before as he did on the bench now.

The older photos nearer to the courtroom echoed the current ones: Jules's father, Ansel Clement, was framed above the office dates 1966–1972; Scotti's great-uncle Tomas had ruled as county attorney and judge for twenty-five years, from World War II into the early sixties. In a county with only one hundred years of history, such a chunk of time meant having your name on at least a street. There was a Scotti Avenue and a Scotti wing on the hospital and a Scotti band shell. Even Ansel Clement had rated a playground. His photo was also displayed in the west wing of the building near the sheriff's department, part of a small panel dedicated to what Jules thought of as the working dead. The end of Ansel's tenure, 1972, had also been the year he ticketed the wrong trucker. Jules had been thirteen, past the age to find a playground with his last name much consolation for a father's shotgun murder.

In the property records room he checked through deeds and surveys, scanning the shape and ownership of Magpie Island back to the first records. The ass end of the island, the downriver tip, had been much bigger in the 1940 survey, having gained considerable ground in a 1921 flood, and had lost this same ground gradually over the next fifty years until another big flood in 1993 changed its shape. The current owner was absentee, and the former owner, now deceased, had owned the land through the sixties and seventies. He'd bought it in 1966 from Joseph Clement Ganter, who'd acquired it in 1936 as part of an inheritance from his grandfather, a homesteader named Jens Ansel Clement.

The family relationships weren't spelled out, but Jules knew them because they were—again—his own. Joseph was Axel Scotti's father-in-law and Jules's second or third cousin, though Jules regarded him as an uncle; Jens was Jules's great-

great-grandfather. Jules's own grandfather Charlie had gotten a 640-acre parcel for an eighteenth birthday gift, too, but he'd pissed it away and died before World War II; his widow had married an equally short-lived pharmacist. As an end result, the Ganter side of the family had fifteen or so thousand acres, and the Clements had two small bungalows in town, a collection of old cars, and the habit of travel.

Jules drummed his pencil violently until the clerk looked up in annoyance, and then he simply stared blankly into space. Through the glass wall he saw Neil Amundsen, tall and graceful, strut down the hallway toward a dark-haired woman in a deputy's uniform who was talking to a parole officer. Neil smiled and spoke to the woman, and Jules, rather than waiting to see if the woman smiled back, lurched to his feet, threw the files back into the drawer, and headed for the hall to break things up.

Neil was joking about a lunatic Caroline Fair had ferried from the Greyhound station to the hospital the afternoon before, then retrieved from the hospital and brought to the jail that morning after the man's medication had worn off and a doctor had quickly and accurately diagnosed him as criminally insane. "Peter needed a can of Lysol to introduce himself."

"He was fairly fragrant," said Caroline mildly. "They were going to try to clean him up at the hospital."

"Well," said Neil, "he'd wiped himself with you-know-what."

Caroline looked blank.

"Excrement," said Jules. "That's shit to you, Neil."

Neil stared. Jules decided to be unrepentant. "Your day getting any better?"

"It was," said Neil.

"Well," said Jules, "I'd hate to get in the way of progress. He turned to Caroline. "Did you get anywhere with Mary McLinchey?"

"I ran more pictures by her," said Caroline, glancing nervously at Jules, then at Neil's angry back.

"Anyone look familiar?"

"No, but she keeps going for the same physical type, brunette with light eyes, blue or gray. She's been comparing other people's heights, and she thinks he was between five-ten and six feet."

They started walking toward the station offices. "Can you take my Thursday shift?" asked Jules.

The look she gave him was mildly bemused. Caroline specialized in such looks, from heavy-lidded eyes. Her face was fine, very pale compared to her almost-black hair, but with gazes that said "Are we both speaking English, little boy?" she became austere and forbidding. Jules thought she was beautiful. Peter thought she looked cold, which didn't mean he didn't agree. "For the Contway trip? When are you planning to leave?"

"Tomorrow morning, early."

Bemusement turned to disbelief. "In a blizzard?"

"What are you talking about?"

"Ed said we were getting a blizzard at the end of the week, that there's a front moving down. He said you could see it starting in the air."

Jules turned to stare through a window at the dulcet afternoon and found that the air was crisp but otherwise invisible. Ed Winton was the oldest deputy, and his sense of humor was ripe. "You believe everything he says to you?"

"Not everything," said Caroline. "But when I took this job, I remember you telling me to listen to Ed."

When she'd taken the job there'd been the implicit notion that she'd listen to Jules.

ABSAROKA COUNTY, MONTANA, was six thousand square miles, a long, narrow county in the southwestern part of the state, running down the border of the Rocky Mountain front to Yellowstone Park. It had lush valleys and trout-laden rivers, forbidding mountains and unkind weather. The people were similarly varied and always had been: on the one hand, Montana had sent the first woman to the U.S. Senate before women actually had the right to vote; on the other hand, Blue Deer schoolboys had been allowed to carry guns to the classroom until 1911.

Jules ate a sandwich in the sun in the back parking lot of the station, leaning against the building with a newspaper spread on a car hood in front of him. It was the one place the mayor, who always parked in front so that people knew he actually worked, would never find him. While he ate, he read the weather forecast in Monday afternoon's paper, which promised that the world would continue to be "mild and seasonable." Not that *seasonable* meant much in Montana, but only the most paranoid individual would take it for a blizzard forecast. Possibly Ed was using Caroline for an elaborate joke.

Jules walked back inside and approached Grace Marble, the station's sixty-year-old dispatcher-commandant, at an angle. She finished with a nasty-sounding dog complaint and glared up at him over her glasses.

"What time are they taking off from Deer Lodge tomorrow with that asshole?"

She raised a single eyebrow. "Mr. Contway and his escort were planning to leave after lunch and be here for dinner. I had the impression regular meals were important."

"Will you call for the new weather report?"

The other black eyebrow arched as she reached for the phone. Grace had a talented face, and with it had trained almost everyone to follow silent commands. Five minutes later she marched to his desk, cleared her throat, and read aloud from notes.

"We can expect snow above five thousand feet, locally heavy, before dark tomorrow. The lows shouldn't be too bad, ten or twenty, but the white stuff should continue through Friday."

"How much?"

Grace smiled sweetly. "Hardly anything in town, but a shitload where you're going, dear."

Jules mimicked this last clause as she walked away and he dialed. It was mid-October, after all; at eight thousand feet it might as well be January. Given a choice, why would anyone sleep outside in such a season? The warden of Deer Lodge sounded nonplussed when Jules stated the impossibility of a fifteen-mile round-trip on horseback in two feet of new snow. The warden suggested he send Wayne Contway that afternoon anyway and let Jules store him in Absaroka County. Wayne was all packed, it seemed, and that way Jules would be ready to go into the mountains at the drop of a hat. Maybe Wayne would feel more at home in Blue Deer, volunteer some information. Jules should also know that the horseback idea had an innate flaw: Wayne had found considerable solace in prison food.

"We're not just talking chubby," said the warden.

Jules added another item to his day's list, a reminder to request the outfitter to bring along a draft horse. They set the departure date for the following Monday, and the warden promised he'd send good help. Jules shook off a vision of pit bulls in crew cuts and tried to get off the phone, but the man had one last thought: just between him and Jules, no one would be heartbroken if Wayne should fail to make the return trip. A coronary would be likely, and Wayne was the right shape to roll down an incline like a greasy snowball.

"He's a pain in the ass?" asked Jules.

"He's a world-class whiner," answered the warden. "It's hard to put into words."

Ah, thought Jules, staring at the calendar after he'd hung up. Another reason to go on living.

ANYONE WHO'S BEEN shot, battered, ridden horses, incurred a hangover, or been in an auto accident has a personal concept of the fragility of bones, but in Jules's case all these pleasant experiences had been amplified by a Scandinavian sensibility and a previous career as an archaeologist. Jules had not only sifted through bones but thought about them, deeply and at length, and for once could actually bring real knowledge to bear on a job riddled with gas station robberies, domestic abuse, mistreated animals, and bad checks. He understood, more thoroughly than most people who attempt to keep public order, how recently a shell of civility had covered life.

Much of the digging Jules had done around the Mediterranean had revealed violent death, but such death had been run-of-the-mill. Sack, rape, burn, and break the crockery for some poor studious fool to puzzle over centuries later, smug in the belief that it would never happen to him. Even lovely Blue Deer could erode such a feeling of safety, if you saw it from the inside out as Jules had over the last three years. When he'd come home and decided to be a cop, he'd underestimated the vast difference between wiggly live problems and long-dead ones. If he'd had any sense, he'd have continued his earlier career in his home state by excavating Paleolithic campsites and buffalo jumps. Instead he'd fallen into his late father's profession out of a combination of laziness and a fuzzy sense of duty, tumbled into what his mother, who'd recently been reading a good deal of popular psychology, called "the father thing."

That morning he'd loaded his old tools—screens and brushes, picks and shovels—from a large dusty crate into his patrol car trunk. It was almost two by the time he moved a stack of mail and a spool of measuring tape so that Ed Winton could fit his ample butt on the passenger seat. Wesley Tenn followed them over the island bridge in the county van. For the first half hour they checked out the lay of the island, cleaning up obviously recent trash and finding a sun-bleached rib in the willows near the northern edge in the process. A vertebra poked out of the eroded bank, but no one had noticed it, and possibly no one would have if the camper hadn't dug an impromptu latrine. The bones were deeper where the bank had eroded, buried by successive layers of silt while the top half gradually disappeared downriver in flood after flood. The foot discovered under the rock was only eight inches deep, and whoever had buried the body had probably thrown it in that way, hastily and facedown and on a slant, heaping it with rocks that still showed clearly under the silt in the bank.

Perhaps someone had found the missing spine and ribs and skull decades earlier, far downriver. Jules would have to call the departments along the length of the Yellowstone, maybe even a chunk of the Missouri—could a skull navigate a dam? Wesley Tenn pointed out that where he came from, in New Mexico, stray skulls were always bobbing out of the gravel, freed from old graves; everyone assumed they were native, and no one worried much about them. This was probably just another forlorn settler buried in the wrong place. Jules decided that he liked this theory.

Harvey Meyers showed up at five, just in time to relieve Ed

and take part in the heavy digging. Harvey, who always had to take an unhappy stand on something, bemoaned his luck for the next hour until Wesley, who'd started the job only that summer and was still capable of being annoyed, began deliberately shoveling sand in his direction. They staked the area, boxed cross sections of the silt, and removed the dirt above the skeleton itself, moving up from the feet. The exposed tibia were long and elegant, and there was clear evidence of a well-healed break in the right ankle. The legs weren't old relative to others Jules had dug from the ground—the man had died sometime in the first half of the century—and from another perspective they were big strong young bones, from a man in his prime, no younger than twenty or older than thirty.

"You're sure?" asked Wesley, confused by Jules's unexpected expertise.

"Or a six-foot woman who never reached puberty," said Jules, labeling another manila envelope.

He wasn't really being glib: the pelvis was almost certainly male. The remnants of clothing—pale canvas pants and cotton boxers, a simple leather belt with a buckle shaped like a horse's head, and equally fine shoes—were post-World War I but probably pre-Korea.

Wesley turned the buckle over in his hands. "Brass," he said, "but still shiny. It's pretty."

"That's gold," said Jules. "This probably wasn't your ordinary cowboy."

The shoes were beside the feet rather than on them. Ed, who'd stayed on to watch, was amused and popped a second beer while he opined that removing shoes seemed more the sign of a suicide than a murder.

"He didn't bury himself," said Jules mildly. And whoever had buried him hadn't done so with respect. In almost a decade of digging up bodies, the only times they'd ever faced the earth had been in mass graves, and then only when buried by their enemies. A half hour later they found two flattened slugs in the sand inside the pelvis. Even Ed agreed that not many people intent on peace shot themselves twice in the gut.

It was a beautiful afternoon, sixty or so in the sun and typical of an exceptionally late and easy fall: one hard frost in early September that a few lucky gardeners had managed to survive, good fishing without much wind yet, almost too hot for bird hunting. It wasn't like a fall day in the Midwest or Northeast, with the cold wet sweet smell of dying leaves and apples; or the fecund dormancy of the South; or the frozen, dusty air of the higher Southwest, which felt as if everything once alive had simply blown away.

From where Jules stood on the river, fall smelled of clean clay, water, moistened rock and drying grass and pine. If you were to die of a belly wound, facedown in the wet sand, this was as beautiful a place to do it as any. The soft breeze blended with the sound of water and swirling aspen leaves, and they dug in the midst of violently colored gold-and-orange willow saplings and garnet dogwood. Jules filtered sand, scraping patiently away at a top layer of teenagers' cigarette butts a few feet in either direction around the body. His familiarity with this end of the island dated back to high school, when it had been the best place to drink and smoke. It still was, despite several new houses and a sheriff whose life experience had made him scarily attuned to misbehavior. Both he and Harvey had giggled out here twenty years earlier, and giggled again now when they found an especially antique roach clip. They didn't show it to Ed, who was now in his mid-fifties and had once been their worst nightmare.

Within the bones they found the remnants of what might

have been a leather wallet with some coins, a nail scissors, and no trace of identification. Most of the coins were from the twenties and thirties, with a couple of strays, higher in the sand, from later decades. They also found a piece of tattered plaid, a tin of chewing tobacco, and, beneath the pelvis in the finest sieve, a nice pile of blond pubic hair. Jules felt pretty smug about this last, and even Harvey, almost pigment-free himself, became punchy toward dusk and made jokes about naturally blond cowboys.

Wesley, whose middle name was Arturo and whose mother had been born on a Sonoran ranch, wondered how people so waxy had won the West.

"We bred like rabbits," said Harvey, one of eight children. "Still do."

"I come from a pretty big family," said Wesley. "I have six aunts, seven uncles, and God knows who's past them."

"We bred at the right time in the right place," said Harvey. "Gave everyone smallpox and moved on in."

Jules, lying on the still-warm sand with a beer, recalled that Harvey had been surprisingly fond of history in high school. "You ride, Harvey?"

"Pardon?" He looked alarmed, light blue eyes bobbing up and down. "Horses? Is this about riding in with Wayne Contway?"

Jules closed his eyes.

Harvey was querulous now. "Are you asking if I can or if I will? I have Donnie's game on Monday, and my back's been bad since that shoplifter took me out. I shouldn't be looking for any goddamn body in the mountains."

So much for the pioneer cowboy. Jules opened his eyes again on Wesley, in his early thirties and robust. "How about you, Wesley?"

"Asthma. I'd stop breathing after ten minutes." He smiled. "I'd love to go back in those mountains, but being near a horse'd kill me."

Horses. Jules's broken jaw ached on cue, and his ass felt a great anticipatory weariness.

"Take Caroline," said Wesley. "I think she's pretty comfortable on them."

Jules scowled and finished his beer. There was the greater problem of being uncomfortable around Caroline. "You're not off the hook, Harvey."

"Contway doesn't want to show you where he buried that lady," said Ed, who weighed two-fifty and would have killed a horse. "He just wants to run away. You'd best wear that bulletproof vest."

TO GET TO Joseph Ganter's ranch, Jules took the freeway east for ten miles, then cut south toward the already white Absaroka Range for another six or so, climbing above the creek bottom on a winding clay-and-boulder road. Jules would have driven it a dozen times a day for the sake of living there. Great gusts of wind made the chokecherry and aspen leap and shimmer on the hillsides; six experimental wind generators were perched on the bench above, only a mile from the tiny and rarely usable airport. Farther up the road, on a hillside, lay a tiny cemetery and a boarded-up Lutheran church.

By the time Jules crossed Mission Creek it was almost too dark to see anymore. He drove another half mile along a road lined with willows, past great round bales of hay, a large wooden barn, and assorted sheds and machinery. Joseph's house was large and stucco, with a deep-eaved wraparound porch and a dormered second story, functional rather than showy. He'd returned with an Italian wife after World War II and built the house for a large family, a self-fulfilling prophecy.

Jetta Scotti, Joseph's daughter and Axel Scotti's wife, was in the kitchen surrounded by charts and lists for her parents' fiftieth anniversary party, scheduled for that Friday. Her friend Flo Amundsen, Miles Birdland's daughter and Neil Amundsen's mother, was in the process of peeling the foil from a bottle of wine. Jetta smiled but looked weary; Flo pretended Jules didn't exist, which was par for the course, but automatically poured a third glass of wine. Jules, usually temperate before card games, noticed it was one of the good bottles ordered for the party and decided not to be rude by declining.

Jules heard the sound of a shotgun. Flo twitched.

"Dad's out behind the barn," said Jetta. "Taking his mood out on the old roosters."

"Since all the hens have been gone for a year it only makes sense," said Jules. "But why now?"

Jetta shrugged and looked out the window. "He's got the corral light on."

A blast echoed on cue. Flo jumped again and looked pained. "This is just awful," she said.

Jules wasn't sure if she was referring to the roosters' fate or the general mood. "He's still not happy about the party, huh?"

"My best hope is that they'll celebrate their fiftieth with a divorce," said Jetta.

"Where's your mother?"

"She ran away to town a couple of hours ago."

"You should cancel while you still have a chance," said Jules. "You should never have given them a choice on food."

"I didn't," said Jetta testily. "He had a shit fit about the mail order from the place Alice recommended. And it's not just the menu, it's the guest list, the decorations, everything. He has one of those headaches, and the roosters have taken to crowing all afternoon and never in the morning."

Jules's enthusiasm for cards continued to dwindle. "What did he want to eat instead of Italian delicacies?"

"Beef."

"He doesn't even *like* beef." Joseph had often said he'd seen too many cow assholes to want to eat what grew around them.

"I know."

"Who doesn't he want to come?"

Jetta shrugged, looked miserable, and took a healthy gulp of wine. She'd inherited classic northern Italian looks from her mother: blue eyes, gold skin, chestnut hair. Laura Ganter had been a little snotty about Jetta's having crossed "the veal line" to marry Axel, a definite Sicilian.

"He's being very difficult," said Flo emphatically. "No appreciation at all for what we've gone through."

It was typical of Flo to include herself in whatever drama happened to be playing out in someone else's life. She looked just as you'd expect from her name, big and bumptious and curly-haired. Another ten pounds and she'd be bovine rather than cherubic, lumpen rather than bouncy all over. Neil had the same good-natured look on an angular frame; it didn't mean a thing, and the impression disappeared as soon as he opened his mouth. And Flo's veneer was growing thin as she aged. It wasn't the fact of the wrinkles, but where they lay, the expression they'd entrenched: a peevish, wronged look that no number of strained smiles could quite dispel.

Flo made money off the county, like everyone else in her family. She counseled part-time, a bizarre career choice in that she was possibly the least empathetic person Jules had ever met, with a high-pitched voice that echoed in his head after the briefest conversation. It wasn't hard to imagine where Neil had come by his single drip of compassion. Miles Birdland, to give him credit, rarely sentenced people to consult his daughter.

Jetta rattled on about the horrors of party planning, the constant arguments between her parents about the guest list, the menu, who should be encouraged to give a toast and who should be shot dead if they so much as opened their mouths. It was incomprehensible to Jules that an otherwise rational woman in her forties still put up with this kind of infighting. The other four children were all flying in just in time for the party, and Jules, who liked Jetta's siblings well enough but thought this was unfair, hoped that the cleanup was just as messy as the planning.

"It would be helpful if you could get him out of here," said Flo, "so we can do the seating chart in his absence."

Jules had wondered why she was surrounded by paper circles and tiny yellow name tags. "That's why I'm here," he said. "Poker."

"What's new in town?" asked Jetta. She was sticking the yellow name tags on the fingers of her left hand, looking as if she'd like to cry. "I feel like I've been up here for weeks."

"Not much," said Jules.

"I heard something about a body on the scanner this afternoon," said Flo.

Jules hated scanners. He would have thought Flo, a true snob, would be above them, and withheld comment to torture her.

Jetta slapped a half dozen slips onto one circle. "Natural, or something for you and Axel to worry about?"

"Don't leave Neil out," said Flo.

Two more gun blasts. Real progress was being made. Jules considered the promise of Joseph in a foul mood and wished he'd called in sick for poker and simply gone to bed. He imagined the old man pulling the birds from under mangers, tracking them down behind saddles. There were at least six roosters, five too many. "Hard to tell. The guy had been there a long time."

"What do you mean by 'long'?" asked Flo. "Months or years?"

"Years." Another two explosions.

"Axel's going to love this," said Jetta.

"Maybe he'll give the case to Neil," said Flo.

"There's not much chance of it turning into a case after so long," said Jules. "But I happen to know Neil has plenty to do."

"None of it's interesting," said Flo. "Top of his class and he's handling DUIs."

Jetta finished another circle for the seating chart and tossed it to Flo like a Frisbee. To Jules, the table looked like a crime scene map or some horrible record of a nightclub fire.

"It's his first year out of law school," said Jules. "Why shouldn't he handle DUIs?"

Flo's mouth tensed but she studied the seating chart table instead of biting back. "Jetta, will this work, or were Merle Ott and Rance's wife naughty together once upon a time?"

Jetta peered at the circles. "I forgot. They had an affair when we were in high school. Better move Rance to Boskirk's table."

"Don't," said Jules. "Rance shot Boskirk's dog. Why are you inviting him?"

Jetta lifted an eyebrow. "We're inviting everyone. Since when did it matter if they like each other? Weren't you here to talk to Dad?"

"Is Axel playing tonight?"

"Yes," said Jetta. "Please lose to him. I'd like a vacation when this is all over."

Another shot echoed, and the last of the sparrows flew out of the cottonwood next to the kitchen window. "He always hated those roosters," said Jetta. "Not that Mom liked them."

"What about chopping off their heads?"

"I think he finds this more satisfying," said Jetta. "He said he was going to shoot them like skeet, but with his old Colt. And if they run away he doesn't have to actually catch them."

By the time Jules walked behind the barn, Joseph was digging at the edge of the circle of light behind the stable next to a heap of bloody feathers, while Max, the ancient barn cat, boxed at the still-jerking legs and wings. Joseph arched an eyebrow at Jules and went back to chipping at the ground with as much ease as the rock and clay and arthritis would allow.

"I was finally in a bad enough mood to take care of this problem. If I hadn't done something, I would have kept the bad mood and lost at cards."

"And now you'll win?"

"And now I'll win."

Joseph Ganter was normally a subtle man, hard to read and hard to annoy. He was seventy-six, tall and unstooped, with long straight arms, slightly bowed legs, a high domed forehead, and nearly white hair. Joseph was elegant, handsome, and more than a little arrogant. He reacted to most problems with humor, and you could grade their importance only by the bite in the jokes, but tonight Jules sensed an inky mood.

He leaned against Joseph's old Scout, eyed the Colt on the hood, and cleared his throat. "Not even going to make stock out of them?"

"No," said Joseph. "If you'd watched them pecking holes

into the hens and each other for the last few years, you wouldn't, either. I pulled a few feathers to tie flies."

Jules watched him work for another minute before he volunteered to take over. "I'm fine," said Joseph, but he handed the shovel over a minute later. He dragged a camp chair from the side of the barn and sat heavily, lighting a cigarette.

"Why be pissy about your children throwing you a party?"

"It's only Jetta who's working. The others are just flying out to drink for free. And why would I want to celebrate my marriage surrounded by assholes? Why, I've had cause to wonder of late, would I want to celebrate my marriage at all?"

"At least you haven't had cause to wonder for most of the last fifty years."

Joseph gave him a withering look. "Aren't you here a little early for cards?"

"Who didn't you want at the party?"

"None of your business."

Jules pried up a large rock. One of the chickens was still twitching, and Max the cat now watched it closely from the hood of the Scout next to the gun. "I found a body on Magpie Island. An old one."

Joseph didn't respond immediately, and Jules turned to see he'd shut his eyes. "Are you attempting to further undermine my evening, or is this gossip?"

Jules hauled the stone to one side. "A couple were camped on the downriver end yesterday, and the man noticed some bones when he made a hole back in some willow saplings. According to the records, you used to own the land, and I wondered if you remembered anything funny happening out there back then."

"Jesus," said Joseph. "Back then when? I owned it for thirty years. Who'd you find?"

"I don't know that yet," said Jules. "The top half washed away. The bones have been there at least forty years, maybe longer."

Joseph reopened one hooded eye, then another, and stared for a long moment up the dark hill. "I like the idea of a hundred," he said.

"Sorry," said Jules. "The tip of the island didn't exist until the 1921 flood."

"I sold that place in 1962, got it before the war."

"You inherited it in 1936."

"Huh," said Joseph. "Well, I can't know what's tucked in every corner of my own house, let alone the ranch, or why some asshole would end up on land I haven't seen in thirty years."

Jules tossed the roosters in the hole. "Why assume it's a man?"

If Jules had been younger, the look Joseph gave him now would have puckered him into silence. "I've observed throughout my life that men tend to die in strange ways, due to testosterone and an innate lack of practical intelligence. Is it?"

"Probably. Anyone live out there when you got the place or when your grandfather owned it?"

Joseph put out his cigarette. "Not on that end. Too low. My grandfather owned it for forty years. I don't remember hearing a thing, but maybe you need to ask someone really old."

"Some coins on the body date it after 1937."

Joseph raised an eyebrow. "A lost boy, lying low during the war. Someone who came in with the train."

"I think he was young," said Jules. "But someone bothered to bury him."

Joseph shrugged. "As you say. Are Flo and Jetta still haggling over the guest list? Is my wife still hiding?"

Jules finished hilling the grave and started to pat the

gravel down with the back of his shovel. Joseph had always had a talent for simply ending a conversation; these days Jules, as sheriff, could simply continue it. "We found some bullets under the body."

Joseph lit another cigarette and took a long drag, the better to regard Jules as coldly as possible. "What are you getting at?"

Jules stared at him. "What's eating you? I'm going to ask a lot of people if they remember anyone disappearing back then. You would have been about the guy's age, and you owned the island, so it's natural to start with you."

Joseph started to speak and shrugged.

"What'd you use the land for?" asked Jules.

Joseph, in the process of pulling himself out of the camp chair, seemed amused. "I thought of building a place there, but every few years it'd get wet. So I sat on the land and watched the value rise and leased it out for pasture."

"To whom?"

"Jesus, Jules."

They started walking toward the house. Through the kitchen window, Jules could see Jetta pouring herself another glass of wine. "Who leased it?"

Joseph stopped walking. "You want me to remember a deal fifty or sixty years ago? You think I haven't been doing much in between? I don't remember who used to keep what animals on the goddamn island."

They neared the house. Joseph looked at the kitchen window at Jetta's and Flo's profiles and sighed.

"How long have they been friends?" asked Jules.

"Sunday school. Jetta would have been three or so, 1949 or 1950. The real question is why."

"True," said Jules. "Maybe Flo was a cute three-year-old."

"Not particularly," said Joseph. "She used to stand in a corner and wet her pants and scream when she was over to play and Laura wouldn't give her what she wanted. She looked like a calf then, instead of a cow."

No one had ever said Joseph was a nice man. "What would she want?"

"She had a fondness for Laura's polenta cake."

Jules raised his eyebrows. "So in 1949 Flo was fond of polenta cake, but you can't remember who you rented a pasture to in 1939."

They'd reached the front porch steps. "Let me tell you something you'll understand eventually, if you ever have kids," said Joseph. "The odd tendencies of a three-year-old, even if she's not your own three-year-old, are still more interesting than any business deal. Now let me dart inside and slide in my third-growth teeth and we'll go play poker."

"Why not," said Jules. "I'll wait by the car."

"Chickenshit," said Joseph.

THE WHY NOT of poker proved to be forty dollars. Peter lost, too, as did Joseph's old friend Merle Ott. Axel Scotti, a Forest Service ranger named Patrick Ankeny, and two geriatric good old boys broke even. Joseph won big, and Jules, after some whiskey, began to believe in the concept of roosters as a ritual sacrifice.

Much of the night's conversation concerned Ankeny's winter research, a study of temperatures of hibernating grizzlies that called for Ankeny to crawl into dark dens with a thermometer and a flashlight, aiming for bear assholes.

"Do you have some deep, dark reason for valuing your life cheaply?" asked Joseph.

"He got divorced last year," said Jules. "Peter handled it."

Peter smiled bleakly.

"I'm fine now," said Ankeny. "And I think the bears have made me begin to value my life again."

They played on the mezzanine of the Baird Hotel, and from this vantage Jules could (*a*) watch a bachelor party in the lobby below and think of how poorly so many men handled marriage and (*b*) keep tabs on his sometime friend Edie Linders, who due to poor planning was stuck working the front desk in the midst of these festivities. As a result, by the time she went off shift at eleven, Jules, the man she'd called a self-centered prick that Monday morning, seemed like an enlightened, compassionate diamond in the rough, or perhaps a turd of coal that hadn't yet endured sufficient pressure. She left for home with the understanding that Jules would follow her there after he drove Joseph home; he couldn't quite believe their earlier argument could have been put on hold so easily.

Outside on the sidewalk, howls from the bachelor party, which had moved to a room upstairs, followed them to the car.

"If you were to do that, I somehow sense the style of the celebration would be different," said Joseph. He was moving slower than usual, the rooster massacre having taken a toll.

"Thank you," said Jules. "That's nice of you to say."

They looked up at the party suite window in time to see a balloon with a nipple painted on one end float down toward them. A moment later it was brought up short by a dart that plummeted to the street a foot from Joseph's boot.

"You want me to arrest them?"

"Nah," said Joseph. "Let's just get out of here. I'm too old for this shit."

"So am I," said Jules.

A.C.H.S. AGENDA, OCTOBER 19
DECISIONS TO MAKE:

Design.

I'll pass around the carpet and tile samples. We've settled on oyster white walls throughout; Bilton's is donating six dozen gallons.

Organizational.

See attached map of museum for suggestions for how to arrange exhibits. Rough headings members have previously suggested:

- Fires & other acts of God (earthquakes, floods, droughts, windstorms, avalanches, etc.)
- Schools (eighteen county-wide in 1910)
- Sports (rodeo, prewar basketball champs, early horse racing, white-water rafting, etc.)
- Local tribes & pioneers (inc. archaeological exhibits)
- Weddings, funerals, births & customs (combine with above?)
- Mining, timber, railroad, ranching
- Crime (Jules Clement says we can have whatever we can find in the department's old storage locker)

- Medicine (inc. Dr. Craitson Sr.'s father's operating room equipment!) & other early professions
- The wild life: one half upstairs hall on animals, terrain, etc.; other on bars, fights—the Wild West (combine with Crime?)

Monetary.

According to my last discussion with our contractor, we're running about $20,000 short, due to the wiring and asbestos problems. Who haven't we hit up for funds yet?

Publicity.

If we can approve and refine some topics, I'll start writing the regular weekly column, to be published beginning Jan 4.

I still need help with cataloging, fund-raising, and a prospective membership list. Let's get the dirty work out of the way before the holidays.

—Alice

THE SNOW HAD STARTED THAT MORNING, AND Alice Wahlgren was almost beside herself at the idea that winter had already begun. A measly twelve days left to October, and then November would kick in. Alice hated November more than any other month, more than virtually anything on earth short of an ex-employer or two, or tomato worms. She was a premier case of solar deprivation effect, and Peter was already running scared, watching her covertly when she was reading or cooking, larding conversations with mentions of this or that friend who'd found equilibrium with Prozac or Zoloft. Their first long winter in Montana had been spent on an isolated ranch, and Alice had chosen that November to quit smoking. Peter had never recovered from the way she'd constantly volunteered to chop wood in the basement, and she couldn't really blame him.

The ladies didn't know this about her. Jules and Peter had made fun of all the things they didn't know, now that she was a club-joining matron, curator extraordinaire. Alice had spent a decade getting her ya-yas out in New York, but she suspected the ladies at the Historical Society guessed the truth and wouldn't have hired her without the mileage.

She'd guessed the truth about them, too, according to Jules who had a horrible memory for truly awful things, a wonderful one for good-bad stuff. The group included the immortal Bertha Nickelskin, who'd run Blue Deer's last escort service; Cicely Tobagga, antiques store owner, renowned for her gin consumption and enthusiastic dancing; Angelina Smarts, former county clerk, whom Merle Ott claimed had once given him an astounding blow job under a table at a Cattle Association banquet; Mabel Hicks, the open-minded wife of the Methodist minister; Venus Meriwether, a Radcliffe graduate rumored to have once consorted with Howard Hughes; Indabel and Etoile, the Whitsan "girls," who'd retired recently from teaching and living the free city life in Seattle; Horace Bolan's wife, Ella, who'd just the year before stripped her shirt off to swing dance at a wedding. Jules's own mother, Olive, had been responsible for God knows what sort of damage in her youth. Jetta Scotti and Flo Amundsen were probably the most conservative women in the bunch. Jetta was wonderful, funny and graceful and intelligent. Flo, Alice's neighbor, was another matter.

One by one the ladies finished reading the memo and folded their reading glasses. Alice tried to imagine them in the same classroom sixty, seventy, eighty years earlier, owl-eyed kindergartners cowed by the size of the building, the smell of chalk and a teacher's pointer, mysterious closets, and long halls. The museum, scheduled to open May 1, had been Blue Deer's grade school for half a century and still had chalkboards, boarded transoms, boy and girl stencils on the bathroom doors. Alice had been stripping linoleum for the last month, clearing the basement and back rooms and trying not to panic.

Venus Meriwether, ninety-one, adjusted herself in one of the armchairs and sighed. "I gather this is a working meeting."

"It was bound to happen sooner or later." Alice filled her glass with ice tea. They were on the second floor, arranged in the old music room, which held an ancient Bakelite-and-chrome space heater. The room faced south onto the white Absarokas, though currently a person couldn't see across the street for snowflakes. Alice had dragged in the dozen comfortable armchairs in the museum's collection, horsehair and silk and leather and velvet; she'd even cut the last of her cold weather flowers, larkspur and lavatera, and arranged them in a massive crystal vase on the broken grand piano.

Alice needed them in a good mood—they had too many decisions to make to afford crankiness. She was now officially curator of the not-quite-existent Absaroka County Historical Society (ACHS—or the Aches, as Jules called them, in reference to the geriatric membership: a dozen women with an average age of sixty-two), Flo and Jetta were the youngest members besides Alice, the baby at thirty-four. It was time, as Cicely Tobagga had suggested dryly, for a membership drive.

"What topics do you have in mind for the column?" asked Indabel Whitsan, seventy-eight.

Alice looked down at her notes. "You've suggested about two dozen, including that shotgun wedding at Bobbin in the 1890s, a piece on sanatoriums, the World War II Japanese balloon alerts, the drought and exodus of 1916, the shooting of the sheriff in the late twenties, infant mortality during the influenza epidemic in the teens, earthquakes in the thirties, a lynching in 1905, a rash of rapes in the thirties—"

"This seems like an excessive amount of crime," said Venus.

"These are all suggestions from previous meetings," said Alice. "Or stuff I've picked up from the newspapers. Newspapers don't change."

"I believe we were *talking* about many of those things, not suggesting that they be publicized," said Flo. "There's a difference, Alice."

Flo and Alice tried to be cordial at Aches meetings. Alice said, "Of course," pleasantly enough and resolved to let her dogs piss on Flo's shrubbery. "But we've planned a whole exhibit on crime. People want to hear about the Wild West."

"I recall the late thirties as happy years," said Cicely with a sly smile.

"I'm sure they were," said Alice. "But I can't write about the happy stuff unless you tell me."

"I was happy in 1936," said Etoile Whitsan, Indabel's younger sister and one of Cicely's schoolmates. "I went to Seattle for a high school graduation present, and I got engaged that July."

"What happened?" asked Flo acidly.

Etoile looked apologetically at Indabel, who rolled her eyes. "He flipped his car on the Clyde City road, broke his neck."

Indie Whitsan guffawed. "Second car the idiot totaled that summer."

In a town like Blue Deer, where the melting pot reached its final glory in the loneliness of the prairie, names were often idiosyncratic. Etoile and Indabel (two other sisters, Retsina and Lucretia, had died in the aforementioned influenza epidemic of 1918) had been born to a mother who had so treasured her honeymoon grand tour that everything afterward became a confused tribute to Eurasia and a denial of life on a ranch. Not that Indie and Ettie (the nicknames sounded to Alice like twin racetracks) had inherited this attitude. They'd worked for forty years in Seattle, always wanting to be home. Ettie was failing a bit, perhaps a victim of what Venus called "the dreaded A."

"Surely there's some other crime to mention from the thirties besides those rapes," said Venus. "I won't be a party to publicizing such nastiness."

Alice looked through her notes. "An embezzlement scandal at the River and Park Bank in 1934; Opera House arson in 1938—"

"Both of those sound very interesting." Venus's voice was brisk.

"Well, they're not," said Alice. "Only five hundred dollars was embezzled, and they never caught the arsonist. You mentioned a KKK bomb plot in 1934—"

"No, no, no," said Venus. "We get enough bad press these days. Something else."

Thirty minutes later the first bottle of sherry had been opened despite the hour and they'd gotten nowhere with topics or money sources beyond muttering about old boyfriends and long-gone trust funds. By the time the bottle was gone, they'd decided to give the archaeological and native collection a place of honor in the old speech room upstairs. It would include the prehistoric and pre-European piles of arrowheads and buffalo bones from ten-thousand-year-old encampments, sleds and tepees and beadwork and skins recording the first encounters with smallpox and doom, and the original cast from the ancient camel skeleton found on the edge of town, now thousands of miles away in the Museum of Natural History. The mining and railroad and logging and early newspaper equipment, being heavy and large, would be set up with partitions in the gymnasium, downstairs; Dr. Craitson's circa 1920 operating room would fit right into the old kitchen.

Alice opened a second bottle and asked for cataloging volunteers. Half of the museum collection had been in storage for thirty years, and not even Venus knew what they might find.

"Probably a hell of a lot of doilies," said Angelina Smarts.

"Wait till you get to our trunks," said Ettie. "You won't believe your eyes. Have you found the keys yet?"

Not that Ettie could remember what she'd packed, but she brought it up every meeting. "No," said Alice wearily. "I'll get Sheriff Clement to help open them. I promise." Alice had suggested Jules for the task the week before, when he'd promised to give a talk, and Ettie had locked on to the idea. Jules was a deliberately moving target; usually Alice could pin him down only by promising to feed him.

AT THE SHERIFF'S department, everyone worked on everything: the staff was too small to focus on any single crime and remain ignorant of another. They took turns patrolling, and paperwork was split as evenly as possible; normally, on any case that seemed destined to last longer than a day, two people were assigned. Some combinations had always worked, while others were innately flawed, but Caroline Fair's arrival in June had upped the ante. Only Wesley Tenn, who had been hired at the same time, seemed completely at ease with her. Jonathan Auber, twenty-five, was pink and speechless in her company, a vast improvement over his usual asinine verbosity. Ed Winton had started doing sit-ups for the first time in a decade, and considered it his duty to advise Caroline on all things local: weather, politics, wildlife and some euphemistic tips on the sexual habits of repeat offenders. Harvey Meyers, always touchy about his height (five-five), had been initially ornery about working with a taller (five-eight) female cop but now preened whenever they found themselves on a sidewalk together.

Everyone, in fact, was at their best with her except for Jules, who tended to be dour when uncomfortable. Despite (or possibly because of) this discomfort, he scheduled himself to work with her more than anyone else.

This morning they'd had two problems to bear down on, and only three people on duty, which meant that Jules, who felt a bit grainy between poker and a not entirely pleasant night with Edie, would work on both. Caroline Fair and Wesley Tenn flipped a coin, and Caroline won the dead problem of the island body, Wesley the live and ongoing one of Mary McLinchey's rapist. They now had a clear link with earlier attacks, a blatant serial problem: on the theory that it was unlikely the rapist had started from scratch in beautiful, pastoral Blue Deer, Jules had Wesley begin a state-by-state troll for similar rapes.

Caroline and Grace cleared an old banquet table in the far corner and helped Jules lug cartons of ancient records from a dim corner of the courthouse basement. Caroline lifted a pile of records from the first carton, labeled "1925 to 1929," and dropped them on the table. A gray mushroom cloud of dust erupted and dissolved again in a puff of cold air and snowflakes from the open window.

"Do you know how to ride?" asked Jules, apropos of nothing.

Caroline wiped at her face and looked wary. "Yes."

"Western or English?"

"Both. For Wayne Contway?"

Jules nodded. Caroline flipped open the first ledger.

"Well?" he asked. "You're fairly good?"

She looked impatient. "I had my own horses when I was a kid, and I used to jump. And I spent summers out here breaking colts when I was a teenager."

Jules's expression must still have been dubious. Caroline held up her left hand and wiggled three crooked fingers. "Would you like to see more proof?" she asked with great sarcasm. "The funny bumps on my rib cage?"

He didn't have the guts to say yes.

ALL JULES KNEW about Caroline Fair was from her résumé: she'd grown up in Philadelphia, gotten a BA from Columbia, intended to go to medical school but realized in junior-year anatomy that happiness did not lie in this direction (Jules had asked at the time of the interview if he then could count on her throwing up at her first bad car accident, just like everyone else, and Caroline, with her first smile, had told him he could). After a few years in a Washington lab, she'd moved west. She hadn't volunteered much else, though she was thirty-three, and some years were missing. When Jules asked why Blue Deer, she said she'd visited as a kid and it was the only place she could think of when the time came to run away from Washington. She hadn't quite put it that way, but Jules had run to and from Blue Deer himself and had an imagination.

Where Caroline was concerned, he'd gradually noticed he had too much of one. Whenever he caught himself looking at her, or trying too hard to please her, he slammed his mind shut. He had a horror of seeming a fool and was embarrassed by the very idea that he had a small crush on an employee. As a result, he'd at first seemed arrogant and officious. In later months, after a few encounters with his slightly bizarre sense of humor and after watching him with everyone else in the station, Caroline had decided he was an intelligent manic-depressive who didn't, for whatever reason, like her.

After a half hour of squinting at cramped, dusty accounts of disaster, Jules was a twitchy mess. He stood and put on his coat. "I'm going to talk to Mary McLinchey," he said.

"Well, good," she said.

"Then I'm going to lunch."

"Another good idea," said Caroline.

His face was hot when he walked out into the snow.

RAPE IN BLUE Deer was fairly rare and usually involved a known quantity: date rape or a friend of the family or an estranged husband proving his clout. But Blue Deer lay on the interstate, just as it had been serviced by the railroad for the previous hundred years, and though it had plenty of homegrown problems it also had its share of Greyhound wanderers, closed-face hitchhikers, overtired truckers. The town was just small enough for it to be probable that a local woman would recognize her assailant if he lived there, too, just large enough for this theory not to be foolproof.

The last two rapes, one in mid-August and the other on Labor Day, had seemed random. The first woman had been drunk and sick in an alley when she was accosted, and her memory had been entirely lacking in details; she actually thought the whole nightmare had been just that until she found blood on her clothes the next morning. Jules doubted she would even have come in if she hadn't been the sister of a Missoula cop who'd driven south four hours to bring her to the Blue Deer station. When Jules talked to her twenty-four hours after the fact she was humiliated, shell-shocked, and still hungover. She remembered only two things beyond the fact that the man was entirely average: he had dark hair, and he sounded asthmatic. She had some bruises, small deep ones, but couldn't remember how she'd gotten them.

The second woman had been asleep alone in her own bed when a man climbed on top of her and put what she assumed was a knife against her throat. He had a flashlight; he held a sheet over her eyes while he held the light at her crotch. She could tell from the heat. But she never saw him, could only tell from his weight that he was neither heavy nor light. He was there less than fifteen minutes, smelled of nervous sweat, and bit her a half dozen times on her inner thighs before he raped her. He'd broken in through the old-fashioned window in her kitchen.

Jules knew Mary McLinchey, though not well; had known her older sister, who now lived in Alaska, very well almost twenty years earlier. He'd been fond enough of the sister to run interference twice that summer when Mary was close to being arrested for bad check charges. In August she'd gotten a job at the supermarket, and things had looked up.

Mary walked back to her kitchen table after she answered the door, pulled out a chair for Jules, and pushed a packet of pictures to one side. The top photo showed her two children and an older woman in the kitchen where Mary and Jules sat now, the one with the windows that lacked locks. Mary resumed eating canned tomato soup and a grilled cheese sandwich. After every third bite or so, she offered some of the food to the baby, who accepted each spoon without pulling her eyes away from Jules and gripped the chunks of sandwich so tightly she left five perfect dents in the toast.

Mary McLinchey was soft and rounded, with red-brown hair and milk-pale skin from a lifetime of working too hard indoors. The bruises on her face and her throat were plum-colored.

Jules took her through the story one last time, but she couldn't add much to Caroline Fair's file notes. After the man had left at four, she'd showered and lain down in her children's room until it was time to take the oldest to school. She knew it had been the wrong response, and she was sorry, but she'd had to wash herself. The hospital tests were therefore mostly worthless. She'd fought, but she hadn't made noise; she hadn't wanted the man to notice the baby, and was glad her older child was also a sound sleeper. She was even glad for the first time that they lived in such a shack, because the kids slept in a lean-to-style bedroom that didn't look like more than a closet from her bed. He hadn't been a large person, as she'd said before; he'd worn a mask, but the hair on his arms was dark and bristly. Two of the bites on her legs had broken through the skin. He'd been five-ten or so, didn't seem heavy, had horrible breath and wheezed like a smoker. "It sounded like he had a bad cold or asthma or maybe emphysema." She smiled. "Wouldn't that be nice."

The flip tone didn't quite come off, and she cried silently and briefly, tears plopping into the tomato soup while Jules made faces at the round little girl.

They covered window locks, door locks, why buying a gun

for a house with children could cause more trouble than it might prevent, when the tests for venereal disease and AIDS would come back from the lab, who among the three local counselors Jules thought might be best for her, how he'd make sure she had locks installed on the windows that lacked them. Caroline had probably said most of it the day before.

The baby gave up on Jules's poker face, suddenly noticed the sandwich clenched in her hand, and whooped. Mary McLinchey managed to look amused, which was truly impressive.

"His voice," said Jules. "Anything about his voice beside the wheeze?"

"He didn't say much," said Mary. "It wasn't low, it wasn't high, anything in particular. When I thought about it last night it seemed familiar, but now I'm not so sure."

"Not young, not old?"

"No. Forties, maybe."

Jules drummed his fingers on the table and let the baby lurch forward and cover them with grease.

"I've been thinking about it," said Mary, "and it's as if his mouth and eyes didn't have any expression. Or maybe it's me who's gone blank."

"Have you thought through everyone you know? Neighbors, old boyfriends, people you've worked with? If it's not too much, try to keep it in mind when you're at the grocery store or the bank, places like that. Just to see if it's someone you see but never think about."

"I thought about it all night."

"That's not good," said Jules. He pried his fingers free and closed his pad, then started to doodle on the cover, unwilling to give up. "Nothing else, nothing he had on or brought with him?"

She didn't respond and he looked up. She was flushed and miserable. "Mary," he said softly. "It's okay. Tell me."

"He had a flashlight," she said abruptly. "I thought he was going to shove it up me. He'd covered my eyes, so I couldn't really see, but I saw light and first it was cold and then it started to burn me."

Jules looked out the window, then down at the drawing of an eye on his notepad. Mary McLinchey stood and cleared the lunch dishes. "You'll drive by, right?"

"Everyone will come by a few times a shift. If it helps, I think he'll keep looking for new people."

"Helps me," she said. "Not you, if you think he's the same man who did the same to the other women."

"We'll figure it out," said Jules.

He walked outside into gently swirling snow. Mary McLinchey remembered an average man who carried a flashlight and wheezed and had come in through a kitchen window with no locks. Jules could kiss goodbye the hope that they were dealing with a random series of unrelated attacks. He walked back toward the station very slowly, wondering how he could begin to track down an utterly anonymous serial rapist with bad lungs, a bad smell, and a hot flashlight. Then he veered north and picked up the window hardware himself. Mary McLinchey was surprised to see him again, but he knew it was the best and only thing he could do—besides making sure that the *Bulletin* ran a cautionary story on the front page about an unidentified victim.

JULES WAS NO fan of organized religion, but he did believe in the importance of ritual in daily life. He'd made up his own wherever he'd lived, but somehow the regular morning ride on the F train out of Brooklyn had never quite compared to an annual May dip in the frigid Yellowstone, walking to a particular valley in the Crazies after the snow thawed every spring, or the rite of pissing on Judge Birdland's hedge on his way home during his biannual drunk.

Wednesday lunch at the Bucket was such a ritual, as well as a necessary, perverse, inedible luxury. Like Tuesday poker, it was a bow to small-town tradition and necessity. Jules, having forgotten where he'd stored his uniform parka the spring before, was wearing a big Filson jacket that was covered with funny stains. He and Peter took their time on the three-block walk, moving at the same pace because they were roughly the same size, Peter six-one and slightly top-heavy, Jules two inches taller, skinnier and less obviously coordinated. They didn't bother commenting on the failing light, the increasingly dark lid of clouds and density of snow-flakes, or the temperature, which had dropped ten degrees in the last hour. They took a table in the corner under a collection of ceramic schnapps bottles. Every time the door swung open the inhabitants of the bar, most of them over sixty, shuddered in a draft.

Jules and Peter decided to celebrate the onset of winter with a beer and the day's specials, chicken soup and meat loaf sandwiches. In their fifteen years of knowing each other, they'd never tended toward healthy lunches; neither at the University of Michigan, nor in New York, nor finally in Blue Deer after Peter and Alice abandoned Manhattan and drove west and Jules gave up digging bones on the other side of the world.

Today they needed to figure out how to evade another invitation to become Elks initiates without offending the chunk of Blue Deer that felt they should belong. Peter had heard there was a goat involved in the initiation ceremonies and didn't want to ride it; Jules didn't want to listen to the "in *my* day" chitchat, with its implied criticism. Everyone seemed to think they were older than they were; everyone—including Axel Scotti (Elks and Ducks Unlimited) and Alice (the Absaroka County Historical Society)—let them know there was something snotty about remaining aloof.

Still, the Elks were too much to face quite yet, and they conspired to blame their workload. "Not to be callous," said Peter, "but you have a serial rapist to chase, bones to identify, teenagers on crystal meth to straitjacket. You don't have time for billy goats and gratuitous social drinking."

Jules nodded and waved at the waitress. Peter continued. "And I have dozens of bad check writers, wife beaters, and petty dealers to defend, not to mention the record number of drunks you've pulled over. Neil's trying to turn everything into a capital crime." (Peter liked to pronounce the name "Ka-neel," as in the courtroom line "I'll see *Ka-neel* on his knees.") "I can't go for his throat, either. Given our current problems."

Flo lived across the street and downwind from Alice and Peter in a pretty Victorian house gussied up with gingerbread trellises, a perfectly raked lawn and geometrical shrubbery. Alice's and Peter's bungalow was one of the messiest-looking homes on one of the town's nicest streets. Alice's ideas about what constituted a yard differed from her neighbors' at the best of times. She loved to garden but wasn't lawn-oriented, and still occasionally took pleasure in smearing dandelions on her hand when bored; she tended to dig holes for shrubs she didn't always get around to planting, booby-trapping her own property. She enjoyed fluffing her leaves on windy days and watching them blow over the fence and across the street, and couldn't comprehend Flo's rage when thistles and clover set up colonies in the neater woman's emerald carpet. Flo constantly called the department to complain about Alice's and Peter's yard and the things that came flying out of it, and had once successfully had them cited for growing weeds.

"It'll come to blows," muttered Jules darkly. "You've got to fix your fence, keep those dogs in your yard. She already suspects that it was Alice who shoved the dandelions into her geraniums."

"It was funny at the time," said Peter.

"I was laughing out of fear." Jules shivered in another cold blast and turned to see Miles Birdland stalk to a booth, followed by a smaller, beaming man with a pronounced limp and papery gray skin.

"Who's Mr. Sunshine?" asked Peter.

"Nestor Amundsen. You've met him."

"No, I haven't."

"Yes, you have. We picked mushrooms on some of his ground last spring. Neil's other grandfather. Flo's father-in-law. He eats here all the time."

"The ranch below Joseph's?"

"Yeah. Stop staring," said Jules. "He does look like shit." He accepted soup from the waitress with his version of a blinding smile and a request for Tabasco.

Peter peered down into his pool of noodles and broth. "Alice wants you to come speak to the ladies on the history of crime in the county," he said.

"I know that," said Jules. "I need to talk to her anyway. I need some help. The ladies might have a clue about the bones on the island, and I don't have time for old bones."

"I'm sure they'll be thrilled to help," said Peter. "But why even bother trying to identify half a body?"

"A body's a body," said Jules. "It's not as if we find a dozen mutilated corpses a year. I'll drop off a list of candidates in your office by the end of the day."

"No," said Peter. "You won't. I'll just forget to give it to my sweetheart and be stuck in the middle of your pissing match. You're afraid of what she'll say about Edie, right?"

Jules craned his neck, ostensibly checking on the meat loaf's progress.

"You and Edie all happiness again?" Peter asked.

"A temporary rapprochement was achieved after poker. It didn't last long, but we're better off than before. It's not that we don't like each other." But he wasn't truly sure they did, and he had a feeling they'd have to give up seeing each other entirely to relax around one another again. They were running on urge rather than any gentle emotion.

"You treat each other like furniture."

"How so?" asked Jules coldly.

"You sleep on each other when convenient, instead of with each other," said Peter.

They exchanged a long look before Jules gave Peter the finger. "Anyway, I'll find Alice after lunch."

"She said she'd be at the museum all afternoon. Milk and cookies and Mabel Hicks's homemade wine," said Peter, stirring his soup. "Woooeee."

"Bourbon, more likely," said Jules, wanting one. He'd known Mabel Hicks since he was born, and she enjoyed winding down no matter the time of day. The potential that any Ache would serve lemonade was low.

They slurped companionably for a while. Jules couldn't quite make out the conversation between Amundsen and Birdland, but it didn't sound relaxed. Nestor, normally a tidy picture of health, despite almost eighty years and an artificial leg, now seemed too animated for his evident frailty and was doing most of the talking. When the door opened again, both the old men smiled in relief. Jules turned to see who or what they had in common.

It was Joseph Ganter. He gave Jules and Peter a dismissive nod as he slid into the booth next to Miles Birdland, who inched toward the wall.

"Well," said Jules. "I never. He and Nestor only talk about lost cows, and I've never even heard him say Birdland's name." In small towns, it was natural to assume similar people knew each other and liked each other, went to the same parties and shared an easygoing history. There were few coincidences in acquaintanceship. But even though the Birdlands and the Ganters and the Amundsens were strung together by the courthouse and Axel's and Jetta's marriage, he'd never once seen the judge and two of the county's biggest landowners exchange a word. It was just the way things were, nothing dramatic; maybe they'd had a bad day at recess seventy years earlier. Only now, when Jules saw them together in the same booth, preparing to eat the same bad food, did he realize how foreign the sight really was, and note how uncomfortable it made the three men.

Peter was twirling his fork. "Has it ever occurred to you that you might not know everything about everybody?"

"Yeah, yeah," said Jules, still annoyed by Peter's comments about Edie. In a lifetime of hearing Joseph's caustic and memorable character assassinations, he couldn't remember a single comment against Birdland, a natural target.

When the meat loaf arrived, they reached for the mustard in unison and fell quiet. Across the room Nestor Amundsen was still talking, and if the other two men were listening, they didn't show it. Miles Birdland rubbed his forehead and stared at the hokey hunting print above the booth, and Joseph surveyed the room with large gray hooded eyes.

Peter was watching them, too. "How old is Birdland? How soon will he retire and make our lives easier?"

The "our" was amusing, in that Jules and Peter were theoretically opponents. Jules chewed and thought. "Seventy-five, more or less. He'll never retire, and Scotti wouldn't be a bed of roses, either."

The judge seemed to be complaining about his soup, and the waitress looked as if her blood needed antifreeze as she backed away toward the kitchen.

"Maybe I'll just quit," said Peter. "Build cabinets for a living."

"You don't even know how to make a sawhorse," said Jules.

"I'll learn. It seems so relaxing, such a doper pastime, fiddling with wood all day. Like when you used to fiddle with bones."

The waitress brought sandwiches to the old men's booth, but no one thanked her. Birdland was holding forth; he could be a real talker out of court, as was Nestor. Jules might have considered such traits fondly if he'd ever had a drink in a bar with either man, but some circles never intersected, and never would until he broke down and went goat riding.

Though Jules knew Birdland as a man not at all, he had considerable experience reading his moods, and the judge was obviously enraged, hissing and gesturing, for once not caring about appearances. Nestor looked flushed and cornered. Joseph wore a look that had once caused a six-year-old Jules to wet himself in fear. Most of what they said was unintelligible, but Jules heard fragments from the most familiar voice, Joseph's: "Is this some goddamn joke?" and "Wait until Nina comes back," which sounded more like advice than a threat.

Three old assholes, still being assholes together, probably after decades of dissension. The men didn't seem to be having the classic, peaceful shoot-the-shit lunch you'd expect from longtime friends. Jules wondered if they got together out of boredom.

His plate was empty. "Blecchh," said Jules. "Why do we keep doing this?"

Peter smiled. "My turn to pay."

"I'll just say hello to the boys."

"I'll say a prayer for you," said Peter, fishing through his pockets.

The men fell silent when he was halfway across the room. "Judge Birdland, Joseph." Jules nodded politely, then smiled to the left. "Hi, Nestor. How are you doing these days?"

"Just grand, thanks," said Nestor.

"What are you gentlemen up to? Catching up?"

"Yes," said Joseph with a smile. "We played basketball together, the championship team of 1936. Believe it or not."

For a split second Jules had trouble believing it, before he remembered their picture on the wall in the high school gym. Joseph still had long arms and deft hands, but the other two hadn't aged so well. Birdland, though tall, was twitchy and bloodless; only his long fingers were still athletic. At five-six, Nestor Amundsen had to be one of the stubbiest Scandinavians in the country. It was easy to see which grandfather Neil had gotten his height from.

"Maybe you'd forgotten that I helped teach you to play," said Joseph mildly. He and Nestor looked amused, but Miles Birdland was sunk in a private misery.

"You tried to," said Jules.

"Now, now," said Joseph. He had an oddly gentle smile, one that cracked the rest of his forbidding face in half. "You had at least one good season with the cheerleaders."

In terms of cheerleaders, that season had actually been an utter failure; in terms of those girls who had no interest in cheerleading, it had been an unqualified triumph. Though not so triumphant that it was worth reliving at the moment. "I wondered if you had a chance to remember who you rented that land to."

Jules smiled at Joseph; Joseph smiled at Jules. "Are you riding my ass because I won money from you last night?"

"You always were a fine player," said Nestor, a little flushed, coming alive like an old machine.

Miles Birdland gave him a sharp look, but Joseph looked amused. "I'm riding your ass because I found a body," said Jules. "It's what I'm paid to do."

"Well, hell," said Nestor. "You talking about that body on the tip of the island? That on the land Joey owned? Miles here used to lease it for Ruth's horses." He looked at Birdland. "Didn't you?"

Birdland had been studying his chicken and biscuits, and his head came up with a jerk. He stared at Nestor in utter incomprehension.

"Wasn't that after the war?" asked Joseph.

"You know, Miles," said Nestor Amundsen, looking amused again. "Joey's land. Nothing but a sand spit now. He always knew when to sell."

"We leased it right after we married," said Birdland slowly. "Before I went to school in 1939." He finally looked directly at Jules. "I had no idea you'd found the body on that end when I asked you yesterday."

That was possible, though Jules couldn't recall Birdland ever seeming curious about anything in the past. "Any idea of why a man might come to be buried there?"

"None," said Birdland. "Though I didn't spend much time there. My wife was the rider."

"Perhaps I should ask Mrs. Birdland," said Jules.

"She's indisposed," said the judge, using the same tone he might have for the phrase "He's in Deer Lodge for life." "If she'd seen a soul out there, she would have told me."

"She might not have if you were in law school in Missoula," said Jules mildly.

Birdland's expression was not pretty.

"It used to be a quiet place back then," said Nestor. "That bridge scared the shit out of most people. When I was a kid I'd only cross it on a dare."

"Well," said Jules. "Sorry to bother you."

"Who do you think it is, out there in the sand?" asked Nestor.

"Not a clue," said Jules. "That's why I'm asking around. A tall dead guy."

"How do you know he's tall if you've only got the bottom half?"

"Oh, for God's sake. Long legs, Nestor," snapped Joseph. "Don't you know what Jules used to do for a living?"

My, they seemed to be having fun together. Jules turned back to his own table, where Peter was struggling with his coat.

"SHIT," SAID PETER, wincing in the sidewalk cold. "Where's my hat?"

"I'll get it," said Jules. "I left my gloves." It was the same thing every winter, a matter of getting used to excess baggage. A few steps inside the Bucket, as he retrieved the baseball cap and leather gloves from the table, he noted that Nestor Amundsen and Miles Birdland were apoplectic, hissing at each other, too enraged to notice either Jules's presence or the check the waitress dropped lightly on the table from arm's length.

"I wasn't asking your goddamn opinion," said Nestor. "I'll do what I want to."

Joseph picked up the check, his face impassive. "Of course you will, Nestor. You always have."

WHEN JULES RETURNED from lunch, he found a heavyset blond woman sitting next to his desk and holding a leash attached to the world's fattest English pointer.

"I'm Amber Jump," she said.

"Oh," said Jules, taking off his coat. Grace was typing violently in the corner, deeply put out.

"This is Serena. My husband took her again yesterday."

"Ah," said Jules. Serena, the county-famous sausage dog; Peter represented her other owner, Carl Jump. "I heard."

She stomped her foot; the dog didn't move. "Aren't you going to do anything about it?"

"I'll call him and ask him not to take her without your permission, but otherwise it's a civil matter."

"The number's one-five-four-zero," she said. "I'm waiting."

She didn't just wait; she talked. Peter had warned him about this. "It's quite something," she mused while Jules dialed her husband's number, "waking up one morning and looking over, and realizing your husband is a raving asshole, a sad, sick man . . ."

Jules drummed his fingers and raised his eyebrows, realizing that this woman would never finish her sentence. An answering machine came on, and he left a message. "Mr. Jump, this is Jules Clement of the sheriff's department. I'd appreciate—"

"I had all the evidence," she said, "and you'd think the feeling would have grown on me, but no, it came as a thunderbolt—one minute I thought he was perfectly reasonable, and the next he didn't deserve to live."

"Let's not escalate," said Jules, hanging up the phone. "Let's get you two back on the custody agreement."

"Serena isn't coming close enough to his doorstep to fart on it until the month is out, and if that sack of shit snoops on my property again I'll shoot him."

"Has it occurred to you that your dog might enjoy hunting? If he's bringing the dog back to you each evening—"

"Are you here to uphold the law?"

"Yes," said Jules. "But that doesn't mean I have to agree with all its possible applications."

"I don't care if you agree," said the woman. "I don't feel like being reasonable. I'm pissed off."

Jules opened a drawer and pulled out a complaint form. "I'm happy you two aren't arguing over children," he said. "I'm happy you don't have five dogs."

She leaned toward him. "You know what I hate?"

Jules, who didn't particularly want to know, kept his mouth shut and started filling out the form.

"I hate people who assume children are more important than pets. What do you think about that?"

Wesley and Caroline and Grace were watching from the far side of the room. It was only one thirty, and Jules wanted a drink, a nap, anything but the rest of the afternoon.

"I think there's no finite rule to affection," he said carefully. "Who am I to tell you who or how to love?"

Amber Jump's eyes softened, and she stroked the fat, sleeping dog while Jules finished the complaint.

WHEN SHE LEFT he walked over to Caroline, who sat on the floor covered with dusty journals.

"Anything?"

"I'm up to 1948, with a dozen possibilities out of the missing persons entries."

"Ew," said Jules. He cleared a place for a chair with his toe and noticed her hands were black with dust. "Let's not bother with anyone who disappeared after 1955 or was younger than twenty."

"You're sure?"

"I'm sure." He wanted to say that he'd had a life before he'd come to this pass, that she shouldn't think he was an average dweeb cop, whatever that was.

Caroline raised her eyebrows and looked at her list. "Could the blond hair you found have bleached over the years?"

"I don't think so. The soil's pretty alkaline, and the color was uniform. I'll ask the people at the lab."

"Your uncle owned the land? Did you ask him about it?"

"Yeah. He didn't have much to add."

"Anything?"

"He used it for pasture and leased it out for a while in the thirties and forties."

"To whom?"

A sense of being second-guessed solidified. For some reason, Jules protected Joseph; he didn't tell her his uncle hadn't volunteered the information. "Judge Miles Birdland leased it for his wife's horses. He actually asked me about the body yesterday. What you might call a coincidence."

He had some satisfaction from her expression. "Well," said Caroline.

"Would you like to talk to him about it? I just saw him, and he didn't have much to say."

Jules caught a glimmer of a smile on Caroline's lips, still a rare occurrence after four months. "No thanks."

They simmered into silence and read. A few minutes later she pointed to the missing persons report files. "How are we supposed to figure out who they ended up finding?"

"The ones who turned up weren't recorded?"

Caroline shook her head, and the promise of an easy solution vanished. "Goddamn it," said Jules, flipping open the next volume in the pile. "Fuck a duck."

Caroline eyed him. "We'll just have to call around, right?"

"Death records," muttered Jules. "If we're lucky, some relatives will have filed for the people who never came back after seven years, to straighten out property and inheritance."

"The first dozen aren't in there," said Caroline, pointing to another stack of black ledgers. "I already checked."

Jules had noticed over the last several months that Caroline was not like Harvey or Jonathan, or even Ed or Wesley, in that she went to the next step without being asked. Sometimes she went to the next step before Jules had considered the next step; sometimes, in all honesty, the next step would never have occurred to him.

"The two dozen you mentioned all matched up?"

"All taller than five-ten, all within the age span, light blond and in possession of both feet."

"Goddamn blondes," said Jules, snatching a notepad.

"Fuzzy pink people who think they own the world," said Caroline evenly.

Jules, who had chocolatey hair, stared at her. She shrugged and gave him an almost-smile.

THE FIRST SNOW of the year brought out the Texas driver in everyone. Though the storm was nothing like what they'd been told to expect, most of that afternoon was given over to weather-related traumas: people from the Carolinas who kissed ditches and realized they'd planned trips to Seattle a little late in the season; quickly canceled reports of missing hunters and hikers; and complaints against landlords who'd neglected to repair furnaces. Someone had broken into the bakery, and an itinerant was found under the freeway overpass, suffering mild frostbite. None of it resulted in a single hospital check-in, which was miraculous, and nobody would be fishing the Yellowstone, stumbling over accordioned divers.

At four, Jules and Wesley returned from the continuing search for Alston Hantz, the county's most relentless alcoholic. Caroline, in the process of wrapping a series of wool scarves around her neck and head, handed Jules a neatly typed list of missing men. "When are you planning on the Contway trip now?" she asked.

"Early Monday."

"Who's going?"

"So far just Harvey and me and whoever they send along from Deer Lodge."

"Should I plan on it? Do you want me to go?"

"Yes," said Jules. "That would be wonderful."

JULES PHONED THE forensics lab in Missoula, the recommended pathologist at the Smithsonian, and the anthropology lab at the college in Bozeman, where they normally handled dinosaurs and Plains Indians. Missoula won: he packed up the island bones, clothes, in situ photos, the bullets, some soil cross sections, and his notes, and shipped the lot off to them.

Alice was locking the front door of the museum when he pulled up. "I need help," he said, leaving his car running, checking one pocket after another of his wrinkled coat for the list of names.

She beamed and reinserted her key. "So do I. We have a few trunks we can't open, and I'm putting you on the lecture list. And by the way, it's been a full forty-eight hours since Flo has complained about something the dogs have done, so maybe you could put us on the patrol list tonight."

"Not now. Shut that door and listen."

Alice lost her always-tenuous sense of humor. "Pardon fucking me."

"It'll be fun."

"Fun would be help with the trunks and your promise to give a talk."

Jules rubbed his forehead. "I promise. Please. We found someone out on the island, and I want you to ask the ladies who he might be."

She looked over his list. "You missed this week's meeting."

"Goddamnit," snapped Jules. Little things were beginning to miff him. "I thought you met Thursday evenings."

"Good God," said Alice. "You're just as pissy as Peter was this morning. We usually meet then, but half of us are getting together to do the Ganter flowers tomorrow night."

"Then you can discuss mysterious tall blond boys over bouquets." He finally found the list in one of the coat's inside pockets, along with a grocery receipt from the previous spring, some bar matches, and a five-dollar bill. Most first snowfalls delivered better perks. "Ask them about these guys," he said. "See if any of these Romeos ever came home again, or maybe if there are some others no one ever reported. We're looking for a missing blond, probably disappeared in the thirties or forties, fairly young, fairly tall."

"They'll love this." Alice looked down at Jules's scribble and snorted. "These names are incredible. Avery, Lars, Oleander."

"Try telling them you want to do a series on county murders. See what they come up with."

"I'll ask," said Alice. "They like to act like they're down on crime these days, but they'll know it all. This is probably a laundry list of old boyfriends, and they'll tell me where the other bodies are buried."

Jules didn't want to know about other bodies.

BY THE TIME he finally drove over the island bridge on his way home, the landscape glowed gray-pink with white snow and the half-moon and the lights of town and the sawmill. The willows and dogwood and wild clematis were draped like furniture in a wealthy summer home, and the bone hole was a gentle depression. Jules walked to the far channel, swinging one foot before the other to shower the fluff to either side.

The river channel looked shiny, like mercury, and the snow absorbed all its noise. Jules tested the wooden footbridge gingerly, then stood in the middle and bounced a bit, feeling like a kid. The same flood that had eroded the bones and reduced the last concrete bridge on the other side of the island to gravel should have taken this one to Big Timber, forty miles downstream. His mind drifted until he caught a blot of color in a gravel spit twenty yards downstream. He made his way along the mainland bank, sinking through the snow into half-frozen mud before he executed an awkward leap to the spit. It was a bouquet of iris and alstroemeria with puffs of snow on each stem and blossom, blues and pinks as bright as new, and only one stem broken.

He looked back to the bridge and across to the island, water sliding east on either side of him. The bridge was really only a few yards from the tarp and the hole, and without the snow you could probably make out the hole from the center of the wooden span. The flowers might have traveled down the river a mile before they washed ashore. Jules would have been likelier to think it a romantic gesture to death or dead love if it weren't for the fact most of the town was still ignorant of the bones—the *Bulletin* had run only the briefest mention in the Tuesday paper. The simplest explanation had to do with an incident Harvey had dealt with the night before on the island road, a couple's slugfest. Perhaps someone had brought the wrong flowers or given them too late. Perhaps Jules should take it as a hint and give Edie a call.

4 The Elements

WHEN JULES SLUMPED DOWNSTAIRS AT SEVEN THE following morning, his thermostat read 10° Fahrenheit, a dry, truly unseasonable chill that had kept the snowfall down to a measly eight inches. They were halfway through the grape harvest in the south of France, still fanning themselves on porches in the Florida Keys, while he had chosen a place where a hummingbird could freeze in mid-flight and where happiness was not having to patrol more than once a week.

The pansies in the windowbox under the thermometer, planted by Alice, looked deceptively bright and perky, enjoying a brief suspended animation before they thawed and turned to soup. His backyard bird feeder was empty, and various lawn chairs lay on their sides against his johnboat. One life preserver had blown into the shrubbery during the winds the week before, and now he'd have to pry it out of the ice or wait for a thaw. He'd left the back gate ajar and broken since his dog had died, three years earlier, and now he saw that one of Marv's old buddies had hauled a discarded antelope spine into the yard, perhaps as an offering.

A token piece of poor-white America tucked behind an upstanding citizen's house. Just thinking of crawling around to clean up spare animal parts put him in a fouler mood; thinking of a day of patrolling made him slam his refrigerator door a little too hard, and in the echo he heard the door shelf give way, launching fifty-some condiments into a few moldy containers of leftovers.

Once in his office, Jules decided to take his mood out on Ralph Rouse, the guy who'd duked it out with his girlfriend on the island bridge two nights earlier. Ralph was a repeat customer, and deputies had had to peer into his unhappy private life several times in the last year. The phone woke Ralph, and Jules began to cheer up.

"Buy her flowers? Of course I didn't buy the bitch flowers."

"Never have, never will?"

"Fuckin' A."

Wesley Tenn was watching him from Grace's counter. Jules realized all these questions, his very curiosity, were inexplicable.

Ralph raved on. "Why would I start on the day she tells me she's sucking someone else's joint?"

Men were forever doing unlikely things. Jules asked how long they'd been on the island road before Harvey joined them. Fifteen minutes, more or less; Ralph and the lady in question had met on the bridge because it was a halfway point between her house, on the island, and his, near downtown. They were there for the possessions swap; she had some of his tapes and a pair of pants, he had her underwear and a paperback and a hairbrush. No one had interrupted the fray proper, which had begun when Ralph's erstwhile love had tossed his pants into the river, but he remembered an old lady walking by when he first got there, because she had come out of a woods path and stared at him like he was dirt. No, he didn't remember what she'd looked like, just old, and not real fast on her prissy little feet.

Venus Meriwether, an island homeowner and president

of the Absaroka County Historical Society, had probably been checking out the bird population. She didn't answer her phone, and a neighbor told Jules that Venus had gone to a meeting of the Audubon Society in Helena the night before. Just your average ninety-some-year-old, driving two hours through a blizzard for birds.

When Jules had bad news for Axel Scotti—for instance, that they had no suspect for the rapes and no identification for the bones—he liked to get it over with quickly. Instead he and Neil Amundsen had to share the secretary's office while on the other side of a door Peter and Axel screamed at each other about some unfortunate felon. Neil regarded the diplomas on the wall and ran his finger along the line of his chin in such an admiring way that Jules wanted to kick him. The feeling grew so strong that he tried friendly conversation out of desperation.

"Are you going to the Ganter party?"

"I might."

"Want to help me set up? I need to get chairs and tables at the Lutheran church, and you have that new pickup."

"No."

Jules stared at him. Neil was now exploring his cheekbones. "I think my mother's helping enough for both of us."

Jules felt a rare pang of sympathy for Flo. Neil finally gave up on his face, straightened in his chair and looked at Jules directly. "What's with the uniform?"

"Patrol day," said Jules, gritting his teeth.

"Who's working tomorrow night?"

"Why?" asked Jules suspiciously.

"I thought maybe I'd get to know Caroline better."

The door to Scotti's office opened and Peter slammed past them, leaving a wake of Scotti's cigar smoke. "Offhand,

I can't remember the schedule," said Jules. "Call her. She's off today." It was a lie; he knew she didn't work Friday night.

"I'll just stop by her house," said Neil.

Jules stalked into Scotti's office to spread the mood.

THE WIND KICKED in that afternoon, and they closed the freeway's most exposed stretch after a double-wide on its way to Billings blew off a trailer and shattered. The bad news about the wind was that it redistributed all the light-and-airy snow; the good news was that the wind was a chinook and the temperature would rise forty degrees by dark, which meant that all the drifts would melt.

Jules only liked to patrol when he could manage to forget why he was driving the squad car. Most days the landscape put him into such a good mood that he had by far the lowest ticket rate of his department. Today the landscape had its work cut out for it, and he cited four drivers in the first half hour.

He tried not to anticipate problems or fall into cheap generalizations; he liked to give people the benefit of the doubt. When he pulled over a Camaro for passing at eighty on a double yellow line, he actually waved the cite book back and forth until the pot smoke diminished, then nailed the obese, gray-skinned driver for an expired license, lack of proof of insurance, speeding, and the open can of Old Milwaukee that gradually spilled around the accelerator during their conversation. When he pulled over a Nevada speeder in a late-model white Cadillac, a man with a hairpiece and bumper sticker that read I DON'T BELIEVE THE LIBERAL MEDIA, he struggled to not assume the driver was an asshole until the guy proved it by offering a ten-dollar bribe. On the other hand, once the man proved himself an asshole, Jules relished the discovery of six outstanding tickets and the desperate pleas during the ride to the station.

By mid-afternoon he was in a fine mood, dawdling on the eastern border of the county, just south of the Crazies, when his beeper went off. Grace had an edge to her voice as she gave him the address. "That's Peter and Alice's house," said Jules.

"Yep."

"Is it Flo again? Send someone else."

"Everyone else is busy, sweetheart. She's all yours."

"Who called it in?"

"Both."

"Who started it?"

"If I knew that, do you think I'd be answering phones?"

Flo, it seemed, had observed both of Alice's and Peter's charming dogs out of their yard and in hers without an escort or a leash, and called Marlene, the romance-reading brunette in charge of most animal matters. Marlene arrived to discover both dogs in Alice's yard and no sign of damage to Flo's lawn, though Flo tried to show her a wet spot between blades of force-fed grass. The dog warden said she could do nothing besides have a friendly talk with the owners, neither of whom happened to be home (Jules imagined Alice hiding in her basement, nervously doing laundry). Flo did not take this news well, and when Peter arrived home, Earl, the older dog, reeked of some sort of air freshener, and Pearl, the puppy, was hiding under the porch.

It was a strange revenge. By the time Jules drove up Flo was long gone, having once again started something without weighing its consequence. He'd dealt with her other vendettas: the clerk at the market she'd thought had looked at her cross-eyed, overcharged her, stuck a fingernail in her plum, on and on, ad nauseam; the lay minister at the Episcopal church, who'd suggested Flo not chair the Sunday school drive after she was heard telling a child he might go to hell for denuding an Easter lily; the lady at the clothing store, who refused to give Flo a credit for stretch pants that showed unmistakable signs of having been stretched. When you pinned Flo down about these things, she could be quite persuasive. It was only later, muddling it through, that Jules had come to wonder why all these people would volunteer time to persecute poor Florence Josephine Birdland Amundsen.

Jules sighed deeply and stared across the narrow street at his friends' small house, not such a bad place if you didn't take offense at the dogs' stuffed toys. Pearl had inherited a host of rabbits, marmots, Cookie Monsters and Santa Clauses from Alice's small niece, who now preferred Star Wars figures. The wind had pasted these prizes and the puppy's other belongings—chewies and old sneakers and bones—against the wavy wire fence and flattened the dormant grass so that lumps of puppy shit stood everywhere, like tiny volcanic islands. If and when Peter and Alice had a child, Jules could imagine Frisbees and squirt guns and Barbie limbs and the unidentifiable plastic parts to a score of $4.99 toys accumulating there as well.

Alice was putting on lipstick, a recent fetish. Peter was changing, having gotten wet while giving Earl a third bath.

"Listen," Alice said. "I lived in New York for ten years. I worked with two dozen gay cooks, and I worked with producers, and I worked with magazine editors. I'm used to extreme behavior, and I've never in my life seen something quite like that. She needs medication and she needs a nice rest in Warm Springs."

Jules rubbed her neck. "I promise to be good," she said. "And if she says anything and I hit her, I promise to go quietly."

"Thanks," said Jules bleakly. "I just came to advise you

that it would be illegal to allow your dogs outside of your yard within town limits without a leash. Okay?"

"Okay," said Alice.

"Okay," yelled Peter from upstairs. "Meet you for a drink in an hour?"

"Okay," said Jules, deciding the day had officially ended.

HE CHANGED OUT of uniform and slid down wet sidewalks to the Blue Bat. There he found Patrick Ankeny, engrossed by the *Bulletin*. Jules bought him a drink and let Patrick think it was a gesture from the heart for a full five minutes.

"Want to help me find a body next week?" asked Jules. "I meant to ask during cards, but I didn't want everyone else to feel left out."

Ankeny had a fine-boned nose, sharp chin, and pale blue eyes; the rest of him—smooth dark skin, soft black eyebrows and hair—was pure Crow. The combination made him particularly difficult to read, especially during poker games. Now he regarded Jules with what might have been amusement, put his beer down, and swung a knee swaddled in Ace bandages onto the bar. "This is a sprain. Sorry, but I've been out on search-and-rescue four times already, once just yesterday, and it's only the beginning of the season. We haven't even lost an elk hunter yet."

Jules peered at the knee. "Is that how you did this?"

"I did this in my driveway last night. Found the guy, drove home, got out of my car, and fell down on the ice."

Jules bought him another drink, this time a gesture born of true compassion. Peter walked in ten minutes later, while Ankeny read the paper and Jules daydreamed about variations of camping with Caroline. No, Peter didn't know if Alice had gotten anywhere with the ladies and the list; she was at the Baird right now with most of the Aches, arranging flowers for the Ganter party.

"How do you think it's going over there?" asked Jules.

"Badly," said Peter. "I dropped Alice off on my way here. Joseph and Laura were talking in Italian, Flo was crying, Jetta and your mother were drinking, and Edie was asking everyone to be nice."

"I don't like the idea of Alice and Flo in the same room if there's alcohol involved," said Jules.

"Not much of a way of avoiding it in this town," said Peter. "Don't you ever miss New York, going whole days without seeing someone you know?"

"Sometimes," said Jules.

Patrick put the *Bulletin* on the bar with a thunk, and Jules picked it up. Professionally speaking, he rarely considered his hometown paper pleasing entertainment.

DETAILS ON ISLAND BODY

Authorities have released some additional information about a body found on Magpie Island last week, in the hope that someone may be able to provide identification.

The geriatrics in town would now file in and donate memories of lost friends, which was just as Jules wanted it. Better endless cups of coffee with people who had something to remember than the juvenile shoplifting beat.

"Why don't they use dental records?" asked a tourist, reading a second copy down the bar from Jules.

"No head," said Patrick Ankeny.

"Eww," said the man, taking a long pull on his beer.

Patrick smiled at Jules, who was safely disguised as a normal human in a pair of jeans and a flannel shirt.

The tourist persisted. "Maybe they can match up an X-ray, figure out where the guy had the broken ankle set."

"Not many X-ray machines in Blue Deer in the thirties and forties, probably," said Peter.

The tourist tossed his paper on the counter. "I like the way they wait till the end to tell you the guy died before Korea."

Jules raised an eyebrow and read the full account.

> The body is that of a light-haired Caucasian male between 20 and 30 years of age, and between 5'10" and 6'. The man had suffered a broken ankle at least a year before his death, and was slightly bow-legged.
>
> The Absaroka Sheriff's Department has received assistance on the case from the FBI, whose forensics experts estimate the individual met his death 40 to 70 years ago, or between 1925 and 1955, and who confirmed that death was due to a firearm, and unlikely to be a suicide. Sheriff Jules Clement has confirmed for the *Bulletin* that neither his department nor the now defunct city police investigated a similar shooting between those years, and says that additional evidence places the death after 1936. The department is now investigating all appropriate unsolved disappearances, and Sheriff Clement asks that any long-time citizens who may have information call him. "Unless the man was an itinerant, I have faith that we'll identify him," he said. "Blue Deer is a town of long memories."

"And the lady in the mountains, the one the guy chopped into bits and just now admitted killing. This shit happens in cities," said the man down the bar. He said "in cities" twice, so that Jules, who was staring blankly into space, would have to respond.

"It happens everywhere," he said mildly. Murder predated cities. Odds were the man on the island had died because of land or money or a woman, because of drink or greed or arrogance, died maybe from a combination of all these things, horribly and slowly from those two bullets in his gut. Jules had seen the fragments of maggot husks under the belt, the egg-bearing flies having arrived even before the man had been buried. Maybe the person with the gun had enjoyed watching the whole show before he threw the body facedown in a sandy pit.

"Well, sure," said the tourist. "But I don't remember stuff like this in the town where I grew up in New Hampshire. Two bodies in a week, three if you count that guy who tried to go swimming, plus a rape. This is the goddamn Wild West, right?"

"Two of them are old," observed Patrick Ankeny.

Jules looked into the back bar mirror at the reflections of the other drinkers who'd flooded into the bar as it grew dark outside. Blue Deer's own rapist, the oldest problem in the world, could be in the same room, having a beer and laughing with the others. So far, the guy had stuck to town; Jules tried to remember how secure Edie's windows were. He moved on to the small item on the bottom right front page, three paragraphs on the rapes with no names, lots of "No comments" and warnings from "a sheriff's department spokeswoman" that the women of Blue Deer needed to be wary of strangers and invest in window locks. Jules hadn't particularly wanted to discuss their lack of progress, but he'd wanted the story longer and up front; his conscience would already be wracked when and if another woman was raped, and a blatant warning might help. Though the wording would be difficult: Beware men with flashlights; try not to live alone. Try not to breathe.

He looked out the Blue Bat's narrow strip of windows and watched someone's fancy cowboy hat sail past the post office.

"Where'd the head go, anyway?" asked the man.

He was full of pesky Yankee curiosity. "Maybe it blew away," Jules answered.

The tourist gave him a look of disdain and departed, blasting the bar with light. Jules had the satisfaction of seeing him recoil in a gust. He'd done his bit for limiting immigration that day.

"He thought you were joking," said Delly.

Blue Deer's local hero was the wind, and the wind's most dramatic season ran from October through January. It shot north up the Rockies, funneled through the upper Yellowstone valley, and swooped east over Blue Deer, not slowing for the corner. The wind gave Blue Deer its greatest notoriety after its fabled trout waters: though the Rocky Mountain front near Browning received mightier blasts, Blue Deer was rumored to be the second most beleaguered town in the country. They needed as many words for wind as the Aleuts had for snow. When it kicked in every fall, the bleariest citizens took on the air of embattled warriors. Even the most rabid land-use fiends, the men and women who would be happiest in a fully paved county-wide shopping mall, were secretly proud of their weather and the first to run to their favorite tavern to discuss gusts of ninety miles an hour during forty-below cold spells, always with the hope that someone else would buy them a drink. When the gusts or the "snap" continued, they were the first to whine and run for a weekend in Las Vegas on $49 round-trip tickets. When they returned crooning Humperdinck songs, the true winter bar brawls ensued, surlier and longer-lived than the summer variety.

This, at least, was Jules's perspective. He also secretly loved the wind, cackled deep in his heart every time a loaded freight car or semi or Airstream simply gusted off a track or road, though he was now the one to have to clean them up. He liked the fact that it crumpled experimental wind machines and antennae like tinfoil, stripped storm windows and roof shingles and sent rocks flying on the river's banks, bent trees and hopelessly inadequate snow fences right off the ground. He enjoyed phoning old friends in New York to announce that, with wind chill, the temperature had reached one hundred and twelve below zero. Such calls reeked of bravery and usually produced sympathy and stray presents, sometimes music, sometimes a bottle of unobtainable Armagnac or Calvados or fine tequila, sometimes fragrant, illegal packages that made Jules happy that he'd vetoed local funding for a dope-sniffing dog at the post office. He'd called it, quite honestly, an unnecessary expense.

The *Bulletin* weather box was right across from the rape article and told Jules that winds had averaged 40 mph and a 74 mph gust had been recorded that morning. At that speed a pinecone with the right trajectory could pass as a deadly weapon. A small chart informed him that a gale was defined as 39–46; a "strong" gale, 47–54; a "storm," 55–63; a "violent storm," 64–72; and a hurricane, 73–82.

Jules looked at Ankeny, who'd flipped his wallet open at

the bar and was prying out money. "So what happens after eighty-two? You're part of the organization that decides such things."

"Huh?" Ankeny peered down at the paper. "Why would you expect the Feds to be good at details? I dunno. *El gusto grande?* The big cold air balloon in the sky farting on us on its way east?"

Jules considered the image of icy, stinky cosmic gas. Patrick cleared his throat and shredded his bar napkin. "Any luck with the dead guy?" he asked.

"Nah. Some poor sucker is going to be eating a sandwich downriver, thinking it's the Pillsbury Dough Boy floating by."

Peter made a face and chugged a beer. "Not the idiot who jumped off the bridge," said Ankeny. "The bones on the island."

"Nothing yet," said Jules. "Probably nothing ever, with no skull."

Ankeny lit a cigarette. "My grandmother knows I know you, and she called to remind me her brother disappeared in the summer of 1939. Just poofed off without a trace. He was working on a Mission Creek ranch up by the old Agency. He said he was going to town one day and that was that. His name was Malcolm Gray Crane."

"Malcolm Gray Crane." Jules echoed the name, and the corner of his mouth on the broken side of his face curled up.

Ankeny didn't notice the smile. "Yep. In his mid-twenties. Her brother, my great-uncle."

"Patrick, that's not a very Anglo name. I'm looking for a blond."

Ankeny grinned. "You know that for sure, huh?"

"We're positive. A real Saxon mother's son."

"Huh," said Ankeny. "Well, anyway, Malcolm wasn't the kind not to come home."

"I didn't see his name on the missing lists," said Jules.

"I imagine my family saw no point to asking the cops for help back then."

"I imagine not," said Jules glumly. A Montana cop had been likelier to beat an Indian than find him in the thirties, or at least beat him after he found him.

Down the bar, Peter and Delly and the man who'd taken the tourist's seat were still talking about the wind. "My tripod blew over," said the new man, gesturing dramatically. "I was out on the park flats below Gardiner, trying to photograph a herd of elk, and everything went down."

"You two met?" asked Ankeny.

They hadn't. The man's name was Carl Jump, and he had the predictable subtle recoil when he found out he was drinking with the law. He was in his forties, with a four o'clock shadow, dark brown hair and a bad cold that didn't seem to dent his sense of humor. He and Peter were telling dog jokes, and Jules finally understood: this was the other owner of Serena the sausage dog, Amber Jump's bird-hunting ex-husband.

"I can't comment on your case," said Jules, "but I'll admit that I don't always agree with the county attorney's office."

"You don't usually agree," said Peter.

"The county people aren't that bad," said Jules mildly. "And most cases are rote."

"Well, this is just silly," said Carl Jump, who seemed more confused than outraged.

He and Ankeny knew each other, too; they'd met when some of Jump's photography students had wandered the wrong way in the Absaroka-Beartooth Wilderness the fall before, and Ankeny had been on search-and-rescue. "You like to hang out with a man who crawls into grizzly dens?" asked Jules.

Ankeny snorted. "You should fucking give me shit. My job's never put me in the hospital."

"I recall a case of smoke inhalation and some minor burns last fall."

"I wanted a vacation."

Neither he nor Patrick had chosen plum professions.

"Photography sounds like such a civilized occupation," said Jules.

"Not really," said Carl Jump. He had his own store, developed film, handled parties, a bit of everything. "Animals are the easy part."

"I'd think weddings and graduations are especially bad," said Jules.

Jump shrugged. "Some are fun, some are nightmares. Tomorrow night I've got a fiftieth anniversary party at the Baird, which should be fun, but it's looking like a nightmare."

Peter snorted.

"Oh, you poor sucker," said Jules. "Let me buy you a drink."

5 *Dancing*

Please join us for a Celebration of Patience
on the occasion of Joseph and Laura Ganter's
50th Wedding Anniversary

6:00 P.M., OCTOBER 21, AT THE BAIRD HOTEL

An Italian Buffet including:

PROSCIUTTO DI PARMA, TOSCANA SALAMI,
COPPA AND MORTADELLA

ROASTED OLIVES, SAVORY BREADS,
AND ASSORTED CHEESES

INSALATA DI MARE

BRODETTO AND LASAGNE DUKES OF FERRARO

ARISTO OF VEAL WITH ROSEMARY

RISOTTOS WITH BABY ARTICHOKES AND WITH RAGU

ROASTED BALSAMIC VEGETABLES AND MASHED
POTATOES WITH BASIL

FRESH FIGS, POMEGRANATES, AND CHAMPAGNE GRAPES

SWEET POLENTA CAKE WITH THIMBLEBERRY SAUCE,
PLUM TART, AND ZABAGLIONE

WINES FROM THE ESTATES OF GIUSEPPE
QUINTARELLI, GIACOMO BORGOGNO & FIGLI, AND
MARCHESI ANTINORI,, AS WELL AS A SELECTION OF
GRAPPAS AND OTHER BRANDIES

BEEF FOR THE HOMEBOYS

No gifts, please

EARLY FRIDAY MORNING, JULES, WESLEY, AND JON-
athan stood in an orchard at a bend in the valley road, re-
garding what they could see of the second automobile fatality
of the year. Al and Bean, the county paramedics, were on
their way with the jaws of life. Jules had told them not to
bother hurrying; he and Wesley, sizing up the situation, had
approached the car very slowly indeed. Only Jonathan, who'd
radioed them to the scene, had been optimistic enough to
rush to what remained of the driver's window and peer inside.

"Eat a peach," said Wesley. The van had traveled over
fifty yards of thawing snow, glacial rubble, and two fruit
trees to accordion definitively on a third.

"That's a plum," said Jules. "Peach trees explode in cold
snaps around here."

"What are you talking about?" asked Jonathan, wiping
away tears.

"Before your time, hon," said Wesley. This was disingen-
uous; almost everything was before Jonathan's time.

"The van? It's got to be at least an '81."

Jonathan was worsening a mess by trying to wipe flecks
of vomit off his uniform. "Never mind," said Jules, grabbing
the handkerchief and deftly wiping away the evidence. "Go
home. Your shift was supposed to be over an hour ago. Call
in the license plate and have Grace start on an ID and next
of kin."

"Male or female?" whispered Jonathan.

Jules and Wesley exchanged a look. Wesley shrugged,
and Jules walked reluctantly back to the van and stared in for
some time. "Male," he said finally.

Jonathan wandered off to his patrol car, staring at the
sunlit valley below the road like a man overwhelmed by the
earth's beauty.

"I just missed you at the Bat last night," said Wesley. "Then I ran for my life. Ankeny was in the mood to go late, and this would have been a bad thing to see on a hangover."

Jules was pacing off the van's ruts to the road. The chinook had continued during the night. The wind felt soft and balmy on his face and the world looked fresh. "He still seemed to be in a fine mood when I left. Just medicating that knee."

"Yeah. For a change he's drinking because he's happy. He's in love."

Jules snickered. "He didn't tell me that. I'm glad he finally has a reason to take his vitamins. Maybe he'll agree to a desk job again."

"Well, as usual there's a problem."

In the year since his divorce, Ankeny, who'd been the friend to recommend Wesley call Jules for a job, had specialized in picking impossible cases. "What now? Is she psychotic? Underage?"

"No, he says she's just right except there's some other guy she's still seeing sometimes. He didn't want to get into it, but he did, you know. I think he knows the boyfriend, so he feels guilty."

"It's not as if the town's swarming with women," said Jules. "A little guilt might be worth it."

Wesley, who had moved to Montana with and for someone, was happy enough to not have noticed the town's poor male-female ratio and found this amusing. "I gather you speak from personal experience."

"Long ago," said Jules. "These days I'm so good I squeak."

ALICE'S LIST WAS on his desk by ten. He found her new efficiency rattling, especially given the reports of dissension from the party front.

Jules:

Here's the dish from the Aches on your missing boys. A big Bronx cheer but for Lars, Ed and Atticus. All of the below were tall & blond & younger than us:

Avery Wale: to California after W.W.II.

Lars Edsendatter: No clue. About the right age, faded off on a trip to Missoula in '38 or '39.

Oleander Prine: Dead of drowning in the late forties or early fifties.

Perry O'Driney: Dead of drowning with Oleander, drunk. They used to do the dirty together.

Ed Compson: No clue, too young for the Aches, last seen in late fifties, early sixties. You might find family in Dillon.

Bill Pope: To Texas.

Bob Kahuc: To Nevada.

Atticus Rinkle: Gone since early forties, big mystery. No one knows. *Very* handsome.

Marvin Datschel: Still kicking in Billings in the sixties.

Sam Millard: Lost a leg in North Africa.

Leslie O'Rourke: To Spain in forties; no one knows.

Gerald Faust: Living in Salt Lake with "his fat wife" (Cicely).

Karl Rothenberg: Cancer, early seventies.

Ford Holleyman: Ran auto parts store in Belgrade, dead in sixties.

Lawrence Sevrier: Living in Great Falls with "his fat third wife" (Cicely, again).

Venus says she didn't buy anyone flowers, so bug off.

I expect you at the hotel to help at four. I hear Neil won't donate his pickup. Peter wants to stick an open can of Spam under the seat when things heat up next spring.

What gives with you and Edie?

Love, Alice

Caroline was on the far side of the room, snickering with Grace about something. Jules waved after he tore off Alice's parting salvo. "This is what my friend Alice Wahlgren came up with. Do you know her? She's running the Historical Society."

"I've talked to her about Flo Amundsen's complaints. I thought Venus Meriwether ran the society."

Apparently everyone had dealt with the Flo-and-Alice conundrum. Jules gave them another month before it came to violence. "Venus runs Alice, and Alice does the grunt work. This is what she gave me on the names you got together. I asked her to take the ladies through yearbooks and come up with some other nominees, but it seems like she's trying to forget. You could get together with her and ask the ladies to come up with some other boys."

Caroline scanned the list and nodded. "So only Lars and Atticus and Ed are really left as options."

"I think Ed's too recent."

"Perry and Oleander must have been quite a scandal."

"I'm sure they were," said Jules. "I'm sure the Aches would love to tell you all about it. Their meetings are usually Thursday, but maybe you could get Alice to speed things up."

This was called passing the buck. It was only after Caroline left that Jules thought of all the disadvantages to Alice's and Caroline's knowing each other, all the ammunition

Alice had collected on him in the last decade. The thought weighed on him until lunch, and when he headed out to pick up Mexican takeout he drove toward Alice's house, prepared to barter for silence. It was too late; Caroline's patrol car was parked out front.

ABSAROKA COUNTY HAD ten thousand people, with not quite half of them in Blue Deer. A few, like Jules, were third or fourth generation, which was as old as it got for a white person; aside from some gold mining in the valley during the 1860s, the Bozeman Trail had been too dangerous to settle until the railroad came through and the Crow were banished in the 1880s. The railroad was still the county's biggest landowner, despite the initial ranching and farming acreage grab; others came for ongoing, not particularly profitable, gold and coal mining, timber, and the trains themselves, which were repaired in massive brick shops on the north side of town.

Then as now, those who didn't come for the trees or the trains or the gold had moved out randomly, either not quite making it to the coast or believing the beauty of the landscape might equal grace. Mostly people saw the place, wanted to live in it, and then flailed about, trying to dream up the how after the why. This was different from the way people moved to, say, Indianapolis or Houston or Hartford. For a long time the Blue Deer Chamber of Commerce had trumpeted about how inexpensive the town was to live in, which was shorthand for admitting that the going wage for a teacher or a printer or a cook averaged six dollars an hour. And it wasn't true anymore; you could no longer buy a house for $20,000 or even $40,000, what with the trust fund ski fiends and retirees and the flotilla of city exiles, all creatively self-employed and computerized. Blue Deer was beautiful, but still a place half the population—possibly the sane half—left after high school.

Jules was bargaining on the few who'd never left, or who'd returned after retiring from jobs in Denver, Salt Lake, or Billings. All afternoon calls came in about the newspaper article. Everyone over sixty had known someone who'd left too abruptly and too finally, and Jules gradually realized that there was a nostalgic tendency to remember short, homely, balding men as long, lean, and golden. Everyone he knew on a first-name basis—almost all the elderly men—wanted to meet for coffee to discuss it all; the ladies wanted him to stop by. Most weeks Jules would have been happy to miss work and sop up loneliness, but this week he couldn't make anyone happy.

Almost all the callers were vague or easily shaken on details. It might have been a broken ankle, though it could have been a collarbone or a rib. The missing man's hair was really light in the summer, when he was out in the fields, but dark in the winter; Jules didn't bother with pubic hair questions. Some of the men had vanished at the turn of the century; others had possibly headed for Canada during Vietnam. Someone's brother Elmer, only missing since 1959; an albino cousin named Dwight who went fishing in 1945; an arrogant asshole named Henry who'd broken his right leg, or was it his left ankle, in a 1938 fracas. Jules wrote down all of them and left his notes on Caroline's desk.

Two conversations stuck out, both of them anonymous. The first voice was whispery, an aged woman. She wanted to speak to the sheriff and seemed dubious of the idea that he might answer his own phone. It took Jules a while to bring her to the point.

"I think my brother killed a man in 1939," she said finally. "Maybe you found the man he killed."

Jules thought about where to begin. "What was the name of the man your brother killed, ma'am?"

"I can't tell you."

"Did he shoot the man?"

"I think so. Yes."

"What did the man look like?"

A pause. "Dark. That's what confuses me. The paper said the dead man was fair, but if the man's head is gone I thought perhaps you were jumping to conclusions."

"We're quite sure the man was fair," said Jules. "But even if we haven't found the man your brother killed, I'd like to know more about your brother and who he killed and how and when." Why, too, though saying he'd *like* to know any of it was a lie. Ignorance, these days, was bliss.

"I'm sorry," she said. "If it's a different body, mine's best left to lie. It was just one of those things. Have a nice day."

A half hour later, after an arduous conversation with a slightly deaf grandmother of missing twins, he had a male caller who tried several strained accents before settling on a rattly whisper.

"You think this man you found had some height?"

"We think so," said Jules. "Like the paper said."

"Maybe you should think about what that means," said the man, his voice very low.

Jules rubbed his eyes and plugged a welling sense of self-pity with the image of the morning's car accident. Once upon a time, he'd actually campaigned for this job. "Maybe you should tell me what information you have," he said patiently.

"Just pointing out that he was a tall boy," said the man. "A tall boy who died before the war."

"Or after," said Jules. "We don't have a sure date."

"Before," said the voice on the phone as the line went dead.

Jules sat for some time before he yelled at the phone. "It means he was tall, you asshole!" The hint was as subtle as a club: Two days earlier he'd talked to three old men who had some connection to the body, and they'd mentioned a sport that involved height. If the man on the island had played basketball in the same decade, they'd have known him, probably well; it was even possible that the caller had been one of them, though Jules was sure he'd have recognized Joseph's voice.

Jules, who was used to believing his uncle, began to get a bad feeling. He wanted to clear it up, make it go away, but he wasn't eager to sic Caroline on Joseph. He tried calling the Ganter ranch himself, but nobody answered, and nobody probably would until after the party.

MILES BIRDLAND'S SECRETARY was chain-smoking and sorting a mountain of paper, acting far too relaxed for her employer to be anywhere near the building. "Did he already head home?" asked Jules.

"I doubt it," she said. "Friday afternoons are his wind-down time. He'll be driving somewhere until he takes over with his wife at dinnertime. That's the regular schedule, more or less."

In hindsight, that whole wing of the building felt empty. "Are they all gone?"

"Well, Axel has to help with that party."

"How about Neil Amundsen? He said he was too busy to help."

"I try not to notice his existence," she said. "I'm usually

successful. But their secretary just told me he took a long lunch, had a quick hearing at three, and headed off again. Dollars to doughnuts it's a girl. He's a looker."

"Ecch," said Jules. "Don't bother the judge if you see him. I hope you have a wonderful weekend."

GRACE WAS STARING into space, looking glum. "Sorry about yelling," said Jules. "An informant was being coy."

She shrugged, but her expression didn't change.

"Don't let me ruin your day," snapped Jules.

She gave him a blank look. "If you'd heard a rumor about a man, and this man asked out a friend, would you tell her about the rumor?"

Grace was usually brutally direct. "Are you worried about damaging the man's reputation?"

"I don't like the jerk, but I want to be fair."

"Is it something harmful to the woman, like a sexual disease?"

Grace's forehead turned pink under the gray frizz. "Not a disease.

"Tell me," said Jules.

"I've heard the man's not always . . . patient."

Jules drummed his desk with a pencil. "Not many people are, these days. You mean rough?"

She nodded. "Abusive. Beyond pushy."

"The 'I know what you really want' sort of thing?"

Grace lurched in her chair as Jonathan blasted through the back door, picking his nose.

Jules suddenly felt his blood pressure skyrocket. "Is it Caroline? Caroline and that prick Neil?"

She nodded.

"Has Neil ever been called on this?"

"I don't think so. I heard it through Bonnie."

Bonnie was Grace's daughter. She owned a hair salon; she probably knew more deep, dark secrets than the town's sole psychiatrist. "Of *course* you tell Caroline," said Jules, enraged. "Are you out of your mind? Did he ask her out? Did she say yes to him?"

"I don't know," said Grace. "Maybe you should mention it to her."

"Somehow I think it would be better coming from you," said Jules.

"It might be too late, anyway," said Grace.

THAT AFTERNOON, WHEN Jules left work to help set up for the party, the temperature was seventy, and he could think of a thousand other things to do with the evening, most of which involved his own porch. Maybe it had been the sight of the man who'd died on the plum tree, or Mary McLinchey's face as she said the word *flashlight*, or a photo Jules remembered of the woman Wayne Contway had buried in the mountains ten years earlier—whatever the reason, Jules wasn't particularly eager to celebrate fifty years of combatant love, especially when the celebrated couple seemed to be having the worst disagreement of their married life.

Eager or not, he and Peter and the owner of the Baird retrieved banquet tables and folding chairs from the Catholic school and the Lutheran church basement and unloaded them into the Baird lobby and dining room, then rearranged everything twice as Jetta and Alice and the owner's wife refined their plans. Alice and Jetta were wrangling about wine; Flo, it seemed, had wanted all of it in a corner location, to slow people down and have the bottles look more plentiful, and Jetta didn't want to risk angering her. Peter and Jules had first moved everything according to Flo's wishes, then moved it again according to Alice's, then let Axel Scotti move things where he wanted them.

Flo didn't arrive until five thirty, a solid hour late, and everyone began to yell at once. Flo immediately burst into tears, which made her look larger and pinker than usual.

"Give her something," muttered Jetta to no one in particular. "We don't have time for this. I have to go find that old asshole."

"What old asshole?" asked Jules.

"My father," she said. "Mom says he wouldn't get in the car with her."

When Scotti said something acidic about Flo's table-setting pace, she choked her way into a monologue. She was late *because* she'd been watching her mother *because* she, Flo, suffered for everyone and *because* her father had to work late *because* Axel was a lazy asshole, on into infinity. Perhaps, thought Jules, Neil was a lower life-form *because* Flo had always used that word for an answer when he asked questions at age two.

Jules had these evil thoughts from an armchair in the corner of the lobby, where he and Peter were blowing up balloons and sipping double whiskeys while everyone else argued.

"Flo planned to put the gifts on that table," said Jetta wearily.

"Well, I haven't seen Flo do anything but plan, so she can put them up her ass," said Scotti.

"She was taking care of her mother, Axel."

That shut him up; death and its entitlements. The problem in this case was that Flo wasn't the one who was dying, though the distinction seemed lost on her.

They watched the chaos grow. It reminded Jules of Alice's catering days in New York, when he and Peter would be suddenly called upon to drive forty blocks for an extra lobster or a pumpkin-colored tablecloth or the trays of appetizers Alice had inevitably left on top of her refrigerator. There had been the notable incident when the Volkswagen had been towed away for double-parking in the midst of unloading on Fifth Avenue; Alice's whole profit had changed hands for the sake of a speedy retrieval.

Such fiascoes had only been made bearable by drugs and alcohol, no longer entirely viable options. Jetta shot off to find Joseph, and Jules was amused to see the hotel owners exchange a look and escape by the back door. Alice walked over and drained half of Peter's whiskey.

"Did you talk to the ladies about new candidates for the missing list?" asked Jules.

"No, but Caroline and I are getting together with them at the next meeting."

"When?"

"Thursday."

"That's not exactly jumping all over the problem."

Alice narrowed her nearsighted eyes. "Everyone's coming to the party tonight, and no one wants to meet tomorrow. Mabel and Angelina are going to Billings on Sunday and won't be back till late, and Caroline's leaving with you early Monday morning and won't be back until Wednesday night at the earliest. So the regular Thursday night meeting wins the prize."

"You could call around," he sniped, not caring if he sounded pissy.

"Waste of energy," said Alice, finishing Peter's drink. "They play off each other, and half of them need to read lips.

And it seems to me that if no one's missed the body in fifty years, another week won't make much of a difference."

She wandered into the bar, passing Carl Jump, the photographer.

"It's going be like this, is it?" Jump asked forlornly.

"Nah," said Jules. "Everyone will have fun once the food comes out."

THE ONLY HIGH point of the early evening, beyond the prosciutto and cheeses and wine, was the sight of Neil Amundsen arriving alone, having obviously begun drinking earlier in the afternoon. Flo watched him like a hawk. She seemed tremendously agitated and busy, but Jules saw her check the same table setting four times without doing more than adjusting the salad fork.

Mental illness took so many forms. Jules mentioned this to his mother, Olive, who muttered something about God's infinite capacity for variety and humor. It was her favorite new concept, picked up due to her new job at the admissions desk of the hospital—her early retirement from the Forest Service had lasted four months.

Joseph appeared at Jules's elbow at seven, an hour late for his own party. "Where the hell were you?" asked Jules.

"Burning trash in the gully after my wife took the house to pieces."

"This your week of destruction?"

He smiled. "Apparently."

"Is this a specific argument or a general mood thing?"

"Oh, it's specific all right," said Joseph a little giddily. "I'd give you anything for a sip of that drink so I can stand in this corner for another three minutes without talking to people."

"I'm not people?" asked Jules.

"Not really. Take it as a compliment."

Joseph had two minutes before Laura, tall and regal in black, swooped down upon him. The three other corners of the room were taken up with couples who looked as if they didn't appreciate their good fortune. Peter and Alice weren't actually married, which was probably part of the problem; Jules expected them to change this situation within the year. To do them justice, this argument looked minor, probably having to do with Peter's problems in cocktail pacing. Axel and Jetta Scotti were huddled together near the stairs, and Axel was wearing the expression he normally saved for the judge's chambers, an I Am a Truly Intelligent Yet Thoroughly Humble Human look that didn't seem to be getting him far with the rancher's daughter. Jules deduced the struggle might have something to do with a waitress named Ben who was caroming through the room with a tray of prosciutto and cheeses, caramel locks flying prettily every which way. Jules assumed this because Ben had once told him, when she happened to be sitting on him, that she'd known the prosecutor quite well too; wasn't that a coincidence? Scotti was about as Italian culturally as SpaghettiOs, in that his family hadn't visited Naples or even New York since 1860 or so, but the last trait to go was the conviction that men would of course stray, and other men, even relatives of the wife, would never question this or take it amiss. It had kept Jules from liking him openheartedly as a cousin-in-law even before their work began to set them at odds.

The room was filling up with people who circled and gestured and hugged. Jules watched the men and women and wondered who had called that afternoon, talking of dead dark men and tall boys. Ben the waitress winked a soft green eye at him. Jules winked back and took another no-nonsense slug from his whiskey. The couple of honor now held the corner nearest him, and off and on he could hear their endearments; Laura had just called her husband of fifty years an old prick and a liar in still-accented English. Her Italian mouth made the very crisp word extra long, *prrricccckkk*, a verbal roller coaster of derision. Joseph was attempting, a little feebly, to defend himself, and said something very soft in Italian.

This last actually made her smile, and she pinched his ear. Joseph's long arm disappeared behind her, returning the favor. At least, thought Jules, averting his eyes politely, they didn't take each other for granted. Alice was smiling now, too, with Peter's arm draped around her shoulder; Scotti wasn't smiling at all, and Jetta was nowhere in sight.

The other hundred people, half of them white-haired, thundered away at each other while various Ganter offspring and staff monitored their happiness. Flo Amundsen was chasing the determinedly cheerful photographer from group to group; Edie was helping bartend at one of the drinks tables, not the one Jules had visited. She was wearing a tiny black skirt and a low white blouse, and Jules tried to think pleasant thoughts. But nothing was entirely pleasant anymore, even Edie in a short skirt; they'd lost most of their empathy, and with it most affection past lust. He cared that she might like someone else, sleep with someone else, but not as much as he should care. He didn't give a shit about much of anything, a sure sign that winter was looming.

Jules looked away from them all, through the windows into the dark, windy night. A couple was walking bent in the wind toward the hotel, but they passed the awning; Jules enjoyed the idea that someone in town had somewhere better to go than the anniversary party. The man was turned away from Jules with his arm around the woman's shoulders, talking to her while she looked past him through the hotel windows and straight into Jules's eyes. They stared at each other and then she was gone.

It was Caroline.

Jules looked around the room for Neil in vain and put down his empty glass. Ben, intimate to county law, was offering oysters and had to say his name twice before he noticed her presence or her tray.

After a dangerously long cocktail hour they took assigned places. Jules was with his mother at a table with a retired minister, Cicely Tobagga, and Horace Bolan and his wife. Olive and Cicely and Ella Bolan talked about Cicely's granddaughter, who'd just moved to town in the midst of a disintegrating relationship, and how Blue Deer might not be the best place for a single woman. Or person, period; they kept including Jules in their conversation, as if he'd have inside information. The minister, Jules, and Horace, who was a doctor, talked about death; the minister, who was slightly daffy at the best of times, chugged red wine and began to refer to his tablemates as fellow "Horsemen of the Apocalypse." Jules, glazing over, came out of his trance to notice that Neil Amundsen had taken a seat next to his mother and that Carl Jump was watching him with loathing, undoubtedly thinking about Serena.

The sappy toasts from friends took an eternity. Actual relatives thought it most apt to give a sort of Top Ten list of Ganter arguments, decade by decade, starting with the one that had followed Laura's horrified first sight of her home in 1945. No stucco churches, soft olive groves, glowing frescoes, real vegetables; she'd tried, incoherent and five months pregnant, to immediately board an eastbound train. The argument for the fifties had to do with renovating the ranch house after child number three, something about Laura's ordering tens of thousands of dollars' worth of furniture from Chicago. In 1964 they'd returned to Europe for a sort of honeymoon and Joseph had caught Laura kissing an old boyfriend; in the mid-seventies Joseph discovered that Laura had known for some time that most of their children (and nieces and nephews) smoked pot in the tack shed. In the eighties they'd actually separated (no one mentioned that this had been spurred by the revelation of Joseph's long-term affair with Cicely Tobagga, who drank heavily through this portion of the evening) and had sent their children back and forth with messages in Italian. The current decade's argument seemed to be fomenting, and no one had the nerve to ask for a topic.

Dancing kicked in right after dinner, with the cutting of the anniversary cake scheduled for later. Jules leaned against a register, letting his ass absorb the heat while he watched the couple of honor waltz and while Alice and Peter began another argument. Alice had a long "seemed fine" stage while drinking, during which she was witty, voluble, and energetic. But when this stage ended, it was a bit like seeing a two-year-old hearing one too many no's.

It seemed to Jules that such a moment might be approaching. He wandered off to tail Edie, who'd begun to look friendlier as the evening wore on. Once he started, a sense of urgency grew. She consented to dance only after he began to apologize in front of other people, and once they began to dance he finally succeeded in making her laugh by whispering about his house, or a room upstairs, or possibly the basement couch. Success was near when Ben's dear hand clamped down on his shoulder.

"You have a phone call."

She pointed to the lobby desk and headed in the other direction. Edie was gone in the next second.

Jules knew it would be Grace. Someone had misjudged a curve, misunderstood the domestic contract, incited a summer-style bar fight.

"Is Nestor Amundsen there?" she asked.

"Not that I've seen. He's not much of a partygoer."

"Are you sure?"

Jules swiveled to inspect the room. Most of the rancher types had run for the bar when the dancing started, and he dropped the phone to check there, too. In the process, two people started conversations with him, and it took two or three minutes to get back to Grace.

"Well," she said crabbily. "Then I have a welfare check for you."

"Are you kidding?"

"No, I'm not. Nina and the ranch manager are in Denver, and Nestor didn't pick up when they tried to phone in with the details of some deal or another. They say he's all alone on the ranch, and he has a cold, and he was supposed to call this afternoon. The last they talked to him, he'd planned to come to the party."

"Humph," said Jules.

"Find Flo Amundsen; send her," snapped Grace. "They left a message for her earlier and she hasn't called back."

"Aargh," said Jules. He'd last seen her lurching through a swing number with Merle Ott, and Merle was having trouble holding on.

"She's drinking?"

"So's Neil."

"That boy wouldn't check on a body in the middle of a road, let alone a grandfather fifteen miles away."

AN UNFORTUNATE PRAIRIE OCCURRENCE   99

As if Jules would argue. "Nestor's probably stuck with some goddamn cow problem."

Grace plugged on, though he could sense she was losing patience. "They say he hasn't been out after dark in a decade. He should be out at the far house, the hands' house, but he isn't answering the phone. They know that the weather's better, but they're worried he got his vehicle stuck in the mud and might try to walk home across the ranch, and you know that would take all night."

As if it was Jules's fault that Nestor owned too much land to cross in a polite period of time. "Or he's on his way in to the party now. Or he forgot to call, felt yucky, went to bed early and isn't picking up. Or the wind blew the phone lines down. Or he left the phone off the hook by accident. No neighbors who could run over?"

"You're eating with the Ganters. The people to the north don't pick up, and anyway they just moved from California. They wouldn't know where to start."

Jules kept trying. "I've had a few drinks."

Grace snorted. "That's never stopped you before."

"Call them one more time, make sure he hasn't checked in with them."

"Call them yourself," said Grace. "They're at the Brown Palace."

"Just your average thrifty ranchers," said Jules. "This is a bad night to do anyone a favor. The old asshole's probably tucked in with one of his sheep, or with a girl who looks like a sheep."

"Hey," said Grace huffily. "I'm calling you from home. I was supposed to be at that party, too, but I've felt crappy all week and needed a break. Nina couldn't get anywhere with Richard at the station, so they got me out of bed, and two-tracking around for an old asshole, if he isn't my old asshole, isn't in my job description, is it? And it's in yours, isn't it?"

Jules sighed, took the number and muttered.

"What?" asked Grace.

He enunciated clearly. "Smart-ass."

She laughed and hung up. He stayed at the phone, playing with the idea of begging Edie for a quickie. He was just drunk enough to be desperate, locked into an idea of pleasure like a child promised a toy. But she was dancing with Joseph now, giggling and oblivious.

Jetta was wrestling with the cake in the cloakroom while Flo watched critically. Jules rummaged through the coats, swearing.

"What are you looking for?" asked Jetta.

"My goddamn coat. I've got to find goddamn Nestor Amundsen, make sure the old goat hasn't fallen out of bed. You hear from your father-in-law today, Flo?"

He'd rarely seen an expression so blank. "Never mind," he muttered.

"Nestor?" said Flo.

"Nestor," snapped Jules. "He was supposed to be here tonight, and he was supposed to call Nina, and he failed on both counts. So I'm going to make sure he's just sucking his thumb in bed."

"Why would he come here?" asked Jetta. "He wasn't invited. He and Dad haven't spoken for years."

Jules didn't care to argue. "Where's my goddamn coat?"

"I put them upstairs," Flo whispered. "Along with everyone's who came early. I'll get them."

He followed her, feeling contrite, threading through the people crouched with drinks on the steps along the banister and the wall. "Have you seen him lately?" he asked.

"Not since yesterday," said Flo. "I brought him dinner and dropped off something for tonight, too."

"I don't suppose Neil would want to check."

She stopped and gave him a panicked look. "Don't you dare send him."

Jules stared at her. "He's had wine," said Flo. "What if he got a DUI?"

Not "What if he had an accident?" Here was a family who put an emphasis on judgment. Jules focused on her plentiful backside as they continued up the stairs and wondered what she'd have to say if the sheriff came up with a DUI that night.

They faced a wall of people; the mezzanine had its own bar table, plus a view. "Wait here," said Flo.

Jules waited on the stairs and watched the party below. Edie was now dancing with Peter, Alice was dancing with Joseph, Jetta was tangoing with her errant husband, and Neil was locked together with Ben the waitress, who was possibly in search of fresh courthouse blood.

"Watch out," yelled one of the watchers on the mezzanine.

Jules looked up to see his coat floating down toward him, and his first thought was that Flo had finally begun a tantrum and thrown it. His second thought was panic: Flo was floating through the air after the coat like the Macy's Bullwinkle balloon, with an amazing look of concentration on her face and an abundance of not very appetizing cleavage. Jules clutched the banister a second before she landed on him, and they slammed into the marble wall three steps down.

"My leg," howled Flo. She had her arm wrapped around one of his thighs, and he was fairly sure his spine had cushioned most of her fall.

"Uh," said Jules.

"I've broken my ankle," she moaned.

He finally managed to inflate his lungs but decided he shouldn't use them to comment.

FLO SOBBED THE whole way to the hospital. After a couple of attempts to comfort her, Jules opted for silence, then dumped her with the emergency ward nurse. Back at the Baird, he had a quick brandy, turned down a chance to pose for a group shot with the family, looked for Neil in vain, made Edie promise to sleep in his bed, and limped back out into the night.

The warm chinook had shredded the Baird's new awning, but it rocked him and cleared his head. He took the back road, all dirt, forgetting stretches of it would be a mud wallow after the thaw, and after one particularly loose maneuver on a switchback he pulled over and very deliberately recited the alphabet. He took the next two miles east at a crawl, then cut north onto Nestor's land at the Hancock church.

The road was Nestor's driveway, and for the next ten miles Jules glided through the dark, humming and enjoying the wind. There was still plenty of moon, and the wind sucked at limestone outcroppings as if it could make the mountains tidal. Jules traveled along a plateau, level with the dark shapes of tree tops rooted in the creek bottom, past a sign that said SPEED CHECKED BY RADAR. It had been there for at least a decade, and was someone else's silly idea. Blots of juniper on the hillsides sometimes moved and became blots of cattle, but he saw no buildings for three miles. He reached the dark ranch house and main barns and kept going, turning northwest when the road splintered into three smaller lanes. After four more miles on slippery clay, the ruts shiny in the high beams, he made out the porch light of the guest house shuddering through the old willows that lined the road.

Jules turned off his engine. There was no other car in the yard. There hadn't been at the main house, either, but he supposed there were several places to stow a vehicle on fifteen thousand acres. As he crunched across the driveway to the house he was sure no one was home; the muddy gravel he walked on, from Nestor's very own gravel pit, glowed pink and shiny with mica and travertine in the moonlight. There was fresh horse shit near the front porch, but no horse; Nestor was probably taking a warm night ride, either chasing stragglers or ministering to sick bovines or possibly just enjoying the change of weather and the nearly round moon. Or he'd fallen off for the first time in sixty years and was dying slowly on the chilly, wet dirt of one of the hundred gullies he owned.

The cabin stove was still warm, and someone hadn't washed a plate that held the remnants of not-completely-dried-out baked beans and the crust of a sandwich. The bedroom and the bathroom were empty of bodies, though tissues were piled by the bathroom sink and there were small drops of blood on the gray linoleum floor.

Jules called Denver from the cabin phone. Yes, said the ranch manager, Ira Meidenhaft, Nestor had been prone to nosebleeds—hiccoughs, too—and he'd probably leave all his dishes for their return or the once-a-week maid, and he wouldn't put it past Nestor to be out late riding on a chinook night if there was animal trouble. Still, eleven was unheard of. Period. It shouldn't be hard to find Nestor; if he was in trouble, Jules would hear the border collie, Ralphie, barking.

Nina Amundsen got on the phone. Did Jules remember

the case a few months ago that hadn't ended well, the murder of a wealthy rancher whose glasses had been discovered in the mud of a stock pen? Jules did; he pointed out, politely, that that man had been worth ten million and his murderer, a hired hand, had confessed.

"It's stupid, I know," said Ira, retrieving the phone and asking Nina to go back down to the lobby for some tea. He thought it likelier she fretted about the example of Nestor's "little" brother, Gott (age seventy-four), who'd committed suicide with a .45 on a cold spring day earlier that year.

Without saying that Nestor had lied about being invited to the party, Jules tried to suggest that he might have headed to town for the anniversary party and decided on a poker game instead. No, said Ira. Nestor never gambled. Jules mentioned the absence of a car and asked if it was possible that Nestor's had broken down, and if he might have taken a horse to go fix it. "It's a new Suburban," said Ira. "But he's always ripping them up on boulders. That's probably what he's doing, instead of just waiting until morning. It embarrasses him when he screws up."

Jules promised to call back that night, one way or another. He hung up and stared at the cabin living area again. A finished beer by a pile of old stock receipts; playing cards in a messy pile by their box on the coffee table. He walked into the bedroom and regarded the sheets and blankets, which were pulled halfway off the bed and onto the floor, though Nestor had taken the time to fold a pair of jeans on a trunk and had tossed his laundry in the corner. A suit jacket, a white shirt, and a pair of slacks and good shoes lay under the bedding on the floor. Party clothes, for sure.

Jules drove above the house to the east for a mile. Halfway up a stubby butte he climbed out and looked and listened, bending forward in the wind. Nothing but the glow of the porch light and the dim flicker of a car on the main road, several miles to the northeast. He walked west a hundred yards to see around a hump of rock, saw the porch light again, and retreated for the car, squinting toward the first glow he'd seen, suddenly sure it was a fire but unable to make out any details.

Nestor, the asshole, had apparently decided to camp out in late October on his own land, a concept so Norwegian as to be beyond belief, so annoying that Jules longed to ignore it. On a windy night that would be bad form. Fifteen minutes later Jules was lost and had taken a year off his pickup's already extended existence, but he finally reached a reliable-looking two-track. He followed it around a rise and faced the source of the glow, Nestor Amundsen's dark green Suburban, now black and nestled within some charred juniper bushes.

Jules's lights played over the back end, the scorched grass and shrapneled fragments of a metal can. He parked and found his flashlight and circled around toward the front of the Suburban. The vehicle creaked and ticked, still cooling. The wind barely touched this coulee, and the needles hadn't dropped on the burned junipers. A few tiny, cindered aspen were interspersed throughout, all the shrubs there because of a small oozing spring that made the soil around the Suburban mud and recorded what looked like a single set of prints leading to the driver's door. There was little doubt who they belonged to: a left footprint next to a round, deep impression; another round, deep impression a foot and a half to the right. Nestor had been using crutches instead of his artificial leg when he'd gotten in; offhand, it didn't seem he'd ever gotten back out.

Jules was sweating despite the wind. He looked up to the sky before he stepped closer to the still-radiant Suburban and pointed the flashlight. Nestor's teeth, white and gleaming against a charred background, grinned back at him. One arm propped him up on the seat, and the other was curled under his chin. The posture was oddly relaxed; he might have been thinking about life.

After Jules got rid of his roast veal and vegetables, his risotto, seafood salad, numerous glasses of Barolo, fine grappa, and a plum tart, he called the station from the cabin, then aimed his truck lights again and walked above the coulee, trying to take in the landscape. The right side of the Suburban abutted rock. Jules moved the truck and crawled around on that side to ensure that nothing illuminating lay on the pink travertine. Then he walked up to the blown-out passenger window and peered into the Suburban again. That was when he saw the dog.

After a second cleansing, Jules radioed and curled up in his truck cab to wait for Harvey and Ed, the van, and the equipment.

AT 3:00 A.M., in the midst of a monologue from Ed about how Nestor had a real sense of timing—a grass fire would have started for sure if it hadn't just snowed—the patrol car radios all squawked simultaneously in the warm night breeze, and Jules sped back to town with his lights on, no siren.

The woman's name was Rosa Bouleouw, and she was a forty-year-old Dutch member of their local New Age cult. She was covered by angry red bite marks and had a welt on her left cheek where she'd been knocked to the ground by the rapist, who'd once again worn a ski mask, a sweatshirt, and jeans; carried a knife; and entered through a rickety back door while she slept. Her estimate of his height was taller than Mary McLinchey's, up to six-two. Rosa was shorter than Mary, and Jules took this difference in perspective into account. The man had sounded perfectly healthy physically, if not mentally. He said he'd kill her if she yelled, and he'd laughed toward the end. Rosa Bouleouw had found this particularly scary.

Jules had dealt with her earlier that fall, when she'd complained of harassment by some teenagers and he'd managed to catch them red-handed, spraying anticult slogans on her car. Her English was British-accented and precise; she called the flashlight a "lamp" and the hospital an "infirmary." She didn't want to go for the lab work, and Caroline had spent the last hour coaxing her. Rosa Bouleouw finally agreed to go when it became evident that Jules would dedicate the same amount of time to the argument. She was obviously leery of him: The cult had been around for a decade and hadn't been well treated before Jules's tenure.

The three of them climbed into the squad car for the drive to the hospital. Caroline looked as if the call had gotten her out of bed, but she still smelled faintly of perfume, and her lips were too red.

She caught him looking. "Well, where were you? Did the party run late?"

"I'll tell you after we finish up here," said Jules.

6 *Cactus*

10/16. Watch out for Rm 203. Tiffany said he paid for a beer and hamster or bird food fell out of his pocket, also suspicious white gooey stuff on one bill. Has anyone seen anything? Smelled anything? Checked the closets? *AH*

10/17. Alvin needs medication. Left message for Abby at Social Services after some asshole there told me it wasn't our business to monitor their clients, even if they do sleep in our rooms and piss on our floors. *AH*

Guy from bar was sleeping in front of 320 at 4:00 a.m. He tried to kick me so I called it in; Officer Auber took him away. *DM*

Changed rooms for Levi's commercial crew to 206, 210, 212. They complained about being on bar wing, said they needed more room for equipment, couldn't hack the stairs from 4th floor. Pissed off that we don't have 2-hour dry cleaning service. I said they should try Billings for their next shoot, if they wanted big city conveniences. *Hoo hoo hah hee hee. BH*

10/18. Mrs. Ganter wants to know if we can get in midnight blue tablecloths for the Friday party.

Sez she's not in a white mood. Does anyone know where the linen sample book went? *BH*

10/19. Warn Barbie that Jetta Scotti's pissed off about the flower order, and Flo A. (psycho bitch) will be calling about more roses and vases (do we have fourteen matching?!?). *EL*

Alvin told me the third floor ghost ate his favorite book. I'd appreciate it if everyone bothered Abby about the prescription. *EL*

Tawna didn't show to clean. I think this is fourth day in a row. I finished all rooms except 410. Everyone should go up and see what's hanging from the ceiling fan. *EL*

10/20. River Drug called to say Social Services called in meds for Alvin, could we pick them up, and did we think they really meant to put Alvin on gout medication. I said I thought gout might be the only thing he didn't have. Left message at SS; Alvin headed off for a walk in shorts. Bank clock reads 9F. *EL*

Tawna's asshole boyfriend came looking for her so I called the station again, got that dweeb Jonathan instead of that cutie Wesley. Next time I'll just throw Tawna's asshole boyfriend out the window myself. *BH*

10/21. Edie—your boy the Law phoned, sounding contrite. Hubba hubba. Are you working the party tonight? *AH*

10/22. It's 4:00 a.m., the lobby's still styed out, and a lady is screaming bad words in what sounds like Italian on the fourth floor. They don't pay me enough. *DM*

Technically, I think it's too late, but will someone please warn Ben that Neil Amundsen is a raving prick? *DM*

SATURDAY WAS A LOVELY DAY, THE RIGHT KIND OF DAY FOR fishing or a nap in a hammock or reading a cheap novel on a front porch. During his two hours in bed, Jules had secretly hoped for a record blizzard that might erase or at least postpone every problem in life, including flight arrivals and crispy bodies and girlfriends who'd left fuck-you notes on his kitchen table. But that morning at ten, following a long talk with a distraught widow, Jules stood in the basement of the hospital, looking down at the way Nestor's burned flesh had pulled back from the round bullet hole in the temple, postmortem heat cracks radiating away from the opening in his skull. They'd just lifted him from the scale, where they'd discovered Nestor had lost at least a quarter of his body weight to the blaze.

The plum tree man was a blob under a plastic sheet on the next table. His blood alcohol had been .18, not quite high enough to make it clearly an accident that he'd accelerated, rather than braked, as he rounded the orchard bend; his foot on the gas pedal had been one of only two intact body parts. Fifty-two, recently divorced, no note, no children, no siblings, parents, money, or pets.

Horace was bending over Nestor. "What was he wearing?" asked Jules bleakly. Vomiting at his first sight of Horace's current subject hadn't saved him from a slight hangover, nor had staying up all night, drinking coffee with a traumatized woman. Whenever he managed to put aside thoughts of Rosa Bouleouw, the word *grappa* kept echoing in his mind.

"Something thin and waffly, like long underwear." Horace Bolan pointed to a bumpy pattern in Nestor's charred skin. Horace, an internist, had been Absaroka County's temporary and highly reluctant medical examiner for two years.

"Shoes?" Jules corrected himself. "A shoe?"

"Something thin, like a slipper. Something that just melted." He gestured to the gummy sheen on the bottom of Nestor's withered foot.

Jules thought of the dainty crutch print in the mud outside the driver's door. "Did you know his brother shot himself?"

Horace nodded. "Not to mention his father, who was one of my first nonpatients," he said quietly. "An instructive example of the destructive capabilities of shotguns."

Jules looked outside in time to see one of Scotti's campaign posters fly by in the wind. "How many people kill themselves in their pajamas?"

"I'd guess beds are one of the most popular locations," said Horace. "Guns and pills, usually. They go together. People think they'll be able to relax."

"Pajamas *outside*?"

Horace grinned without looking particularly happy. "I bet cars run a fast second to beds. Maybe Nestor mixed his metaphors."

Jules drummed his fingers on the steel table.

"Listen," said Horace. "The one thing I know is not to expect anyone crazy enough to kill himself to be reasonable. And it looks like Nestor was reasonable enough to pop himself before the fire got to him. He probably hoped the fire would incinerate everything, clean up the mess so his family wouldn't see anything bad."

"He failed," said Jules.

Horace looked down at the contorted black lump and nodded. Nestor Amundsen had assumed the fetal position, ending life as he'd begun it.

"Any health problems?"

"An enlarged prostate, probably precancerous."

"Do you think he knew?"

"I told him myself a couple of months ago."

Another classic presuicidal straw, the shitcanning penis, added to centuries of Norwegian tradition. Jules began to perk up. Horace noticed and threw another bucket of water.

"He didn't seem heartbroken. He said something about being lumped in with half the other assholes who'd reached his age and said he hadn't had good sex for five years, anyway. His other foot was getting funky. He said I was welcome to snip whatever whenever, but he didn't seem to want to bother."

Jules felt his groin quiver and traced Nestor's outline on the examination table, edging toward Horace's true opinion. "Any problem with the wound or the gun placement?"

Horace shrugged. "Nah. You said the gun hopped around the car like a Mexican jumping bean, right?"

"Yes."

"Was he left- or right-handed?"

"I haven't asked Nina yet," said Jules. They looked down in silence for a while. "You'll take tissue samples, won't you? When you're done, call Babaski."

"I've already taken some samples," said Horace. "But I don't want to be the one to cut him open, mess around with that hole in his head. I'd just as soon you sent him north to the state lab in Missoula before the funeral home."

Jules made a face. "Not enough left for you to test?"

"No," said Horace with a small smile. "No, I just found one thing I didn't like, and because the damage is so extensive I'd just as soon they look at that bullet hole, too."

"Didn't like" was Horace code for something's being horribly wrong. Jules felt his breathing slow with dread. "What?"

"Well, first look in his mouth."

"Oh, goodie," said Jules sarcastically. He peered in with the proffered flashlight. "I see a black palate and a shriveled tongue. I already knew Nestor had a good set of teeth for his age."

"You see that funny stick on the roof, way back? Got little webs coming out of it?"

"Maybe." Jules stood straight. "I can't look in there anymore, Horace. I just can't."

"Well, I pulled this out of his throat."

Horace was holding a discolored, misshapen white feather. The kind of feather, Jules realized, that was probably duck or goose and probably came out of a pillow. "Oh, fuck me," he said.

"Now, let's not go jumping to conclusions," said Horace. "He might have kept a pillow in the car, used it when he shot himself. God knows what happens to feathers during a fire."

Jules rubbed his head with both hands and sat down on the wall radiator.

"No chance that he kept poultry on the ranch?" asked Horace.

"What, and ate them raw and unplucked?" Jules cast a bleak look in the doctor's direction. "What do you want

Missoula to check with the wound? How long it had been there before he burned?"

"Yes."

"And whether he was still alive when the hole got there?" Horace nodded and covered Nestor with a plastic sheet.

"Any other signs that he might have been smothered?"

"Missoula might be able to see something. He's too charred for me to see bruising."

"I'll get Harvey to drive Nestor up this afternoon," said Jules. "Harvey has family up there."

But first he had Harvey and Ed keep Nina Amundsen and a growing covey of mourners safely in the main house while he dusted the bunkhouse, finding prints from at least a dozen people, and took tire impressions from the yard and the road leading to the shell of the Suburban. Five cars had pulled through the mud after Wednesday's snow disappeared: the county van, Jules's pickup, Ed's patrol car, the Suburban itself, and another vehicle with worn Goodyears. Jules couldn't swear to it, but this last looked to be second from the bottom, on top of the Suburban but below the others; whoever had driven it had parked twenty yards from the inferno, where a nice long rock ledge led straight to Nestor's last parking place.

Jules crawled around in the drying pink mud for another hour, looking for oddities while a tow truck prepared to remove the scorched Suburban and Harvey took molds of the tire prints. The car's doors had had to be pried open the night before, and Nestor's crutch print and footprint had been obliterated in the fray after Harvey had taken photos. Jules found nothing but an arrowhead and a petite and hardy cactus, whose thorns would remain with his knee for some time. A herd of yearling Angus watched him, and he wondered if they'd watched Nestor burn the night before. The tow crew politely avoided looking at him directly, as did the Amundsen clan when he stopped again with more questions, his hands and knees filthy and dried grass in his uncombed hair.

Ira Meidenhaft, the ranch manager, was succinct and businesslike despite red-rimmed eyes. Nestor had been in fine spirits lately; he'd chosen to skip the Denver trip because he hated to fly. Nina had arthritis in her back and wasn't up to a day in the car, and she was the one who really enjoyed some days in the city, especially with Christmas coming up.

Jules had never used "coming up" to describe an event two months distant, but he wasn't the sort to argue with a widow. Nina, who passed for sixty most days, now looked as if she'd given an extra pint of blood at eighty. She spoke in a monotone without moving except to occasionally push back the cloud of soft gray hair that kept slipping out of a chignon. Ira Meidenhaft stood protectively behind her while a growing cloud of women, many of whom had danced until midnight the night before, swirled in and out of the kitchen: Laura Ganter and Cicely Tobagga, testy as always with each other, Indie Whitsan, Ella Bolan and Mabel, Jetta with a big bowl of fruit and a bottle of cognac. Jules's own mother, Olive, wore dark glasses and arrived with the special inedible meat loaf she brought to every house in mourning. Flo lay on the couch in the living room with her arms folded over her head, every so often giving a long, shuddering sigh. He noticed that her ankle was in an Ace bandage instead of a cast, and resisted the urge to kick it.

Jules took Nina to a glassed-in side porch, warm in the sun. She refused to believe her husband had killed himself, though she also refused to believe he'd been murdered. Jules tried discussing Nestor's mood and mentioned his brother's death, the rancher's precancerous prostate, the poor circulation in his remaining foot, the death of their only child, Neil's father, five years earlier. She heard him out patiently, then shook her head. "It's always something at our age," she said. "His body still worked, and his brother and our son had been unhappy for years. It was a relief when they found peace."

Jules found this equanimity hard to believe. "I saw Nestor a few days ago and he looked awful."

"He'd had a cold," said Nina, waving feebly to a new arrival.

"This was more than a cold," said Jules.

She stared at him for a moment, then roused herself. "Life," she said in a sharper, deeper voice. "There were many things to make Nestor unhappy, but that does not mean he killed himself. He would have told me, at least left me some word if I didn't want to go with him."

Jules was used to each suicide's next of kin feeling that way. He still hadn't come up with a graceful way of disagreeing.

"We were married fifty-five years this August," Nina said gently. "He always gave me a note when we were going to be apart, and either left me a rose or sent one wherever I was staying. Always. This time was no different."

"Can I see the note?"

Nina's thin gray skin turned rosy. "They were personal, funny." Jules thought it over.

"It had to be some sort of accident," she insisted.

She was smart enough to understand, when she was ready, that no one accidentally shot himself while wearing pajamas and after shooting his dog, dousing his vehicle, and lighting a match.

"Who might have seen him last?" asked Jules.

"Probably Flo. Nestor had planned to eat with her and Neil Thursday night."

"What does she say about last seeing him?"

"I haven't asked. Laura says she's crying in there because I didn't call her myself this morning. Flo's a fine daughter-in-law but she's not, not—"

"Empathetic," said Jules suddenly, surprised by himself.

"Is that like sympathetic?" she asked.

"A bit," said Jules. "But what about Neil?"

She looked harassed. "Neil won't have a clue. All I want to do is go to our bedroom and be alone and think about Nestor. Then I'll deal with the rest of them."

"I need to have a real pathologist look at him," said Jules. "It might take a few days."

"It doesn't bother me," said Nina. "I'm in no hurry to go to his funeral. But do we need to tell anyone?"

"No," said Jules.

"If they don't know what questions to ask, maybe they'll button up. Ira and I can handle things." She gestured toward the living room. "The last thing I need right now is an argument with Flo about flower arrangements."

Jules smiled. "I don't think even Flo would try to argue with you today."

"She already did," said Nina. "The other reason she's out on the couch sniffling is because I said I wanted to pick Nestor's casket myself."

Jules helped Laura Ganter take Nina to her bedroom with a glass of water and a smidgen of cognac. Nina slumped in an armchair in the sun, facing south into the mountains. "Where was Nestor?"

Jules felt alarm. "Where? Last night?"

"When you saw him in town, when you said he looked ill. What was he doing?"

"Having lunch at the Bucket."

Nina Amundsen smiled. "Good."

Jules started to shut the door. "I'll call tomorrow."

"With friends?" she asked, outlined by the sun.

"With Miles Birdland and Joseph Ganter, talking about basketball." He nodded to Laura and backed into the hall. He was halfway to the kitchen before he realized the last expression on both their faces had been shock.

Jules helped Jetta and Ira move furniture around for a buffet table, carried some beer in from the minister's wife's car, and gingerly took the minister himself through likely safe dates for the funeral. Flo's sighs from the couch grew more resonant, and finally, after an especially vibrant moan, Jetta threw down her oven mitt, marched into the living room, and slammed the door.

Jules was in a corner of the kitchen, trying to suggest to Olive that she simply label the meat loaf and freeze it, when the door swung back open and the volume went up several decibels.

"You're saying it was my fault."

"No," said Jetta patiently, "I'm not."

"Nobody even told me. I had to go to the airport for Nina and Ira, find the cops waiting there—"

"Get a grip, Florence."

Olive was in such a hurry to get out of the line of fire that she actually slammed the meat loaf into the freezer without taping a warning label on it first. Flo's eyes settled on Jules.

"Wasn't it your job to tell me?"

Jules felt his evil twin take over. "Sorry, no. But let's go talk."

He put her back on the couch and placated her with some of Jetta's cognac. Flo had last seen Nestor Thursday evening, when she'd brought him some food, including his favorite kind of game stew for dinner Friday night.

"Nina said he'd intended to go to the party last night, and there were some nice clothes laid out at the cabin."

Her eyes fogged with confusion. "I can't imagine that," she said. "He and Joseph weren't very social."

Jules had told everyone else; he might as well tell her. "I saw them at lunch just this last week," he said. "With your father, in fact."

Flo stared at him with her mouth open, no one's smartest look.

Jules stood wearily. "Glad to see that your leg's better."

"What do you mean?" she asked blearily.

"Your leg. From falling last night. You're not even limping."

"How dare you?" she hissed.

"Jesus, Flo, the last time I saw you we were at the hospital and you thought you'd broken an ankle. So it seemed like a normal comment."

"You're just rubbing it in, humiliating me."

Her voice had started to rise, and he had the horrible feeling Flo would be testing her soprano range soon. "I fall down all the time myself," said Jules. "I'm *glad* you're feeling better."

"You could have asked earlier," she said. "Of course, I'm just an old, low-priority bitch, hmm?"

Jules opened his mouth and shut it.

Jetta spoke up. "Florence, stop it right now. The man's been busy."

"Your baby cousin," said Flo, raising her chin.

"Where's Neil?" asked Jules. It wasn't as if there was a pleasant mood to preserve. "Is he off running errands?"

"He's too upset. He's not feeling well."

"Maybe he caught his grandfather's cold when you all had dinner Thursday."

"We didn't have dinner Thursday," said Flo. "Neil was working late. And anyway we'd never planned any such thing. Nestor and I barely talked. Otherwise I would have been able to tell something was up, being that I'm a trained counselor."

Jules thought that Flo's level of training made cosmetology school look like four years of MIT. He shuddered every time one of his arrests brought someone to her office. "What did Nestor have to say?"

Flo glared. "I said, I just dropped food *off.* I'm a busy woman. I had to go help with the party flowers."

People usually romanticized their last encounter with a loved one, and he was surprised that Flo, given her love of drama, would pass on the chance to wax eloquent about Nestor's last words.

On the way to his car Jules counted seven sets of Goodyear tires out of the eighteen cars parked in the driveway. Flo, Laura Ganter, and Jetta all had them; so did his own mother. And all of them were covered with Nestor's special pink mud.

EDIE, DIZZY FROM boomeranging wine and sex and sleeplessness, was having a bad day. Two toilets had backed up in the south wing, the computer had crashed for an hour, and she'd had to clean five rooms herself. All this before the four o'clock clerk called in late. Alvin the monthly, an ex-physics professor, was cutting loose in the lobby for the third time that week, and she grew tired of having to be resourceful. Normally, when a guest began gradually but obviously to disrobe, and didn't respond to requests that he remain clothed, and flitted back down the stairs each time she hauled the bouncer out of the bar or tucked him into his room herself, she would have called the sheriff's department. But Jules was due any moment anyway, whether or not she really wanted to see him.

Alvin was flapping the loose end of his belt about in the air, pretending to duel a display of real estate flyers, rattling off some convincingly foreign phrases. Edie could hear Alice giggle on the mezzanine above. She was ostensibly alphabetizing index cards for the Historical Society, as the Aches' furnace was in the process of being replaced, but was in actuality nursing her hangover by sunning her legs near the French window and reading the hotel stash of fashion magazines. A couple edged down the stairs and veered toward the far exit; Alvin waved goodbye. Edie sighed and rubbed her eyes and walked over. He'd been going for an hour straight, and she tried the secret weapon.

"Alvin, how about some hot cocoa upstairs? I'll bring it up with some new magazines. You look cold."

He froze in mid-gesture. The words *hot cocoa* and *magazine* and the suggestion that he might be chilly had brought about the reliable Pavlovian response, and he hugged Edie ardently.

"You wouldn't mind?" said Alvin. "Such a kindness." He was South African, with the manners of a colonial Brit. Maybe collective guilt had sent him over the edge.

"Not in the least," said Edie, stepping into the role. "You start up."

She made a carafe of cocoa and checked the empty

prescription bottles again when she delivered it, once Alvin was tucked into an armchair with a quilt. He only slept sitting up, which made it easier to give him a free room. Edie then called one of the social services workers at home for the umpteenth time as she marched down the stairs with her cordless phone. Alice gestured toward her, but they both heard the main door slam open, and Edie continued down.

It was Joseph Ganter, looking very large and angry for a man of almost eighty. The words were polite, the inference not at all. "Has my wife happened to check out yet?"

Edie, flustered, tapped the phone against her leg. "Ah, no. She said she'd be keeping the room tonight as well." She tried to smile. "She said you had a full house."

Joseph stared at her for a moment. "The full house can move to the goddamn hotel. What room is she in?"

Edie opened her mouth and closed it again.

"What room is she in?" asked Joseph a second time. "I spent the night there but I can't remember. I'll look it up myself if you can't bring yourself to."

"Four-sixteen," said Edie abruptly. "Would you like the elevator?"

"If we're lucky the stairs will tone me down," said Joseph, halfway up the first flight.

Edie stayed rooted in the center of the lobby. After a full ten seconds, as Joseph's heavy steps echoed higher and higher, Alice's head appeared over the mezzanine rail. "Your day isn't getting any easier."

Edie shook her head mutely.

"Be nice if Jules would show up on time, for once. Or if maybe you'd gotten off shift when you were supposed to."

"Hah," said Edie bitterly, looking at her watch. "I can't believe they're still acting like this after fifty years."

"I can," said Alice. She went back to sorting and counting the index cards on housewares, and Edie, with too much nervous energy for computer work, began to sweep. Ten minutes later the door swung open again, with the same drama and the same sense of doom, revealing another elderly man, tall but somehow smaller and balder and less assured. He scanned the lobby and approached Edie slowly, without looking at her directly.

"I'm looking for Joseph Ganter."

Again, due to some combination of fatigue and shyness, words failed her. He was familiar, though she couldn't place him, with sparse dark hair and beaky features.

"That's his truck running out front, and someone at his house said I might find him here."

The voice was gravelly and heavy, and she remembered him now: he'd presided over her divorce. "Four-sixteen," said Edie. When the going got tough, the tough gave up.

She didn't offer the elevator this time around, and the man started up the stairs. Edie followed as far as the mezzanine, where she tiptoed around the corner and sat in a chair next to an owl-eyed Alice.

"What on earth?"

"I have no idea," said Edie wearily. "Maybe I'll get my teaching degree after all. Maybe middle schoolers would be easier to deal with."

"Do you usually let irate husbands head up to rooms with no warning?"

"Stuff it, Alice."

Five minutes later, in the midst of index cards for hat pins, ivory figurines, and silverware, they heard voices in the stairway and both eased deeper into their chairs, though a partition protected them from view.

"We did not begin this thing, Miles." It was Joseph, not sounding as if his mood had sweetened.

"We knew. No one will split hairs," said the other man.

"Well, he's made up his mind. He thinks it'll set things right, and he says he doesn't owe anyone anything."

"People will ask why."

"You bet they'll ask," said Joseph. "And he fully intends to answer."

They were on the mezzanine level now, blocked from view by a paintings exhibit, and Miles Birdland's voice was sarcastic. "You're not worried?"

"Sure I'm worried. It makes me want to drink like a fish."

Birdland's voice crackled with disgust. "That was the old solution. I lost my appetite long ago."

Then the two men were outside. Alice stared into space and Edie peered down through the window. "What's it mean?" Edie asked.

"I don't know," said Alice. "More proof that people don't always get nicer as they age, but I was already my own lab experiment that way."

The bank clock showed that it was sixty-one degrees at 4:34 in the afternoon, October 22. Cars came down the street in spurts, which meant the police were still directing traffic around the overturned semi a few blocks away. Which might, to be fair, explain Jules's lateness.

Down below, Joseph Ganter reached into his truck and turned off the ignition key. Edie could still hear bits and snatches of conversation between gouts of wind; the words seemed conciliatory. "It's a shame," Joseph was saying. "To suffer like that. I can understand—"

And then the voice was gone again. Birdland passed beneath her, his pale bald head glowing in the sun, and Joseph headed back toward the hotel. "Eeek," said Edie, backing away from the balcony. She and Alice sat in silence for a full five minutes before Edie had the nerve to edge along the wall toward the stairs and reappear in the lobby as if she'd been checking rooms far, far away.

Joseph was sitting in an armchair, staring out the window. "I'm waiting for my wife to come down, if you're curious," he said. "Then we'll attempt to have a civil cocktail together in your bar."

"Well," said Edie. "Would you like the paper while you wait?"

"No thank you."

She started to sweep. Alice leaned over the balcony and said hello. A glimmer of amusement passed over Joseph's face. "How long have you been up there?"

"Too long."

"Did you end up dancing on the food you conned my daughter into ordering?"

"No," said Alice. "I went home early. There was nothing left anyway."

Joseph grinned. "I had probably commenced to dance myself at that point. So what are you doing up there?"

"We're finally cataloging the museum collection."

"Counting arrowheads?"

"Counting everything," she said. "Two floors full of crap. Crates that haven't been opened in fifty years."

Joseph looked out the window, thinking it over. "Time capsules. How long do you suppose this will take you?"

"Well," said Alice, "the basic inventory had better be done by Thanksgiving, so we can strip the building by Christmas, so we can start the renovation by New Year's. If we're open by May Day, we might have the bugs out by Memorial Day."

They were all quiet for a few more minutes. "Has Jules been late his entire life?" Edie asked.

It was a few minutes before Joseph roused himself and answered. "He was actually quite prompt until he took this job. Why did he leave so early last night?"

"Somebody was raped, and somebody else died."

"Who?"

"I don't ask." In truth, Jules hadn't volunteered any information until after they'd been in bed together for an hour, which was when she'd left; Edie couldn't make peace with the idea that Jules could go from a dead body to hers with hardly a pause. He claimed the one canceled out the other, but Edie didn't see this as her role in life.

Joseph sighed and rummaged for cigarettes in his coat. "I hope he quits before the somebody is him."

IT WAS ALMOST three by the time Jules drove into town. He wanted a Bloody Mary but settled for a malted and a hamburger at the Fry & Chew, which was about to close for the winter. The order girl pointed out that his right front tire was low. Jules kicked it twice when no one was looking, drove slowly down Main to the nearest tire shop, and started out on foot for the station, intending to make that stop as fast as possible before he moved on to the Baird and Edie.

Jules hadn't much noticed the wind while crawling over dusty rocks at the Amundsen ranch, but his car radio had blared of nothing else. Harvey and the highway patrol had diverted semis from the high freeway bridge over the Yellowstone, only to have one sway neatly onto its side downtown, taking out two signs, a light post, a trash can, and someone's Harley. Jules wandered through the wreckage, angling to make it through the wind, and saw a camper fly from a pickup bed into a parked car. Jules looked around guiltily, saw no witnesses, and pressed on, leaving the problem for Harvey.

He rounded the corner of the post office and leaned into a wind tunnel, but kept moving so quickly that the Oldsmobile coming out of the Baird alley nearly hit him. He gave the driver a killer look before he recognized Miles Birdland and decided to seize the opportunity. This despite the fact that Birdland was obviously in no mood to talk; Jules had to run along and rap on the hood to get him to pull over.

"Sorry to bother you."

Birdland glowered. "No, you're not."

"I am," said Jules nastily, "but it's quite important. When you had lunch with Nestor Amundsen the other day, did he seem out of sorts?"

"What kind of question is that?"

Pretty goddamn simple, thought Jules. He had the feeling that if he let go of the rearview mirror the judge, not in one of his finer moods, would lay rubber; clutching it also helped stabilize him in the wind. "It looks like Nestor killed himself last night, and I'm interested in his state of mind."

"Oh, my God," said Miles Birdland, mouth gaping. "Oh, my precious lord." The Olds started to roll, and he slammed it belatedly into Park. "There must be some mistake."

Jules decided to take the innocent approach to the last comment. "He's definitely dead. I'm sorry, I didn't know you were close."

"We weren't," said Birdland, some of his acerbity returning. He stared up at the Baird Hotel and shook his head several times as if discarding a series of private images.

"Did he seem troubled to you at lunch?"

"Not at all. But he wouldn't confide in me; we didn't talk

about anything important." Birdland gave a last shake of his head. "When did this happen?"

"Last night."

"How?" He stared straight ahead, his eyes blank.

Jules watched Birdland's profile, the sharp chin and gaunt cheeks, and shrugged when the judge finally, reluctantly, met his eye. "We're working on that. I won't keep you."

He let go of the mirror and gave a little wave. The judge pulled away slowly, then sped up as he turned on to Second, wire hubcaps glinting prettily in the afternoon sun.

There you go, thought Jules. The world was filled with medium-sized Goodyears.

When he opened the hotel door, Joseph was the first person he saw. "What were you doing talking to that prick?"

"Well, hello," said Jules. "Business. Why else would anyone talk to that prick?"

Joseph drummed his fingers on his knees and eyed Jules.

"So where the hell did you go last night?"

"Me?" Jules was watching Edie, who was playing with her computer, pretending to ignore him. Planning on a private talk in Blue Deer wasn't always this much of a joke. "A welfare check."

"Did you find whoever you were looking for?"

"Yep," said Jules, knowing it wouldn't end there.

"Who were you looking for?"

"Nestor Amundsen."

Joseph raised his eyebrows. "It's good he turned up. Nina called here looking for him last night."

Jules sighed. "Not necessarily. He was dead. Didn't Laura and Jetta tell you?"

Joseph's face worked for a moment. "I've barely talked

to them," he said finally. "Did he have a heart attack? His mother died of a heart attack."

"I think this looks more like his father's death," said Jules carefully. According to Ed, Joseph had been one of the neighbors to help haul Nestor's father home from the high benchland where he'd blown his brains out.

"What does 'looks like' mean?"

"Pending the usual bullshit, it seems that he set his Suburban on fire and shot himself in the driver's seat."

Joseph blinked and lit a cigarette, and his hand was actually shaking. Jules couldn't remember ever having seen such a sign of frailty in his uncle.

"That little coward," Joseph said. "Viking bullshit at the end of it all. I'm surprised he didn't take his cows and his wife with him to goddamn Valhalla."

"He took his dog," said Jules. "She burned in the car with him."

"Asshole," said Joseph. "She was such a nice collie."

7 *On Safari*

WAYNE CONTWAY, TRUTH-SEEKING CONVICT, LUMBERED through the jail doors Sunday at noon. He'd once been good-looking but had gone loose and soft, with gray hair, pink eyes, and dusty white skin; he resembled a jelly-filled powdered pastry gone bad. It was impossible to believe he'd once made his living as a hunting guide. Jules asked his two local prisoners, near-permanent guests of the county, to be polite. This didn't prove to be much of a problem, as Wayne Contway was bubbly, quite evidently overjoyed to have a change of scenery. He immediately took their photos with the small Instamatic that was evidently his prize possession.

The crime Wayne Contway had finally confessed to had begun with innocuous kindness. In September 1985, his friend and neighbor's wife, a thirty-year-old dark-haired woman named Mirabel Jordan, had felt sorry for Wayne after his divorce and the loss of his job at a local auto dealership (not apparently believing the violence that had led to both) and asked him to help repair her back deck. Her husband worked sixty-hour weeks at the train rebuild shop and was good with metal, not wood; he was simply happy that Mirabel was able to bear Wayne's whining. Everybody, including Wayne (before he admitted to killing her), described Mirabel as kindness and patience personified.

Wayne had been working on the deck for two weeks when Mirabel was last seen in the grocery store. Wayne said that she'd confided in him, and intended to leave her husband, and that he'd helped out to the extent of giving her most of what he had left in savings and doing work on her old Volkswagen to make sure it made it over the state line. Wayne said she was probably heading to Louisiana, where she still had some family; Wayne said he loved her, and was grateful for the moments they'd shared, and hoped she'd find happiness in a warmer climate. He'd been away hunting for a few days before she disappeared, he said, and when he'd come back he'd simply assumed that she'd run away and that he should keep working on the deck.

Mirabel never showed up in Louisiana, and her Volkswagen was found in Gillette, Wyoming. Wayne's explanations turned gloomier: She was so trusting that she could have given the wrong man a ride; she was so despondent over her marriage that she'd probably driven to Yellowstone, given her car away, jumped into a hot spring, and disintegrated. None of these stories made sense to her family or friends or other neighbors. Raking hot springs for stray bones proved nasty and futile, but hairs in the backseat of the Volkswagen proved to belong to Mirabel and Wayne, and though they could have dropped in there naturally enough, several of them were matted together with her blood. Blood was also found on a board edge abutting a patched section of the deck, and Jules's predecessors headed to Wayne's house with a warrant. Ed had already been on the force for ten years at the time, and Harvey had just started; they were the lucky deputies who found more blood under a cabinet in a corner of Wayne's basement shop, and Harvey had been resourceful enough to pull up a basement sink trap and discover gristle that later tests showed to be human.

Wayne had no explanation for the blood or bits of tendon other than the hypothesis that Mirabel's husband had chopped up his wife at Wayne's house while Wayne was hunting in the Crazies, or that Wayne had inadvertently borrowed and cleaned the tools Dennis Jordan used to kill his wife. Wayne had the Jordans' key; they had his. The Absaroka County Sheriff's Department checked every dumpster and gravel pit and riverbank for a hundred miles before the county attorney, a freshly elected Axel Scotti, decided to proceed with the case without Mirabel, corpus delicti, and successfully asked for life without parole after a trial presided over by His Honor Miles Birdland.

There was no real reason anyone could determine for Wayne to burp out the truth at this late date. He'd never spoken during counseling sessions, confided to a cellmate, or shown a smidgen of doubt about his own eternal salvation. Mirabel's widower shot himself on Christmas Eve two years after his wife's disappearance, so that additional guilt was hardly recent. Wayne's life sentence wouldn't be shortened by the truth. And aside from suddenly announcing the location of Mirabel's body in the Absarokas south of town, seventy miles from where he'd claimed to have been hunting, Wayne offered no further explanations, no whys or hows.

Wayne had confessed nine years to the day from Mirabel's disappearance; perhaps the particular look of the fall air, some echo in the lighting, had bothered him. That Sunday afternoon Wayne's eyes had locked onto the sunlit window of the Blue Deer interview room the way a baby might stare at a Christmas tree, while Jules made him go over the map one last time. But Wayne marked exactly the same spot he had for the Deer Lodge authorities, a small valley about eight miles in, a half mile past a high lake Jules remembered camping near as a child. Jules read the altitude rings and wondered if the thawing chinook had reached 7,900 feet. He'd pack a pickax.

Wayne was watching paper trash pirouette across the parking lot, his bleak, puffy face rapt on the equally bleak scene. Jules, who'd been up much of the night absorbing and adding to Edie's unhappiness and his own failings, looked at him in disgust and wished the whole situation would simply go away. He felt empty-hearted and defeated, which meant he was in the mood to ask Wayne Contway pesky questions.

"Why'd you take her in so far?"

Wayne pulled his eyes away from the window and smiled pleasantly. "I don't know. It was a nice day, and I didn't mind riding. I didn't want her to be able to find her way out."

Jules, startled, thought of the flesh Harvey had found in the sink trap. "You weren't sure she was dead?"

Wayne was ogling the paved view again. "Anything seemed possible."

THEY HAD A quick staff meeting that afternoon. "I love the timing of this," said Neil. "Did you actually forget my grandfather killed himself the other night?"

"I know that," said Jules. "But there's nothing I can do for him, and we've just gone from a month-long interval between rapes to four days. And Harvey and Caroline and I are leaving in a few hours—"

"What do you mean?" asked Neil sharply. "This doesn't seem like the time for a convention."

"They're looking for Wayne Contway's body," said Scotti. "It's not a field trip."

Neil looked at Caroline, who was staring out the window, possibly not listening to any of them.

"Any suspects in the rapes?" asked Scotti.

"Not really," said Jules. "We've been keeping an eye on a bank clerk who assaulted a babysitter a couple of years back, but he has an alibi for the last two attacks. Wesley's wading through about three hundred potential interstate tie-ins."

Wesley would be mired in accounts of foul psychological problems for the foreseeable future, and looked very tired.

Jules started in. "The man is Caucasian, anywhere from five-ten to six-two and a hundred and fifty to two hundred pounds. No prints; he wears gloves. He's worn a condom each time but we've found enough semen to type his blood as O positive. His eyes have been described as light, probably either gray or blue, and his hair is brown, both from the victims' observation of arm and chest hair and from pubic and head samples found on the scene. They estimate he's anywhere from twenty-five to forty-five."

"That's great," said Neil sarcastically. "Even sounds professional, like you do this every day. But what's he *look* like?"

Jules wanted to say "Like you," but this was wishful thinking; the description could apply to half of Blue Deer's men in that age bracket. Harvey was blond and tiny, Ed was fat and old, Jules possibly too tall and Jonathan too young, but Wesley, Peter, Neil, Axel, Al, Bean, and countless bartenders and bankers and carpenters fit right in. Everyone had wheezed at some point in life; everyone had bought a flashlight.

"He wears a mask."

"Like Zorro?"

"Neil," said Scotti, "muzzle it. I don't find anything funny about this."

Jules tapped his pen on his palm. "A synthetic cold-weather face mask, black or navy, nylon or polypropylene."

"Anything else?" asked Axel.

"He carries a knife with a three- or four-inch blade, maybe a switchblade. He carries a flashlight, and he bites the women on their arms and legs."

"He doesn't really bite them," said Caroline moodily. "He *chews* on them."

"This last one was a ditzy stargazer, right?" asked Neil, looking through the notes. "She'll be great on the stand."

"She'll do fine if we ever get that far," said Jules.

AN HOUR LATER, as Jules tried to bully the week's paperwork into order, Neil Amundsen wandered back into the station room.

"Can I help you?" asked Jules.

"No," said Neil, starting to walk out. "You can't."

"Wait," said Jules. "I heard you took Friday afternoon off. What were you up to? I remember you were too busy to help with chairs."

"Why is this any of your business?" asked Neil.

"I'm asking everyone," said Jules. "I need to figure out what Nestor was up to that afternoon. I thought you might have seen him."

Neil looked confused. "I thought you said he died at night. Why do you care about the afternoon?"

"I said he burned at night. It's possible there was some time in between."

Neil grimaced in disgust.

"So," said Jules. "What were you up to?"

Neil looked at him a minute, thinking it over, then surveyed the station room. "It's not just a question of my privacy," he said. "I was with someone, and I'd hate to have her suffer professionally."

Jules followed his eyes. They were trained on Caroline's desk.

"I was with this person most of the afternoon," said Neil. "Except for a hearing at three. We had lunch and this and that, before and after the hearing."

They looked at each other. "Do you want the particulars on the this and that?" asked Neil.

"No," said Jules. "I sure don't." He cleared his throat, fighting the desire to break Neil's tidy face against the nearest wall. "That night, at the party, you absented yourself several times."

Neil looked wide-eyed. "Ben Wingate?" asked Jules.

Neil grinned. "Hey," he said. "What's a boy to do? Just don't tell my mother or I'll get a lecture about trailer trash."

WAYNE CONTWAY'S ESCORT was named Barney Bell, and he'd never been on a horse before. Deer Lodge had assumed the trip would be on foot, and when Jules explained that they'd be gone for a week if they opted for independent locomotion over horses, Bell was nonplussed.

"How can I keep an eye on that asshole Wayne if I have to be figuring out a horse?"

This was a good question, and Jules continued to get a sick feeling about the trip in the pit of his stomach. He still had it at 4:00 a.m. Monday morning, as he and Caroline sat glumly in one car waiting for the outfitter to finish fussing over packs. Harvey and Barney Bell were shooting the shit with Wayne in another.

"Are you worried about this at all?" asked Caroline.

Jules watched her blow on her coffee. "Yes."

"Because you think he has something in mind?"

He nodded. "I can't think of any other reason for him to finally open his mouth. Can you?"

"Boredom," said Caroline.

Jules didn't say anything, and they both looked out opposite windows.

"I think we should have just left her back there," said Caroline. "Her parents are gone, her husband's gone. I wouldn't mind being buried back there."

The outfitter waved.

"I know how you meant it," said Jules, opening his car door, "but don't say stuff like that, okay?"

BARNEY BELL CAME down with stomach flu at dawn, and had not, sadly, packed a full change of clothes. No one had the heart to be critical, though the outfitter was heard to grouse about the potential harm to his saddle.

Jules rode behind Bell, finding it hard to imagine such a level of misery, wondering if it was possible that Wayne had slipped his guard some Ex-Lax. He'd offered to have Harvey or Caroline ride him out again, but Bell had pointed out that would leave only two cops and the outfitter; at the very least, Jules would be wide open to a lawsuit if Wayne acted up successfully.

They followed the creek gradually upward through tall conifers and along scree edges, across lush meadows with flattened rounds of grass where deer and elk had bedded down. Wayne had brought four rolls of film and shot away merrily at every pretty view, his escorts, the horses, the sky. One hour into the ride he began to talk, a free-form monologue on everything from magpies to mining to the best Deer Lodge work details and the worst cellmates and their toilet habits. By ten o'clock, Jules's temples were pounding. He stopped in the center of the trail.

"Wayne, shut the fuck up or I'll drag you facedown behind your horse."

Wayne's mouth puckered in confusion and hurt. "It's the fresh air," he whispered. "I feel so fine."

"Then I'll tie an evidence bag over your head," said Jules.

After another hour and mile of trail, Wayne, who was handcuffed in front for purchase on the saddle horn, cleared his throat and said his stomach bothered him. Jules stood four feet from him as he squatted in the snow behind a juniper making vain grunting sounds and occasional farts.

"Getting close, huh, Wayne?"

"It's not funny," said Wayne.

"To where you buried her," said Jules. "I don't care about your digestive process."

Wayne buckled up with difficulty, handcuffs clanking. Jules didn't volunteer to help. "I guess so," Wayne said. "Everything looks different in the snow."

At midday the path widened and Jules came alongside Caroline. "I meant to ask you this days ago, but it's been a long week."

"You could say that." She gave him a sidelong look. "Ask me what?"

"Last Friday we had an anonymous call, someone who inferred the man out on the island had been a basketball player here before the war. So I thought you could go through the team photos with the Aches, make sure everyone was accounted for, when you get together about Lars and Ed and the other one."

"Atticus," she said. "Atticus Rinkle. I found him in a 1940 yearbook, and he actually looked like Gregory Peck."

Jules, who looked nothing like Gregory Peck and knew it, said, "Huh."

"Throughout the thirties?" she asked.

"I guess," he said. "The caller said before the war."

"I looked through your notes about Joseph Ganter and Miles Birdland having to do with the land back then," said Caroline. "Are they about that age?"

Jules concentrated on Wayne's wide back. They were crossing a rope bridge, and the mention of his uncle's name brought on a sudden, defensive, protective rage, just enough testosterone to want to tip a fat murderer into a rocky thirty-foot gorge. "Joseph was born in 1918, so that would be about right."

"So he would have graduated in '35 or '36 or '37."

"I guess," said Jules. "He's seventy-six."

"Huh," said Caroline with a funny expression on her face.

"Something wrong?" asked Jules. "Would you rather not deal with Alice or the ladies?"

"Oh, no," she said. "It'll be my pleasure."

THEY REACHED THE lake just after noon and began to set up camp. Caroline hobbled all but two of the horses while the outfitter handled the mules and started on the tent with Harvey. Barney Bell set off moaning for some private place, and Wayne said he felt bad and lay down on the gravel by the half-frozen lake, then insisted he had to make another trip to the shrubbery.

Jules studied the pretty scenery again, trying to ignore the utter desecration of the landscape by Wayne's white struggling ass. The sun was warm now and tufts of grass stuck out of sticky snow, and the slush on the trail threatened to give way to mud.

He chewed on an old blade of grass and wrinkled his nose. "You don't seem to be getting anywhere, Wayne."

"You sure don't like me, do you, Sheriff Clement? I think you're quite uncharitable."

"I think killing Mirabel was quite uncharitable. I think it was uncharitable of you to wait to confess until there was snow on the ground."

Wayne snickered. Jules kicked slush toward the white vision. "Let's get a move on. If it's flu, you'll know when it really kicks in."

They headed down the trail again with two horses, leaving the outfitter behind to set up. Barney Bell insisted on going the last half mile, having, as he put it, suffered so much already. They moved through a thimbleberry thicket with only Caroline and Wayne on horseback, then headed up again to a thickly wooded rise with cliff faces on either side, a hundred yards apart.

"This look about right?" asked Jules.

Wayne, staring at the sky, didn't respond. Something began to unsnap in Jules's brain. "Wayne. You there, ladykiller."

He flushed a bit. "Sheriff Clement."

"Are we close to where you buried her?"

He looked about, still not quite focused. "It looks so different in this season, leaves down and all."

Jules stared at him. "Wayne, we're in a goddamn coniferous forest, same season as when you killed Mirabel. If there's so much as an aspen, it's currently out of sight."

Wayne shrugged. "The grass was lush; the air was warm."

Jules grabbed Wayne's remaining hair and jerked him off the horse. "Walk and talk."

In twenty yards they came to a clearing like the one

Wayne had described earlier. Barney Bell exited left in a lurching scoot.

"How's it looking, Wayne?"

"It's looking like I have to go, too."

Jules turned to Harvey. Harvey shuddered.

Wayne suddenly glittered with good humor and winked at Caroline. "Maybe Harvey will actually wipe my ass for me."

"You're getting weird, Wayne," said Harvey, leading him toward a dense thicket.

Caroline stared after them, then cleared her throat. "I'd like to backtrack a little, see if those thimbleberries had fruit this year or if it was too shady. I'd love to come here next summer."

"It was too shady," said Jules absently. He sat heavily on a log and watched her swing gracefully off her horse and head for the berries. He turned to the cliff wall, looking for other landmarks Wayne had described, but Caroline's movement and shape replayed in his mind, and when he stood he literally shook himself, like a dog flinging off water.

Wayne had given very specific directions: Mirabel lay fifty yards south of the trail and away from the creek, in another thorny patch twenty yards from a gray rock overhang and fairly near a downed lodgepole pine. He said he'd piled some rock and a nearly rotten portion of the log over the grave when he'd finished. Jules saw a gray rock overhang, one of only five thousand or so in the Absaroka-Beartooth Wilderness. He saw the top of what might have been a thorny patch, roses or more thimbleberries, these receiving plenty of sun. He saw two dead and tilted lodgepole pines, a tree that usually traveled in packs. He waited alone on the path, hearing only Wayne's intermittent monologue and the whine of a late bee.

Then he heard a sound like a thud, snapping wood, feet sliding, and Caroline screaming *"Stop!"* for all she was worth. Jules made out Wayne's head as the man hopped around bushes and over hummocks of grass, heading for the rock wall.

Wayne didn't have supplies, matches, keys for his handcuffs, or guns—unless, as was likely, he had Harvey's or Caroline's. Plenty of places to hide, but not much of a vacation destination. Jules was running now, too, screaming Caroline's name and wondering if she was dead, and what had happened to Harvey, and whether Barney Bell might possibly be able to pull up his pants and aim a gun.

Jules vaulted a log at the same time that Caroline's horse seemed to leap over him, a shock that sent him face first into a snowdrift. She didn't bother to apologize, but rode Wayne down like he was a polo ball and her shotgun was a mallet. The blow took him to his knees but didn't stop him, and Caroline, who kept one hand to her mouth, had trouble slowing her horse and turning. Wayne had a gun but seemed too intent at forward motion to pause long enough to use it. He waddled at high speed, even when he was bouncing off rocks and sliding on icy snow. Jules was still twenty yards behind when Caroline managed a second pass and he saw that her face around her hand was red; she stopped trying to hold her teeth in for long enough to club Wayne again. This time she got his shoulder, and the blow seemed to cause him considerable pain. Wayne howled, and stopped, and started fumbling with Harvey's pistol. Jules accelerated one last time, clubbed Wayne's skull with his own gun, and this time the man dropped, exhaling like a cheap armchair.

Jules recuffed Wayne with his hands behind his back and stood in silence for a while, feeling shaky, wondering about closed head injuries and deciding he didn't care. Barney Bell approached at a weak and desperate run, followed by Harvey, who had blood dripping over his ear. Harvey had a nice little subdural hematoma but said he felt fine, though he was glad Wayne had two or three similar lumps. Jules turned to Caroline, who'd found a handkerchief in her pocket and clamped it over her mouth. The handkerchief was leaking blood; Jules walked over and asked her take it away.

Caroline shook her head.

"Just let me see."

He flinched and she actually laughed.

"Eww," said Harvey. "How's our dental insurance?"

"Oh, hush," said Jules, reaching out to tentatively tap her oddly angled front teeth. They moved slightly, and he brushed her hair away from her face. "Must hurt."

"Not really," she whispered thickly. "Are they going to fall out?"

"I don't know," said Jules, "but you may never eat corn the same way."

They packed her mouth with several changes of snow and gave Wayne a few more minutes of solid rest while they weighed options. Caroline, who needed hours of dental work, claimed to be in no hurry. Harvey, resident medical expert, gave her a codeine pill and patched her split lip with some fancy bandages, then used one on the side of his head and several on Wayne, who'd woken up enough to tell them all to die.

They led him under the cliff wall and tied his feet together. Jules retrieved a shovel from the mule, who'd watched the whole drama with utter patience, and wandered through the grass and slushy snow, trying to decide which downed pine looked most promising.

"Hot," said Wayne blearily. "Cold. Lukewarm."

Harvey kicked him in the ass. Barney Bell didn't protest.

Jules tried one promising hummock and hit a tree root, moved a yard away and tried another, in vain. He walked off the fifty yards from the path again, this time ignoring his compass and going by the faint sun, and wound up at the other end of the bramble patch, looking at another hump of disintegrating log.

Harvey, dragging Wayne behind him, pointed a few feet away. "Bear shit. Pretty fresh."

Caroline, whose lips were swelling as the side of her face grew orange-shaped, giggled. Harvey and Jules exchanged a look. "Sit down, honey," said Harvey. "Don't worry about a thing."

"I can't wait," said Caroline, beyond caring. "Really."

Jules dug into the soft log, working through centipedes and ants still insulated enough to be active just under the surface. Then he hit some loose unlikely rocks and allowed himself to hope. He stabbed around with the tip of the shovel until he located a rough rectangle and started to dig in earnest with Harvey while Barney Bell and Caroline and Wayne watched.

"Fuck you," said Wayne.

"Ditto," said Jules, beginning to sweat, not quite able to believe any part of the day might prove easy. "Maybe we won't mention this set-to to the warden. Now that you've been so helpful, they'll probably take you out of solitary, and this time next year your ass will be too wide to stay on a horse. You won't even notice flu anymore."

"I bet your dick's an inch long," said Wayne.

His vocabulary had fallen apart, but then Jules hadn't begun on a high note. He and Harvey slowed their pace, then Jules got on his knees and used a trowel to clear the surface of a discolored canvas bag, like an extra-large bat bag. Harvey reminisced about Wayne's past life, which had included coaching junior high softball. A zipper gradually emerged, and when Jules pulled gently he found, to his surprise, that it still worked.

Caroline sighed, and Barney Bell made a funny noise and retreated. Mirabel's head lay under the top end of the zipper, her long dark hair still attached to her small and dainty skull, which was nestled in her ankles. Jules thought for a moment that Wayne had managed to fold her in two, then looked at her spine and flinched. He saw a wedding ring, bits of skin, a pair of glasses, and an assortment of knives, but no clothes; she'd been buried nude.

Barney Bell was back. "Should we just lift the whole thing into the body bag?"

"I don't think the canvas will hold." Jules turned to look at him and instead met Wayne Contway's smiling, fascinated face. "Get that smug fuck out of here."

Bell and Wayne retreated. Jules looked back at the bones nestled in the rotting canvas and tried to regain his train of thought. The canvas shredded when he tugged gently. He took some photos, put on gloves and lifted the bones one by one into the new bag, listing each for Caroline's pen. She wouldn't be guilty of Harvey's usual misspellings of *lumbar* or *humerus*. He'd moved from the vertebrae to the pelvis when Caroline tapped him on the back.

"Are you sure it's her?"

"The hair matches, and this person was short and small-boned. And I can tell someone cut her in half right above the hips." He pulled a vertebra out of the bag and showed her the saw marks.

"Golly, Wayne," said Harvey. "No wonder something got stuck in the sink."

Wayne had gone back to staring at the sky. "It was easier to carry her."

"Wayne told me he was worried she might walk out again," said Jules mildly.

No one had much to say to that. The light was failing when they headed back to camp, drained of adrenaline, taking all of Mirabel they'd found and leaving the area tarped and staked. The outfitter, who showed no interest in their bloody lumps and bruises, had set up one large communal tent with what looked like a bunch of gym pads inside for mats. The food was awful, but Wayne gobbled it up, and Jules killed what was left of his appetite by mashing up the undercooked beans until Caroline could negotiate them, while Harvey bullied the outfitter into making some cocoa. Her good humor had passed, and he distributed a fresh round of codeine, some even for Wayne after Caroline pointed out he'd keep all of them awake if he didn't have a capsule. They tied Wayne up in a corner and played euchre until the outfitter's snores abated and Caroline listed to one side.

THE NEXT MORNING Wayne was a new man, and after they finished excavating Mirabel's grave he tried to charm, wheedle, erase his misdeeds the whole way out.

Jules watched him talk, amused. "You want me to say I hit Harvey and Caroline?"

"Of *course* not," said Wayne.

He talked about the snowpack and tried to discuss mountain lions with the outfitter, who looked as if he ate them for breakfast. He wanted to discuss mutual Deer Lodge buddies with Barney Bell, how nice or instructive thus and such a guard or counselor was. He complimented Caroline on her shiny dark hair, which made the rest of them remember the long hair still attached to Mirabel's small skull.

Monday afternoon's warm sun had turned the trail to slop, and the going was much slower. They passed two groups of guided hunters, men who wanted to talk about elk until they focused on Caroline's face and Wayne's handcuffs. After a spell of silence in the mid-afternoon and another flurry of photo-taking, Wayne tried again. "I want to volunteer some information which may or may not be of use to you."

"Talk away," said Jules, not bothering to turn around. He'd moved up a spot after the hair comment, making himself the buffer between Wayne and Caroline. Wayne had taken two pictures of her hair, and Jules didn't want to think of how he might use them.

"I hear you're looking for a fuck geek."

Jules watched Caroline's back stiffen. "Sadly, they're a dime a dozen," he said slowly. "We're always looking for fuck geeks."

Wayne persisted. "I know of a man in your area who's good with light. A friend, a teacher."

Jules still didn't turn around. "What's light got to do with anything?"

"I heard a couple of you talking."

"We've already checked to see if anyone's been on a flash-light-buying binge, Wayne. You'll have to do better."

"He's in for the long haul, and he can make your life miserable," Wayne insisted. "You know, once you start it's hard to stop."

"I'll mention this at your next parole meeting."

"I'll get out. Another ten years or so."

They were in the middle of a beautiful meadow. "Keep talking."

"No."

Even Wayne's horse stopped. Jules glared at them both. "I can't do a thing for you, Wayne. You assaulted two officers in front of witnesses. There aren't any walls to walk into out here. So keep talking and stop expecting anything. Give us some more information or shut the fuck up."

Wayne scowled. Caroline had turned to watch and met Jules's eyes with a look that said *Are you sure?* Jules nodded.

An hour later, nearing dusk in another beautiful meadow, Wayne burst forth again.

"All you have to promise me is that I keep my old cell and don't have to share it."

"He can't promise you anything like that," said Barney Bell, who'd eaten six eggs for breakfast and glowed with health. "You're shit out of luck."

"Well, fuck all of you," said Wayne. "This guy is gonna bring you down. He's not a *nice* guy."

"Like you," muttered Jules.

"Like me."

Jules turned to stare at him, but Wayne made a zipping motion.

This time Jules stopped the procession and circled around until he came even with Wayne. He reached out slowly, brought one finger back, and flicked, hard, in the middle of a bruise. "I'm going to try to make sure they double your sentence, so you can die scrubbing the urinals, never use your education."

Wayne made sniffling sounds. Five minutes later, Jules looked up to find Caroline's worried eyes on him again. He mouthed *Let him stew*, and she shrugged.

THEY CAME OUT of the mountains at eight o'clock on Tuesday night. Jules sent Caroline home with Harvey, put the evidence boxes and bags in the back of his pickup, thanked the outfitter, and headed north on the side road.

Edie was out in the yard, standing in boots and a bathrobe waiting for her elderly springer to get around to a shit, smoking a surreptitious cigarette at subfreezing temperatures so that her sons wouldn't realize she hadn't quite quit.

Jules parked and got out. "I'm sorry," he said.

"You were only honest," she said. "We're just doing things out of habit, anyway."

Jules rubbed his face. "Maybe we deserve more credit than that."

She arched an eyebrow. "Actually, I called today. Grace will tell you, even though I didn't leave a message."

Jules beamed. Ten feet away, the springer awkwardly and apologetically assumed the position. Things were looking up.

"Still," said Edie, "don't you think this is a little arrogant, showing up like this?"

"Maybe," said Jules. "Or desperate."

"Oh, *I* see," she said, shifting from foot to foot to stay warm.

"I'd fall to my knees if we weren't standing on gravel," said Jules. "I'll do it anyway, if you want."

"Do it," said Edie.

He did it, but he also shoved his cold hands up under her nightgown for revenge.

THE NEXT MORNING Edie was appalled to discover that a skeleton had spent the night in her driveway, more evidence of Jules's antiseptic heart. When he got to work at eight he visited the jail first, to see if by some miracle Wayne felt more forthcoming about flashlight-carrying rapists. Wayne, who'd just finished breakfast, felt forthcoming about his stomach, which he said really did bother him now; it was a good thing he and Barney Bell weren't taking off until after lunch. But he didn't feel like volunteering information and ended the conversation by saying that he hoped Jules had a sister and a mother and a wife, and that they all had a visitor with a flashlight soon.

Jules, normally not a fan of capital punishment, felt his ethics waver on the way up the stairs. The mayor, Travis Brushcobb, was waiting in ambush near Grace.

"Where were you? I tried you last night at home and I tried you early this morning."

Jules scratched his head and edged past the man to Wesley's desk. The deputy wouldn't be in until four, and Jules left him a note to concentrate on a Deer Lodge link when he scanned the files of the county's sickos, to check through counselors, cellmates, guards for anyone who might have been "a teacher and a friend" to a fat killer.

The mayor persisted. "Where the hell is Nestor Amundsen? His family wants to bury him this afternoon."

They stared at each other. Brushcobb was large, round, and bristly, and had obviously had too much coffee. He was in the process of accepting another cup from Grace, who'd only once seen fit to cart some to Jules. Jules started to get a bad feeling. "Jonathan, did anyone talk to the lab in Missoula?"

The room—Grace and Jonathan and a DMV clerk—froze.

"Why would he be in Missoula?" asked the mayor querulously. "You mean you sent him to the state lab?"

Jules felt sick, ground his teeth, and counted to five. "Did you all just think they'd guess the funeral time and deliver?"

"They called and I forgot to call them back," said

Jonathan, standing. "I spent the whole day patrolling and dealing with that baseball bat guy. I thought maybe Ed or Wesley handled it."

Jules looked at Grace. She was magenta.

Meanwhile the mayor lost another notch of color. Jules held up his hand and looked at the clock. "Jonathan, go make sure the van has gas. Grace, call Babaski at the funeral home and tell him they might have to slide Nestor in really fast. And call Nina Amundsen and tell her everything is just fine."

"It's Flo Amundsen you should talk to," said the mayor. "She said not to bother Nina."

"Leave it, Grace," said Jules hurriedly. "I'll make the call."

The mayor found a chair, looked fretfully at the piles of paper on Jules's desk, and quickly recovered his usual pink and righteous state, what Grace called his "underline" mood. "Don't you people have anything like a *schedule*? Don't you give your employees *reminders* about unimportant things like *bodies*?"

"I was a little out of range for personal reminders," said Jules, hating the man, hoping the office coffee worsened his evident hypertension.

"You *wanted* to be out of range!" shrieked Brushcobb. "You could have waited to make that trip until everything was nice and *organized* here. You and that girl and Harvey Meyers out being *Boy Scouts*, and here we have a grieving family with no *body* to *comfort* them."

"Nestor," said Jules icily, "was not what I'd call a comforting sight. Do you want to take a look at a picture?"

The mayor recoiled. "Well, he may not have looked *good*, but that's no reason to send the poor man all the way to *Missoula*. Can't Horace even handle a simple old *suicide*?"

Jules leaned back in the chair. He might as well enjoy the moment. "Horace turned up possible evidence that Nestor was smothered."

The mayor exhaled so sharply he seemed to visibly shrink in bulk.

"It was a possibility we had to check into, even though I'm sure Missoula will come up with an explanation. The Amundsens will get Nestor back in plenty of time if Jonathan drives as fast on duty as he does off, and I think everyone will understand. For Christ's sake, he's already cremated."

"Does the family know?" asked the mayor.

"Nina does," said Jules. "And she's the only one who needs to."

The mayor agreed heartily and left. Jules sat at his desk, rocked back, and looked at the ceiling. Grace cleared her throat, but he ignored her, counted to ten, and dialed the crime lab. Grace kept clearing her throat while he was on hold, and he continued to ignore her.

He got the man who'd worked on the island body, a forensic anthropologist who specialized in the long-dead, and told him Mirabel Jordan was on her way north. "Stiffs scraping pelvises on I-90," joked the scientist. They were returning the island man; they didn't have much of anything to tell Jules beyond what he'd already guessed. The bones were forty to seventy years old, give or take five or ten; the man had died at the approximate age of twenty-five, no younger than twenty, no older than thirty. The bones had been buried in the grave after a slight delay, just enough lag time for a fly population to colonize. Ten minutes would do in midsummer, and these husks of maggots under the body almost certainly pointed to a warm-weather burial, sustained warmth, not a spring thaw or an Indian summer day. Perimortem nicks on the pelvis and lower vertebrae confirmed the bullets found within the skeleton; the leg bones pointed to a considerable height and strong build, and the hairs Jules had found were in fact pubic and pointed to a fair-haired boy. The man had probably been slightly bowlegged, whether from work or heredity was unclear, and he'd had a mild case of polio as a child as well as the ankle break. Otherwise the only helpful detail was an anomaly in the knee and shin, a tiny spur usually found only in people of Scandinavian descent.

The possibility of Scandinavian heritage wasn't as promising as it might have seemed, despite the fact that at least one of the holdouts on Caroline's list, Lars Edsendatter, had obvious fjord rompers in his background. Absaroka and neighboring counties had been so overwhelmingly Norwegian in the early years of white settlement that Blue Deer's Lutheran church hadn't offered a sermon in English until World War I. When Caroline got back from her two-day dental repair break, he'd sic her and Alice on the Aches together, see how many Olafs and basketball players they could drum up.

The forensic anthropologist rattled on. "Actually, we have another body in your place that's causing a problem down here," said Jules apologetically. "I need to talk to the pathologist who's handling a man named Nestor Amundsen."

He was on hold for several minutes, during which time Grace waved to him fretfully; Jules made faces at her until Nestor's pathologist picked up. She had a wonderful, patient voice, but it gave him bad news. "Sorry, but you can't have him. I left a message on Monday, as soon as it was clear we'd be needing extra tests. Didn't you get the message?"

"Don't worry about that," said Jules. "Just let me know what I should really be worried about."

"This is not a sure thing," she said. "I wouldn't bother talking to anyone about it yet, until we complete this second set of tests."

This request seemed easy; Jules didn't want to talk about Nestor, period. "Please tell me," he said plaintively.

"There's bleeding in the brain in the area of the entrance wound, so it would seem likely that the head wound was the absolute cause of death. We didn't find smoke in his lungs, but he could have lit the fire, kept the window down until he was sure it was really going, rolled it up and *pow*."

Pow. "Just hit me with the problem," said Jules. "I'm one of those masochists who likes bad news on a platter."

"Two of us looked at him. One person thought the damage to the skull could be consistent with a close-range .45-caliber bullet and subsequent fire."

Could be, thought Jules. "And the other thought not?"

"The other thought he was dead as a doornail by the time he shot himself, due to a blow to the head in the same area. There's some evidence of a tapered object entering the skull at a different angle in the same place."

"I'd guess that this is your opinion."

"Yes," she said.

"Nothing to show where he might have been killed, if it didn't happen in the car?"

"Nothing but the feathers. Not many fibers make it through a fire like that."

"Any way of telling how long the fire burned?"

"Not with that body. You might have more luck with the car."

"Yeah," said Jules. "I'll just ship that Surburban off to the FBI arson building in Manhattan."

"We have a guy up here who's pretty good," she said

mildly. "He's on vacation right now, but he'll be back in a week or so."

The Suburban, tarped behind a chain-link fence, wasn't going anywhere.

"So right now we can only agree that he was dead before the fire burned him," she said. "But you already guessed that. It's quite difficult to determine bruising in the throat area after charring. If someone put a pillow on his face, they didn't use enough pressure to leave evidence. So I can't tell you what the feathers mean. Sorry."

The silence spread out. Jules was wondering how long it would have taken to haul Nestor from his bed to the gully, not trying to make the pathologist feel personally at fault, but the lull had the effect of goading her on.

"But I can say I've never heard of two feathers in a gunshot or fire victim's mouth before. One of those cowplops you sent us from the interior of the car—"

"Sorry about the dog."

"I'm not talking about the dog quite yet. One of the cowplops was a down jacket, old-style nylon, and though that was past comparing to the duck feather we took out of the guy's mouth, and though that sort of jacket should be all down, you'd be hard-pressed to say it didn't match. Unless you actually found a pillow that did match."

Jules ground his fingers into his temple, trying to remember what Nestor's bed had looked like.

"Hey," said the woman. "The gunshot wound is in the classic place for a suicide, the A-number-one pick for a man who's made up his mind. And the dog was shot in the head, too, definitely in advance of the fire. No smoke in the lungs at all. We opened her up when things were inconclusive with the old guy. So it's just taking a second look at that head wound."

"Thanks," said Jules. "You say that was a duck feather in his mouth?"

"Yep. No high-quality goose down." She sounded troubled. "You know, it's still possible Mr. Amundsen shot himself."

"But it's likelier," said Jules, "that someone hit him, smothered him—"

"Vice versa. I believe the blow to the head was fatal, and the smothering only caused him to lose consciousness."

"—and then shot him and burned him up?"

"Yes." The next pause was long. "Off the record, this whole business redefines the word *hinky*."

Of course *hinky* probably hadn't rated an entry in Webster's Dictionary yet. Jules hung up and looked down at his notepaper, where he'd drawn a dog. He stared into a long vacuum of suspects, motives, imagined the wrangle over whether or not to hold an inquest, imagined the jury's blank looks, the jokes afterward at the Blue Bat about three bodies in a matter of days. He wished he could demand a firmer opinion: Don't worry about a thing, the old asshole swallowed those feathers and bashed his head against a fence post just to make your brain cells shrivel another collective centimeter.

He called Nina and gave her the choice of an empty casket or a delayed funeral. Nina chose empty and saw no point to illuminating anyone, including next of kin or the minister. Jules called Babaski and explained, then called Brushcobb and asked him to keep his yap shut.

Grace marched over and dropped a newspaper on his lap.

"Soren Rue called from the *Bulletin* five times while you were gone. I had Ed talk to him."

Jules looked down at Tuesday's paper and saw the

backcountry trip on the front page. He hadn't bothered to notify the *Bulletin* and had thought it was even ignorant to the fact that Wayne would be spending two nights in the county jail. But in an unprecedented series of deductions, Soren Rue, star reporter, had ferreted out some of the truth and accompanied it with a charming stock photo of Wayne at the time of his arrest. He was fifty pounds lighter, with a bow tie and blown-dry hair, God's gift to womankind circa 1984.

Jules wished they could have put off the story for one more day, until Barney Bell and Wayne were driving northwest on I-90. Grace read his mind, or maybe she'd just been moving him in that direction.

"We didn't think there'd be any problems from it, but there have been," said Grace.

Jules turned slowly and regarded her. She still looked abashed about forgetting Nestor; Grace wasn't used to making mistakes, and now she was hinting at two.

"There's someone who's been waiting to see you in the kitchen. He came in yesterday afternoon, too, but I said you weren't back yet."

Jules knew he'd been set up and was too disgusted to ask for a name before he walked down the long drab hallway. A gray-haired man was sitting at the kitchen table and stood to offer his hand.

"Jules Clement."

"Woodrow Jordan. My son Dennis was married to Mirabel Jordan. The lady Wayne Contway killed, the one you went to find."

The last sentence was unnecessary, as all the echoes clicked one by one in Jules's mind. "I'm sorry," he said.

"My son killed himself."

"I know," said Jules. "That's one of the reasons I'm sorry. Have a seat."

Woodrow Jordan sat, and so did Jules after he poured them coffee. "I'm here to turn myself in."

Jules spilled milk on his hand. "Excuse me?"

"For murder."

There was no point in saying "I don't understand." Jules put down his mug and stared.

"You know Archie and I are buddies?"

"No," Jules said slowly. "I didn't know that." Archie was the jailer, and his private life would quite likely always remain a mystery.

Woodrow Jordan sipped his coffee. "We visit all the time, evenings, and soon after he mentioned a few nights ago that Wayne Contway would be here, I am afraid that I gave Archie something to cause headaches. Nothing so bad that he'd miss work, nothing to do lasting harm." He smiled. "I was a pharmacist until I retired last year."

Jules stood slowly, his eyes not leaving the man's face. "Don't blame Archie," said Woodrow. "He thinks I'm okay now, as I was joking about leaving Wayne to the married life in Deer Lodge. This morning, knowing of these headaches, I stopped in with something I told him might help, and Archie took it, a big ol' dose of Demerol. I then told Wayne that I was from County Health and that there had been some problems with the jail food, and that I needed to give him an antibiotic. And he took his shot, too, didn't recognize me from the trial. A massive dose of Procaine."

They were moving down the hall now, Jules dragging Woodrow Jordan behind. "There's no point in hurrying," said Woodrow. "Archie's just asleep, and Wayne's heart's blown up."

They ricocheted down the stairwell. Archie was face-down at his desk. Jules slammed Woodrow Jordan into an empty cell, grabbed the keys, and charged toward Wayne Contway's cell, yelling his name.

"Well," muttered Archie, managing to turn his head slightly.

Wayne didn't move at the sound of the lock. The moon face was already tallowy, past all memory of circulation. Jules touched him, found no pulse, and knocked Archie out of his chair.

"FUCK!" SCREAMED AXEL Scotti. "*Fuck!*"

Horace estimated Wayne Contway had been stone dead for half an hour when Jules found him. He said that by the time Wayne felt considerable pain, paralysis would have prevented him from crying out or moving. Jules had already forced Woodrow Jordan to strip and searched his clothes for more fun packets—even though Woodrow said he had no interest in suicide; he hadn't felt this happy in ten years. The surviving two inmates kept quiet, especially after Jules asked them if they had noticed anything funny about their eggs that morning.

No one had ever died on the department's watch before, no shoestring suicides, let alone murder, since a probable lynching in 1901. At the hospital, Archie wept and said he wouldn't sue for Jules's punch. He felt he should resign. Jules told him to shut up.

The warden at Deer Lodge didn't seem heartbroken about Wayne; though Montana had only 1,600 inmates, versus Texas's 100,000, the state hotel was full up. The pathologist in Missoula actually laughed when Jules called a second time to explain the new situation. Barney Bell, who'd spent the morning fishing, simply said "No shit?" a half dozen times in a row and used Wayne's death as an excuse to stay another night.

After his initial comments, Scotti was beyond speech for better than an hour, a new record, then roared to life with a vengeance, granting interviews with any state paper that would have him, effectively moving attention from Wayne's death to the woman retrieved from the mountains, to the pursuit of the rapist, and to Scotti's own conviction rate.

At three thirty, Jules drove to the funeral home and oversaw the fiction that Nestor really lay in the pretty pine casket. At the Lutheran church he found a back pew, waved to his mother and Joseph and Laura, near the front, and managed to doze with a look of great concentration on his face.

8 *A Leg*

BLUE DEER BULLETIN
SHERIFF'S REPORT, WEEK OF OCTOBER 17–23

October 17—A man reported shots ricocheting in his yard. An officer investigated but failed to locate the offending hunters. A local hostelry requested help with a drunken individual. An officer responded.

October 18—Deputies responded to a loud music complaint at the Baird Hotel and reported that a party was going on.

October 19—Help was requested because of a disorderly individual who broke several glasses and urinated on a floor at a business. An officer responded.

October 20—A woman reported her kitchen window had been opened in her absence. An individual who caused damage at a local business for third time in a week was invited to be a guest of the county.

October 21—Officers removed eight cars from county ditches.

A deputy was called to the bus station to help control an unruly individual. The deputy stayed until the right bus arrived.

A welfare check was requested by out-of-town family. An officer responded.

October 22—Officers investigated a report of a man beating on a house with a baseball bat. The man was questioned and released.

October 23—A woman complained about items blowing out of her neighbors' yard and into her own. An officer advised she consider purchasing a snow fence.

PETER LET A DIVORCE FILE DROP ONTO A PILE ON the floor and gave a gurgle of weariness. He looked out his dark window at the county building across the street, his eye catching the small, dusty button he'd propped on the sill when he first started working as a lawyer again: IN NONLEGAL PARLANCE, YOU'RE FUCKED. It was seven o'clock, and time to stop worrying about it. He picked up his coat, ignoring his briefcase, and started across the street to see if Jules wanted a quick drink.

When he and Jules had wound up in Blue Deer together they'd fallen into the habit of winding down at the Baird or the Blue Bat after work. Within a year, Alice's mild sarcasm about the phrase "a quick drink" had turned into outrage; she saw them falling into the pickled pattern they'd shared at college in Ann Arbor and later in New York. Not everyone required three double whiskeys to relax, Alice pointed out; not everyone needed ten hours of sleep after an additional bottle or two of wine and a heavy dinner; not everyone thought thirty-five was an appropriate age at which to give up the fight against a potbelly. She'd forced Jules to admit that when he went home alone he'd fallen into the habit of channel surfing instead of reading, and that when he went home with Edie he was not quite as ardent a boy as he'd been before he and Peter regularly resorted to the communal rubber mallet.

This lecture was visited upon them during a dinner in November, with Edie looking on warily. When Alice popped, she skipped the middle ground and became viciously articulate. "Alky pin-dick cocksuckers" was the least-imaginative line Jules recalled her using. Peter decided to wallow in a last bottle of wine, but Jules, who saw himself as Captain Virtue that night, fought back and eventually bet Alice three four-course meals that he could dry out for a month, *like that*, Christmas season or not.

And he did, though it didn't necessarily make the people around him happier. As soon as Jules moved at a faster speed, he expected others to do the same. The plus side for Harvey and Jonathan was that he no longer lost his temper when telling them they were slow, stupid assholes; he remained calm and enunciated every word. Peter dried out for two weeks and stayed moderate for some time; Alice and Edie, on the night of the first four-course payoff, split a bottle of tequila after dinner and shared the bathroom until morning.

But it was late October now. It was the weather thing again; it was hard not to seek comfort when the sun kept forsaking you. And this wasn't the sort of day to even attempt sainthood. Peter found Jules slumped over the mound of his desk, tagging lists with Post-its, ignoring a stack of firearm applications waiting for approval.

"I expect Scotti headed out for multiple doubles after burning me in effigy," said Jules in an underwater sort of voice.

"Probably," said Peter, dropping some folders to the floor from the spare chair. Jules probably only piled them there in hope the mayor wouldn't sit down. "I'm just thinking of a glass of wine, what with poker and all."

"Poker," said Jules. "Oh, God, I keep forgetting."

"They postponed the game from last night especially for you," said Peter. "You'll need the wine, because Axel will be there, after those martinis, and so will his dog Neil." He scanned the desk. "Where'd you get those flowers? You finally convince Edie it was all her fault?"

Jules regarded the wilted bouquet. He'd completely forgotten it existed, and, in fact, it was partially barricaded from his view by paperwork. One last dark blue iris had managed to open. "In the river, a week ago. Out by the island. I thought it might have something to do with the skeleton."

Peter arched an eyebrow. "You've got a poisoned murderer and a scorched rancher on your hands and you're fucking around with bones."

Jules tilted back in his chair to stare sadly up into the fluorescent lighting. "I don't like loose ends," he said. "Joseph used to own that land."

"So?" said Peter. "He didn't live there. Ever hear of a coincidence?"

All the time, thought Jules. There was the coincidental way Joseph and Miles Birdland had been connected to the island body, and the coincidental lunch they'd had with Nestor a few days before Nestor had killed himself—or, as seemed more likely, been murdered—and the coincidental phone call mentioning a coincidental sport. Three men who have avoided talking together since World War II—a gap that echoed the age of the bones—suddenly have lunch, and one of them winds up dead a few days later. That lunch was the salient oddity of Nestor's last week, perhaps the only oddity in decades of even-keeled existence. "I don't want anyone saying I looked the other way," he said stubbornly.

Peter shrugged, lit a cigarette, and smiled at the disapproving dispatcher. "So what's the deal with Nestor?" he asked. "I heard something about a feather."

Jules stared into space for a long moment. "We'll be having an inquest."

"Based on a feather?"

Jules decided to sandbag for a while. "Based on a few things. As of this morning, I wouldn't have had more than a moment's doubt, and I never would have if Nestor had walked to some high place on the ranch and stuck a shotgun in his mouth. The pillow and long underwear and the crutches wouldn't bother me if he'd done it in the morning, when he got out of bed. Why have party clothes laid out if you're not going to a party and don't intend to shoot yourself in them? I don't get the dog, either, and we didn't find the bullet that killed the dog in the car. If he shot the dog in the yard I didn't find a bloodstain—"

"Oh, come on," said Peter. "Any yard's filled with grass and oil spots and gravel, all sorts of shit. How could you expect to find a dog's bloodstain in all those thousands of acres?"

Jules sighed. "Whatever. So Nestor didn't bother changing into the clothes he'd gotten out, and he took his leg off for the occasion. He shot the dog and carried the body to the car for company, even though it wasn't a small dog and he was using crutches. He drove out to a spring gully, doused the Suburban with barbecue starter, swallowed two feathers, got in with the dead dog, and shot himself."

"Right," said Peter. "Only his prints on the gun, right? Or no prints because of the fire?"

"Just Nestor's. They made it through the fire much better than his fingers."

"You found a crutch print in the mud, right?"

"Someone might have wanted it to look like he got to the car on his own steam."

"How about the gas can?"

"Itsy bitsy pieces. The crutches bother me, too," said Jules. "I don't understand why he'd take his leg off before the end of the day."

"Maybe his stump was sore. Maybe he took it off for a nap, first. Maybe he had the flu and had talked himself into thinking it was leukemia. Maybe he didn't want a lot of plastic and metal mixed in with the ashes, just wanted him and the dog together forever."

"If you wanted purity, would you burn yourself up in a Suburban?"

Peter dropped his cigarette butt in an old soda can near the back of Jules's desk. "I'm just asking everything Scotti's going to ask. Do you have anything in your drawer?"

Jules pulled one handle and looked into a fright wig of neglected paper. He saw no containers of liquids, which was a shame.

"Try the bottom drawer. I think I'm having a flashback."

Jules jerked it open and found a pile of faulty handcuffs, a half-empty bottle of pepper spray, and a secret stash of travel magazines. "Your flashbacks used to be more reliable."

Peter rubbed his face. "Axel's probably not so much pissed by the idea that Wayne died on your watch as having to prosecute a man as sympathetic as Woodrow Jordan. And he might make you fire Archie."

"He can't make me," said Jules, knowing he sounded like a five-year-old.

"He can give you the option of having charges filed against the old idiot, or maybe the county proper. Maybe Wayne still has a mama or a papa who'll want to sue."

Jules snorted in disbelief.

"Everybody was somebody's baby once," said Peter piously.

JULES PULLED ON his coat for the walk to the bar. "Actually," he said, "there's this other problem with Nestor."

They had Manhattans, a private, convenient joke. "Why wait to tell Axel? The delay will just give him another reason to want to kill you."

"Because you said he's bringing Neil to play tonight," answered Jules.

"Get it over while they're in the same place," said Peter. "Maybe this will keep Neil from talking about his dick size."

Jules folded a napkin into the shape of a turtle. "Neil's not a prosecutor on this. He's a suspect."

Peter stared. "He's a relative."

"Sure," said Jules. "But he should still take himself off the case. I'm not accusing him necessarily, but who profits? Nestor was sitting on more than fifteen thousand acres, and he owned them free and clear."

"Neil would inherit anyway."

"So it would seem, but he could be in a hurry."

"The wife," said Peter. "She's sixty-something but beautiful."

"Seventy-something, and she was out of town with the ranch manager."

"They were having an affair and hired someone."

"Maybe," said Jules. "Though they've all been on that ranch together since 1950."

Peter played with his ice. "Flo."

"Inheritance probably skips her."

"Don't they both have alibis?"

"I think so. We'll go over it all tomorrow."

"Neil's getting a bundle of money through Ruth Bird-land," said Peter. "He says he and Flo will split a few hundred grand. Birdland's father-in-law was a banker."

"Nice," said Jules. "Couldn't he keep his mouth shut for a week or two, until his grandma pops?"

"No," said Peter. "Which is why I can't see him having the patience and the cool to kill someone and not have it be obvious. And his mother is even less capable of rational thought. You know what she just did?"

"No," said Jules, eyeing him warily. "What?"

"While you were in the mountains with Wayne, she taped a note to the door alleging that our spruce tree needles had wound up on her sidewalk during that last big wind. Then Monday night someone dumped a load of Styrofoam popcorn in our car."

"No one saw this happen, of course."

"No," said Peter. "But if I were a neighbor, I'd stay out of it, too."

It was time to leave for poker when the Bat door opened and a large skinny man staggered in. "I'll have to meet you later," said Jules.

"Why?" asked Peter, fascinated by the man's progress.

"That's Alston Hantz. I had Birdland sign a warrant for him a week ago. I had a feeling we'd end up in the same place sooner or later."

THAT NIGHT'S POKER game was hosted by Ed Babaski, whose actual home had been co-opted, somewhat ironically, for a baby shower. The game had been moved to the side chapel at the mortuary, where they played surrounded by various crematory urns and casket wood samples. Babaski had decided to embrace the ecologically friendly funeral before it embraced him, and started the night out by showing them a simple fir model while he discussed recycling formaldehyde; after many congratulations, all the players cleared their throats in concert, uncomfortable to a man with the surroundings. This translated to drinking heavily—and quickly—with Jules continually being sent to the embalming room cooler for ice cubes on the grounds that he was "used to such things."

By ten o'clock even Joseph, winning again and not shy about pointing this out, was looking bleary and mean. The jokes about Wayne Contway and jail food had been endless, and there was some good-old-boy implied criticism about Caroline's injury: Merle Ott had seen her at the dentist's while having his bridge repaired and said her face looked "just like a prizefighter's." Whereas Jules was sitting there just fine, at least to the naked eye. The conversation made Neil Amundsen so happy he won three hands in a row. Since Scotti had ostensibly brought Neil along to cheer him up after his grandfather's death, Jules supposed everyone should be overjoyed.

Two hours into the game, Peter ran out of money. "Would anyone like my house?" he asked politely. "Alice probably wouldn't mind sharing the deed with someone else."

"Who'd want to own your house?" asked Neil.

"Why don't I just give you fifty dollars and stop playing myself," muttered Jules. He was down ten dollars.

"Do you suppose people really used to bet the works?" asked Peter. "Houses, wives, cows?"

"All the time," said Merle. "At least in the old days."

Whenever that was, thought Jules. "Joseph, what was that story you told once about the guy betting his acreage?"

"I have no idea what you're talking about," Joseph replied. He was squinting at his cards with his head tilted back, and had been pissy all night, having brought along the wrong glasses.

"You said you played once with some rich kid, a real asshole who lost everything."

"I wouldn't play with anyone who put up land," said Joseph evenly.

"Well, sorry," said Jules, amused. "But you did. You told me the story when I was in college after I pissed away two hundred dollars you'd loaned me on a controlled substance. You said it didn't matter, because some of your gains were ill-gotten."

"Maybe I was trying to make you feel better. I'm stunned you think you can remember anything from those years."

Jules stared. Nothing like this had ever happened before. "Joseph."

"Maybe I was lying."

The words were bitter and sharp. You could have heard a single card collide with the pile carpet. The other men shifted unhappily, except for Scotti, who opened his eyes wide, and Neil, who stared as blatantly as a child. Merle and Ed Babaski started talking about the winter's heavy snow forecast, and Jules stared at his cards, hopelessly confused.

Neil stood. "I'm on to better things," he said. He shrugged his leather jacket on in a practiced, fluid motion, and a wave of aftershave hit Jules's unhappy nose.

They stared at him. "Really," said Joseph. "Family things?"

"Woman things."

"Ho ho," said Merle. "*Sex*, Joseph. Imagine it."

Joseph didn't look like he wanted to. The heavy chapel door shut behind Neil, and Jules decided to air another grievance. "I would never have guessed that you and old Nestor Amundsen and Miles Birdland were friends," said Jules. "Can you believe they all played basketball together?" he asked the table.

Scotti and Babaski looked dubious, even shocked. Merle Ott, always a happy drinker, beamed. "I was on that team, too."

Joseph shrugged. "That was almost sixty years ago now."

"So you all got together regularly?"

Joseph laid down his hand. "No. It was just an impromptu thing. Nestor seemed fine, if that's what you're driving at."

"Be hard to know what was ordinary for a man you almost never saw."

"True," said Joseph softly.

"Aren't you being a little uppity, Jules?" asked Scotti. "What is this?"

"Just questions, Axel. I needed to get them out of the way sooner or later. Who had the idea of meeting?"

"Nestor called me," said Joseph. "I don't know if it started with him or with Miles."

"There you go," said Scotti, draining his cognac and inspecting a cigar. "A last look at old friends before he blew his brains out."

Everyone stared at him.

"Fucking A," said Scotti. "I like it when things make sense."

AN HOUR LATER, Scotti drove his father-in-law back to the ranch, and Jules walked home with Peter in the cold, crisp night. His head gradually cleared, but the anger stayed and the sense of righteousness. He delivered Peter to his doorstep, and as he left he saw Flo Amundsen silhouetted in her living room window across the street, in the still, half-alert position of someone who's watching television. Miles Birdland's car was only three blocks away on Jules's homeward path. He could check Flo's tires, too, but she'd have gotten mud on hers when she brought Nestor his last supper.

The Birdlands lived on Cottonwood in an austere brick Victorian surrounded by grim juniper bushes and a sharp and forbidding iron fence. Fifteen minutes later Jules was crouched in their dark driveway, chipping and prying at the judge's Goodyears with his pocket knife until he had several nightcrawler-size chunks. The dried pink mud glittered in the dark, and Jules gloated over the open plastic bag. Then he heard a car accelerate up Cottonwood and decided to absent himself.

But he was dizzy from bending over for so long, not to mention being legally drunk. At least .15, he estimated as he scooted through the backyard, not wanting to chance being seen by the driver of the car on the street. There had been a point to not driving that night. Maybe .2, he conceded as he narrowly avoided a neatly pruned raspberry patch and a birdbath and accelerated. Maybe even better than .2, he thought as his shin smote a metal guy wire holding up a nice new maple tree near the back fence and he went sailing.

At first he didn't feel a thing, and he took this rightly as a bad sign. A few minutes later it was hard not to scream, and he hissed out a stream of imprecations until the pain began to subside and he felt gingerly for the tear in his pants and the gouge beneath his knee. Then he lay there for a few more moments, soaking up icy dew, trying to determine if he'd broken anything and looking up at the light in the open upstairs window. He heard a querulous sound and Miles Birdland's voice above it, soft and warm and comforting and human, at once familiar and utterly foreign. At 1:00 a.m., there was music on in the background and Birdland was singing a lullaby. Jules listened, tentatively flexing his leg, and when he realized the song was "My Funny Valentine" he lay for another long moment with his arms over his head.

Then a light came on in the house next door and Jules pulled himself to his feet and hobbled on, stuffing the sandwich bag of clay and gravel in his pocket. The warm stuff heading toward his sneaker was blood. "Son of a fucking bitch," said Jules aloud when he was a block away. He'd broken the leg years earlier, and wasn't sure this was so much better. Maybe he'd reopened the old seam; maybe an attached leg could have its own kind of phantom pain. He was a lightweight—imagine Ruth Birdland's cancer and the pain of even trying to sing to her; imagine the pain of an amputation; imagine being coordinated enough to get around like Nestor.

"Son of a bitch," he said again. Jules paused in mid-limp and stared up into the scudding clouds, the cold yellow moon.

Where the hell was Nestor's artificial leg?

AN HOUR LATER he was at the hospital for stitches, not particularly happy to see that his mother was working the admissions desk. She looked him up and down.

"You're drunk."

"Oh, please," said Jules. "Treat me like a citizen."

"At least you're walking. Is this work-related or recreational?"

He tried to remind himself that much of her dry humor stood for affection; he tried to remind himself that they'd both seen his father quite suddenly dead in this same hospital and that Olive had a horror of seeing her son the same way. On the other hand, his leg really hurt, and there was his mother, utterly devoid of empathy.

"Don't you even want to see it?"

Her face softened, and after dutifully eyeballing the gouge and saying "Ick" and patting his head, she asked him how he'd come by it. He told her.

"For God's sake, Jules."

"Well, what the hell was he doing at Nestor's?"

"Have you asked him?"

"No. But he didn't exactly volunteer the information."

She shrugged. "Ask. He's a truthful man."

"He's a prick."

"His politics stink, not his ethics." A nurse appeared and peered at his paperwork, and Olive patted his head a last time. "And your ethics stink, no matter how fine your politics."

JULES CELEBRATED HIS dozen stitches by sleeping until seven and taking several ibuprofen on arising. At the station, on learning that Harvey had called in sick with Barney Bell's stomach flu, Jules muttered "sissy" and tried not to limp in front of Grace, who would eventually hear the story at bridge from his mother. By ten o'clock, after the revelation of a minor burglary at the hardware store and a tractor-trailer accident, Nestor's absent leg had become just another confusing detail in an overwhelming world and the bag of shimmery dried mud in his pocket was mildly embarrassing. Jules checked through his original notes, saw no mention that a prosthesis had been found in the car or cabin, and put the matter aside.

Jonathan had finally concluded his skull assignment, having recorded every cranium ever found along the downriver

Yellowstone, no matter the year or circumstances. Jules scanned the list of skulls found before the turn of the century and in the late eighties, skulls of women, children, and in one case a gorilla, skulls still attached to flesh, and even a trophy from each of the world wars, one supposedly German and one Japanese. The only towns Jonathan had not yet cataloged were Forsyth, where the sheriff was in the hospital with a heart attack, and Big Timber, where the man in charge had reacted in a thorny fashion: Absaroka County was welcome to dig through moldy records on its own. Jules told Jonathan that Caroline would finish up later, and sicced him on the hardware store burglary.

The FBI had finally sent a rapist profile based on the information Wesley had given them a week earlier. Jules limped behind Wesley to the kitchen and reached for a second doughnut from the pile Grace had brought in; this was her kind of apology for the mess of the previous day. His shin was hot and tight and pierced his slightly dehydrated brain with pain whenever he put weight on it. "I'm ready for good news."

Wesley lifted his eyebrows and consulted the fax in his hand. "They say that if he's consistently been described as 'average, ordinary,' stuff like that—the five-ten to six-foot, dark hair, hundred-and-seventy-five-pound, thirty-something thing—that he could seem average to people he knows well, too; that he keeps his weirdness pretty well buried so that friends might at most say he's a little lonely or maybe aloof. They say he's likely to be smart, imaginative-slash-creative-slash-delusional, and that he has a problem with women."

Jules started to giggle hysterically out of sheer fatigue, and put the doughnut down to wipe his eyes. Wesley peered at him, worried. Someone ought to be, thought Jules. "Really," he said. "A problem with women. I'd have never guessed."

Wesley cleared his throat and continued. "They suggest looking for someone who had a shitty mother."

"Oh, Jesus," snapped Jules. "What with average this and average that, we've now winnowed our suspects down to about five hundred men out of five thousand in the county. What do you mean, 'shitty mother'? Bad enough for the kid to have been taken from her?"

"Not necessarily," said Wesley.

"Of course not," said Jules. He met bad mothers every single day on the job, and they always shocked him. It would seem his own prying, bad-tempered, absentminded mother had been so loving as to make the others incomprehensible. "Anything else?"

Wesley sighed. "We should expect him to continue. People like this don't just stop."

Neither of them said anything more for a few moments. "Well," said Jules finally, "we'll just have to make him stop, won't we?"

THE WILTED BOUQUET Peter had pointed out was somehow representative of Jules's physical state. After lunch he took it to Blue Deer's only florist. Yes, the owner had sold the bouquet; he recognized the ribbon. Yes, he could probably figure out when, but only because of the flax in the arrangement; they didn't usually have flax. Yes, it was possible he'd sold it to an old lady; he probably sold most of his bouquets to old ladies in a variety of shapes and sizes.

He looked in an order book and confirmed that the flax had arrived the previous Tuesday morning; he commented on how well it had held up while he stared intently at the wilted mess. Jules shifted his weight to his left foot, wincing at the last flashes of horseback riding pain in his buttocks and the split shin traveling up his sciatic nerve.

The owner flipped open a fat account book and actually said "Aha." He happened to remember this bouquet because the purchaser had been hurried but specific about colors, and he'd had to fish through the alstroemeria for the right shade. The owner had made a note of her tastes because the buyer had received so many herself and stood to receive more: she was Ruth Birdland, the judge's wife, and he'd heard she was dying of cancer. The owner had been shocked to see her up and about for someone else. Just a few days later—last Friday, to be precise—Jules's own aunt Laura had sent Mrs. Birdland her own get-well bouquet, and by then the poor lady had been bedridden.

"That's how fast things can change," said the florist. "She went down just like that, and she won't be up again. It's never too soon to start having checkups."

Jules wondered how old he looked that morning.

THE JUDGE'S CAR, covered with Jules's fingerprints, was in the courthouse parking lot, and Jules recalled that Peter hadn't been looking forward to the day's schedule. This meant the coast was clear, and Jules drove to the house.

The door swung open before he could knock, and there was Flo, juggling keys, a bag, and a wheelchair filled with an old deck blanket of rich red and gray wool. She blinked once, a habit much like her father's, then smiled sweetly, as if she hadn't misbehaved badly the last two times they'd met.

"Thank you for helping," she said.

Jules had been reaching for the wheelchair handle when he made out a waxen oval in the midst of the blanket, Ruth

Birdland's disembodied face. Her eyes were trained on the sky past his shoulder, and Jules avoided a second direct look as he grabbed the door and the chair.

"Thanks," said Flo again, rummaging through her purse once they had the wheelchair on the sidewalk. "Dad's not home."

The glimpse of Ruth Birdland's tiny face had rattled Jules, and he had to force himself to look again. She had been watching him from under a lopsided turban, and now gave the slightest nod.

"Well," said Jules, "I—"

"Shit," said Flo, dropping her purse to the sidewalk. "I forgot my checkbook. Can you wait here with Mom?"

"Sure," said Jules. Flo bounced back toward the house, and he crouched next to the wheelchair. "I'm sorry you're feeling poorly, Mrs. Birdland."

Ruth Birdland gave him a mirthless smile.

"I found a bouquet near the river the other day. I gather it was yours."

She nodded slowly.

"You'd left it there deliberately?"

She considered him. "I like flowers," she said finally, in a virtual whisper.

Jules heard a door slam inside the house. "I wondered if you left them because of the body we found out there. I wondered if you knew anything about that man. I've been told you used to ride out there."

Ruth Birdland shut her eyes.

"Did you ride out there a long time ago?" Jules asked, feeling stupid.

"Yes. It's still a pretty place." She opened her eyes again and watched Jules.

Flo came pounding down the walk. "Can't you see she's too tired to gossip, Jules? Don't you think you're being just a bit insensitive?"

Jules slowly rose, using the wheelchair for leverage. "I'm sorry," he said. "I'd heard Ruth was doing better."

"She was," said Flo. "Now she isn't." She fumbled with a pack of cigarettes, lit a Marlboro, and sucked so hard he could see the ash grow.

"I'm sorry," said Jules again. "Do you have help?"

Flo shrugged. "Hospice and Jetta and Laura and Nina and all sorts of other ladies." She took another desperate drag. It seemed to harden her up. "Is it true that Nestor might not be a suicide?"

"Now who told you that?" asked Jules, looking down at the forgotten woman in the wheelchair and trying to decide if she was listening or dozing.

"Jetta, of course."

Jules considered her for a moment. "It's possible," he said finally. "One of those things we have to clear up. I'm asking everyone if they saw Nestor at all on Friday."

Flo pointed to herself. "Me? I told you I saw him the night before."

"Everyone," said Jules, trying to smile as nicely as possible.

"When I dropped off his food he said he was planning to repair fence on one of the north sections," said Flo. "If anyone did stop by, he wouldn't have been near the house."

She flicked her cigarette into the lawn, then had second thoughts and bent to find it. Ruth Birdland's hand clamped down over Jules's. Jules leaned over the old woman, looking questioningly into her face.

"Let it go," whispered Ruth Birdland, her eyes locked on his.

"Jules!" Flo pulled the wheelchair away hard enough to make her mother lurch as she released his hand. "What are you bothering her with now?"

Ruth Birdland spoke, or rather whispered. "I was simply saying goodbye, Florence. I've known the sheriff since he was a toddler."

Flo huffed and started to roll the chair to the street. Jules had no last look at Ruth Birdland's face. The judge's wife had never dandled him on her knee; Olive Clement had always called her a snooty bitch who'd never acknowledged knowing Olive even when she'd been a sheriff's wife, much less a sheriff's mother.

He walked down the sidewalk in the opposite direction, toward his car. Of course he could ask the judge himself: Why is your dying wife tossing flowers in the river near an unidentified male skeleton? What precisely might she want me to let go? By the time he started the car, his arms were covered by goose bumps, a wave of bad feeling he'd decided was totally illogical by the time he was two blocks away.

Grace's voice crackled out of the dashboard. "Jules?"

"Yes, ma'am."

"Get your ass over to five-oh-nine North Ellison. Someone's in bad shape."

"Spell it out."

"You'll be there by the time I can tell you."

Caroline pulled up behind him in front of the peeling wooden house, still fumbling with her tie as she climbed out of the car. Her face was purple with bruises, and he stared despite himself. "I told you to take more than a day off," said Jules.

Her expression, though bumpy, was clearly incredulous. "I've already been to the dentist and to Big Timber. Harvey can't leave his bathroom, and Wesley worked all night, and I couldn't reach Ed and Jonathan—" She didn't bother to finish the sentence. "And it looks like a rape. I'd asked Grace to call me."

Jules, as a policeman, had witnessed all sorts of things. He'd seen a fair amount during two years as a social worker in New York, too, but that had been mostly gray, after-the-fact pain. Somehow even a charcoaled Nestor was easier to handle than a naked, writhing, bleeding woman on a floor. The sharp bone of her upper nose jutted through thin skin, and her belly was blueing and swollen. Red-streaked excrement smeared the floor beneath her, and the ropes were so tight around her wrists and ankles that he could make out the flex of a ligament when she drew back in pain from the touch of Bean, one of the paramedics. This time, most of the man's bites had broken the skin.

Jules was still helping with the cords around the woman's ankles when they lifted her onto the stretcher. She was a bird of a girl, carrot-red hair, twenty on the outside.

"Jesus," said Al, the other paramedic. "She's just a tiny thing. A hundred pounds, tops."

Caroline started to climb into the back of the ambulance.

"She can't talk," said Bean. He was the slower driver, and usually took the back. "There's no point quite yet. Give her a few hours."

Caroline stood next to Jules on the sidewalk. Up and down the street, people retreated through their front doors. "You think she's got a few hours? She's bleeding internally."

The girl was in shock; it was almost eleven, and she'd probably lain on the floor for at least six hours. Most of the blood came from cuts to her genitalia and her head, but the real damage came from the way the man had apparently crushed her stomach. "Either way, she can't talk," Jules said quietly.

The woman who'd found the girl was huddled up on a plastic chair on the front porch. She'd stopped to pick up Joy Adele Schwartz for their lunchtime waitressing shift and had looked through the window before giving up and driving off. She didn't know Joy well, and she didn't know where she was from—Utah, maybe, or Nevada. They'd worked together for only two weeks, but she thought Joy was in her early twenties and she was pretty sure she had no boyfriend or family in town.

Jules and Caroline let her go and walked around the house. They found the same setup: the old, easy-to-jimmy window in an old, obviously poor house. This one was neat and clean, like Mary McLinchey's, but inside there was hardly any clutter, scant evidence of the victim herself beyond the mess on the kitchen floor. They found a knapsack with a pack of snapshots, cherry-flavored lipstick and a wallet. The driver's license was from Montana and new; Joy Schwartz was twenty-two, red-haired, gray-eyed, five-two and 110 pounds. In the photo her young cheekbones stuck out like a dust bowl mother's, and the neck was a tiny stalk. Maybe the man had stomped her stomach because he couldn't bear to touch that particular neck. Mary McLinchey's neck had been the only badly bruised part of her body.

They photographed, bagged, and dusted. They split the kitchen, and discovered a cheap, plastic-handled paring knife, flecked with dark spots, half under the refrigerator. After Jules finished the living room he looked at the contents of the knapsack again, double-checking the wallet and sliding the photos from their envelope.

Caroline was on her hands and knees in the victim's

bedroom, wielding the small vacuum they used to gather evidence. She didn't seem sore from riding or from nearly having her teeth clubbed out of her head. Jules crouched next to her in pain, unable to whine about his leg. "Is this the girl? Her sister, maybe?"

Caroline's ruined face had taken on a sheen of fingerprint powder. He held the photo gingerly, by the edges, and she peered at it, craning her head. "It must be her," she said finally. "The features are the same, and she had a mole on that cheek. How old is the snap?"

The developer's envelope had been filled out just the week before, but the photos themselves had all been camera-dated the previous January. In them, Joy Schwartz was curvaceous and pink, downright plump. The photos showed a family gathering; it was easy to pick out the likely father, mother, and brother because they all had the same orange hair.

Jules carried the photos back to the kitchen and bagged them. "Any letters, personal papers to show where she moved from?"

"No," yelled Caroline from the next room.

"Maybe the landlord will know."

"Maybe."

"Or we'll get something off long-distance records."

"Maybe."

Jules peered through the door. Caroline was half under the bed. "Find anything?"

"Dust bunnies and a very old condom stuck to the bottom of the rug."

"How are you feeling?"

"Great."

"You and Alice finally talking to the Aches tonight?"

"Yep."

"Are you going to be able to hang on to your teeth?"

"More or less. I go back in tomorrow."

"Great," said Jules. She hadn't bothered to pause, turn to him, ask any of her own questions, but he was equally annoyed by the fact that he couldn't quite tear his eyes away; while most people looked terrible in police pants, what he could see of Caroline looked just fine.

He decided to retreat and thus avoid wondering how he'd offended his deputy, imagining her line of thought: If Jules hadn't been such a hard-ass with a live, talkative Wayne Contway, they might have learned more about the man and might have prevented Joy Schwartz's long night on the kitchen floor.

Outside, in the beginning of a drizzle, he found no footprints in the weedy turf under the window, but after fifteen minutes he discovered a bloody, heavy, army-issue flashlight in the ratty spirea near the back stoop.

JULES GOT ONE brief glimpse of Joy Schwartz before he was shooed from the operating suite. He found Al and Bean sipping coffee together in the cafeteria. Alberto Ramoski, like his name, was a goofy mix of Latin temper and Eastern European opacity; he was also a very good diagnostician and intended to give up ambulance driving for medical school when and if he received a scholarship—unlikely given the current political climate.

Bernard Gleason, who was Jules's age, lacked such ambition and seemed to be a genuinely happy, preternaturally calm person, which was especially surprising given that his working hours were spent with people who were at the very least panicked. He had three kids and a wife who taught grade school; in his time off he smoked dope and raised and trained hunting dogs. He saw Jules coming first, and stuck out his tongue, grinning.

"Just another happy day—right, sweetie?"

"Huh," said Jules. "How's she doing?"

Al ran through it all while he tied a daisy chain of coffee stirrers and Bean ate a bag of chips. Not good, in the short answer; especially because it seemed likely that Joy Schwartz was anorexic, and her system had been in crappy shape even before someone trampled her. She'd spent at least eight hours, maybe more, on her kitchen floor, and had likely developed an abdominal infection. She hadn't said a word beyond "Stop" when they moved her at the hospital.

"Her belly looked pretty bad, all red and swollen," said Bean, crumpling the empty bag of potato chips. "White count was through the roof. I wouldn't bet on her."

"How much longer will she be in surgery?"

"An hour at least."

"I'll tell Caroline to go home, wait until tomorrow before she tries talking to her."

"If the kid wakes up, Caroline'll be a reassuring sight," said Bean, starting a second bag of chips. "Welcome to heaven, where we all look like you.'"

Jules, who thought Caroline still looked fine with snaggly teeth and a melon jaw, was mildly offended.

9 Snakes

A.C.H.S. Memo, 10/27

Sheriff Clement has asked us to continue helping him with the identification of the man's body found on Magpie Island. Of the missing persons' names provided by Sheriff Clement and Deputy Fair only three—Lars Edsendatter, Ed Compson, and Atticus Rinkle—remain possibilities. Facts to bear in mind:

- The man was 5'1" to 6'3", 20 to 30 years of age.
- It's likely that his build was slender.
- Based on coins found underneath the body, it's likely that he died after 1936; based on lab tests it's likely he died before 1955.
- He'd had a very minor case of polio as a child and had suffered a bad break to his right ankle at least a year before his death.
- He was wearing canvas pants and lace-up boots (good quality) with silk boxers. He had a leather wallet (empty), an unmonogrammed handkerchief and a belt with a gold buckle in the shape of a horse head.
- He'd been shot twice in the stomach area and buried facedown.
- He was probably Scandinavian.

- Sheriff Clement has reason to believe that the man once played high school basketball here.
- He was a blond (even in private places).

"THE IDEA THAT ANY OF YOU WOULD KNOW SUCH a detail," wondered Flo Amundsen.

Venus refused to be sidetracked. "I simply can't believe they'd let such a thing happen," she said. "To send you out with a murderer, a murderer of women, and fail to lend adequate protection—"

"I wanted to go," said Caroline mildly. "The trip was probably less dangerous than the average traffic arrest."

"Give it up, Venus," said Cicely. "The girl takes care of herself."

They were an hour into the meeting, and everyone wanted Venus to leave Caroline alone. Flo's comment merited a few amused eyebrows. The other ladies were still reading.

Alice heard a choking sound and turned, alarmed.

"It's so sad," said Etoile Whitsan, tears flooding down her cheeks. "I suppose it was just one of those things."

Her sister, Indabel, put the list to one side. "It happened a long time ago, honey."

Alice cleared her throat, happy that they'd at least worked through the regular agenda before the cocktails kicked in and the conversation degenerated. She had a decade's worth of yearbooks in hand, ready to make everyone look at boys in glorified underwear, and she wanted the mood to improve.

"So none of them—Lars, Ed, or Atticus—played basketball?" Alice began.

"Well, we'd have to double-check," said Mabel.

"We will," said Alice with a touch of sarcasm. "Now, we've

decided Ed Compson was too young and too short, and Bertha seems to remember that Lars had been born with a clubfoot."

Bertha, given her past career as a madam, was also the person likeliest to know about blond pubic hair. She beamed at her companions.

"Now, what was the rumor about Atticus?" Alice asked. "Just that he went camping and never came back?"

"He was younger than me," said Cicely quietly. "Angelina's age."

Angelina's eyes filled, and she shook her head mutely.

Cicely gave Alice a pleading look. "I don't think he ended up on the island, honey."

"Well," said Alice, "let's move on." She spread the flagged yearbooks on the card table and rummaged through her desk for a half dozen magnifying glasses. "You all look, and Caroline and I will listen."

They lined up. Etoile Whitsan plucked at Alice's sleeve. "It sounds just like our brother Henry," she whispered, "but the boys put him on the train to New York. And we had two cousins who looked something like that, but they lived in Fort Collins. And you know our father was quite blond and tall, but he—"

"But he was sixty-two when he died, and we know where he's buried," said Indie, turning in line and clenching her magnifying glass. "For God's sake, Ettie, we're Norwegian. We all look like that."

Indie was four-eleven and a near-perfect sphere, with dark gray hair. But Ettie, though now bent and diminished, with a cloud of snowy hair, had in her glory days been a tall blond. She didn't seem to notice the faultiness of the criticism and blinked back fresh tears. Indie scowled and looked in the other direction.

The mood in the room had gone downhill. "The idea," muttered Flo again, stewing in her chair near the window, still locked on the dead man's pubic hair.

Caroline poured another round, with extra big glasses for herself and Alice, and tried another tactic, a general discussion of crime and other, not-so-mysterious, bodies: so-and-so who'd probably poisoned her husband, the rumored series of rapes in the thirties, thus and such a tramp who'd peered out of a boxcar just as it coupled and been beheaded by a slamming door, various shotgun slayings of itinerants and miners, never prosecuted.

Then there were the bodies still to be found. "I expected a darker body when I heard they'd dug someone up," said Cicely, looking meaningfully at Angelina.

"Who?" asked Caroline.

Angelina and Cicely both looked defensive. "Someone got in the way one day," Cicely said.

"Not a blond?"

"No," said Cicely. "An Indian."

"So they never found the body?"

Cicely shrugged.

"They never looked for the body?" asked Caroline icily.

"Maybe the belt buckle would help," said Alice nervously. "A gold horse head."

"It only means he was a rodeo boy," said Mabel. "In those days everyone rode."

"Henry won roping two years in a row," said Ettie.

"See what I mean?" asked Mabel.

"Everyone had a gold buckle?" asked Alice.

"Of course not," said Cicely. "Just the fancy boys."

"What about my trunks?" asked Ettie.

Alice rubbed her eyes. "Sheriff Clement has promised to

open your trunks at the next meeting. Maybe he can give his lecture then, too."

"We don't have time for Sheriff Clement's stories," said Flo. "We have a museum to open."

The royal we, thought Alice.

"You promise?" asked Ettie. "Next meeting?"

"I agree," said Indie. "We should pay attention to other things."

"Next meeting he'll go at them with a pry bar," said Alice. "Not the trip to the Ganter ranch, but next Thursday."

"You're wasting my time," said Flo, growing pinker and pinker by the second. "You've dedicated yourself to making my life miserable."

Alice slammed down a stack of yearbooks. "You burn my ass," she said.

"Whoa," said Cicely. "Hello."

Flo left, and the bottle went around again, but they'd dried up, wouldn't admit to knowing the when or who or how of old crimes, and drifted on to other topics while Caroline sat back and watched with something verging on disgust. By the end of the night they'd added another six or so names, none of them likely, though Caroline and Alice found the yearbooks fascinating anyway: boys who looked blond even in bad black-and-white photos, hair darkened and pasted back with oil, boys who'd probably broken bones if only because almost everyone had sooner or later broken something. Three were ranch boys who'd faded off sometime during the thirties and forties, men whose absence was noticed only when a yearbook reminded the Aches they'd existed.

For Ettie's sake, Alice put Henry Orien Whitsan, twenty-two, at the top of the list, despite the fact that he'd headed east in the summer of 1939 following a disagreement. He'd been the center on the 1936 championship team, the tallest player of a group in which Nestor Amundsen was the shortest. Alice tried to pry into the argument as delicately as possible, but she was let to know it had been a family-ender, and very private.

The next nominee came from Angelina Smarts, who remembered an exceptionally handsome veterinarian's assistant named Alonzo. He'd been around in the summer of either 1938 or 1939, but none of the women could remember his last name. Olive Clement, younger than the others, recalled a very blond and very mysterious music teacher, circa 1948 or so, but Mabel identified him as Frank, let them know she'd slept with him, and pronounced him a failure who'd returned to family in Macon, Georgia.

"He was a snake," said Mabel.

"Alonzo was a snake, too," said Angelina.

"I'll say," said Cicely.

Caroline and Alice stared. "Look at my poor shocked granddaughter," said Cicely.

"Jules didn't tell me you and Caroline were related," said Alice.

"He probably doesn't know," said Caroline.

"Jules is still probably trying to see north of your neck," said Cicely.

The following week they were scheduled to visit Joseph Ganter's Mission Creek ranch and look through the tack and branding equipment he was donating to the society. Venus also wanted to explore the old cemetery and the old Crow Agency, some logs of which were still visible. They decided to go Saturday, rather than use up another meeting; Caroline observed that no one mentioned asking Joseph if Saturday agreed with him.

"Caroline dear," said Cicely, "that man does what we ask."

Olive Clement looked at the list about the island man a last time before she folded it and placed it carefully in her purse. "Why facedown, do you suppose? Do you think the killers were just in a hurry?"

"I think someone wanted him to contemplate hell," said Cicely Tobagga, walking toward the door.

JULES HAD A drink with Peter and Patrick, ate leftovers, argued with Edie over the telephone, and decided against starting a book or revisiting the bar. At eleven o'clock he walked to the hospital in the wind, under a quarter moon and clouds that looked as if they were on speeded-up film, and slid by his omnipresent mother, who was reading a paperback at the admissions desk. He waved good-naturedly at the nurse who'd mended his shin on her previous shift and glided into Joy Schwartz's room to discover Caroline dozing in a chair, her lap covered with files and books that were about to descend to the floor. He reached down to stop this from happening, and she opened her eyes. One moment of confusion, then a smile, and then she frowned and sat up and pulled the files out of his hands.

"The Aches are hard on a person," said Jules.

"I knew what I was getting into."

"Alice warned you?"

"Cicely's my grandmother."

Jules stared at her.

"That's why I moved here. I thought you knew. I thought people here knew everything." Caroline gave him a suspicious look. "Why do you have that look on your face?"

"It explains so much."

Joy Schwartz sighed.

"It doesn't mean a thing," said Jules. "She hasn't moved."

Caroline stretched. She was wearing a thin sweater, and Jules could hear his blood hum. "It isn't likely she'll wake soon," he said.

"But you wanted to see for yourself."

He shrugged. "I live near here."

Caroline grinned. "A nurse named Renee told me you visited last night, too."

"Har-de-fucking-har," muttered Jules, taking the chair on the far side of the room. "We're neither of us prime physical specimens tonight."

She nodded in the dark. "You've been drinking," said Caroline suddenly.

Jules smiled to himself. Her voice and movements were a little looser, her ponytail lopsided, and she'd survived a three-hour meeting with some of the scariest humans on the planet. "So have you."

Neither spoke for a bit. Jules listened to the whoosh of the respirator, the hum of the bed light, the voices and steps and rolling sounds in the hall. Every five minutes a machine in the corner clicked on and took Joy Schwartz's pulse.

"I got some names from Sweet Grass County today," said Caroline. "I'll check on them tomorrow."

"Great," said Jules. "So what did the ladies come up with?"

"Lars and Ed and Atticus are probably out."

"Lars and Ed were always longshots."

She sighed. "It seems likely that Atticus blew out his brains up in the Crazy Mountains. They never found his body but they did turn up a note and his car. That was a whole long story; they kept getting off on a tangent about other things that happened during the same period, dead Indians and bums and some rapes."

"I've heard something about an Indian," said Jules. "Any details on the rapes?"

"Absolutely nothing. Everything they said dissolved as soon as we questioned it. I thought Alice would go out of her mind."

"Not a far reach."

"She did better than I would have done," said Caroline.

Jules, who knew Alice's lack of patience firsthand, found this insight slightly unnerving.

"Mabel thinks it might have been the slow kid who grew up down the road from her, but Angelina says he was sent to an institution. Ettie thinks it might have been her brother, who did play basketball, but according to Indie he moved to New York after an argument."

"I'd go with Indie if I were you," said Jules. Indie had always been sharp, and Ettie seemed fuzzier all the time. Not that either was that reliable—he'd seen Indabel just a month before when she'd reported a burglary. The missing jewelry case had been located behind a bureau, and after Jules had replaced it he and Indie had watched her fat white cat knock it aside again to make room for his spacious ass.

Caroline fumbled through the pile on her lap and pulled out two yearbooks. "The only other basketball player over five-six unaccounted for was a red-haired boy, and Bertha vouched for that being his natural color. Half of them had a field day with the whole natural color thing, and the other half were offended. Flo was offended. Is she mentally ill?"

"Well," said Jules, "I don't know that anyone's ever bothered to put it so bluntly. I don't know that anyone really wants to think about it if they can help it."

"Does she see anyone?"

"She's supposedly a counselor."

"No, I mean sexually. Romantically."

Jules wrinkled his nose. "I don't know, and I don't want to know, unless it's a boyfriend who helped her kill Nestor Amundsen."

Caroline stared.

"Nothing's definite," said Jules. "But it's likely someone carried Nestor to that car."

"Ah," said Caroline, her eyes widening in the dark. "How likely?"

"Pretty goddamn," said Jules. He tapped the picture. "Anyway, this guy's legs are all wrong. He's knock-kneed and long-waisted. These sort of proportions on our guy would take him to six-four."

"Is that so?" said Caroline.

"Yes," said Jules. "It is. What's interesting in the other yearbook?"

She flipped it open and handed it to him. "This."

The boys were lined up in order of height, with Nestor at one end, Joseph at the other, the tallest but for Henry Whitsan, Indie and Ettie's New York-bound brother. In between were Miles Birdland, Merle Ott, and six other pale teenagers, half of them familiar to Jules as cranky, slow-moving men he ran into at the bank or post office or barbershop.

The caption underneath described how this team, the first to win state, was also the tallest to come out of Blue Deer High School, with an average height of five-eleven, quite extraordinary for the thirties. Hence their nickname, the Tall Boys. It had a nice native feel, especially when paired with the regular team name, the Blue Deer Braves.

Caroline was watching him. "That's the phrase the caller used, right?"

Jules didn't look up. Caroline pointed. "Two at least are dead, not counting Nestor, and five still live here, Birdland, Joseph Ganter, Merle Ott, Ames Beal, and Einar Anderson, who used to be a banker until he had a series of strokes." She pointed to a series of faces. "These four all left. New York for the Whitsan brother, Denver, someplace in Wyoming, and Texas for this shorter guy."

Caroline sat back while Jules flipped through the pages. "I don't know how to say this, but your uncle Joseph—"

Jules was looking down at Cicely Tobagga, nee Ullrup. Caroline had inherited her grandmother's haughty eyes and the general shape of her face; Caroline's full lips and long sharp nose came from Laurens Tobagga, a handsome cop who'd been too nearsighted to serve in World War II. Cicely had been "the Queen of the Braves" in 1936, whatever that meant, and Joseph, looking smug next to her, had been king. It was gradually dawning on Jules that his adored uncle might have been the kind of prick he remembered from his own high school, the popular renaissance boy who never, ever lost. Might still be that kind of prick, in fact. "My uncle Joseph used to own the land and he also played basketball during those years. It's occurred to me."

There it was again, the knee-jerk protectiveness. Caroline tilted her head back a notch. "Have you ever really questioned him about the man on the island?"

"I've talked to him several times. He leased it to Miles Birdland. I told you."

"And you left it at that?"

"You're saying I should treat Joseph as a suspect solely because he owned a remote piece of land that proved to contain a body?"

She had no expression.

"Does Joseph strike you as a violent or dishonest man?"

"Of course not," said Caroline, losing her temper. "But neither would Wayne Contway if I'd met him at a dinner party."

Jules gave her an icy look. "I see."

"Listen," said Caroline, frustrated now. "I'm simply saying it's likely that if anyone knows anything about the man on the island—or about Nestor Amundsen, who seems to have been on a basketball team with them—it's Ganter or Birdland. I'm not necessarily suggesting any of them were ever connected, but it's ludicrous to ignore the likeliest sources."

Ludicrous. Jules glowered at her. Caroline glowered back. "And I know he's probably wonderful to you, but my grandmother says there was no more arrogant, righteous asshole than Joseph Ganter before he left for the war."

"What the hell does that have to do with it?"

"I don't think you're seeing him clearly."

Jules made a last attempt at patience. "Your grandmother has a right to her opinion, but don't make the mistake of thinking people are wise just because they're old, or that they drop their grudges."

"What do you mean?"

He blew. "I mean that my uncle and your grandmother used to know each other pretty well, and that she'd recognize Joseph in a lineup naked without seeing his face, and that I wouldn't trust either of them past my own dick about each other."

Caroline was flushed, even in the hospital half-light. "My grandmother was happily married to my grandfather for thirty-some years and hasn't slept with anyone since he died."

Jules stared at her in disbelief. "Maybe she wasn't in the habit of dozing off, but let me assure you that Cicely has led a healthy private life. Joseph was still parked at her house when I was walking to high school. I don't know what it meant to his marriage or hers, but I do know it started when they were in school together, probably back before this photo was taken. Maybe you just never asked."

They both kept silence, staring fixedly in the direction of Joy Schwartz as if turning a neck would admit defeat. Jules's anger faded quickly, and sadness followed as the essential hypocrisy of wanting to please a man like Joseph, no matter the cost, hit home. As a child he'd tagged along like one of his uncle's setters, wanted to capture all Joseph's calm and intelligence and reserve and cram it into his own awkward, lanky young body. In his mid-thirties, he'd mostly forgotten this mimicry, and didn't have a clue that he'd largely succeeded.

He'd known for a long time that Joseph was capable of being a shit, and here was Caroline, discovering with no warning that her grandmother was no Betty Crocker. "Christ," he said. "We'll run out to Joseph's ranch together. Maybe not tomorrow, maybe Saturday so we can see the ladies in action. Unless you'd prefer to patrol with Jonathan, but it really is a beautiful ranch."

"Isn't that your day off?" she asked.

"I don't really have those," said Jules. He didn't even need them these days.

They were quiet for a while. Caroline reached out and gently tapped Joy Schwartz's knee. Nothing happened. "How'd you hurt yourself?"

"I tripped over a staked wire for a new tree in the dark behind Miles Birdland's house."

The long, peaceful profile turned toward him, open-mouthed.

"I'd just chipped mud out of his tire tread after poker the

other night," said Jules, past shame. "I was drunk and started to run away. That's one of the things I want to do tomorrow."

Caroline was wide-eyed, even in the dark. "Get drunk or run away?"

"Go to Amundsen's and make sure the mud matches."

THE MISSOULA PATHOLOGIST called a few minutes after he arrived at work on Friday morning. "So," said Jules, his fingers cramping on the phone receiver.

"Murder," she said. "It's pretty conclusive. Someone jabbed him with a tapered object in the side of the head, then shot him in the same place at a later point."

"When?"

"Can't tell you. More than a half hour, less than twelve."

"Jesus," said Jules.

"This is not a pristine corpse," said the woman dryly.

"What about the feathers?"

"Someone smothered him, then jabbed him, then shot him."

"And then burned him."

"Yep. What you might call overkill."

"What do you mean, 'jabbed'?"

"It wasn't a knife. It had a sharp point and a wider base that crushed his skull. Like a cow horn without much curve."

Jules shut his eyes and tried to imagine how to sugarcoat the succession of violence for the widow. "Any funny gardening implements on the scene?" asked the pathologist. "I use something called a dibble when I plant garlic that would be about right."

"I'll check," said Jules. He sighed and hung up.

The certainty that Nestor had been murdered was paralyzing, and he forced himself to think of a less painful problem, that of the island man. Caroline had already been and gone, off to the dentist and back to Big Timber to check on the most recent batch of names. None of them sounded likely. All morning Jules had been thinking of Peter's line about everyone's having been someone's baby once. He'd only dealt with two runaways since he'd taken the job, but he didn't kid himself that life had grown more precious since the island man's burial. Maybe he should be looking for someone people wanted him to find, like Ankeny's great-uncle, Malcolm Gray Crane, rather than Nestor, or a man everyone seemed happy to forget.

JOY SCHWARTZ WAS still heavily sedated, mute. Ed and Jules talked to her landlord and coworkers and came up with a complete blank. She'd placed no long-distance calls, and Jules noted that her listing in the phone book had been careful, just an initial and no address. They tried the Department of Motor Vehicles and discovered she had no record of a license before she applied in Montana. She'd been prosecuted for a reckless driving charge in March—no alcohol, just high speed—but there was no helpful information in the file, and Harvey, who'd been the arresting officer, couldn't recall a thing about the incident. They tracked her Social Security number to the Provo area in Utah, and determined that she'd received it in the mid-eighties, but the Provo authorities couldn't match her with anyone on their missing persons list, and Social Security would take days to give more information. The post office couldn't recall forwarding mail, the town's hospital and doctors had never handled her. So far her fingerprints hadn't matched any in the system. The old condom Caroline had found under the bed had probably come from the restaurant's dishwasher, who said it was a one-nighter and that he thought Joy Schwartz was from somewhere like Texas or California, "someplace hot." Despite the fact that her snapshots placed her in Blue Deer six months earlier, and despite her penny-red hair, they could find no evidence of a previous job.

Eventually they'd give her photo to television stations and newspapers, query eating disorder clinics and churches, and dig through Utah's birth certificates and the whole miserable system. For the remainder of Friday morning, Jules and Ed settled for a visit to the local photo store, where Joy Schwartz had taken her film. It was the only place, besides the restaurant where she'd worked, they knew she'd visited.

It took two minutes before Carl Jump materialized from the back. "You survived the anniversary party," said Jules.

"More or less," said Jump. "I could say the same for you. I wish I had a picture of you rolling down the stairs with Mrs. Amundsen."

Ed raised both bushy eyebrows.

"It's not what you think," said Jules.

Jump didn't recognize the girl or her redheaded family, either from her driver's license photo or the heavier images his store had developed. He would have waited on her, though, because he'd lost a clerk weeks before and as yet had no replacement. Maybe she'd been wearing a hat; maybe he'd been developing right before she came in, which made him squinty in the light.

"You develop any of this boy dancing during that party?" asked Ed. "We could use some blackmail material in the office."

"I'd like to find my favorite lawyer in a compromising situation," said Jules.

"Peter?" asked Ed. He was pulling small items from the shelves, lens caps and cloths and camera batteries.

"No," said Jules. "I was being sarcastic. I'd like a picture of someone on his way out the door to visit his grandfather."

Ed stared at him. Jump turned from one to the other, bemused. "If you'd like the Ganter party photos, I'm afraid you'll have to ask Mrs. Scotti. I finished developing them a couple of days ago."

"I will," said Jules. "Thanks. Let's go visit some Latter Day Saints, Ed, see if our girl sought spiritual guidance."

Ed nodded and pulled out his wallet to pay for his purchases.

"The girl was a Mormon?" asked Jump.

"It's just a possibility," said Jules. "Her Social Security card was issued in Utah. Want to take a second look at those pictures?"

Jump looked them over again, drumming his fingers on the counter. He had dark ink on his forehead and smelled of chemicals. "Hang on a sec," he said, and came back with an account book, which he quickly paged through. "A couple of months ago I sent two prints to a girl's family in Nephi, Utah. I asked the girl what kind of name that was, and she said Mormon." He found the entry and pointed. "They went to an Opal and Isaac Schwartz in Nephi. Could that be right?"

Jules beamed down at the entry.

"But I still don't recognize the girl, even with the hair," said Jump, nonplussed. "She wasn't skinny and she wasn't fat. Is one of these photos really old?"

"No," said Jules, scribbling down the address. "But I think her weight went up and down really fast. Maybe you saw her in between."

"By the way," said Jump, giving Ed change, "if you ask Jetta Scotti for those proof sheets, tell her to put in her order soon. Christmas is right down the pike. Why do you want to see them?"

"Just curious," said Jules.

As he started the patrol car he thought of how much more fun it had been to be curious as a child. The downside of having found Joy Schwartz's next of kin was that he'd have to call them. Ed, who wasn't in an inquiring mood at all, made growling sounds all the way to the Bucket.

Jules waited for lunch to arrive before he finally asked. Ed was selecting a half dozen packets of saltines from the basket on the table.

"Ed, did you get Nestor's artificial leg out of that cabin?"

"No. Why?"

"Just checking. It wasn't on Harvey's list. Is it still there?"

"I don't know. We found what was left of the crutches in the car." Ed crumbled a dozen crackers into his gluey chowder, turning the bowl into a white pyramid. "I didn't see the point to looking for a leg, frankly."

Jules, who thought chowder in Montana was an innately flawed concept, shook the hot sauce vigorously. The sky was dead gray outside, and he felt the need for liveliness. "We'll go up there after lunch. I've been meaning to since I got back with Wayne. Nina sounded fine this morning."

Ed nodded and delicately inserted his spoon into the mound of crumbs. Not one fell to the counter. Jules watched for a moment, fascinated.

"Maybe he threw the leg out before he killed himself," said Ed after his first three bites. "Maybe it was a symbol to him."

"Of what?" asked Jules. He'd gone too far with the sauce, and sweat beaded his forehead.

"Of what he couldn't do anymore."

"He needed that leg to ride or walk, and he did both just fine," said Jules. "I never even once heard of him mentioning that leg with anything but affection and humor. He'd had it for almost twenty years."

"Hey," said Ed. "I know that. I had a beer with the stubby angel once a month or so up in Clyde City. But he kept his mouth shut about things that mattered."

"Like what?" asked Jules.

"Like his prostate. Like the little matter of his brother Gott blowing his brains out," said Ed. "Like the fact his dad had done the same thing, and so had his great-uncle. It's a fucking family tradition, being too impatient for chemo, and his son was dead, too. His dad and his great-uncle picked the same high spot on the ranch, nice patch of prairie where they could see the whole place. The only thing that confuses me about Nestor is why he skipped the view."

Jules sighed. He started his sandwich and gave Ed enough time to read the *Bulletin*'s Club Notes column, probably seeing if his name was mentioned in the Masonic minutes, before he cleared his throat politely and gave Ed the pathologist's news.

Ed stared sadly at the carrot cake displayed by the cash register. "Is this a sure thing?"

"Ninety-nine percent."

"Why," asked Ed icily, "would a murderer kill a person three times over, then take a fake leg?"

"I dunno. Maybe the leg will turn up. We'll just ask, and anyway we need to go over the place again."

"I feel stupid asking. I hate feeling stupid."

Jules drained his soda. "Join the goddamn club. I've got a question like that myself."

Ed raised an inquiring eyebrow.

"You ever hear of anything funny about Neil Amundsen and women?"

IN THE COLD sunlight on the way out to the Amundsen ranch, they passed a frost-stunned rattlesnake warming itself on the bumpy clay of the back road. Ed, pointing to a nearby pasture of horses, made Jules back up and crush the rattler. The sight of a snake still made him feel automatically ill; he'd never grown used to them and hadn't touched one live since the last time he'd felt sufficient peer pressure to try, at about age twelve. On a similar fall day when he was seventeen, after a valuable foal died from a bite on the nose, he'd helped Joseph and his hands dynamite three dens below the house on Mission Creek, watching hungover and shuddering as shreds of hundreds of rattlesnakes foamed into the air with frozen mud and ice crystals.

Nina Amundsen responded to Nestor's multiple causes of death stoically enough, but when Jules asked about artificial limbs her lovely face crumpled. Hadn't they taken the leg when they'd gathered up Nestor? Nestor had only had one; could it have melted, and they mistook the metal for part of the Suburban's hand-operated brake system? After she said the word *melt* she began to sob in earnest, gesturing to the paper, saying she'd been upset anyway; so much evil in the world. An article on Joy Schwartz's rape faced up, and Jules admired her attempt to avoid the main event for someone else's misery. It reminded him a bit of the suffering Ruth Birdland buying a skeleton flowers.

Perhaps the common thread was Flo, out to help Nina sort through Nestor's belongings. Jules had begun talking to Nina in the living room, but Flo had interrupted every other minute about what Nina wanted to do with thus and such pair of shoes, tie, or photo. Nina tried to suggest that Flo wait a bit until Jules was finished and Nina could look at each item.

"Nonsense," snapped Flo. "Looking at this directly will cause you too much pain."

No matter that she'd dangled Nestor's underwear in his widow's face. Jules's mild aversion to Flo was turning into active antipathy. He didn't believe she so much as farted out of pure generosity; she was either looking for things of Nestor's she might want for herself or her son, or she was being nosy about their conversation. When she whirled off toward a ringing phone, Nina leaned forward. "I wish she wasn't in such a hurry to clean things up. I'd rather wait. I don't want him to disappear yet."

"Tell her that," said Jules.

"I tried," said Nina. "Sometimes it's just too exhausting to cross her."

Jules could understand wanting to avoid a Flo-style scene. "Get someone else up here, like Laura or my mother. They'll tone her down."

Nina gestured hopelessly.

"How'd she and Nestor get along?"

"Well, like with anyone. It can be hard, hitting a balance with Flo. Even after almost thirty years." Nina rubbed her eyes, then smiled and rolled them at Jules. "Let's go in the kitchen."

Ira Meidenhaft was peering into the refrigerator. "Wake turkey for lunch?" asked Nina. "Again?"

"Wake turkey's just fine by me. Get a list ready for me and I'll go to the store this afternoon, get us some variety."

"I'll go with you," said Nina.

"No reason for either of you to make a trip like that,"

said Flo, who'd materialized carrying a toilet kit. "You give me the list. Now, shall we pitch this old thing, give it to the Salvation Army?"

Nina glanced, squinched her eyes, and reached for a jar of pickles. "Couldn't Neil use a nice toilet kit?" asked Ira politely.

"Neil got a nice Coach kit for his college graduation." Flo grabbed the pickles from Nina's hand. "I'm not sure this one even rates the Salvation Army."

"I'll take it," said Ira.

"Maybe you should ask Nina if that's all right," said Flo, wrestling with the lid to the pickle jar. Jules offered to open it, hand outstretched, but Flo jerked away the jar and whacked the top on the sink two more times.

Jules seized the pickle jar, wrenched off the top, and slammed the jar on the table so that juice shot up in the air. "Since you want to handle everything yourself, Flo, maybe you could answer one or two questions. Was Nestor wearing his leg when you brought the meals by Thursday night?"

"Sure," she said warily. "He always wore it."

"What do you mean about bringing meals?" asked Nina. "Nestor told me the three of you were planning to eat together."

Flo flushed. "I did not neglect Nestor. We still had a visit, but Neil needed to work late so he didn't come along."

"Have you seen the leg around the house?" asked Jules.

"Like I told you," said Flo acidly, "he always wore it. Did you lose the leg when you lost him? Neil says your evidence room is a disgrace."

Their evidence room was actually a glorified closet, and to the best of Jules's knowledge, Neil had never seen fit to look inside. He preferred having others fetch and deliver.

"He wasn't wearing the leg," said Jules patiently.

Flo's eyes clouded with confusion. "But—"

"Florence, please don't argue with the sheriff." Nina was hacking at the turkey with a long carving knife. "I'd appreciate your helping him determine how Nestor died."

Flo built up steam again. "That's easy. He shot himself in the head."

"That's enough," snapped Nina.

"If the leg wasn't in the Suburban with him, maybe he was too cheap to let it burn. Maybe he thought we could resell it. That's probably why he left his nice clothes out. I mean, look at the worn-out stuff he still used."

Jules thought this was an interesting insight, albeit a strange one to air in front of a widow. Nina slammed the knife into the pickle juice puddle and headed for the porch.

"I'm a counselor," said Flo stubbornly. "People who kill themselves aren't reasonable."

"How perceptive," said Jules, wanting to choke her. "Your sensitivity stuns me, but I'm afraid we're no longer treating this as a suicide."

Flo gaped. "You're insane."

"This isn't something I just dreamed up to make my days more interesting," said Jules. "I'll have to ask you to put the cleanup project on hold until after we go over the property a second time, ask everyone the same questions all over again."

Flo threw the toilet kit at his head. Jules raised an eyebrow.

"Did you think of asking *her*?" She gestured angrily toward Nina, on the porch. "Ranch manager my ass."

"I'll talk to her," said Jules. "And if you prefer, you can visit the station later today or tomorrow—"

Flo stalked out of the house. Ed, who'd seen fit to keep his mouth shut throughout, began to hum while he wiped off the table. Jules walked down to the driveway, rubbed the pink grit between his fingers, and filled an empty plastic bag with a few tablespoons. Ira Meidenhaft had come out of the barn and leaned against the squad car and watched. He owned 360 acres on the verge of the Amundsen ranch where he raised lamb for local restaurants and wool for a cottage slipper industry. Before he'd fought with Nestor in World War II and been discharged with a "mental collapse," he'd been a jazz pianist in Greenwich Village. Jules had taken lessons from him for a few years before high school.

Jules walked over. "What happened to Flo's husband anyway? He died before I got back."

"Nol Amundsen?" asked Ira. "Popped through the guard-rail about five years ago on his way home from Butte. Drunk, probably. That's what he spent most of his time doing."

Jules nodded. "Do you think Nestor could have killed himself?"

Ira watched the clouds. "Might have later on, but he didn't seem ready quite yet."

They were both leaning against the patrol car, staring out over the high windy flat of prairie. Jules gave Ira a sidelong glance. "Why didn't he seem ready?"

The old man nodded toward the house. "He loved her too much to leave her early." He toed the quartz gravel. "That place you found him is where we used to burn garbage. It's out of the wind, but I can't see Nestor picking a place to die just for practicality. We found his dad in a real pretty place, nice high prairie where he could see everything. Why don't *you* think he killed himself?"

"Ah, well, who knows?" said Jules. He was fairly sure that Nina confided in Ira; it was likely they were both being coy. Sooner or later they'd search the house and the grounds a second time, anyway, so there was no point in hiding the news.

Ira answered routine questions about Nestor's health and insurance policies while Ed and Jules searched the cabin a second time. No leg, but they found three pillows, all old and stained and mismatched and probably plucked from various empty rooms in the main house: a foam, a rag, a goose down. Nestor had liked to sleep with lots of pillows, and Ira hadn't a clue to how many might usually be on his cabin bed; neither would Nina, who had never felt comfortable in her husband's hideout.

Nor could the old man dredge up any memories of creepy hired hands, poisonous age-old animosities, other women, or unhappy heirs. On the other hand, Nestor had been deeply depressed since his brother's death, troubled over the prostate problem he'd shrugged off with Horace, and was entering the season of icy driveways, when his center of balance became even more tenuous and his stump ached. No, he wouldn't have let the sadness out with anyone but Ira and Nina. If Nestor had faced other problems, "outside" business problems, he might not have told them, and he certainly wouldn't have confided in his daughter-in-law or his asshole of a grandson. Anyway, money trouble was hard to imagine; the old man was swimming in acreage and retirement funds, his only vices an occasional new car for Nina and a yearly trip with her overseas. They'd been slated to visit Australia in February; the year before they'd gone to Crete and Istanbul.

This adventurous aspect surprised Jules, and Ira said it had surprised Nestor as well, once he and Nina started traveling, that he'd prefer a camel to a cruise chair.

Jules and Ed dusted the whole cabin again, even taking prints from the food in the fridge, the stew Flo had left for her father-in-law's Friday dinner, and some tipped-over Coronas. There were three empty bottles in the trash, and Jules hoped that Nestor had been fuzzy, daydreaming about a next trip to a warm and exotic place, by the time someone visited a succession of injuries upon him. He bagged the bottles just to make sure.

Jules would have given his eyeteeth to be sitting on a rock on Crete that afternoon, maybe with some wine and an octopus salad and the woman he'd traveled with ten years earlier. Ed just wanted to sit on a toilet. Something had been funny about the chowder, or maybe Barney Bell's flu had infected the station, so Jules drove back to Blue Deer at ninety miles an hour with his lights on and enjoyed passing terrified motorists.

EVERYONE MET IN the station kitchen at three. "We've got a wide-open time period here," Jules said. "A gap between death and burning that could be minutes or hours."

"What time do you have for the burning itself?" asked Caroline.

"Somewhere between seven and nine," said Jules. "During which time everyone seems to be accounted for."

"Who's everyone?"

"Everyone Nestor was related to," he said morosely. "Everyone I'm related to. They were all eating at the goddamn party."

"It could have been a crazy," said Harvey.

"How would a crazy get close enough to him to use a pillow without a struggle? We didn't find a mess up there."

"I don't know, but why would anyone who knew him keep his leg? A stranger might think it was a novelty. And why not just finish him off with the pillow?"

"To stage a suicide," said Jules.

"Deliberately render him unconscious without killing him?"

"Maybe they didn't know we'd be able to tell he was alive or dead when he was shot. Maybe they thought they could make it look like a stroke, something natural, and then when they realized he was still breathing they moved on to plan B."

"It's not as though people act rationally when they're doing such things," said Caroline. "If they were rational, they'd find another solution to their problems. People make mistakes, and mistakes snowball."

He'd never heard her talk so much. Flo's lines about suicide had been quite similar, and he wondered now if they stemmed from recent experience.

"Do you want us to do this quietly?" asked Wesley.

"Please," said Jules. "And bear in mind that if they haven't killed him they'll be mourning him."

JULES MADE MORE lists. If he played his cards right, he could offend everyone in town. He'd discovered no extant insurance policies held by Nina, Flo, or Neil, no crafty will changes—Nina had inherited from her husband, as expected, and Flo and Neil seemed to have a comfortable amount of money through Flo's mother's family and no large outstanding gambling debts, Mafia dues, or expensive drug habits.

Jules spun in his chair, forcing himself to pause once a revolution to review another gun application. It was a shame, really—Jules could daydream for hours about sending Neil and Flo away for life in Deer Lodge, but it didn't seem possible that they could have killed Nestor even if they'd wanted to. Nina and Ira Meidenhaft had been in Denver, and Flo and Neil had been at the anniversary party from six o'clock on. To the best of his memory, almost everyone Nestor knew in Blue Deer had been at the same party. There was a huge extended family to consider, a few dozen cousins with names like Nels and Natalie and Norbert spread throughout eastern Montana, but this tack didn't seem likely. And as for employees, no one remembered Nestor's firing anyone since Eisenhower.

Jules had spent the hours since leaving the Amundsen ranch talking to a variety of sources, and no one, in fact, remembered Nestor's losing his temper since Truman's term, when he'd given up drinking. Now, when Jules tried Ira Meidenhaft for a second time, Ira couldn't recall Nestor's so much as spanking his dead son.

As Ira wound up a story about some impoverished child Nestor had sent to forestry school in Missoula, no strings attached, Jules gnashed his teeth. If Nestor had been fiction, no one would have read the book. "So basically, he hadn't so much as harbored an unchristian thought since the last Klan meeting his father hauled him along to in the twenties."

Ira hemmed. "I'm not saying I knew everything he thought. He was always one to give a lecture on no one's knowing what they're capable of, good or bad, until push came to shove. And he wouldn't go to church, even for most weddings. It made things awkward for Mrs. A."

"Something happen in the war?"

"Not that I know of. He was in France and Germany, so he saw plenty of shit."

"Which made him love all of mankind somehow." Jules tried to flip an M&M into his mouth and missed. Grace, packing up her purse at the end of the day, snickered.

"He had people he'd just as soon not deal with, just like everyone," said Ira defensively. "It's not like he was *too* nice. Nina's good friends with Ruth Birdland and your aunt Laura, but Nestor and the judge and Joseph wouldn't say a word to each other. Gene Zatow screwed him on some sick calves, and Nestor always sat on the far side of the room from him in Rotary. And I know he thought the minister was an asshole."

Jules stopped sorting colors into columns on his desk. "Why'd he dislike Miles Birdland?"

"I don't know," said Ira. "I mean, Miles Birdland *is* an asshole, so it never occurred to me to ask."

Jules started to say something, paused and started over. "Anyone else unlikely? Any other acquaintances—neighbors, maybe?"

"I don't think he much cared for any of the neighbors. We've got that Japanese hydroponic company and the California goofballs who burned down their own barn last summer."

"What's wrong with the Ganters?"

"I'm sure it was just about who owned what and how much. What Nina would call a boy thing. They were always perfectly civil with each other about stray animals and ditch problems, always said hello. They just preferred to be invisible with each other."

Joseph was good at making people feel invisible, but it wasn't Nestor's style.

"It wasn't like with the minister," Ira said. "Nestor just shook with rage when he saw that man. I believe he and Joseph and Miles Birdland had been tight, and I guess they just came to a parting of the ways."

"About what?"

"Before my time, and probably not that interesting," said Ira. "I was never really a local boy, and nobody saw fit to fill me in."

Jules rubbed his head. "How long you been around, Ira? You planning on staying for Nina now that Nestor's gone?"

"You fit in a lot of questions just now."

"I guess I did," said Jules. "I've been asking everyone un-popular questions lately."

"I have my own land here, and I intend to stay and help out as long as Nina needs me to. I met Nestor in the war, came out here to visit afterwards and never left. So if I read you correctly, and you're thinking we're a triangle, it's a pretty old one, and I'm definitely the short side."

"How's that?" asked Jules.

"I got a medical discharge. I was a sapper and a pen-cil bomb blew in my lap. So though I can say honestly that I love Mrs. Amundsen, I've never loved her, if you get my drift. Poor girl had one old man missing a leg and another missing a dick." Ira laughed merrily.

Ho ho ho, thought Jules. He said goodbye and ate the rest of the M&Ms one by one with his feet up on the desk.

AXEL SCOTTI WAS staring bleakly out his office window when Jules wandered in. Even robust, deeply unreflective Si-cilians were apparently falling victim to gray skies, and Jules wasn't there to make the day any sunnier.

"We're going to need an inquest on Nestor," he said a few minutes later for the fourth time. "There's just no way around it."

"Maybe he gave the leg to Goodwill before he offed him-self. Maybe he did something creepy and whatchacallit, au-toerotic, with the pillow."

Jules felt a glimmer of compassion for such desperate wish fulfillment. Scotti would do almost anything to get out of an inquest. "At seventy-something, in a car, with a dog?"

"Why not? Did you check his dick?"

"It burned right off, Axel. Are you serious?"

Scotti sighed. "I'm always serious."

"Considering the bad prostate, no rope on the scene, and an unpleasant outdoor temperature, I'd let that theory go. Especially given the head wound."

"You got a weapon?"

"No," said Jules. "But we've got two pathologists who aren't going to check off the box for natural causes."

Scotti made a face and covered his eyes. "Who the hell is your suspect anyway?"

A good question. Jules rubbed his left temple, where the pain was starting. "Let's compromise and wait a week or so to announce it."

Scotti was suddenly suspicious. "Why?"

"Why what?"

"Why are you willing to postpone? I've never heard of such a thing."

Jules sighed and smiled. "Because as I'm not likely to turn up a witness, I'd just as soon ask questions quietly. If we'd found Nestor in the grocery store parking lot, or if I really thought he'd been done in by a drifter who might float away, I wouldn't be so agreeable."

"Well, of *course* it was a drifter," said Axel. "I mean, if it was anyone. No one from around here set that poor old man on fire."

"Is that so?" said Jules. "Then let's have the damn inquest."

"You just can't bear the idea of a year without a murder," said Axel. "Now, if you'll excuse me, I have to go up to the ranch and spend the evening kissing my father-in-law's ass."

"Doesn't sound like Joseph's thing," said Jules. "But have fun."

"You keep in touch with us on this one."

"Who's 'us'?" asked Jules. "Neil can't work on his grand-father's murder."

"I suppose he should disqualify himself," said Axel morosely.

We should all disqualify ourselves, thought Jules. Just outside Scotti's door he ran into Neil, who was studying Birdland's new schedule on the bulletin board in the court-house hall. Jules wondered how acute Neil's hearing was.

"Just out of curiosity, would you be surprised to learn your grandfathers were friends, really good friends, in high school?" asked Jules.

Neil didn't bother turning to look at him. "Why would I be curious? Why would you be curious?"

"I'm a curious kind of guy."

Even Neil's eyebrows managed to be bored, and his dark coxcomb bobbed as he turned from the schedule. "Not very likely," he said. "In fact, that's bullshit."

"It's true," said Jules. "They played basketball together."

"Maybe they played, but they wouldn't have been friends. I never saw them in the same room except for graduations. We had to have two Thanksgivings, two Christmases, two of everything."

Which was probably as often as he bothered seeing them. "Ask your grandmother," said Jules. "When's the last time you saw her?"

"Which one?"

"Either."

"My grandfather's funeral," snapped Neil. "When's the last time you saw yours?"

"Her funeral," said Jules, smiling. "Just ask."

10 *Wind*

"THERE'S NO ASSHOLE LIKE AN OLD ASSHOLE," whispered Cicely.

Alice's eyes opened wide, but she nodded in agreement. At the other end of the Ganter living room Laura was passing out muffins; they'd been waiting for Joseph to finish "business calls" for twenty minutes.

Cicely had almost no tolerance for delays, but most of the other women in the room seemed happy enough. Venus began to talk again, an informative monologue aimed mostly at Alice. "You'll find the most beautiful stones in this cemetery, and some gorgeous epitaphs."

"'Up or down?' for the old bellboy at the Baird," said Angelina.

"How about 'Miracles happen'?" said Olive. "Poor sucker."

"I like 'Let it go,'" said Indie. "From that one old man who said it to the sheriff as he was dying, the sheriff not realizing the murderer was sitting right there with them."

"'I told you my heart was broken' has always been a personal favorite," said Cicely tartly.

"'All the stars close their eyes for you' is mine," said Mabel. "For that poor girl who burned herself up with her baby after a divorce."

Venus shot an annoyed look in their direction. "I had the

more dulcet inscriptions in mind. There's some very nice poetry and pretty Bible verse—people used to try harder. And anyway, get your facts straight. That girl was divorced, but she killed herself after a different misfortune. And the baby was retarded."

Alice wondered if Venus meant no one should mind as much. "What's a 'different misfortune'?"

"One of those rapes you could never find in the old papers," said Angelina dryly. "You had to know what to look for. A line about so-and-so recovering in a hospital or visiting relatives."

"Or thus and such a housekeeper leaving."

"Speaking of murder," said Cicely bitterly.

"Stop it," said Indie with surprising sharpness. She met Alice's eye. "It's so unpleasant."

Everyone was quiet, watching; even Joseph, still on the phone at the far end of the room, seemed to be listening. Venus tried to regain the advantage. "We had skating meets, skiing in the park with the old rope tow over Christmas. I believe there were many fine weddings that summer—"

"Oh, please," said Ella Bolan. "We've had plenty of violence. Manslaughter they usually label it, and robbery and arson. And those rapes."

Alice looked around the room. "Did they catch the man?"

Cicely shrugged. Indie walked into the kitchen while Ettie, oblivious, talked to a parakeet in the far corner of the room. She hadn't asked about the trunks once so far that day; perhaps she'd taken Alice's last promise about Jules's opening them seriously.

"What was the story of the housekeeper?" asked Alice. "Who was murdered?"

"Just an Indian, sweetheart," said Mabel. "Though I know it's not fashionable to put it that way these days."

"It certainly isn't," said Olive. "And I don't see a point to hiding the past. Bad stuff happens here. Every ten years or so there's something awful."

"That average has gone up a bit," said Cicely dryly. "Just ask your son."

"All of those people died last year," said Olive. "Before that it had been at least a decade. Maybe more. I can't remember anyone dying since Ansel."

No one felt qualified to challenge the widow and mother of a sheriff on her statistics. Things simmered down. Joseph apologized for the delay but made another call. Flo and Jetta brought out fresh pastries, and Olive began telling stories about the family photos on the mantel. Venus commented on the variety of bird feeders, one outside every window; had Laura seen any grosbeaks lately?

Laura, who was busy offering Cicely a scone with a smile that would have shattered glass, didn't have a clue. She came, after all, from Italy, where they'd eaten almost all the songbirds. The feeders were Joseph's; Joseph loved birds. Venus began to calculate the years he'd helped with the bird count, and Alice drifted off. Someone had brought back balloons from the anniversary party, and one of them lived on, bumping the floor instead of the ceiling now with each gust through the open window. Joseph's blind cat tailed it relentlessly around the room, nudging it with her nose.

Then Joseph clapped his hands and told them it was time to go. Outside it was warm and blustery, sixty or so in the sun, probably the last such day for months. This translated to a clutch of octogenarians hopping about, trying to keep their skirts down, especially Cicely, who'd worn a fairly short pleated number.

"I told you all to wear pants," said Venus.

Cicely laughed and smiled at Joseph. Joseph smiled back.

They piled back into two vans and Alice's Land Cruiser for the first leg of the tour, which began where Mission Creek emptied into the Yellowstone. Most of the land they passed belonged to Joseph and Nestor Amundsen now, but the drainage had originally been made up of two dozen smaller homesteads and also encompassed the site of two towns, a school, a post office, and the old Crow Agency. At the turn of the century there'd been a settlement every five or six miles, spaced for half a day's travel. The grass on the bench looked lush from the road, but up close there were larger patches of clay and gravel than green clumps of grass, and small cacti dotted the landscape. With only sixteen inches of precipitation a year, it was easy to understand why the other twenty-some original families had given up parcels that wouldn't support ten antelope, let alone your average nineteenth-century passel of brats.

The only remaining sign of the Crow Agency was a stone foundation for a springhouse and the remnant of a corral. The Agency had once marked the western border of the reservation, when the reservation had included most of southwest Montana; by 1878 it had been reduced to a tenth of its initial size and settlers surged into the void. Alice and Joseph swapped details: During the first summer the garden had flooded, and vegetables had been shipped from Fort Benton. That winter the soldiers and Crow salted ten dozen antelope; by then, the buffalo were already gone.

They explored the old school, the township hall, and the post office, now a chicken coop, and drove back to Joseph's ranch, the ladies having decided they could handle the half-mile walk to the graveyards. Jetta's sons, ages twelve and fourteen, were sent ahead carrying director's chairs, and the group started up the grassy slope to the north of the ranch.

"Where's your granddaughter, Cicely?" asked Mabel, already puffing.

"She said she'd be coming with Sheriff Clement."

"Really?" asked Angelina, trilling her *r*.

"Little Caroline knows Jules?" asked Joseph. "And who, by the way, invited him?"

"Little Caroline works for Jules," said Cicely. "First female in the sheriff's department. Don't you read your paper?"

"No," said Joseph. "I might be suckered into reading the obituaries."

Another ten minutes, another fifty yards. Jetta's sons had slowed down with the camp chairs; the ladies had almost caught up. "Someone's coming," the older boy said, gesturing downhill.

"Oh, my holy saints," wheezed Venus. "I'd forgotten even the hills feel like mountains."

"We're almost there," said Jetta. They'd finally rounded a clump of chokecherry bushes to see a thirty-foot plot surrounded by a Victorian metal fence. The ladies stopped en masse and made puffing sounds.

"It's a man and a woman," said Jetta's youngest son.

"That's Jules," said Olive. "Isn't it, Alice? I didn't bring my glasses."

"It's him," said Alice.

The boys gave a yelp of terror, put on a final sprint, set the chairs up inside the plot and vaulted the far fence to disappear over the rise.

"They ran into Jules for the first time in a professional capacity this summer," said Jetta. "Something about tossing dead gophers off the highway overpass."

"You didn't tell me that," said Flo.

"I probably didn't want to talk about it."

"I'm so glad Neil was never a problem," said Flo.

Alice watched Laura Ganter's lip curl. Jules and Caroline, neither of whom seemed winded by the climb, blended into the group, and Jules held the gate open for the ladies. Caroline's face had begun to fade from purple to yellow; Jules looked as if he'd pinched a nerve in his neck, an expression Alice was beginning to connect to Caroline's presence.

From the graveyard hill you could look down to the facing Crazies fifteen miles away, and between, below the high golden prairie and Nestor Amundsen's land, a train snaked through the low-lying cottonwoods along the Yellowstone. The mountains had hit their prettiest stage, with green conifers, deepening white snow, dormant high-elevation grass looking more golden than dun in the sunlight. But along the cold-looking river the cottonwoods were bare and gray, as moribund and stark in the wind as trees in a flooded swamp. By January, huge black-and-white or gold-brown blots would appear on the high branches as bald and golden eagles started their private fishing seasons.

"So your grandfather Jens owned all this?" asked Alice.

"No," said Joseph. He gestured to the lush creekbed. "I got this section later, built most of the house after the war. I moved his main house down here, from the bench, and added on. No reason to put your ass in the wind if you don't have to."

Venus crabbed over and whispered in Caroline's ear, and Caroline passed the message on to Alice. Her question had been unintentionally rude; they stood on what had once been the edge of Indabel's and Etoile's ranch, lost before the war. Jules had always known this, but never really considered what it would mean to grow up on God's little acre and lose it.

Joseph was watching this and gestured gracefully to Indie and Ettie, who looked especially melancholy and bent in the open air. "This land once belonged to the ladies Whit-san, before they left for their West Coast careers."

"That's where our house stood," said Indabel, pointing out a border of willows and a small orchard of apple and plum trees, the collapsed remains of a barn. "Built in 1919, and it burned in the fifties. We had five bedrooms, a lower wraparound porch, an upstairs sleeping porch, three chimneys and two bathrooms. Twelve rooms all told, including our father's library and a music room."

"You had two cars, too; that was the real wonder," said Joseph, smiling. "The garage was there, next to the stables."

"Father liked Arabians," said Indie.

"That was the root cellar," said Joseph, pointing to a bump in the turf. Alice made out a door. "The scariest place on earth."

"You had your own," said Indie, amused.

"Yours was scarier," said Joseph.

Flo, looking bored, toed a headstone. "What kind of name is Redhot? Some cowboy baby?"

"This was a pet cemetery," said Joseph. "Both families used it. The main cemetery is on the other side of that rise, in the Hancock churchyard."

"Surely, Florence, you've attended a funeral or two there," said Venus sternly.

Flo shrugged. If it never occurred to you others truly existed, thought Jules, it would be easy to forget minor things like death.

Joseph pointed to a double headstone. "Julie and Charlie belonged to my mother and Mrs. Whitsan. They were little English cockers, no more suited to this place than their owners. Nina was Julie's daughter, my first dog. She was eaten by a coyote, broke my young heart."

Caroline straightened slowly from the graves, meeting Alice's eyes with such a shuttered expression Alice thought she must be looking right through her, toward the river valley and the moving train. "What were these other dogs, Nestor and Joey?" Caroline asked, smiling at Joseph.

"I can't remember," said Joseph. "I know they had border collies as well. Our dogs were on this side." He started walking east.

"I'd have thought you'd remember a dog named after you," said Caroline mildly. "And Nina would have been named after Nestor Amundsen's wife?"

"We've all been neighbors since we were born," said Joseph tersely. "Nina's father worked for Nestor's father."

"Can you imagine how pretty Nina was at ten?" asked Cicely. "They all felt protective of her, but Nestor dedicated his life to the cause."

Jules was busy showing Alice the mounds of every mouse, cat, dog and bird he'd ever loved. Only two dogs and one cat and a wild rabbit had rated a stone. Jules pointed to a round granite boulder, half sunk. "My rabbit Ike. He used to box our cat."

"What happened?"

Jules pointed to another stone. "Redhot was getting senile and attacked. He was an Airedale."

"Who was Milla?" asked Caroline. "'The birds fly for you'?"

Joseph was off in a daydream, and at the bottom of the hill the windmill behind the barn shrieked.

"Milla?" prompted Caroline.

"Must have been a gun dog," said Jetta. "But I don't know about the name. Have I forgotten an aunt, Dad?"

"Don't be silly," said Cicely. "For Miles. She was that pretty setter Joseph had right through high school."

Jules stopped in the middle of a story about a one-legged hawk. "Miles who?"

"Birdland," said Cicely crisply. "He grew up out here, too."

Jules was watching Joseph, who turned, met his eyes, and smiled. "Where?"

"With us," said Joseph. "Miles was an orphan. His dad died in Butte, and I think his mother had cancer. He and I shared a room from the time we were five, after his mother died, until we went to college. Milla was a Belton setter, same line as the ones I have now.

"What are you talking about?" asked Flo.

"Surely you knew, Florence."

Jules hadn't, but he kept his mouth shut.

"You're all out of your minds," she insisted. "You're making it up. He would have told me."

"Maybe you never asked," said Joseph mildly. "Did you?"

"You two hardly even know each other," Flo insisted.

"Is that so?" said Joseph.

Jetta broke in. "Dad—"

"Don't worry," he said. "I enjoy Ms. Florence telling me about my own life."

Flo's eyes filled.

"Honey," said Joseph, "you don't have a clue."

They decided they weren't quite up to the overland trip on foot to the church cemetery, and retreated downhill to the cars at a good clip. Jules and Caroline rode with Alice, who had a demonic look on her face as she accelerated out of the yard. Jules noticed that Caroline shut her eyes. Alice slowed down for a steep grade, rounded a sharp corner that made the rest of the car say *Eeep*, and there was the Lutheran church, all that was left of the town, plunked in the middle of the prairie with nothing else around it. The other two cars pulled up a full five minutes later.

From the churchyard you could often see the Little Belts. The view hadn't changed since most of the people in the cemetery had been born; Jules doubted they'd found it comforting or lovely on a cold January day.

"Here's Jules's grandfather Charlie, a real hard-core cowboy. He was more fun than anyone else in the family. He was on the city force for two whole years before they canned him for drinking on the job."

"What you might call a piece of work these days," said Cicely.

"A handsome man, though," said Indabel. "Whenever he brought my brother home for some trouble or another, I'd just stand and stare."

"Why'd he die so young?" asked Alice, relentlessly mordant.

"Appendix ruptured," said Joseph.

"He didn't go to the hospital in time, huh?"

"He didn't go to the hospital at all," answered Joseph. "It was unfortunate timing, during a cold snap in January. He looked funny for a couple of days, then said he had a stomachache and went to bed, then started screaming in the middle of the night so that his wife called us for help. He died after screaming for six hours, which is really quite a long time unless you live way the hell up the Boulder Divide and it's 1936."

So much for romanticizing the past. Alice nodded, as if the story confirmed some deep suspicion about Montana winters, and wandered on. "Here's the girl you said killed herself. And here's another pretty one: 'Your love grows like a garden, still.'"

"She was Nina Amundsen's grandmother. Peas in a pod," said Venus. "The women in that family were always wreaking havoc with their looks."

Alice's few glimpses of Nina Amundsen hadn't brought to mind Helen of Troy, but then the local climate wasn't the type to preserve beauty. The Whitsans' parents were there, and Jules's grandparents and great-grandparents, and the whole Ganter side of the family. All the Amundsens were there in their own wrought-iron plot, along with Nestor's fresh, unmarked grave. Jules helped set up director's chairs while Joseph led Caroline and Alice off for a private tour. Within two minutes Caroline had whipped the 1936 yearbook out of the envelope she'd been carrying under her arm, and Jules watched a familiar, polite mask settle over his uncle's face.

He turned away and found Venus. "Do you have another blood drive coming up soon?"

Venus ran the local Red Cross chapter. "Why yes," she said, beaming. "In just two weeks. Will you have time to help?"

"Love to," said Jules. "You give me the dirt on previous contributors and I'll make the calls to remind them to give again."

"Wonderful," she said. "I'll drop the list off at your house."

He wandered off and sat on a stone, looking at the Crazies. Jetta and Flo were hunkered out of the wind on the church steps, and he heard bits and snatches of their conversation, most of it about Ruth Birdland's illness. Then Jules became aware of a conversation closer at hand.

"Caroline has a friend visiting," said Cicely. "And he's quite something. She's known him for years, and I think they're finally at that point."

The ladies were all smirking, and Jules experienced a troubling and utterly involuntary drop in blood pressure. He wrenched the last chair open and headed for Jetta and Flo, neither of whom looked that happy to see him.

"I need to see those party photos," he said. "Does Laura have them?"

"Party?" Jetta took on a dim look that made him suspicious.

"The anniversary party. Remember, just a week ago? Carl Jump said he gave you proof sheets."

"Oh." Jetta pursed her lips, thinking. "Let me try to remember who has them now."

"Why do you want to see them?" asked Flo. "I don't recall any shots of you and Edie dancing."

"I'm just curious," said Jules. "I missed quite a bit of the party, you know."

Flo flared her nostrils. Jules gave her a big smile. "Where are they?"

"I think they're back at the photographer's," said Jetta. "I think Dad dropped them off."

"I'll ask him," said Jules.

"Or maybe it was Mom."

He squinted, as if she was out of focus. "I can't remember everything," said Jetta, exasperated. "Half my brain died over that party."

A few minutes later Alice began rounding everyone up. "Jules and I'll walk back together," said Joseph. "I need exercise, and he never has time these days."

The look Caroline gave Jules was half questioning, half suspicious, as if she thought Joseph might be pulling him aside to exchange confidences Jules might never pass on. Or maybe she was thinking of Alice's driving and didn't want to die without him.

Halfway up the hill, Jules turned back. The last few Aches—Cicely, Venus and Indie—were still milling around a van, gesturing to tombstones, the sky, the decrepit foundation of the church.

"You've known all of them for a long time," Jules said.

"Most of them."

"Cicely, certainly."

"I'm too old for a lecture," said Joseph.

Jules turned back again and saw that the light had already changed, so that the headstones were whiter and the grass greener. "What was Charlie like anyway?"

"He was a cowboy, and he liked to drink."

"You said that."

Joseph stopped to rest. "I heard a theory recently that these days the people who would have been cowboys in the past are cops."

"Seems to me that they sell dope," said Jules. "You miss out on a lot of profit and excitement in this job."

"Well, you know," said Joseph, "Charlie blasted his shoulder too, just like you, but I think he did it roping, or maybe it was a bar fight. I don't think a gun was involved." He sighed and started walking again.

"Are you making the point that he and I are too alike? Do you think I drink too much?"

"You don't drink like Charlie," said Joseph. "You just drink the way I used to drink."

They crossed the hill divide and looked down to see that all the cars were now at the Ganter house again, all the ladies disembarking for a cocktail; they watched as Cicely's skirt blew over her head again and they could hear the edge of her clear, high laugh.

"Nothing you haven't seen before," said Jules.

Joseph sighed. "You know it's just a blur these days. You're so goddamn moral. Why this sudden fascination with something you've known about for years?"

"You used to tell me the Ten Commandments weren't

just for Baptists. And I'm not being moral. I'm just stating the obvious."

Below them, Cicely whooped again, still twenty feet from the door; round Indie crabbed behind her, trying to capture the billowing hem. "Now, you would need to use your imagination," said Joseph. "Back then she was shaped like her granddaughter, if that helps explain my trespass."

"Since I don't know what the granddaughter really looks like, it doesn't," said Jules.

"Somehow I have a feeling that you will," said Joseph.

Caroline opted to ride back to town with Alice and Cicely—it seemed she had become an Ache, the new youngest member. Jules drove home and started to clean his house before it occurred to him that this would be an opportune time to talk to Miles Birdland.

Flo, a migratory pain in his ass, answered the door. "Are you everywhere," she asked, "or are you just where I happen to be?"

Jules twitched at the latter idea. "Is your father home?"

She half leaned in the doorway, blocking him. "Why?"

"Business."

"So butt out, you dumb bitch?"

Jules's eyes widened. Flo smiled. "If that's how you want to put it," he said.

She colored, and Birdland appeared over her shoulder.

"Florence, please go to your mother. She needs you."

"And you don't?"

"Not right now, dear."

"Well," said Flo, backing up just far enough to let Jules through the door.

"Follow me," said Birdland, ignoring her.

Jules followed, trotting obediently along through a series

of dark rooms until they reached a sunroom at the back of the house. A dozen potted plants, dwarf citrus and rosemary and lavender, lined the windows, and the interior wall was covered with books. Birdland gestured to a chair, and as Jules sat he saw that Flo had followed them and stood in the threshold.

Her father shut the door in her face.

Birdland handed Jules a glass of undiluted whiskey without asking whether he would like a drink, and drained his own, for all the world a character in a thirties movie. Then he flicked on a turntable on the bookshelf and he stared at Jules, waiting, without saying a word, for the music to begin.

He'd put on Ray Charles. Jules cleared his throat. "Did you happen to see Nestor Amundsen again after that lunch at the Bucket?"

"Certainly," said Birdland. "I drove out to his ranch to discuss a mutual problem."

Jules stared. Birdland smiled warmly, like an actual human being.

"It's been weighing on my mind. I felt I should tell you, but I preferred to avoid even thinking of it. And really there was nothing to tell—that evening he seemed just fine, or as fine as an aged, one-legged man can seem. He most definitely did not strike me as someone who contemplated suicide."

"That evening?" said Jules. "You saw him in the evening?"

"Thursday evening. So imagine my shock to learn he died a day later."

"Thursday," said Jules stupidly.

Miles Birdland didn't notice. "I find it impossible to believe he killed himself."

"You didn't go out again on Friday?"

"No," said Miles Birdland. "I drove for a bit, but not out there. I always drive to relax."

Jules looked over the books in the shelves. History, spy novels, gardening texts. "What did you talk about?"

"I believe I said a mutual problem. That shouldn't be hard to figure out."

He turned his head to the curtained glass of the sunroom door. Jules could almost hear Flo breathe, like a bass line in the music.

"How did you know I'd gone out there?" asked the judge.

"The mud on your tires. Nestor had his very own gravel pit, only deposit like it in the county."

Birdland smiled. "It would almost be enjoyable watching this story unfold if I didn't know so many of the people involved. Years and years of dealing with drug and alcohol deaths, husbands who think they've taken out a lifetime lease on their wives' bodies. It's amusing to have a reason to check tire treads."

"Who are the 'so many'?"

"Excuse me?" said Birdland, startled.

"We still don't know who's involved beyond Nestor and some bones on the island. Maybe you could tell me."

"Sorry," said the older man. "A figure of speech."

He smiled. Jules smiled back. "I saw a photo of the basketball team the year you won state. You were all good friends before the war, you and Nestor and Joseph and Merle. You grew up with Joseph."

"Yes," said Birdland. He didn't seem to feel the need to elaborate.

"Can I ask why you stopped being friends?"

"You never really stop being friends," said Birdland. "You simply stop seeing one another."

Jules nodded, beginning to sense that the judge had been at the whiskey all afternoon. "Why did you stop seeing each other?"

"Something bad happened. It infected us; we reminded each other of this event."

"Can you tell me what happened?"

"No," said Miles Birdland. "I can't. I've made a promise, and anyway, it's not one of those stories that redeems a person with the telling. Knowing it wouldn't even redeem you."

THAT NIGHT EDIE came over, with the tacit understanding that they'd proceed in the spirit of friendship and diminished expectations. They had dinner and went to a movie and at midnight were downstairs coming up with a snack from the refrigerator when the phone rang.

"Don't touch that phone," said Jules, balancing some leftover roast chicken, a slightly moldy chunk of Gruyère, and various condiments. "It'll be something nasty I don't want to deal with. It's always something nasty I don't want to deal with."

Edie wrapped her robe tighter and shifted on her tiptoes. The floor was cold. Jules delivered his load to the counter and they both stared at the machine as it kicked on. A voice began to meow, quietly at first and then building to a virtual caterwaul, with soft giggles in between.

Fred, the fat orange cat who still nominally belonged to Olive, walked slowly into the kitchen and stared at the phone.

"Some nice new friend you should tell me about?" asked Edie.

"No," said Jules. He had goose bumps running down his arms.

"Yowl," said the answering machine.

"It's a woman," said Edie.

"It's Flo Amundsen," said Jules. He reached for the phone, enraged, in time to hear her hang up.

JULES HAD BEEN known to simply unplug his phone on weekends; he mentioned this to Edie when it rang again at eight the next morning.

"Let it go," she said. "Did you ever turn the machine back on?"

He hadn't; after nine rings someone gave up. Jules was getting his first back rub in months when it started again five minutes later.

He seized the receiver and growled *"What?"*

At eight thirty he was standing in the Ganters' kitchen, peering at the shotgun pellet in Joseph's upper arm, hoping someone would think to offer him coffee. Jetta, in sweatpants and a T-shirt, seemed paralyzed; Laura was slamming clean dishes into a cupboard.

"Such bullshit," said Joseph. "It was one of those braindead out-of-state hunters."

"Most bad shots notice buildings," said Jules. "You were coming out of the barn, right?"

"It came from the woods along the creek. Someone was aiming in their foreground and I was the background."

"Those trees are fifty yards away, and it's not like you have a little downed barbed wire and one old No Trespassing sign. That's box wire, and you've got a dozen Fuck Off posters."

Jules tried to sound genial, relaxed about it, but this only allowed Joseph to downplay. "Recall the lady who was shot in her backyard for wearing white mittens, or the boys from Pennsylvania who ran from you last year, the ones who shot the buffalo through the twelve-foot game farm fence and claimed they hadn't noticed climbing it. Or all the people who think a moose looks like a horse or an elk looks like a black bear or a mule deer looks like a wolf. Who knows what I looked like."

Across the room, Laura jerked the silverware basket from the dishwasher. "You were wearing a red sweatshirt."

Joseph favored her with a loving look. "You two surely have better things to do."

"Oh, for Christ's sake," hissed Jetta, and slammed down the stairs to the basement. Laura let the silverware drop on the counter and followed her.

"They don't understand how excited these dimwits get when they think they see a deer," said Joseph.

Jules helped himself to coffee. "Probably not," he agreed. "But not even a dimwit uses a shotgun on deer, and I've never met a bird hunter that stupid."

Joseph looked at the floor.

"I'm going to go out and look around," said Jules, "and then I'll drive you in to have that pellet taken out, and maybe we can have a nice peaceful breakfast during which we talk about things like the weather."

"That would be a treat," said Joseph. "You promise?"

"It's Sunday," said Jules. "Tomorrow I intend to be in a different mood."

He couldn't find footprints, tire prints, or an ejected shell anywhere near the two-track along the creek. Nor was there any sign of a trash fire in the gully behind the barn, the fire that Joseph had said made him late for his own party the day Nestor died. Jules walked the area for fifteen minutes, making sure. But the Scout was in a slightly different position, and under a layer of barnyard mud Jules found more pink glitter from the Amundsen driveway.

"What are you doing, Jules?"

Joseph stood by the gate. "I'm looking at your tires," said Jules. "You want to talk about the last time you drove this thing?"

"No," said Joseph. "I don't. And anyway, you promised me the day off."

JULES WAS BACK in bed at two when Nina Amundsen called. She and Ira had searched both houses up and down and come up with three missing items, besides the artificial limb. Nestor had had an 1880 twenty-dollar gold piece, a good-luck item he'd always kept in the bunkhouse medicine cabinet. He'd had a sperm whale tooth from a Navy uncle that Nina thought was usually on the windowsill in the bedroom. And he'd had a nice belt he'd had from the thirties, when he was a rodeo-riding young buck. She'd make sketches of all the items, dropped them off later that week.

Nina's voice was tentative. "Nestor always wore his belt. Wasn't he wearing it when he died? Or maybe he left it out with the party clothes."

Jules tried to imagine Nestor strapping a belt over his pjs before he splashed around gasoline and blew his brains out. No, he said. There'd been no remnants in the car, no belt on Harvey's inventory list. But for the leg, all the missing items were things that could have been taken earlier or given away. Nina knew this, though she thought it unlikely.

"The belt, for instance," said Jules. "Couldn't he have given it to Neil?"

The silence that followed was exceedingly dry. Jules pressed on. "It's the sort of thing you might give to a grandson."

"Neil wouldn't be caught dead in a rodeo buckle. Nestor knew better. The coin maybe."

She seemed dubious about the notion of a burglary, but when he asked again if she had any ideas about who might have had a reason to kill Nestor, she didn't actually answer. "I'll keep thinking about it," said Nina. "I'll call you."

She hung up. Jules thought about thieves, wondering what sort smothers and strikes and shoots a man, then torches him in a car. Not a casual one, certainly, and a prosthesis or a whale tooth wasn't your usual burgle.

WHEN THE PHONE rang again, it was the hospital to say that Joy Schwartz was wide awake. Flo's car was in the parking lot when he arrived, and he peered inside, hoping to discover a stray pillow or gold coin. The car was chillingly clean, and the coffee cup in the holder had teddy bears painted along the rim.

His mother looked up from the admissions desk. "She's here, Romeo."

Jules narrowed his eyes. "What are you talking about?"

"Caroline's with Miss Schwartz," said Olive patiently.

"I didn't come looking for Caroline."

She studied him. "It's always ominous when you lose your sense of humor."

Jules shut his eyes and worked on his surging blood pressure. "Why's Flo Amundsen here?"

"I'm trying to remember what age you turned difficult. Six? Thirteen?"

"Why's she here?"

"Her mother's in for tests."

Jules's face must have said *Why bother?*

Olive shrugged. "Some people won't let go."

"Neil ever been in here?"

"Probably. What business is it of yours?"

"Would you look up his blood type for me?"

"Of course not. Go away."

Jules listened quietly while Caroline dragged monosyllables from Joy Schwartz, who looked as if she'd actually gained weight on an IV. Her mother had made it up from Nephi in time for this reunion, which didn't seem entirely peaceful. Joy Schwartz said that the man had light eyes but dark brows and lashes, but that was as far as she could take the description. She couldn't remember his voice, but she could remember some of what he'd had to say: He'd asked her what had happened to her, yet she was sure she didn't know him and couldn't understand the question. He'd called her a "skinny bitch" and said he'd "fuck her until her bones popped out." When he'd first attacked she'd had a moment of thinking he was familiar, but now she was confused, the eyes so large and enraged and blank in her memory she couldn't tell if the impression was real.

Jules walked Caroline to her car. His mother grinned broadly as they passed the desk; Jules glared.

"What do you make of 'What happened to you?'" asked Caroline.

"She's met him," said Jules. "She just doesn't realize it."

"Do you think that's true of the others?"

Jules shrugged and rubbed his head.

"If he wasn't so goddamn average looking."

Jules nodded. "Though I imagine a lot of men are average in a face mask. That's Flo Amundsen's Taurus, by the way," he said, pointing to the shiny silver station wagon.

Caroline peered at the car. "I'm thrilled for her."

"A week ago she had muddy Goodyears. At least I think they were muddy, and now that she has brand-new Firestones we may never know."

She gave him a sidelong look. "You think I'm insane," said Jules.

"Not all the time."

"When I drove out and found Nestor, the road was solid mud. By the next day it had drained and hardened. On

Saturday I noticed Flo had muddy Goodyears, which was the tread Harvey picked up on the way out to the body. So did half a dozen other people parked in the yard that day, as well as the judge, and Goodyear probably sells half the tires in America, so big fucking deal, right?"

"Right," said Caroline.

"Both Flo and her father said they'd been out Thursday afternoon or evening. But the driveway's shaded by willows and a ridge on the southwest, and it wouldn't have been thawed enough to put pink silt on either of their tires Thursday night, wouldn't probably have gotten mucky till Friday. By Saturday it had dried up, which was why Nestor used the pink stuff to begin with. Everyone else has clay, and they wallow around in it for weeks."

"You can't prove anything with this," said Caroline after a moment.

"No," said Jules. "Maybe the stuff sticks to tires for weeks and weeks. But the judge knew I'd checked his tires, and Flo might have known, and now she has spanking new ones."

"So what do you suggest we do?"

"I suggest we be happy there's only two tire stores in town."

WHEN JULES RETURNED from the hospital, Venus's Red Cross files were waiting on the porch. He skipped through the names in the last of the afternoon sun and found what he wanted after only five minutes.

In the District Court of the Sixth Judicial District of the State of Montana, in and for the County of Absaroka, the Honorable Miles Birdland Presiding

State of Montana, Plaintiff

vs

Alston Howard Hantz, Defendant

(Partial transcript of proceedings, October 31, 1994)

The Court: Is there any legal cause why judgment should not be pronounced at this time?

Mr. Biddle: I have no basis for legal objection, Your Honor.

The Court: Very well. Will you please stand then, Mr. Hantz? It is the judgment of this Court that you be sentenced to the State Prison at Deer Lodge for a term of ten years, the maximum penalty imposed, and of course the reason, which will be stated, is the criminal history of this defendant, showing that he's not responsive to rehabilitation or correction, and he needs to be in prison for the maximum time in the interest of society, or for the protection of society. You're remanded to the custody of the sheriff for the execution of this sentence.

Mr. Johansen: Will that be as a dangerous or non-dangerous offender, Your Honor?

The Court:	Well, I've considered that the defendant is over the age of eighteen years, and has been convicted and sentenced within a period of five years. Considering the flagrant nature of his offense, the Court finds that he's a dangerous offender.
The Defendant:	How in the hell can you find me a dangerous offender? There's nothing in there showing any violent crime. What's wrong with everybody anyway? You take that son-of-a-bitching—
The Court:	That will be all. You're remanded to the custody of the sheriff. Sheriff Clement, you are welcome to remove the defendant.
The Defendant:	You son of a bitch. You bald-headed son of a bitch, when I get out of there, I'll blow your fucking head away.
The Court:	Well, now—
The Defendant:	I hope I get a chance at you, you son of a bitch.
The Court:	Make a record of that statement. Sheriff, bring him back in here. Bring the defendant back in here, I want to make a record of that.
The Defendant:	Fuck you in your ass.
The Court:	The defendant has threatened this Court.
The Defendant:	Fuck you in your ass.
The Court:	All right, you be quiet now.
The Defendant:	You no-good, bald-headed son of a bitch.
The Court:	Get that down in the record, he's threatened to blow the judge's head off.
The Defendant:	Stick it in your mouth you bald-headed bastard. You fucking son of a bitch. You no-good bald-headed son of a cow.
The Court:	If I could, I'd give you another ten years. You may remove him, Sheriff Clement.

Sheriff Clement: I'm attempting to, Your Honor.

The Defendant: I know what you can do. How about coming down here and licking my nuts, you son of a bitch.

The Court: Also include in there a general statement that at the conclusion of the sentencing the defendant threatened the life and integrity of the Court, and called him every foul name he could think of, and resisted removal, and threatened the Court on release. All right, that will be all.

IN TERMS OF CHAOS, HALLOWEEN RANKED WITH the Fourth of July and New Year's Day, though with far fewer drunks of voting age. Jules had no idea why, this year, Blue Deer had begun to go batshit a full week in advance. The weather hadn't been any better or worse than usual, and the impending election was unimportant to most. Hunting season hadn't been exceptionally rowdy, and he'd heard of nothing from the high school to indicate trouble. No remarkable drug invasions, no recent suicides, no standout assholes among the staff or student populations.

But whatever the reasons, the little shits had been relentless. In a week the department had dealt with three sets of slashed tires, five smashed birdbaths—just about every birdbath in town—and a dozen side-panel key scrapes. Wednesday had been broken window night; Thursday night Wesley and Harvey busted a beer party and let all but one of the eight teenagers go (he was the one they'd followed there, the one who'd shoplifted the case) on the condition they behave through Halloween.

On Halloween itself, a Monday, things quieted down after the inauspicious beginning of Alston Hantz's hearing.

A woman shoplifted ten yards of white nylon, which she said she'd needed for her daughter's bridal costume; Harvey subsequently determined the woman had no daughter. A middle-aged man was caught boobytrapping his front porch steps with a staple gun; Jules had him in a cell within fifteen minutes. Everyone else seemed to be saving up their ya-yas for dark.

FLO AND NEIL came in to give a statement mere seconds, according to Ed, after Jules left for lunch; they'd undoubtedly been waiting for him to leave. Ed himself hid in the kitchen so that Caroline won the prize.

Jules read over the statements when he got back. Flo had been monosyllabic about Nestor and quite articulate about what she thought of Caroline and the rest of the department; it seemed she'd just discovered that Nestor hadn't been in his casket. Neil had been politely flirtatious, the perfect altar boy in his mother's presence. Neither had anything to add. Flo had last seen her father-in-law when she'd dropped off food Thursday night; Neil had last been to see his grandfather ten days earlier for lunch.

Jules and Harvey and Caroline and Wesley drove to the Amundsen ranch after lunch, leaving Jonathan to handle the crises of Absaroka County, and Ed to lie on his couch, ruminating over a herniated disk. Caroline hadn't been out there before, and he finally noticed that she had a way of staring at people—Ira and Nina, in this case—when they weren't watching that made him feel like she was absorbing them. It would have been rude if anyone caught her at it, but no one ever seemed to.

They swept an acre around the bunkhouse. It was Harvey, the detail man, who looked hard enough at the interior of a large kindling box to make out a dry blob of henna red at the bottom, within which he found a tiny chip of skull. Nestor had probably been there for quite a while, dead and slowly draining. They found some white hairs and fibers that might have come from his pajamas, but no weapon.

AN ARTIST CAME from Missoula later that afternoon, just in case Mary McLinchey or Rosa Bouleouw or Joy Schwartz could dredge up anything distinctive about the rapist's ski mask or eyes, even the shape of his head, the profile of the nose or chin under fabric. The result was something like a plastic commando doll one of Jules's nephews owned. The eyes were empty and nondescript, and the mask was dark and revealed nothing about the man's mouth or other features.

After the artist left, Caroline brought Jules a cup of coffee for the first time ever, gave him a relatively compassionate look, and explained that they no longer had a single candidate for the island body. None of the Big Timber leads had panned out, and none of the Aches' tips had led anywhere. She'd bully them again, ask them to dredge a little deeper, but for the moment they had nothing.

Today Caroline's bruise was close to chartreuse, with a single magenta circle at the point of impact. She shot through most of her information rapidly, poker-faced, then handed over a typed version. There were no loose ends. Everyone had gone to Seattle, or New York, or Judith Gap; no one had managed to walk off the face of the earth. Jules looked down at the list and back up at Caroline, wondering how to continue. What had begun as mildly interesting historical research had gained too much importance, most of it emotional; Jules no longer knew if he wanted to clear his uncle of involvement or prove him a liar.

"Though we don't really know that," said Caroline. "I mean, we know these men left, but not necessarily that they got where they were going."

Jules looked through the file. "I don't suppose we really know that all of them left."

"I could try to pull it apart," said Caroline. "See who was actually seen getting on a bus or a train, who sent a postcard once he arrived."

He nodded wearily, imagining another foray into the town's fuzzy memories. The switchboard was going crazy, Grace gradually becoming more and more untethered. "Let's do some errands," said Jules. "Let's go find a different sort of dead end."

The owner of the second tire store kept insisting good-naturedly that Jules must be joking, then begged him to come back later, maybe in January; between pre-Halloween tire slashings and the early winter snow tire panic, he'd prefer to not sort through invoices.

Jules was tired of being nice, and paced while the man babbled on. "Here they are," Jules said, pointing to a large set on the overhead rack, shiny soft pink mud still glinting in the treads.

"Hang on a sec," said the owner, sorting through receipts.

"It doesn't matter," said Jules. "I found them. And they were Goodyears."

The owner looked up at the tires and down at his paper. "Nope. Not Mrs. Amundsen. She bought and traded 205/70s. Those are larger, for some four-wheel-drive job."

Jules stared. "Who did these belong to?"

The man shrugged. "Beats me. We don't bother with a name on most receipts if the customer's willing to wait while we rotate or patch or whatever."

"These come in recently?"

"Can't tell you. We reorganized last weekend."

Jules drummed his fingers on his thigh and stared at the sixty-foot wall of rubber. "Anyone who lives up near Amundsen's been by in the last week? Joseph Ganter?"

The owner looked confused. "Joseph's glasses aren't doing the trick anymore. You know that."

"Ah," said Jules. "True. Laura or Jetta or any of them?"

"Not that I remember."

"Well," said Jules, "I'd appreciate a list of the names you do have for everyone who left tires here over the last three weeks."

The owner was shocked. "Jesus, Jules."

"Can you?"

"It'd take a while," he said sullenly.

"I'll send Harvey Meyers over to print this tread this afternoon. You got anything to cover these with?"

They left ten minutes later, Jules backing onto the main drag so quickly that Caroline gritted her loose teeth and shut her eyes. The owner stood disconsolate in front of the garage, giving a halfhearted wave.

"Everywhere I go, I spread love and understanding," muttered Jules.

The corner of Caroline's mouth curled. "Who's the next lucky duck?"

"I'd like to check out my cousin Jetta's tires."

Jetta wasn't home; neither was her car. Jules and Caroline crawled around the concrete driveway and the impeccable garage floor. Up and down the edge of the driveway he found a thin wave of rosy white crystals, washed there by a hose. Jules scraped samples into an envelope while Caroline sat back on her haunches and estimated the number of neighbors who watched covertly. "Normally you'd think it kind of nice, everybody visiting an old man alone on a big ranch," she said.

"Normally," he agreed, standing. "Aren't you on duty again tonight?"

"At ten," said Caroline. "When Jonathan goes off."

Jules had come up with the schedule to avoid having Jonathan around any real trouble. Jonathan lacked perspective; he believed in the letter of the law because he lacked the imagination to grasp its spirit—the discovery of a joint in a pocket was as important as finding a straight razor or a basement of mail-order kiddie porn. Jonathan was no good for nights like Halloween.

Jules decided to do the right thing. Anyone was better than Neil. "Don't you have a friend in town?"

Caroline blushed around her bruise. "Yes."

"I'll drive you straight home then," said Jules. "You might as well have a good time until then, and I wouldn't know one if it hit me."

CARL JUMP WAS in the middle of inventory, and Jules apologized for interrupting. "That's okay," Jump said. "I should have done it yesterday but I played hooky in the park instead."

"You got those proofs back from the Amundsen party?"

"No," said Jump, scribbling a number on his list and setting it aside. He actually kept a pencil above his ear, in his curly hair. "If you want my guess, check with Neil Amundsen's mother. I ran into her at the bookstore two days ago and she started giving me shit about 'showing him in an unflattering light.'"

"Did you?"

Carl Jump smiled wickedly. "Of course I did, when I had

a spare moment. I aimed for that asshole every time I saw him put food in his mouth, every time he pinched that waitress's ass. That's what Flo Amundsen didn't like—she said her boy didn't bother with waitresses."

Jules stared in disbelief.

"Well, it was more than an ass pinch," said Carl Jump. "Mr. Amundsen was getting a hand job under the table, and somehow it came out clear as day on the proof sheet, and I assume things went further in the basement. But his mother doesn't strike me as well anyway."

Jules eyed him suspiciously. "You wouldn't think of using these to get Neil to back off your dog custody case, would you?"

"Of course not," said Jump with a wan smile. "My private viewing pleasure."

"Did you see him go outside at any point?"

"Not that I recall. Unless there's a way out through the basement."

"How long was he down there?"

"Half hour, hour. You trying to figure out if he could have offed his grandpa?"

Jules gave Jump a weary look. "Where'd you pick up that idea?"

"The bar. Where else does anyone pick up an idea in this town? A dead rancher is a pretty big deal."

Jules faced facts: The photographer had too much of an ax to grind to be reliable. "Did anyone else leave during the first half of the party?"

"People were going in and out all the time."

"Flo Amundsen?"

"No. She was on my ass for the duration, until she fell on you."

"Jetta Scotti?"

"She and her husband were arguing. I got the impression she needed some time off."

"For how long?"

"I just saw her leave once, can't tell you when she got back."

"Will you call me when you get those proofs?"

"Sure," said Carl Jump. "But Mrs. Amundsen's probably taken some ink to the ones of Neil."

THE WIND PICKED up again that afternoon, but now it was out of the north, and that night the Bo-Peeps and Bat-men who were literally blown across streets wore parkas and mufflers, and lost plastic pumpkins filled with gritty snow. It was too windy to drape toilet paper in the trees, too cold to take much joy in scraping side panels with keys.

When Jules officially went off duty he stopped in at the one party he couldn't politely avoid, Scotti's government special at the Baird, and discovered Alice as a cocktail table, Edie as Tinkerbell, and Jetta and Flo as rich ladies from the turn of the century, not much of a stretch. Peter was drinking in a corner as himself, with Neil looking more stylish as a baseball player but just as taciturn ten feet away. Just seeing them in the same room gave Jules a stomachache.

Alice was stationed by a large bowl of shrimp, and they worked on it in silence for several minutes. "Caroline stopped in earlier, before she went on shift. It was fun watching her beat Neil back with a stick."

This image of Neil made Jules very happy. "I don't think I've ever seen her out."

"They'd had dinner at that new place in Bozeman, the place with real mussels."

He began to suspect that Alice knew she was toying with him. "They?"

"They," she said succinctly, peeling two shrimp and handing him one with a look of pity. "Caroline's friend is a six-foot Pulitzer Prize–nominated journalist from a wealthy family who looks like a tall version of Mel Gibson."

"He wear a sign with his particulars?" asked Jules after it sank in, trying to sound amused.

Alice raised her eyebrows. "I read a book review in the *Times* or *Newsweek* or some such. And of course Cicely can't shut up."

"I see," said Jules.

He feigned interest in another shrimp, but Alice wasn't going to let him go.

"Cicely says he begs Caroline to come home to D.C. with a dozen weekly roses and lots of other graft and wit, aside from the aforementioned height, fortune, intelligence, and resemblance to a movie star. Are you listening to me?"

Jules tried a look of innocent surprise.

"You are a six-three cop who makes thirty-something a year and looks like . . . oh, I don't know."

She looked around the room for inspiration, and he broke in. "Don't say it, even if you do know," he snapped. "I wouldn't try to touch a hair on her head even if she was single."

"Huh," said Alice.

"We work together."

"I've noticed."

He balled up his napkin. "Get Peter away from Neil and call me if you find the name of the blond skeleton."

"Jules?"

"What?" He felt snappy, busted. He and Alice had

known each other for a long, long time, had briefly known each other a little too well; there wasn't much of a point in trying to bullshit her.

"Caroline mentioned that the guy doesn't have much of a sense of humor."

"They should get along just fine then," said Jules.

They both watched Edie, who was on the far side of the room flirting with the new reporter in town. "I guess it's anything goes, huh?" said Alice.

She seemed to be on a scorched-earth mission. "Can we talk about something else?"

Alice considered him. "You don't know what you want, do you?"

"Nope," said Jules, heading for the door.

Edie waylaid him. The new man watched with interest. He usually never showed much interest past the repartee stage of things, and Jules told Edie so. She pulled away.

"Thank you for telling me that no one really finds me attractive."

"That's not what I'm saying."

But what had he been saying? It took a hour to ferret this out, at which point they were on a couch in the basement with a bottle of the kitchen's wine and his beeper muffled in the dirty linen pile. At midnight Caroline had just deposited another raving asshole in the jail, and she kicked a supply cupboard when she found the station coffeepot was empty.

"Bad night?" asked a genial drunk. They'd run out of room on the booking bench, and he was slumped on the kitchen couch, looking cozy.

"Not really," said Caroline, rubbing her sore jaw. "It's been too windy to throw a pumpkin."

The night dispatcher passed on a report of teenagers "drinking and doing drugs and having sex" in the lot behind the new historical museum, and Delly, the owner of the Blue Bat, had called in about some trouble with a group of fishermen. Caroline, her tired brain still fixed on coffee, decided to give the teenagers time to dress and headed for the bar. The fishermen were long gone, and when Delly asked if she might perchance like a shot in the cup, it took every ounce of moral energy to say no. While she waited, a good-looking man on the next stool stole surreptitious glances.

"I love a woman in a uniform," he said.

"Do you," said Caroline wearily.

"Yes," said the man. "You're even packing a real gun."

"Why do things half-assed?" Caroline took the coffee from Delly, who was looking nervous.

"My thoughts exactly," said the man. "Let's leave now."

"Down, boy," said Caroline.

She drove to the museum, the temperature hovering at freezing, and saw no naked flesh. She thought she saw a light on the second floor when she first parked, but everything was dark by the time she climbed out into the cold, still night.

Caroline circled the building and found the back door slightly ajar. She stood inside for a moment, listening, then stepped back out and slammed the door shut after taking care that it wouldn't lock. Back in the patrol car and off she went for one whole block before looping around and coasting down the alley with no lights and no engine.

She sat for a few minutes, warming her hands on the coffee, which was still hot. When the lights upstairs flicked back on it took her only three minutes to go in through the back door. She heard voices above and crept up the main stairwell. At the top she made out a glowing doorway twenty feet down the hall and two voices arguing, what sounded like the querulous tones of teenage boys.

"But which one?"

"I don't know."

"You want to haul all of them?"

"I don't *want* to."

By then Caroline was standing in the doorway, wondering if rubbing her eyes would make any difference. Jetta and Flo, still dressed in long ball gowns, had kicked off their high heels and were dragging a dusty trunk away from the wall. The perimeter of the room was mounded with junk; on the bare floor dead center sat a open magnum of white wine, a furniture dolly, a burning cigarette on a jar lid, and a snap saw.

"What are you doing?" asked Caroline. It seemed like a reasonable question.

Flo screamed three times.

"We're society members, so we thought we'd hang out here, help organize," said Jetta once the vibrations died down. "Alice is so overworked."

Flo stared at the ceiling. Neither of them seemed very steady. Caroline wondered if they knew they were making her hate her job. "It seems like an unlikely time to help."

"We have keys," said Jetta. "We have a right to be here."

"Of course you do," said Caroline slowly. "But why did you try to hide?"

"Silly panic," said Jetta hastily. "That old school smell will make you revert every time."

"Maybe," said Flo, "we weren't in the mood to see your bumpy face."

"Maybe," said Caroline, "I'm not in the mood to see yours either, Flo."

"Mrs. Amundsen," said Flo.

Jetta buried her face in her hands.

Caroline tapped her fingers on her thigh. "Where's your car parked?"

"Two blocks down Fifth," said Jetta. "A navy Volvo."

"Give me the keys," said Caroline. "They'll be at the station for you tomorrow morning. I can give you a ride home, now, or you can find your own way."

They looked at each other. "We'll find our own way," said Jetta hastily.

The keys were on the floor by the wine. Flo stuck out her tongue when Caroline slid them into her pocket and left. She was halfway down the hall before she heard Flo's last loud comment and came to a halt.

"Nosy twat."

Nice people, thought Caroline. In the car she found the coffee had tipped onto the passenger seat. "Fuck the world," she said.

"Excuse me?" said the dispatcher. "Is this in reference to the problem on the playground? Have you gotten to the playground yet?"

It took a half hour to extricate the couple from the swing set, another half hour before she left the hospital, where they were being treated for exposure. She snagged a cup of coffee from the nurse's station and drank it in a few seconds, before the next call came in. A concerned citizen reported a dark blue Volvo traveling down the wrong side of Glacier Street at fifty miles an hour. So far the Volvo had sideswiped two cars. The woman driving, a curly-headed middle-aged blonde, had screamed obscenities at the concerned citizen and made rude gestures, and at one point when he'd tried to pull her over, she'd swerved toward him.

"Tell the cowboy to lay off," said Caroline. She had the odd sensation that her head might explode, and immediately made a U-turn and accelerated. She caught up with them on Bison, just in time to see the Volvo ride up a curb and flatten a For Sale sign.

In the dark, as Caroline approached, she had the impression of large objects moving inside the car. Nobody said anything for a full minute.

"Turn the engine off," said Caroline.

Jetta did so quickly and obediently. None of her movements seemed drunken, but Flo's pupils lagged.

"For the record," said Caroline, "who was driving?"

"Jetta was," said Flo, quickly and emphatically.

"I was," said Jetta a moment later.

"Why this funny business with your legs?" asked Caroline.

Jetta darkened.

"How dare you, Caroline," said Flo, finally hauling her legs over the console to the passenger side. Her left pump had lost a heel, but she didn't seem to notice. "I was just kicking her because she'd been so stupid."

"How about your legs, Jetta?"

Jetta lifted hers carefully over the gearshift, staring straight ahead. "I was kicking her back. In self-defense."

"Out of the car," said Caroline.

They looked like demented fairies from her childhood collection of *Grimm's*. "If you tell the truth," said Caroline wearily, "I'll simply drive you home. If you lie, I'm booking you. Think of it as a three strikes kind of thing."

"You've been stalking us," said Flo.

"Jesus," said Caroline. "I've just about had it, Mrs. God-damn Amundsen. One more bitchy line and you're in for the night."

Flo slapped her cheek. Caroline came up with a right hook to Flo's chin that surprised even her. Flo went down in a billow of organza.

"Oh dear," said Jetta. "The night's past saving now, isn't it?"

WHEN JULES CAME home at 3:00 a.m., the light on his answering machine was pulsing in the dark. This was exactly what he'd been avoiding with Edie on the couch in the Baird basement.

The voice was Ed's. "Caroline called me with a situation at the station. If you get in before dawn . . ." A slight, ruminative pause followed. "I hope you're sleeping, but if you aren't, and if you get in before dawn, call me at home, or just go down there and help Caroline."

Jules stared at the machine, then reached out and dialed mechanically.

"I thought you should know," said Ed wearily at the end of the story.

It was very cold now, and very still, and the light from the station was not particularly inviting. Inside, though, there were enough bodies to lend the main room a festive atmosphere.

Axel Scotti was sitting on Jules's desk smoking one of Grace's Kools. "We've been here for an hour," he said bitterly.

Jetta was not handcuffed, nor was Flo, who sat on the booking bench bent over a large and fragrant bucket. Her father perched stiffly next to her, watching. Joseph sat on the couch on the far side of the room paging through one of Jules's travel magazines, and Neil was dead center, arguing with Caroline.

Absaroka County's legal system jammed in one small

room, nepotism run amok. Jules sized up his cousin. "What'd she blow?"

"That's a very rude phrase," said Flo, lifting her head from the bucket and gesturing regally.

"There's nothing you need to worry about here, Jules," said Scotti.

"Let him push it," said Neil. "Let him go down in flames. I can't wait to phrase the recall petition."

Jules watched Flo's hands loop through the air, then turned to Caroline, who looked to be in greater pain, shrunken and pale and miserable, than she had after having her face smashed by Wayne Contway.

"What happened?"

Caroline told him in a monotone while staring at the floor. It was a long story, an attenuated nightmare. Jules could overlook small sins—and, in fact, usually preferred to do so—but these were sins he couldn't afford to ignore in a teenager, and he bridled at being bribed to ignore them in two well-connected matrons with no talent for lying, one of them a cousin.

Axel Scotti was watching him, seeing the decision solidify behind brown eyes with growing despair; Axel probably guessed that Jules was fantasizing about having Flo pilloried in front of the post office. He held his tongue, but Neil had no similar wisdom and interrupted three times. The first two times Jules asked politely that he be quiet, and the third time Jules snapped his fingers and pointed. Neil turned purple, and Axel took his elbow. Miles Birdland and Joseph seemed to have bowed out; Birdland had moved to the couch, too, and found his own magazine to page through.

"Honey," said Axel, "just tell the goddamn truth. Then none of this will be a big deal and you can go home."

"If Jetta says she was driving, that's fine by me," said Jules viciously. "Though off the record I'm sure Flo's capable of satanic possession."

Jetta sat with her legs crossed on the bench, bouncing her right high heel, managing to look like she was waiting for a limo despite scuffed shoes and a torn and dirty hem.

"She was driving," whispered Flo.

"Obviously," said Neil, "it's a bit of a joke that we all have to be here."

Jules agreed. "I certainly didn't ask you to come down," he said. "I'd be surprised if anyone in this room really wanted to see your smiling face."

"It's entrapment," said Neil.

"Shut up," said Jules.

"She hates my mother. Back in September—"

"Flo was arrested because she had some of her prize-winning home-canned tomatoes in the backseat when she was pulled over for running a stop sign and she threw a jar of them at Jonathan and bruised his shoulder. And then tried to claim we'd stolen the tomatoes." But he was almost happy Neil had brought up the incident, because it was an established fact that Flo liked to throw things when she'd been drinking and the night went wrong. Jules eyed the slop bucket nervously.

"Who's to say you didn't? Anyway, this woman's been stalking her. Maybe it's unrequited love. Maybe you give out extra credit points. Maybe this is part of a conspiracy against my family."

"Maybe," said Jules, "you're a little prick with a big imagination. You say one more rude thing about my deputy and I'll stick your head in that bucket and lock you up for the rest of the night."

One of Neil's cold eyes twitched. "I am my mother's attorney."

"Neil, you're already the state's attorney," said Birdland quietly. "Pipe down for a bit or you'll lose that job."

Jules would have given a great deal to still be lying on the dirty couch in the hotel basement. "Jetta, let's talk."

They walked down the hall to the kitchen. She collapsed in a chair and sighed.

"What'd you have to drink?"

"About four glasses of wine, since seven or eight. How many have you had?"

"More," said Jules. "But I'm bigger. And Flo?"

"Lord," said Jetta, reaching for an open bag of chips. "Use your imagination. Get that bucket analyzed, if you're really curious. Let's just say I knew she shouldn't be driving."

"Why are you doing this?"

"Off the record?" She smiled glumly. "The shame of a DUI would kill her. She's a judge's daughter. She's got no sense of humor about such things, and she has trouble sorting out what's really important. She's a goddamn mess anyway these days."

Saying that Flo had her priorities twisted seemed like a massive understatement. "You're a prosecuting attorney's wife."

Jetta raised an eyebrow, amused, and swung her heels up onto the table. "I can always change my mind about that, can't I? I grew up drinking Italian wine on a ranch. Shit happens."

"Her father doesn't seem too concerned."

Jetta sighed. "He's way ahead of her."

"This is the second time," said Jules.

"Well," said Jetta, "I don't plan on a third. Axel will probably manage something."

"Huh." He reached for a potato chip. Down the hall, Flo was talking again, and Axel and Neil had started an argument. Maybe Flo would throw the bucket in their direction. Jules and Jetta exchanged a look, neither of them eager to head back.

"Is Flo capable of killing someone?"

Jetta's eyes widened, and she slowly sat up straight. "No," she said. "Are you talking about Nestor?"

"You sure?"

"Flo has trouble squishing spiders. Flo has trouble deciding when to go pee. I mean, look at her. And she hates fire, *hates* it. I've never even seen her light a barbecue."

Jules had the impression that Jetta was talking to make herself feel better.

"And why *would* she kill someone?" she asked huffily.

"I dunno," he said. "Money, land, a chemical imbalance. She called me late the other night, meowing."

"You know for a fact it was her on the phone?"

"Not for a fact," said Jules. He rubbed his face. "Axel's told you Nestor's death looks suspicious, right?"

"He has."

"Did you tell Flo?"

"No, but Neil did. She brought it up the other day."

Jetta looked up and smiled hesitantly. Caroline stood in the doorway watching Jules shoot the shit and eat chips with a woman she'd just arrested.

"Are we holding them or not?"

"Sorry," said Jules, following her down the hall. "I believe we'll have to."

Flo was up and walking, looking like a badly miscast opera diva. Even drunk, she was all pride and self-righteousness and shabby superiority. "Why are we here?" she asked, gesturing expansively.

"Because Deputy Fair had to talk to you twice, Flo. Because you show signs of being intoxicated, and because the car you were driving or riding in caused substantial property damage. And because you resisted arrest."

"Oh, Jules," said Flo. "Have a sense of humor."

Caroline looked as if she wanted to either cry or spit nails; it was a new expression and an unnerving one. "I have a sense of humor," said Jules. "That's why we're here wasting everyone's time. Just tell me who was driving."

Flo gave him a long unsteady look, eyes swimming. "Jetta."

Jules looked down at the floor, then up at Jetta. "Were you driving?"

She shrugged.

"Send them both home," said Axel.

"Caroline's been at this for hours," said Jules. "They damaged property. They lied." He looked around the room. Joseph and Miles Birdland were engaged in a private and apparently humorous conversation, Scotti was on his third Kool, and Neil watched his mother's weaving head with disgust. Caroline stared at the accoustical tiles, obviously hating everyone else in the room. Jules clapped his hands. "Okay, then. Jetta, Flo, both of you empty your pockets."

Which was a silly thing to say, as they were both in black silk. "Off with the jewelry, the shoes and the stockings, and get your fingers ready for prints. Say goodbye to your next of kin until tomorrow morning, after 8:00 a.m. And we have a curfew on chitchat until seven. Jetta's charged with driving while intoxicated, and Flo's charged with assaulting an officer."

"She did not," yelled Neil.

"Look at her face," said Jules.

"How would you tell?" asked Neil.

Jules strode toward Caroline. "This," he said, pointing to her yellow right jaw, "is old. This"—a pink abrasion on the right cheekbone—"is new. Jetta?"

Jetta sighed and nodded.

"Well," said Joseph, climbing off the couch with effort and tucking a flask into his coat. "Let's all get some sleep then."

Flo finally threw the bucket and hit Jonathan's desk, missing everyone in the room.

JULES ASKED CAROLINE if he could finish out her shift. She refused this offer without looking him in the eye or showing much warmth, and led the surprisingly docile women downstairs to the night jailer. Neil was gone, and Axel Scotti was waiting to give Joseph a ride home.

"Jules can take me," said Joseph. "You need to work in the morning."

So do I, thought Jules. But then it developed that Miles Birdland had walked to the station, and Joseph offered him a ride, and the whole project became more interesting.

They said they wanted to ride in back; they seemed to take great joy in being on the wrong side of the grill, and when Jules heard Miles Birdland actually snicker he realized they'd been passing the flask back and forth for some time. He turned up the heat and let the car warm up.

"I believe the girls were sixteen or seventeen the last time we found ourselves together in the back of a patrol car," said Birdland.

"And before that it had been another twenty years."

A smile flitted over Birdland's thin lips. "Of course, I was a watcher myself."

"You were our ace in the hole," said Joseph, "but you had your moments. You and Ruth hooked up so early there wasn't much time for naughtiness."

"But I appreciated it, even after I became a cop."

"Well, look at Jules," said Joseph. "Think of all the awful things he did."

The man in question, driving as slowly down Main as possible, stared at them in the rearview mirror. "You were a cop?"

"A deputy, before the war," said Birdland.

"You're kidding me," said Jules.

Birdland seemed to find this amusing. People probably weren't in the habit of using such phrases on him. "Now, why would I do that? I put in just two years, before law school and being called up." He accepted the flask from Joseph. "I hated it."

"Why?"

"I felt ineffectual. Random and cruel."

"So you saved up money and went to law school?"

"I came into some money, just enough." Birdland floated off for a moment. "Will someone make sure she doesn't lie in her own mess?"

"Of course," said Jules. "And you or Neil can bring a change of clothes when you pick her up in the morning."

"I think I'd rather see how that dress looks in the day-light," said the judge.

JULES HAD THREE HOURS OF SLEEP, AND WHEN HE woke he stayed facedown and spread-eagled under his goose down and tried to think of something besides his love life or rapists or Blue Deer's claustrophobic criminal justice system. He thought of flying to Spain or Greece or Turkey, or maybe taking a road trip to the Southwest, or possibly simply going bird hunting. As he started to doze off again he thought of Caroline, and only made the vision recede with thoughts of Nestor Amundsen.

The alarm rang half an hour later, signaling an end to the day's buffer zone. He slumped down the stairs to the shower, feeling unintelligent and unloved, and stared at the outside thermometer while he brushed his teeth. At the station he found Archie dozing at his desk, his carrot-and-gray hair ruffled by the blast from the heating vent above him, oblivious to the peaceful snores and muffled whines from the surrounding cells. Jules was thrilled to find Jetta and Flo already gone, and risked lawsuits by pulling bottles of aspirin and acetaminophen from his desk and distributing tablets to the unhappy revelers, feeling like Santa Claus.

At lunchtime he and Wesley sat down to a preliminary list of Contway's possible Deer Lodge acquaintances, which was really only a list of men who didn't like women and who had been incarcerated at the same time. They had no idea if the men really knew Wayne; the warden claimed this wasn't the sort of information he could possibly collect. And he couldn't tell them where people lived currently; for that, Wesley had to get a separate list from county and state probation officers, who all pointed out that their information was laughably inaccurate. None of the probationed rapists had registered as a resident in the area, and the full list of ex-cons in southwestern Montana ran two pages. The warden, deeply offended, had flatly refused information on counselors or other staff.

"Screw him," said Jules. "They're state employees. It's public information."

Wesley nodded wearily. "But it'll take a while."

Wesley had learned that there'd been three rapes in the Anaconda–Deer Lodge–Butte area eight years before. The rapes had been similar to the recent attacks. "Bites, a mask, single women," said Wesley. They winnowed the felon list down with these dates in mind and by physical descriptions, and faxed off a request for two dozen mug shots. Jules felt edgy, convinced any delay meant tempting fate. Wesley pointed out that until recently the rapist had gone whole months between attacks; maybe this recent once-a-week pattern was an anomaly.

IT WAS A poker Tuesday, despite the fact that half the players might have preferred a solitary night at home licking wounds. They played in the back room behind the Elks bar. Axel Scotti, far quieter than usual, had three double Bombay martinis in the first hour; Peter started with water and then succumbed to the mood with a whiskey. Patrick Ankeny and Merle Ott, both of whom seemed nervous, carried on a stilted conversation about water rights. Jules, who'd begun to notice that he always seemed to be hungover or tired or both on card nights, drank numerous cups of coffee and twitched.

Only Joseph seemed utterly at ease. "How's your daughter?" asked Jules when it was clear that Scotti was too far gone to be offended.

"Oddly enough, we haven't talked today," said Joseph, grinning. "Jetta doesn't like flogging her failings. You'll note my son-in-law opted to play tonight rather than discussing life around the family hearth."

Axel smiled, but not, possibly, with his whole heart. Jules wouldn't have wanted to be Joseph's son-in-law. Perhaps there'd been a germ of truth in Axel's line about kissing his father-in-law's ass.

"Jetta's a big girl," continued Joseph. "Maybe she wasn't really protecting Flo. Maybe she wanted to get out of driving the boys to a dozen soccer games and piano lessons a week. Alex's decided to take up trombone. And of course Axel's so busy. Half the time he works through dinner."

Axel dropped his cards to the table with a clunk. "Fold."

"Fold," echoed Peter, who'd taken Jetta's case that morning. "I might turn in early tonight."

"No, you aren't," said Joseph. "We need your fresh blood, and I brought a very fine bottle of brandy for the latter part of the game."

The voice of authority had spoken; Peter's butt returned to the chair, having edged only an inch toward freedom. Ankeny looked down at his cards, obviously rethinking his own escape plan. He and Peter seemed to list in each other's direction for safety.

"Isn't this already the latter part of the game?" asked Axel.

"Far be it from me to second-guess a man on the topic of

his daughter," said Jules. "But I have a hard time believing she volunteered for a second DUI to get out of shuttling her kids around."

"The nature of friendship is often a mystery," said Joseph.

"The nature of a friendship with Flo would be exceptionally so."

"I agree," said Joseph. "I have agreed for several decades. I don't like her and I don't trust her."

Ankeny dealt. No one seemed interested in defending Ms. Amundsen. Jules caught Scotti's eye. "I don't want to talk about any of it," said the prosecutor wearily.

But Jules was genuinely curious, not to mention riddled with ulterior motives. "Is Flo much like her father?" he asked Joseph.

"Not at all," said Joseph. "I'd trust Miles with my life. I have trusted Miles with my life."

"When you were young."

"Yes."

"But you're not friends now."

"We'll always be friends. We just don't talk much anymore."

That had been Birdland's line. "Why'd you stop?"

"What is this?" asked Scotti. "Didn't we cover this last time? Have you turned into a fucking broken record?"

"Curiosity," said Jules. "I just don't know what to make of Nestor's and Joseph's and Miles Birdland's last get-together. I'd like Joseph's insight into his old friend's state of mind."

Jules and Joseph looked at each other for a long time.

"Think of it as archaelogy," said Jules.

Joseph shuffled in silence for a minute. "Why would we be friends after high school? Different politics, different pursuits, and we all found wives we liked to talk to better than each other. Nestor was a bigot back then, and Miles left town for law school. We'd always argued anyway. And then there was the war."

"Miles Birdland told me that something bad happened and it blighted things."

"He's right," said Joseph. "Nothing worth anyone knowing. It was a very private thing."

Jules watched him deal. A private thing, private crimes. Most were, one way or another.

"Where is that bottle of brandy?" asked Scotti.

"Friendships fall apart in the best of times," said Joseph. "Surely you've noticed."

Jules had, of course, but he'd left his hometown for more than a decade after high school. He knew quite well that it took more effort for the three old men not to see each other than to have an occasional drink. In a town the size of Blue Deer, you had to wear a sack over your head to avoid another man for fifty years.

Joseph pressed his victory. "What high school friend do you still see?"

"Divvy Ott," said Jules. "Harvey."

"Both work-related, and you and Harvey were never close."

"Jim's in San Francisco, Mark turned into an asshole, and Larry's dead."

"That happens, too," said Joseph. "And Nestor Amundsen's a dead asshole."

Patrick Ankeny cleared his throat. "I knew Nestor," he said. "Pretty well. You called him a bigot, but he was never one to me."

They all stared. Scotti sighed deeply and walked to the bar for brandy glasses. Patrick continued.

"He was generous, and he was funny. He went out of his way to make people comfortable."

"Pardon me," said Joseph. "People sometimes age gracefully. I should have said that he was *once* an asshole, half a century ago. And I should have said that I was one, too, and that I was fond of him no matter what. Please accept my apology."

The table returned to a simmer. Joseph handed over his bottle of alembic brandy, and Scotti poured them each a glass.

Jules studied Ankeny. "How'd you know Nestor?"

"He gave me my first job, irrigating, and he kinda took care of me after that." Patrick looked at Joseph, not quite dropping the grievance. "Paid most of my tuition, helped me out of jams."

Jules thought of the kid Ira Meidenhaft had mentioned, the one who got a free ride at Missoula. Unless Nestor, saint among the swine, had fostered more than one. "When did you see him last?" asked Jules.

"Had coffee with him the weekend before he died."

"How'd he seem?"

Ankeny shrugged and dealt. Jules drained his brandy and let Joseph refill the glass. "Why didn't you tell me this? What was he acting like?"

"Unhappy, but he never got to whatever was making him that way. His daughter-in-law showed up and things got busy and I left. I planned to stop by the next weekend, and then I heard the news."

Jules decided to corner Patrick later, in a more relaxed setting. But the brandy, rather than allowing him to drop all thoughts of charred ranchers, added to his animation, and confusion made him obsessive. After five minutes of listening to blather about great brandies and bad brandy experiences, he burst out with a complete non sequitur.

"Maybe Nestor knew that great-uncle of yours," said Jules.
Ankeny pulled a blank. "Who?"

"Nestor probably knew your missing great-uncle, the one
you thought might be the body on the island. Did you ever
ask him?"

"If he did, he never mentioned it. He knew my grandmother. That's how I ended up irrigating that summer."

Joseph lit a cigarette. "Who was your grandmother,
Patrick?"

"She still is. Lily Crane. She grew up near Nestor's ranch.
Near yours, too, I guess. Did you know her?"

Joseph stared at Ankeny and put his lighter down slowly.

"Did you know her?" echoed Jules.

Joseph nodded. "Lily Crane. Very sweet and very lovely,
mama half French. Tiny, right?"

Patrick smiled. "Tinier all the time."

Hell, thought Jules, turning to consider Joseph. Maybe
he could clear up a body that hadn't yet been found. "Did you
know a brother of hers, a guy named Malcolm?"

Joseph had turned back to his hand and gave Jules a dis-
tracted look. "Of course I knew Malcolm."

"What was he like?" asked Patrick.

"He looked a lot like you," said Joseph. "Shorter though,
and wiry, a real pistol. Nice kid. Why?"

"Just that he disappeared before the war," said Jules.

Joseph shrugged. "I know he stopped being around, but
not that anyone was worried. Maybe I was away at school."

"Probably," said Jules.

"Where'd you go?" asked Ankeny.

"Yale," said Joseph heavily. "From 1937 to 1941, and then
I shipped out."

One boy goes missing, the other goes Ivy League, both

doing what's expected of them. Jules wondered if the ironies bothered Joseph at all.

"Too bad your family couldn't hold on to the land," Jules said to Ankeny.

Patrick rolled his eyes and smiled.

"They never owned land," said Joseph quietly. "They worked for the Whitsans. Whose deal?"

ON WEDNESDAY MORNING Jules was paging through an old issue of *Archaeology*, ogling color photos of ruins on the eastern Mediterranean coastline, when Wesley arrived and nodded hello.

"Happy Day of the Dead."

"What's that?" asked Grace, looking alarmed.

"All Souls' Day," said Jules, "and it doesn't mean a thing for us. This is going to be an easy day up by the Canadian border."

"I didn't say it would be bad." Wesley smiled, but Jules, when he looked out the window, had to admit it looked like the kind of day when you could sit down to read something cheery like *Under the Volcano* without finding the parallels even mildly interesting. The temperature was fifteen; the air was so gray and sterile and hostile it leached at his bones and made him achy. A county clerk pushed through the wind to the building door, staggering in nylons and dirty white sneakers, and across the street, at Peter's office, a man Harvey had hauled in for a DUI emerged and slammed the door behind him. The man had claimed to be sober, despite seven gin and tonics, but Jules had heard Peter giggle while he watched the videotape in the kitchen.

The mug shots and records from Deer Lodge began to appear in the computer. Grace printed them out while Wesley and Jules glumly watched each image materialize. Only a half dozen of the possibilities lived in Absaroka County, and Wesley and Jules whipped through five of them that afternoon. The first two men, one on the upper limit of age and size and one on the lower, claimed to have never so much as talked to Wayne; they were so resoundingly stupid that even Wayne wouldn't have described them as fiendishly clever. The next man had gained easily a hundred pounds in the two years since the Deer Lodge photo, and Man Four had wasted to a hundred and twenty pounds with bone cancer. Man Five, one Bruce Hagne, was a possibility: he was five-eleven, thirty-six, and pale, with a five o'clock shadow and a Marlboro cough. He lived alone after a recent and vicious divorce, and his Deer Lodge crime had been the sober, deliberate beating and rape of an elderly neighbor. Hagne was as jumpy as a hamster, and it was hard not to read his twitches as a bad conscience. But it was equally hard to imagine him impressing Wayne.

Man Six had a thing for kids, and his taste probably didn't extend past ten-year-olds; they'd had him under their best attempt at regular surveillance for the past six months. Jules and Wesley didn't bother to interview him, but watched from the patrol car, forty yards away, as he fed the geese along the lagoon. The lagoon park was separated from the playground, which the man was forbidden to enter, by one twenty-foot strip of blacktop; Man Six often fed these particular geese, whether or not he was aware of police watching.

Wesley was scanning the list of ex-cons in neighboring counties, and Jules was watching the dark back on the bench, wishing he could believe castration would truly work for some cases.

"How far should I go?" asked Wesley. "I can handle the

three in Sweet Grass and Meagher Counties in a morning, even with driving time. Nine in Gallatin will take a full day. Do we look as far as Billings?"

"I don't know," said Jules bleakly. "Still an easy round-trip, but not yet, I guess."

Wesley lit a cigarette. "I think I should go to Deer Lodge, talk to the staff, see if anything stands out."

Jules weighed the lost labor against the image of Joy Schwartz in the hospital bed. "I could call and set it up for tomorrow. But I think it would be better if you drop in."

Wesley nodded. The radio buzzed; Grace announcing an animal disturbance. Neither Jules nor Wesley moved.

"Jesus H. Christ," said Jules.

"It'll be sheep this time," said Wesley. "This feels like a day for sheep."

Grace tried again. The animal disturbance was of "some magnitude." Wesley reached for the radio, and Jules stopped him with his left hand while he pointed with his right. After six months of feeding birds, their local pederast had finally crossed the road and was standing, very casually, ten feet from a loaded jungle gym, a veritable apple tree laden with squirming fruit. Wesley fought the urge to rub his eyes but opted for catching up with Jules, who was moving faster than he had since the previous Fourth of July.

THERE WERE SOME people Jules absolutely loved to lock up, and in this instance even the probation officer was thrilled by his client's timing. What was left of the afternoon kept to this cheery note, thanks to Grace's large animal disturbance. By an astounding coincidence on that Day of the Dead, a herd of three dozen cows and four bulls had walked over a wind-flattened fence and trashed the

Protestant cemetery. The real damage occurred because the bulls decided to fight, and Wesley and Jules spent a half hour perched on tombstones waiting for the Angus to wind down, Wesley chain-smoking happily, Jules reminiscing about familiar graves. They managed to look as if they knew what they were doing by the time the *Bulletin* reporter/photographer, Soren Rue, showed up with a camera. But Soren had always had a faulty eye for framing and a dislike for ranch stock, and instead of photographing foaming, horny, stupid bulls playing peekaboo behind monuments he took close-ups of the rest of the herd staring soulfully into space.

AT DUSK, JULES and Wesley were finished checking names and were drinking beer in the station kitchen, going over the best strategy for the trip to Deer Lodge the next day. The rapist hadn't been officially paroled to Blue Deer; that would have been too easy, and God forbid they be allowed to feel smart.

"It's worth going through simple battery, if a woman was involved, not just rape," said Jules. "Some incident that might have started things rolling. And see if their computer will break it down to birthplace, just in case this is someone coming home instead of landing here by chance. And make them open up on counselors and staff. That was Wayne's only hint."

"It's not necessarily a counselor with a record," said Wesley. "They're worried about being liable, right?"

"Exactly," said Jules. "And while you've got their computer, see if they've ever had anyone with a thing for artificial limbs or whale teeth."

Wesley arched his eyebrows in mild surprise and gave a gentle beer burp.

"While you're at it," said Jules.

Wesley's expression changed, and Jules turned to the door. Patrick Ankeny stood there holding the arm of a very pale, very wet man decked out in the latest from Abercrombie & Fitch. The man clutched a thousand-dollar rod and was weighed down by a creel, a net, a hat, chest waders, and enough fly boxes to render his vest bulletproof.

A forgotten problem came to mind. Jules stood and pushed his chair toward the wet man. "Let me guess," he said. "You found something ugly."

The man stared at him and nodded.

"He came to the Forest Service offices first, for some reason," said Ankeny. "I was just leaving and didn't want him driving."

Jules nodded and waved his arms encouragingly.

"In the river," said the man.

Jules smiled gently. "Where in the river?"

"I'd waded down from the Mallard's Rest access, maybe two hundred yards."

"Downriver or south?" He hated even asking, but new fishermen from out of town didn't always make sense and often assumed all rivers ran north to south. *Downhill* meant "down the map."

The man looked confused. "Down the valley. South."

"On the beach, underwater?"

"Aaahooh," moaned the man, grimacing. "Under some branches, in a nice pool. I touched him by mistake. I thought it was a big chunk of Styrofoam."

The man started crying when Jules suggested he return to the scene, and Ankeny said he was pretty sure he knew the pool in question. Wesley called Al and Bean, and they headed south after dropping the fisherman at the Baird, on the bar rather than the lobby side.

An hour later Jules and Ankeny were leaning against the patrol car watching Al and Bean wrestle with a large rounded object that seemed to glow in the dark. Wesley sat upwind, smoking again; he'd been the one to wade in and flip the diver over.

"I was going to come see you today anyway," said Ankeny, scuffing the sand with his heel.

He sounded unhappy. Down by the water, Bean gagged. Jules wished he liked tobacco. "What's up?" he asked. "You have a problem at the office, or something more about your great-uncle?"

Ankeny shook his head miserably. "Have you talked to Edie in the last few days?"

Jules turned to him, worried. "She having a problem with mountain lions again?"

"No, no." Patrick paused for a long time. "We went to a movie last week, and one this week. Edie told me she was going to tell you before it went further. She said you two had split up, only saw each other once in a while. But I wanted to make sure. That's why I was going to come by anyway."

Jules's ears were ringing. Wesley, out of hearing, sensed a problem and stared.

"She didn't tell you?" asked Ankeny.

"No," said Jules.

"But was she being honest about the rest?"

Jules wanted to smash something so badly his head ached. "Yes, she was being honest."

Patrick peered at his face. "We haven't done much of

anything yet. We might never. But I didn't want to get in that situation until we'd talked."

Ankeny had always been the sort to do the right thing, and this time around his honor was about to cause him harm. "Please go away," said Jules.

AT HOME THAT night Jules made a pile of small Edie items to be returned: a novel or two, a dusty vase, some CDs, a salad bowl, her sons' baseball caps. Upstairs, in the closet, some jeans, a dress and high heels, underwear. There was only one glass of wine left in the bottle in the refrigerator, and he stared at it for some time, fighting the urge to buy more and self-medicate. At 2:00 a.m., when the phone rang, he happened to be awake still, eating a peanut butter and thimbleberry jam sandwich and reading a mindless legal thriller. He regarded the phone with dread and let it ring three more times, knowing the best he could dream for would be a wrong number.

It was Divvy Ott, the new fire chief, obviously calling from a cellular phone. "Hear that?" he yelled.

Jules heard whooshing sounds and gave up the hope that Divvy was phoning in from some personal, mind-expanding odyssey.

"That's your basic *feu*," howled Divvy. "Hike your ass down to the old school and we'll try to save some for you. Harvey's already on his way. Who'd know about gas and electricity?"

"Alice. Call Alice Wahlgren," said Jules.

He hiked, arriving with a smear of peanut butter intact on one cheek. Flames shot out of the windows on the eastern wing, the wing closest to trees and neighboring houses, and he helped the half dozen firemen rout the people inside, inadvertently getting soaked when Divvy's crew sprayed the cottonwoods and shrubs as he charged back toward the school. Jules ran around the building, checking windows and the ground underneath while Harvey put up barricades. The building had been broken into so many times that it was hard to recall what splinters and dents and broken panes he'd already seen, especially when the once-intact eastern windows exuded heat and ash already covered the ground.

Jules gave up and watched, fidgety and uneasy, as the crew attacked the building. There was no fear more primeval than that of fire, short of being eaten or possibly drowning, and the latter two dangers had to be courted actively, even in Montana. His knowledge included a few basic forensic facts: glass shatters clean-edged in heat, jagged from a blow; cigarette butts don't burn and can retain fingerprints through infernos, which fingerprints can be discovered by any of forty-eight combinations of powder and light. Fire burns upward, unless it burns oxygen itself, as in a backdraft, or unless a surfeit of quick-burning fuel is available at ground level.

The odds were against arson—an elderly building under renovation was an accident waiting to happen. Divvy darted about, looking like he was having the time of his life. Most of the time he dealt with barns, trailer homes, grass fires; errors in judgment while dealing with fireworks, coffee machines, and kerosene heaters. A two-story unoccupied brick monstrosity was a joyous change of pace. Divvy was the only obvious pyromaniac on the premises. A dozen people stood against the barricades, openmouthed and dressed in robes or T-shirts and sweats. None of them looked like the kind who'd stick around to watch with a stiffie under his raincoat.

Divvy, whose other talent (his nickname came from it) was the ability to find underground water, paused to wring his hands near Jules for thirty seconds. "Oh, boy," he said. "This is exciting."

Jules gave Divvy a sidelong glance and wondered how long he'd last. After a double fatality, the old chief had quit to build fly rods.

The flames curling out of the eastern window were black, and Jules tried to remember what this meant the fire was using for fuel. Organic stuff: not just wood, certainly, and even layers of ancient institutional linoleum wouldn't contain enough petroleum to produce such a thick, sharp-smelling murk, airborne carbon. Maybe there was old paint in there, cleaning solutions and other solvents. The heat seemed to be moving due east in the persistent wind, fanned and winnowed by all the open windows on the west side. This might prevent the fire from moving in the classic upside-down triangle and taking out the second floor, unless the wind slackened and the fire turned in the direction of the oxygen supply. Jules wondered where Alice and the ladies had stored the collection. He foresaw a number of nineteenth-century table linens and wedding dresses passing entirely into memory.

"Shouldn't they let the wing go?" asked Harvey. "Isn't this shit-pile condemned?"

"No, it's in pretty good shape. The city deeded it to the Historical Society this summer."

Harvey, who believed in new buildings, harrumphed. Now they saw more smoke than flame, gray billows rising into the clear, cold sky.

"It's not a goner," said Jules. "The wind helps, in a way."

"It could pop up through the floor anytime."

"True."

"It's the wiring. It's always the goddamn wiring," said

Harvey. They'd gone up to Missoula together for classes in arson that summer. "Or the gas."

"It's off," said Alice, who'd come up behind them. "They hauled the old furnace out last week. The new one is scheduled to go in Friday."

"Was," said Harvey.

"Is," said Alice, narrowing her eyes. She tended to be nasty when her sleep was interrupted.

"Like I said, it's the wiring," said Harvey. "Or else it's arson. You got it insured?"

"It's still under a city policy," said Alice.

"The place is history," said Harvey.

"It'll be fine," said Divvy, his face filled with glee. "It's going horizontal inside, not even taking out the ceiling. It's got some other fuel besides the building."

"Arson, then," said Harvey. "Smells like turpentine."

"Jesus, Harvey," said Jules. "Give us some time. What's in this wing of the building?"

Alice ran the zipper of her coat up and down, stunned with noise and smoke and the drama of it all. "Junk. Stuff I haven't sorted. Has it been burning on this end since the beginning?"

"To my knowledge," said Jules. "Ground floor. What kind of junk?"

"Crates, arrowheads and stuff, mostly upstairs," she said. "Downstairs we've ripped down a few walls and stored stuff for the renovation."

"Like what?"

"New paint, flooring, tools. The old custodian's room is on this side, and we had to open up the walls to rewire."

Harvey looked smug.

"Oil or latex?" asked Jules.

"What?"

"What kind of paint?" he asked.

She didn't know. She looked like a five-year-old confronted with her first special-effects movie.

Jules studied the crowd again. "You leave any piles of oily rags around?"

"Of course not," Alice said, suddenly coming out of her trance.

"Why'd you have the windows open on the west end?"

"We were painting yesterday. When can I see the inside?"

"No clue," said Jules. "But I'll tell you what it looks like tomorrow morning."

AT DAWN DIVVY let them into the ground floor. Jules and Harvey inched forward with long shovels, playing their flashlights up and down and from side to side. One sweep showed a turn-of-the-century mannequin, so ghostly that Jules's pulse raced; another showed soot-laden spiderwebs, dangling like jet necklaces. They didn't go upstairs because in bad light it was impossible to tell how fundamental the damage might be, and they didn't go into the room that seemed to be the source of the fire, the custodian's closet. Harvey clicked away with the Polaroid, and Divvy ventured into the basement, where he found pools of paint thinner that had apparently dripped from the floor above. Jules spent the time with his flashlight trained on a time clock on the wall near the door.

Divvy mentioned the paint thinner over breakfast at the truck stop, and Jules mentioned the clock, with its automatic puncher for time cards, or maybe a bit of gunpowder. Harvey, cut short in the midst of another monologue about faulty wiring, said "Huh," ate a piece of toast, and launched into a psychological profile of a garden-variety arsonist.

MONTANA HIGHWAY PATROL
ALCOHOL INFLUENCE REPORT

VIDEO START TIME: *11:04* STOP TIME: *11:21* D.U.I. CITATION #: *94-1096*

LAST NAME: *Bondurant* FIRST NAME: *Charles* MI. *F* D.O.B. *6/2/52*

SEX: M. ☒ F. ☐ D/L # *PA720592* D/L STATE: *D. of Columbia*

LOCATION OF ARREST: *300 block West Park* DATE: TIME: *1053*

FIRST INDICATION OF ALCOHOL INFLUENCE: *subject drove up on*
sidewalk while pulling out of parking space then failed to make a full
stop. Subject was visibly impaired and aggressive

　　　　　dry　　　　　　　　　　　　　　　　*48°*

ROAD CONDITION AT TIME OF ARREST:			WEATHER CONDITION AT TIME OF ARREST:		
49.83B46	*MT*	*93*	*Subaru*	*Legacy*	*W*
VEHICLE LICENSE #:	STATE:	VEHICLE YEAR:	VEHICLE MAKE:	VEHICLE MODEL:	COLOR:

YES: ☐ NO: ☒ 　　　　　　　　　　*parked on street*

WAS VEHICLE TOWED?　　IF YES, WRECKER SERVICE:　　IF NO, DISPOSITION OF VEHICLE:

OBSERVATIONS OF OFFICER

CLOTHING DESCRIPTION: *white shirt & trousers*

CLOTHING CONDITION: *neat*

BREATH ODOR: *strong*　　　　　SPEECH: *loud*

ATTITUDE, EMOTIONAL STATE, AND UNUSUAL ACTIONS: *abusive &*
talkative. Attempted to strike arresting officer

SOBRIETY TESTS

LOCATION: *Park St.*　　　　DATE:　　　　TIME:

ONE LEG STAND	0–10 SECONDS	11–20 SECONDS	21–30 SECONDS
SWAYS	*8*		
RAISES ARMS	*6*		
HOPS	*10*		
PUTS FOOT DOWN		*12*	
CANNOT DO TEST (explain)			

OTHER: *subject lost temper* TOTAL POINTS
and failed to complete
tests

WALK AND TURN		
CANNOT KEEP BALANCE ☐	TOTAL POINTS	
STARTS TOO SOON: ☒		
STEPS	1 TO 9	9 TO 18
STOPS WALKING		*14*
MISSES HEEL / TOE:		*12*
STEPS OFF LINE:		*11*
RAISES ARMS:	*8*	
ACTUAL STEPS:		
THE TURN (describe): *pretended to dance*		
CANNOT DO TEST (explain)		
OTHER:		

ALPHABET RECITATION: A B C D E F G H I J K L M N O P Q̲ R S ~~T U V W X Y Z~~

R37 REVISED 7-91

JULES WAS NOT A NATURALLY CHEERFUL PERSON, and when he went without sleep, or suffered a reversal such as the discovery that he wasn't as well loved as he'd hoped, he could carry a Swedish funk like a halo. Because both were true on Thursday morning, and because he hadn't finished at the museum until 7:00 a.m. and had come to the station without showering off the smoke, the aura of despair was almost palpable. He looked like a coal miner. When Grace told him he could have only one doughnut from the pile in the kitchen, he subsided into a computer sulk. He was sufficiently self-absorbed to miss most of what was happening around him, including the fact that Caroline seemed tired, too, and all the whispering being done included neither of them.

Wesley, who wasn't the whispering type, broached the topic when they wound up in the bathroom at the same time, Jules having finally noticed the soot falling from his hair to the keyboard. "Caroline might feel better if you tell her it happens to almost everyone."

Jules realized too late that the hand towels were out of reach as he lifted his wet head from the sink. "What happens?"

"Her friend."

"Her friend what?"

Comprehension finally dawned on Wesley. "Her friend was visiting and got popped for a DUI while he was driving her car. He only blew .19, but he got kinda cranky during the nystagmus test. And there was no proof of insurance in the car."

Jules dried himself like a dog, shaking his head violently on the way to the hand towel machine. This made him dizzy, so it took him several seconds to realize the machine was empty. "Jonathan or Harvey?"

"Jonathan."

Jules stared at Wesley, his dripping hair cleaning rivulets of soot on his face. "How cranky?"

"Took a swing. It's all on tape, and the guy's still downstairs. Jonathan doesn't want to drop it. I guess the man called him names."

"Like what?"

"Jonathan was particularly offended by 'protozoa.'"

Jules opened his mouth, then clamped it shut again and wandered out into the hall. The wonder was that Jonathan had known what the word meant; maybe the college extension courses were kicking in. Axel wouldn't want to drop it, either. Due to previous decades of scandalous favoritism and nepotism, no one in the county would envy a cop's friend or relative charged with DUI. Even before the hiring of Neil, even before the Jetta and Flo show, Jules would have popped his own sister. "Have you seen the tape yet?"

"Not yet," said Wesley.

They watched it together. Wesley was still giggling when he left to visit Wayne Contway's asshole buddies in Deer Lodge.

Caroline's friend had curly black hair and a fine-boned, sensitive face that revealed every facet of his hangover. He wanted to pay Jules to put him on a bus out of town. He had no interest in contesting charges, though he confided that the arresting officer was a few cells short of a rotifer (it was at this point that Jules realized Charles Bondurant specialized in science essays). His conversation with the deputy had been like a bad dream. Bondurant wasn't in the habit of violence, but he'd been invigorated by his company that night, by the crispness and freedom of the mountain air, by—

"Who were you out with?" asked Jules.

"Just Caroline at first, but we argued and she went home

at nine, and I kept talking to this couple she knew, a lawyer and a lady who runs the Historical Society. The man told me stories about the judge. I got the impression the town was pretty relaxed. I'd *already* gotten that impression, what with Caroline's face, and Halloween—"

Jules began to feel personally responsible; he doubted that Charles Bondurant was normally given to slugging cops. Listening to the extended account, he also found it hard to believe Mr. Bondurant had only blown a .19. Then again, he'd had his drinks at the Blue Bat, where ancient testosterone had been known to ooze out of the stinky carpet and into the feet of the most pacifist patrons.

"You're staying with Deputy Fair? Don't you want to call her?"

"No." The word came out like a bullet.

Jules thought it over and made a good Christian offer. "Do you want one of us to call her?"

The man bit his lip and shook his head and looked off in embarrassment. "Has Caroline ever let you have it?"

Jules blinked in confusion.

"Has she ever really read you the riot act?"

Jules rubbed his forehead. "I'm her boss. So far she's kept to the etiquette of the situation."

Bondurant peered at Jules. "You're Caroline's boss?"

Jules raised an eyebrow. "I understand your surprise—"

"Hmmph," said the man, looking sulky.

Jules stood. "Listen, do you know anyone else in town? Otherwise I can give you the name of a bondsman."

Bondurant thought. "Somehow I don't want to call her grandmother. Do you know her grandmother Cicely?"

"Yes."

"Would you call her?"

"No."

"I could call the guy I was drinking with last night, Peter Johansen. We have some friends in common."

Jules tried to smile; it didn't quite come off. "You'll be talking to him anyway, since he's a county-paid defense attorney. Unless you'd prefer a different lawyer, or unless he might have an ethical problem defending you, given that you bought each other drinks."

"What kind of incestuous shithole is this?" shrieked Bondurant.

Ed started to laugh. Jules shrugged. "I won't give you an argument."

"How long's it going take to set things up with a bondsman?"

Jules looked inquiringly at Ed. "I called for someone else," said Ed. "The guy'll be in Cooke City till noon."

The man buried his head in his hands. "I'm already on her list for euthanasia, and I'm not a well human today," he said. "I have to leave immediately. I was drinking for a reason, if you get my drift."

Jules not only got his drift, he adored it. He wanted to make Bondurant happy; he wanted him to be able to leave with grace and speed. "I'll post bond for you," he said. "It's not like I don't know where to find Caroline if you head for Thailand."

"You mean that?"

"Absolutely." Jules gave him a shit-eating grin and ignored Ed's suspicious stare.

He also gave Bondurant a ride to pick up his clothes and ticket (he made it in and out of Caroline's house with his bag in three minutes) and dropped him at his car in the Blue Bat alley.

"Thanks again," said Bondurant.

"Don't mention it," said Jules. He tailed the car until he was sure Bondurant was headed for the airport.

Caroline, when brought to earth an hour later in the station kitchen, didn't care to discuss her erstwhile boyfriend's rich sense of humor and his departure. She didn't seem to notice Jules's ashy appearance; she didn't, in fact, even look at him. She stuck to news; they'd just been notified about a rape that had occurred in Billings on Tuesday night, one that matched up with their series in most respects.

Jules looked at the printout from Yellowstone County.

"No suspects?"

"No." Caroline tired of waiting for the coffee to drip, jerked the pot to one side, and slammed her mug in place.

"How's Joy Schwartz?"

"She went home with her parents Monday."

He should've known this—details were beginning to slide past him. On the other hand, he hadn't had to; Caroline had taken care of everything. Now she replaced the coffeepot and added milk to her mug without casting a glance at his empty, dangling cup.

"She remember anything else?"

"Not a thing. It seems like the only person who might have had information is scheduled to be buried at county expense tomorrow."

Wayne Contway hadn't had a relative who wanted him; Jules had submitted the voucher for his plot the day before.

"Why don't you just say what you're thinking?" he snapped. "Why don't you just say, You dumb fuck, if you'd given Wayne Contway a reason to talk, Joy Schwartz would have kept waiting tables instead of having her stomach opened up, and this poor woman in Billings wouldn't need a visit."

Caroline turned away, but her face was pink.

"Say it," said Jules, further enraged by his own bad behavior.

She grew a shade rosier. "What makes you think you know what I'm thinking? What makes you think you have a clue?"

Jules threw his cite book against the wall, and they watched a flurry of carbons drift lazily to the floor.

"I'm sorry," said Jules after a long moment, bending to pick up the carbons.

Caroline cleared her throat. "Anyway, I thought I'd head over tomorrow for an interview and check out a skull in Sweet Grass County on my way home."

Life was full of surprises. He was still trying to straighten the carbons, and his hands were vibrating with fatigue and tension. "When did you hear about this?"

"Phil Kaimmer called me at home this morning. I'd asked around when I checked their records last week, and someone remembered a rancher named Kirt who kept a skull in his barn."

Kaimmer, a Sweet Grass deputy sheriff, was a handsome asshole who would never have called Jules at home. "How long has Kirt had the skull?"

"Since sometime in the seventies. He pulled it out of the river and reported it then, and for some reason the department gave it back to him a few weeks later instead of burying it."

They probably thought it was an Indian skull. The sheriff throughout the seventies had been an Aryan Nation sort, the kind who believed proper burial should be reserved for the chosen few. "Bring it back, will you?" said Jules.

"Of course," said Caroline.

"When you—" He searched for the right word. "When you came upon Jetta and Flo Monday night, were they anywhere near the ground floor utility room at the old school?"

"No," said Caroline crisply. "But I remember that room. They were in a big room above it, maybe farther down the hall."

She showed no professional curiosity, which was out of character; her nose was truly out of joint. Jules finally poured some coffee.

"Weren't you planning to take some vacation time? I thought you'd asked for the next few days off. I can handle—"

"Save the jokes," said Caroline. "I won't be needing the vacation."

"I'm not joking," said Jules. "If you don't use your time the county will take it away. And everything your friend said on the video to Jonathan was true. I especially liked the part where he volunteered to pee in a straight line. You could at least say goodbye, page him before his—"

"With all due respect," said Caroline, "screw you."

NOT THAT SHE intended to. He worked on a half dozen reports, doggedly trying to clean up loose ends, while Caroline and Wesley brainstormed on the rapist. Jules gave Grace a stack to photocopy and file, and bit the big bullet, the pre-inquest report on Wayne Contway's death.

It reminded him of trying to write a short story in tenth grade, and when he looked up a half hour later, biting his pencil, to find Caroline standing next to his desk, he was sure she wasn't there for the sake of apology. Her mouth was at a dangerous angle.

Payback, thought Jules. He finished a sentence: "Mr. Jordan, a former pharmacist, has been sent to Warm Springs for a ten-day hold for psychological testing, but in my opinion his revenge—however sympathetic—was sane and deliberate." He flexed his fingers and looked at her again. Caroline was holding one of the reports he'd just finished.

"Joseph Ganter was shot on Sunday?"

"A pellet in his arm," said Jules. "His land abuts forest ground. They get a lot of hunters up there."

"He was in his barnyard," said Caroline, staring at Jules in disbelief.

Ed had come up behind her with something for Jules to sign. "We get a lot of hunting mishaps," Jules said. "It was likely a coincidence, which is why I filed a standard report."

"Heck," said Caroline acidly. "Another amazing coincidence."

Ed edged backward. Jules wrote a line of gibberish.

"Maybe it's something about the water up there."

He wasn't sure if he liked her anymore. Perhaps *like* had never been the operative word. "You're welcome to talk to him," said Jules. "Just because I got the report out of the way doesn't mean I'm not keeping the incident in mind. For today, though, I'd just as soon see your report on Jetta and Flo and the museum."

"You have a problem with that arrest?"

"No," said Jules slowly. "But given the fire, I have more trouble with that particular coincidence than the one about Joseph."

"What fire?"

Jules stared in wonder. He now had proof that she paid absolutely no notice to his corporeal self. He explained. Maybe Caroline would like to talk to Flo and Jetta? After all, she'd been the one to find them moving furniture. Had she noticed any boxes of matches, extra Zippos?

"I can't interview them," said Caroline. It was the first time he'd seen her look panicked. "Not after Monday night."

"Chickenshit," said Jules.

THE STATE'S ARSON hotshot, phoned at dawn in Missoula, had offered to make the trip that day. The northern counties, it seemed, had been boring for some time, and this might be his last chance to do some fishing. He arrived at mid-afternoon, by which time eight members of the Absaroka County Historical Society had called. Venus wanted to see the damage immediately, because she might be dead tomorrow; Alice planned to see it by the end of the day or she intended to revoke Jules's meal privileges for a year. He told Alice she could come along for the tour.

Naturally, in the light of day, the place looked horrible. Alice started to make snorkeling noises, and the arson man shooed them all outside, saying he couldn't hear himself think. They killed time throwing pebbles through the old basketball hoops behind the building while Divvy and Jules made Alice see the bright side: Insurance would now pay for all the renovations the society had had difficulty affording. She perked up at the idea of being an obvious suspect.

The man came out an hour later, blinking in the sunlight. "What do you think?" asked Jules.

"I don't yet," said the man. "I'll call in a couple of days."

He threw his satchel into his car and climbed in behind it.

"Hold it," said Jules, bending down to the driver's window. "I've got one other little problem I'd love for you to take a look at."

"What kind of problem?" asked the man. "I don't usually do *little* when I'm out of town. I came down to fish, remember?"

"It's a murder investigation," said Jules blithely. "We've got a timing question."

"Murders are fine," said the arson expert. "I've got plenty of daylight left."

WHEN JULES RETURNED from the examination of Nestor's car, he found Alice in the big room upstairs, sitting on a windowsill and sipping from a sooty bottle of sherry. She offered Jules a sip.

He batted it away. "Divvy left you here alone?"

"Went off to happy hour, left the prime suspect alone to futz with the scene," said Alice. "Yep."

"I'm going to have to lock it up again," he said.

"I know. I'm not in that much of a hurry to clean up. But the ladies are curious. They'll be relentless."

Jules was sure he'd remember to leave the phone to Grace. "No one's getting in until I hear back from that man, and that won't be until at least next week."

"Humph," said Alice. "Maybe Peter and I will leave for the weekend. He needs a break anyway." She chugged her sherry and looked around. "This is meant to be the family collection room," she said bleakly. "How much smoke do you suppose got inside these crates?"

Jules shrugged. "Has anyone been in here since Flo and Jetta on Monday night?"

"You mean besides me and the painters? What are you talking about anyway?"

"They didn't tell you?"

"No, they didn't tell me. Outside of meetings, Flo and I don't talk, we scream over garbage cans. What the hell were they doing?"

"Hanging out, according to Caroline. Helping you

organize," said Jules, pointing to a wine bottle that had rolled under a table.

Alice snorted and looked confused.

"Nothing different?"

She held up both arms hopelessly. "Since I don't know what's in here yet, I can't know if anything's gone. All I can say is that more stuff's piled in the center now."

They started looking; most things had been rummaged through, but off to one side of the heap they found a crowbar next to three large wood-and-leather trunks, which were still securely locked but showed signs of prying. Each had a brass plate with the initial "W" in haughty script.

"Any reason they'd try to get into these?" asked Jules.

"These," said Alice, "are the trunks I've been trying to get you to open for a month, the ones Ettie Whitsan's driving me nuts about. And no, there's no reason. They were probably just trying to see inside of everything."

"What's in there?" asked Jules.

"I have no idea, and I don't think Ettie does, either."

"Where're the keys?"

"Not a clue." Alice handed him the pry bar.

Indabel and Etoile's cat had probably played soccer with them. Jules gave Alice a sweet smile and handed back the bar. "Forget it," he said. "After the cleanup. And I'll need a gun for the locks. If Flo couldn't bite them open, why do you think I'm strong enough?"

MILES BIRDLAND SWUNG open his front door. "What?"

His face sagged in blotches of pink and gray, and he rocked on his feet.

"Is Flo around?" asked Jules. "It's about the museum. About the fire."

Birdland's stare was long and cold. "What fire?"

"The old school burned last night," said Jules defensively, feeling the beginning of a flush. "Just part of the east wing. And since Flo's a member of the Aches, I need to talk to her."

"And since she and Jetta were up there Monday night."

Jules nodded his head, relieved to be understood.

"My wife died last night," said Birdland. "This morning, rather."

"Oh, Jesus," said Jules, going cold. "I'm so sorry."

Birdland looked at a point over Jules's head. "Flo went home to get some sleep. Look her up in a few hours. And I'll tell her to call."

"I'm sorry, sir," said Jules.

"Ruth had had enough," said Miles Birdland. "Don't be sorry. And remind Harvey to be on time tomorrow. That robbery case."

"Right." Jules trudged to his patrol car. He was two blocks away before it really sank in: The old bastard was going back to work before his wife was buried.

JETTA WAS STANDING in her driveway, unloading groceries out of her Volvo trunk, and let him know he could help. "You get your license back for trips to the store?" asked Jules.

"Yes, thanks."

"I wondered what you were doing in the museum the other night," asked Jules.

She sighed. "Jesus, that was embarrassing. I mean, we had a perfect right to be there, but hiding turned it into this sort of teenage mess."

"I'm sure Caroline regarded it as the highlight of her Halloween," said Jules dryly. "But why go there at all? I thought the heat didn't work."

Jetta handed him a bag of kitty litter. "We were sick of Axel's stupid party, and the bars were full of girls in ballerina outfits. Flo didn't want Neil to see her smoking, and we thought we'd get something done while we talked."

Jules could have pushed a guilt button, asked how good a job they'd done disposing of butts. "Any sign anyone had been up there since your last meeting?"

Jetta hefted a bag of produce. "Alice, I suppose, trying to get organized. Alice is always trying to get organized. She had piles of small stuff out to catalog—mineral samples and silverware and old pens. Why?"

Jules looked at her askance. She was pushing her luck.

"Don't tell me you don't know it burned last night."

She gaped at him. Jules shook his head in disgust and started toward the house with the grocery bags. News of a fire was usually faster than news of a divorce. "You should go see Flo," he said.

"She went back?" Jetta's voice was hushed, traumatized.

"I don't know," he said. "I'd been thinking she might have set the place on fire, but that would have made it quite a busy night."

Jetta slammed her bags down on the kitchen table and stuck her jaw out. "I don't know anything about her busy nights. Why aren't you asking her, then?"

Jules opened the refrigerator and looked for a place for the milk. "Her mother died early this morning."

"Oh, geez," said Jetta, freezing. "Poor Ruth. Poor Miles. Is Flo over there?"

"She will be later," said Jules. He moved a jar of Ragú. Scotti the Sicilian, Mr. I Only Eat Homemade, was such a liar.

"Oh, I won't go until she calls," said Jetta, still stricken. "He loved that woman. He won't want to see anyone."

Jules made a face and watched an orange roll across the floor.

"He did," she said gently. "Adored her for fifty-some years. Even an asshole can have someone they're at home with, and now he's lost his."

Jules shut the refrigerator door, wadded up a torn bag and opened the cupboard under the sink, looking for the trash bucket. An antique-looking can of furniture polish fell out and he pushed it with his toe, thinking for a minute, before he replaced it. "So, what were you doing up there?"

She stared at him. "You already asked."

"And you didn't really answer. Why were you moving around the trunks and crates?"

"We were trying to organize by piling them in the center of the room."

"Directly above where a fire would originate two days later?"

"I don't *know*. I didn't know it had burned."

"Where were you last night?"

She gaped at him. "Dinner in Bozeman with an old law school friend of Axel's," she said. "We didn't get home until lateish, midnight or one. And then we went to bed."

"I need to take your fingerprints," said Jules. "I'll take Flo's, too. It's a matter of being able to exclude yours to see if we can isolate the arsonist's."

She nodded slowly.

"It'd be wonderful if you'd warn Flo when you see her," said Jules, "so that she doesn't eat me alive out of paranoia."

Scotti came through the door. "Jules, good lord, a social visit. Are we having you for dinner tonight?"

Jetta shook her head, and Jules almost laughed. "I just stopped by, had a couple things to tell Jetta," he said.

"So we both left work early. Well, she could at least give you a goddamn drink," said Scotti, opening a cupboard and surveying his hoard. "What'll you have?"

"Nothing, thanks," said Jules politely. "I need to get going."

"Nonsense," said Scotti. A minute later he slammed huge glasses of dark brown liquid in front of Jules and Jetta, and drank half of his own in one gulp. "Ask me how I love my job."

Jules smiled. "Seems like you want to just think about it."

"What'd you want to tell Jetta?"

She looked stricken. "Nothing important," said Jules. "But while I have you together, do you know if Joseph has any reason to mislead me about visiting Nestor Amundsen the day he died?"

Scotti stared at him. Jetta turned pearly gray. "Joseph can't drive," said Axel.

"This wouldn't exactly be taking to the highway," said Jules. "This is five miles of dirt, almost no oncoming traffic or curves. And he sees well enough to hunt."

Jetta made a funny sound. "Darling," said Scotti slowly. "Your cousin is suggesting your father is a liar."

"It'd be fairer to say he probably isn't telling the whole truth," said Jules stolidly. "And he said he wasn't going to, either. But I'm quite sure he drove the old Scout to Nestor's that afternoon, and though he told me he was late to the party because he was burning leaves behind the barn there's no evidence of a fire there."

"You know," said Scotti, "screw you. You trying to look under every rock, start a fight with everyone?"

"Jesus, Axel," said Jules bitterly. "I thought you liked it when I tried to solve things. I've got half an old body out on the island, and a dead rancher, and all sorts of weirdness tying them together. Nothing's just going to go away."

Scotti stalked out of the room.

"What was Joseph doing when you came to get him for the party?" Jules asked his cousin.

Jetta hadn't yet regained her color. "Dressing," she whispered. "He was standing in the middle of the kitchen putting his tie on."

"I'm sure it's nothing to worry about," said Jules. "I just need to know—"

"I have to talk to you," she whispered.

"Get him out of here," yelled Scotti through the kitchen door. "He's trying to ruin the rest of my life."

Jetta leaned closer. "I'll call," she whispered.

Jules gave her a curious look, considered several questions, and thought the better of almost all of them. "Can I have those proof sheets while I'm here?"

"Proof sheets," she echoed.

He headed for the door. "The photos from the party," he said, feeling his patience unravel, his fatigue kick in. "Carl Jump's photos."

"I returned them days ago," she said. "I placed my order. So did Mom."

"Jesus Christ," said Jules. "I asked you a week ago."

"Don't be such an asshole when everything's falling apart," said Jetta, wiping away a tear. "Just go get them."

Jules slammed the door.

14 Collectors

THE OWNERS OF THE BAIRD HAD HAD AN OVER-
whelming summer and fall. Now that the fishermen and
Yellowstone tourists had checked out, they faced a different
sort of difficulty: Only a few skiers stayed at the Baird in the
winter, and in a bad month the heating bill for a circa 1900
hotel could run in the thousands. Boilers broke, maids had
breakdowns throughout the year, and every cook they'd ever
hired suffered from regrettable, vicious character flaws. The
bar made money year-round but had lately been invaded by
a crew of morose, middle-aged divorced men in their forties
who inadvertently depressed and drove away other customers
and the owners themselves. Most of the rooms were rented
at a monthly rate in the winter, and there was an informal
award for the staff member who managed to rent to the
weirdest individual. Two days earlier one of the owners had
won when she'd given a room to a man who spent his first
night burning the carpet with candles and his second carving sixes into the wall and cooking a goose from the town
park on an illegal hot plate. He'd been hauled off the next
morning by a sheriff's deputy.

The owners were the kind of couple who do best in per-
petual motion, but every once in a while everyone hits the
wall. The woman had come to a grinding halt after months

of scrubbing rooms and ejecting drunks. The man's father had died in the late summer, and the death had hung suspended over his head since then, never quite lowering and never quite going away.

So they took a couple of days off to simply drive and talk. That Thursday afternoon they'd opened a bottle of good wine on their way up an old mining road above the Yellowstone River valley. It was fifty degrees and windy, with a front moving in, so that half the sky was robin's-egg blue and the other half battleship gray. They steered around a discarded pair of shorts, which made the woman giggle for the first time in several weeks. A mile later their good mood faded when they slowed near a dark object on the side of the road and stared at a T-shirt.

"What's going on?" asked the woman.

"I have no idea," said the man. "Have some more wine."

They drove on. All the blue in the sky disappeared, the temperature plummeted, and huge flakes of snow began to fall. At the middle of a fork in the road they braked and stared at a new pair of running shoes, socks flopping out of the tops.

"They're empty, right?" asked the woman.

"Let's assume so," said the man.

A moment later they passed a man jogging barefoot in his underpants. He waved to them through the soft snow.

"I bet we see the underpants on the way down," said the woman.

"We could always move back to Minnesota," said the man.

The woman drained her glass. "At least we can stop worrying about finding a body."

They reached the old mining town and wandered around in the eerie snow light, just tipsy enough to not want to give up on their mission, and still desperate to avoid Blue Deer and the hotel. They were rewarded by a troop of coyotes, wrestling with something near one of the old mine shafts.

"What do they have?" asked the woman.

"I don't know," said the man. "I can't quite make it out. Something to eat, probably."

"Go get the binoculars out of the car."

"I might scare them away."

The largest coyote escalated the battle by seizing the object and running with it. When the others closed in, he tossed it up in the air, and the owners of the Baird took in the unmistakable silhouette of a human foot, shin and knee.

"Let's go tell someone," said the woman after a moment of silence. "Now."

"They'll wander away with it by the time someone gets up here," said the man.

"What should we do?"

He sighed and walked down the hill toward the coyotes, waving his arms and yelling.

JULES HAD SNUCK home after the mess at the Scottis', and Grace tracked him to earth there at seven. "I thought you should know," said Grace. "Do you want me to send Jonathan?"

"No," said Jules. "I'll go."

The Baird owners had called from a valley bar, reported their find and asked if someone could meet them there to pick up the item in question; they'd decided to have a few drinks and check into one of the rooms out back for the night, whether or not they'd brought toothbrushes. Jules bought them two martinis and suggested they fly to Mexico for a real vacation.

By the time he got back to town, several inches of snow lay on the road and dusk seemed darker than usual. A stray, skinny dog skittered across the road in front of him, and in a surge of loneliness he drove to the Baird and Edie. But when he slowed to park he looked through windows into the warm, bright lobby and saw Alice's and Caroline's profiles and a half dozen gray heads. The Aches had invaded.

So he put Nestor Amundsen's chewed and dented artificial limb in the evidence locker and headed home. Nestor had actually written his name on the inner face of the socket, as if there might be a cloakroom mix-up someday.

THEY'D BEEN FORCED, *forced* by homelessness, to meet at a restaurant, actually the lobby of the Baird, where a nice young bartender had suggested cozy old-fashioneds to counteract the weather. Now Alice was dealing with the effects of alcohol on fragile bloodstreams; there'd been no point in discussing how to cut and organize the collection until they'd wound up and down.

It was astounding, the amount of bullshit collected over a mere hundred years in a county whose population had held steady at approximately ten thousand since 1910 and whose income had never been great. Tons of stuff, mountains of lives, boxes holding everything from baby clothes to letterpress type to chamber pots. In the beginning, Alice had expected to find secrets, but the truth was inevitably more prosaic. So prosaic, in fact, that they'd begun to set aside piles for possible sale to antiques and secondhand stores. She was photocopying the inventory list with Edie in the tiny hotel office, keeping half an ear open to the conversation in the lobby.

"I guess she was quite upset," said Angelina.

"Why now?"

"About the meeting. That we wouldn't postpone it because of Ruth's death."

"Oh, for Christ's sake. Why is she even thinking about the meeting?" asked Cicely.

"Ruth has been dying forever," said Indie. "It's not as if Flo wanted us to pay our respects anyway. Jetta will go, of course, but she's probably the only one."

"At least it was quiet at the end," said Mabel.

Cicely inspected her fingernails. "If you call your lungs bleeding out quiet."

"That stopped in the last couple of hours," said Venus. "It *was* quiet, at the very end, and Nina said Miles had been loading her up with morphine."

Cicely stirred her drink. "I bet Flo wasn't quiet. Poor Miles. That girl has never known when to shut up."

"Okay, everybody," said Alice. "That's enough fun. The sheets I'm passing out now are of inventory, and it's time to make some hard decisions."

"How can we tell what to get rid of without seeing it?" asked Ella Bolan.

"You'll have to use your imagination. Most of this stuff is in six-foot piles, and this way we can do a silent vote without anyone having their feelings hurt."

"Having them hurt directly," said Cicely.

Alice ignored her. "We're looking for redundancies and for items that are either in bad shape or only have personal value. We currently have something like seven dozen doilies, and somehow none of them are likely to be smoke-damaged," she said, checking her notes. "Five full sets of draft harness, eight old sewing machines, and nineteen cast-iron Dutch ovens. For instance. Try to cut a third or a quarter of the list."

"What about our trunks?" asked Ettie Whitsan. "What if someone wants to throw out our trunks before we've even opened them?"

"Honey, I think they were in the room with the most damage," said Indie, patting her sister on the back. "Please don't be upset."

"Nonsense," said Alice crisply. "I saw them myself, and they're still closed tight. Almost everything in that room is fine. A real lucky break."

"There's silver in there," Ettie said. "Silver and silks and jewels and old paintings. Treasure."

"Enough, Ettie," snapped Indie. "Enough about the damn trunks. Just look at the list."

Each of them thought her grandmother's chipped Sevres jug, her mother's battered silver spoon, the ivory picture frame that had been glued together a dozen times by a great-aunt was the most valuable item in the building. The ladies wanted to at least cultivate the illusion of a worldview, and wanted their museum to reflect the century, to display as many arrowheads and buffalo jump bones and turn-of-the-century postcards from Sicily and Stockholm and Cuba as saddles and porter's uniforms and logger's tools.

With this in mind, Alice voted to sell two of the museum's four cookstoves to make room for the lobster chests the Bairds used to send east on the trains for treats, the Javanese shadow puppets Cicely's aunt had brought home in 1922, the cobra skin from Venus's grandfather, and three mysterious items from Olive Clement's "kinky uncle Mars": a silver Italian girdle, a collection of nineteenth-century French pornography, and a pair of elegant handcuffs. Alice needed to ask Jules about Uncle Mars.

"Do you recall that we were going to open them this meeting?" asked Ettie a few minutes later.

The ladies all looked down at their lists politely.

"The trunks? That was before the fire," said Alice. "Now I have to get Sheriff Clement to open the museum and your locks."

"I think our Persian rugs must be in there."

Indie buried her face in her hands. Ettie stared at her, then looked blindly out the window; it was almost dark. "Oh, what the hell," she said softly. "I'll have another Rob Roy."

"Let's all have one," said Cicely happily. "What else do we really need to get done today?"

"Actually," said her granddaughter, "we have a few things to double-check about the man on the island, about who said what to whom. So drink slowly."

The evening continued to go downhill.

AT DAWN THE next morning Jules stood on the side of a mountain with a thermos of coffee, trying to figure out how a prosthesis had traveled forty-some miles, either over a mountain range or through a town, to become a coyote plaything; who had thought to hide it in such a bizarre place; and why. He could still make out some of the coyotes' tracks under the fresh snow, enough of them to know that he wouldn't be finding a land mine of other Nestor evidence. They'd frolicked with the thing for at least half a mile, tossing it in the air and letting it fall. Someone could have left it in the road, or the coyotes could have plucked it out of a trash can belonging to one of the houses down by the river, only two miles away.

He took another slug of coffee straight from the thermos

and stared down at his feet, which were already cold and wet. At least the leg hadn't been found in his uncle's backyard or his cousin's carport. Maybe things were looking up.

"Yippee," said Jules weakly, walking slowly back to his car.

*

Jules—Deer Lodge was a waste of time. No one likely among current counselors, and no one on the premises can recall anyone with a thing for flashlights. They can't locate Wayne's "education" record in his files, though according to other inmates he'd taken four or five seminars. The warden refused to see me, was supposedly off pheasant hunting in Malta (?!), and his underling said he couldn't show me any info on past employees. I've put in a request with the state. Also no additional information on 1986 rapes—struck out on finding current addresses for any of the victims.

Gallatin County turds similarly a bust. One promising, but he's had an arm and collarbone in a cast for the last month (I checked).

Sorry, but nada. —Wesley

At 8:00 a.m., while reading this note, Jules got a call from the Yellowstone County sheriff. "I'd send someone along with Deputy Fair when she comes to interview the rape victim," he said. "The boyfriend's excitable, all pissed off that the girl wants to add insult to injury by talking about the attack. He wanted to take out one of my people yesterday."

"How excitable?"

"Let's just say the girl deserves a different boyfriend and the boyfriend deserves electroshock."

"Okay," said Jules. "I'll let you put it that way to Caroline, so she doesn't think I want her on a leash."

She didn't make it in until eight thirty, and Jules watched her read the note he'd left on her desk before he wandered off to the kitchen while she called Billings. Caroline didn't look happy when she walked in. "So who else is on duty today?" she asked.

"You have your choice of me or Jonathan."

She managed to look amused. "Don't you have lots of important civic mud baths to attend to?"

"Sure I do. That's why I'd love to leave town."

THEY LEFT FOR Billings a half hour later, planning to stop in Big Timber for the skull on their way home. On the way out of town Caroline told him about the most recent Aches meeting.

"Hardly anything. It's like a lockdown. Ettie rambles on about her goddamn trunks, and when Angelina starts nattering about rapes, Venus gives her the kibosh. Not that I want to know about any fifty-year-old rapes, but . . ."

"But violence begets violence," Jules pointed out. "It's worth nailing them down."

"Finally, my grandmother says something off-color about an Indian blanket, and your mother starts asking her how she can dare make such a joke, and Cicely says something about how counting dead Indians out here is like counting dead blacks in Alabama, just a fact of life."

"The dead Indian's come up too many times," said Jules. "We have to figure that one out. If someone's been murdered, we can try to do something about it, but please remind the ladies we're also looking for a goddamn Anglo-Saxon mother's son, someone who could afford a fancy gold belt and a real goddamn doctor for a broken leg." He drew a breath, tried for patience, and drummed his fingers on the steering wheel. "Who are they saying killed him, anyway?"

"They aren't," said Caroline, watching him leerily out of the corner of her eye. "They clamp down. But there was no one like him in the missing persons file."

"I don't think the local Native American population had any reason to love the department back in the thirties," said Jules. "And maybe we need to play bad cop with the ladies, remind them that murder is murder and they're supposed to know better. I don't want their bullshit code of honor. If some white boy killed a Crow fifty years ago, the white boy needs to go to jail in his wheelchair."

"Maybe they don't know."

"They know everything that happens in this town," said Jules bitterly. "My uncle and Birdland and Merle Ott know everything. They snow me; the ladies snow you."

She didn't argue, and he drove on in silence past the gray and blustery mountains, the wind-flattened grass on the wind-shaped golden rises.

"Doesn't that bother you about living out here, that everyone knows your business?" Caroline asked.

"Sometimes," said Jules. "If what's known really matters. But if it's something hurtful, people are mostly compassionate, and if it's embarrassing, having them laugh puts it away faster."

Caroline didn't say anything.

"Often it's a bit of each," said Jules.

She sighed, which for her constituted an autobiographical wallow.

Jules was desperate to make her feel better. "Shit," he said. "Almost everyone who lives a little gets in trouble some time or another."

"I haven't been arrested," said Caroline, clearly implying that she had lived and that he was full of shit.

He floundered. "Well, Ed's hauled me in, and I seem to recall he arrested Harvey once."

Caroline raised her eyebrows. "Did you get a DUI?"

"For some strange reason, no."

"What, then?"

Jules deeply regretted touching on the subject. "Three times, all when I was quite young. A rioting charge and a pot bust when I was seventeen."

Now she raised only one eyebrow. "What was the third?"

Jules tapped the steering wheel for a few moments. "The actual charge was indecent exposure, but it sounds worse than it was. No raincoat on the playground or anything like that. I wasn't actually booked for anything."

"You peed on someone's car?" asked Caroline.

Jules stared at her, flummoxed. "No, no, no. Another person was involved."

"Ah," said Caroline.

"An alley," said Jules.

"Aren't trash cans noisy?"

He felt his face begin to heat up. "A fence, actually, and it was pretty well surrounded by hollyhocks and stuff. Fairly private, I thought. And it was the Fourth of July weekend, not a very quiet time of year."

She guffawed, a deeply unladylike sound of derision. "And Ed didn't just ask you to take it elsewhere?"

Jules completed his transformation to plum color. "I asked Ed to pretend he hadn't seen us. I didn't want to take it elsewhere."

"You didn't want to pull up your pants."

He nodded stiffly.

"Did you have to appear before Birdland?"

"Not that time," muttered Jules.

She stared, and he shook his head. "Do you still know the lady, wave to each other at the gas station?"

"No."

"I bet her name was something like Tiffany."

Jules shook his head. "No. Caroline, let's—"

"Crystal?"

"No." Jules hit the blinker for a pass with such a vengeance they both wondered if he'd broken it. He didn't look at her, but he could imagine another spasm of raised eyebrows.

"You don't remember it."

He turned now, wearing the arrogant expression he usually tried to dredge up when he was losing at poker. "I never knew it, and I deeply regret starting this conversation."

IT WAS OVER a hundred miles to Billings, and they didn't speak for the next thirty. The car became oppressive. Jules, from the corner of his eye, was aware of Caroline's hand on her knee, the way the fingers flexed as if she were a piano player, the occasional tense sigh and the line of her thigh on the car seat.

The truth was brutal, thought Jules, trying not to clear his throat too often. Caroline's employer had been a peckerhead from time to time, a "dope addick," to use the local vernacular, though actually only a dabbler. At college, jerking your brain around had seemed as much a part of continuing education as flailing through Dante and organic chemistry, secretly enjoying Rabelais and economics, having epiphanies about the periodic table and the first moments of language and art. Jules's covert strength as an officer of the law was an ability to recognize what a person might be taking and what language he might speak.

A decade of energetic experimentation had given him the diagnostic skills it took most cops thirty years to acquire through random arrests, and with a few notable exceptions Jules's method had been more fun, though he wouldn't have taken money to live through it again. It took one to know one, and it saved him a good deal of time: Why comb a car when the hit of blotter had so clearly been chewed and swallowed hours earlier? The problem, of course, was that empathy often made him want to skip the arrest to begin with.

And because so much of his knowledge had been acquired far from Blue Deer, it rarely came back to haunt him. The episode with the girl on the alley fence, though remembered by a chunk of the town's population, seemed like good clean fun to them and a drop in the bucket to Jules. A prodigious alcohol intake in his late teens and early twenties had seemed all right, too, because he'd survived it and supposedly grown up, because even in the late seventies it rarely occurred to these amused onlookers that it might take more than just alcohol to get some people to float rapids naked, or ride bulls in the rodeo, or trade Montana for a decade in the wide, mysterious world.

THE BILLINGS INTERVIEW lasted two hours. From the outset Jules knew it was good both of them had come. The woman's boyfriend wouldn't leave and took exception to virtually every question Caroline asked about the attack. Jules ended up babysitting him on the back porch while the man gnashed his teeth and chain-smoked. Jules hoped that, in the trauma following her attack, the woman would find the strength and perspective to see clearly and ditch the asshole, rather than cling to him. When the boyfriend finally left in a huff for work, Jules walked quietly through the rest of the house while the interview droned on in the kitchen. In the bedroom he found the aftermath of an argument, lingerie drawers emptied and tossed around, some soft-core shots of the woman, chunky and rawboned, ripped and dumped into the trash can by the bed.

"I didn't take a formal statement," said Caroline abruptly as they climbed back into the car. "She comes to Blue Deer almost every weekend, has a sister who just had a baby. I'll get it next weekend, when that prick isn't around."

"You hope," said Jules, who saw the wisdom of this plan.

"I pray, fervently. Could you quiet him down at all?"

"He's one of those people who won't get used to not being the center of attention, which means he'll be reminding her of it for a year, never letting things get back to anything like normal. She'll start blaming herself for his inability to get it up."

Her lips curled ever so slightly. "That'll be how the story goes?"

"I'd bet on it, if I really wanted to know the end."

They threaded through the wastelands on the edge of Billings and reached the freeway. She rubbed her eyes. "I wish we'd talked to the people in Big Timber first."

Any way you cut it, the day was long, though they'd relaxed a bit. "Anything else come out, other similarities?"

"Past the window and the flashlight and the bites, the way he looked, the way she looked? Nothing."

"She didn't look much like Joy Schwartz."

"They're all soft-looking, light complected. Maybe he picks women he thinks can't give him trouble."

"This woman was at least healthy looking, compared to Joy."

"Plump," said Caroline, dubious. "I don't know about healthy."

Jules sighed. "Go to sleep," he said. "We've got almost an hour before we reach Big Timber."

THE SWEET GRASS charmer, Deputy Kaimmer, was on duty. He and Jules didn't like each other even in the best of times, without someone like Caroline around to up the ante. They hadn't since an accident a few months earlier on the county line, when Jules caught Kaimmer lecturing a dead drunk driver's sober wife, who'd just seen her husband's head split open. Jules appreciated the desire to take the scene out on someone, but a white-haired widow with broken ribs didn't seem the appropriate candidate. Better the deputy simply kick the dead man's ass when no one was watching.

Now Kaimmer gave directions to the rancher's barn to Caroline while Jules killed time with the old disaster photos on the wall. The Sweet Grass County building had no martyred cops to memorialize, and instead presented various tragic scenes. There was a lightning panel, featuring oddly rearranged trees and boats and corpses, often with sheep watching patiently in the background, and the train crossing panel, with an assortment of mangled cars posed near prominent warning signs. Farm equipment and flooding scenes required more imagination. One tornado in 1926 had left behind a splintered shepherd's wagon, and a couch and a hand peeked out from under a collapsed riverbank. As a collection, the photos would have made a mint at a Soho show.

Kaimmer was now discussing other body part incidents with Caroline. Jules was fairly sure the deputy's honey-colored hair was permed and hoped this meant it would fall out in the next decade. He tugged the file from Caroline's hands and started reading in the wash of Kaimmer's idiot conversation, lines such as "Well, you know they'll never find that hiker's hand" faithfully answered by her inflectionless "Uh-huh." The skull they'd actually come for had been found in a deadfall on a Yellowstone inlet in 1972; no other bones had been found in the vicinity, and the notes said there was "some evidence of prolonged time in the water." That was it for the investigation but for a short notation from the sheriff to the effect that the skull was likely a hundred years old and a relic of the Indian wars.

Jules slapped the file closed and stared fixedly at Kaimmer, who actually shut up. "Thanks for the information," Jules said pleasantly. "We'll copy the file and get it back to you next week."

In the car, Caroline rubbed her forehead. "I never got the directions straight."

"I know where the ranch is," said Jules. "Stubby little prick," he muttered.

Caroline's head jerked around. "The rancher?"

Jules gave her a withering look.

"It's interesting to me that everyone describes you as a nice person," said Caroline.

"You don't think I'm a nice person?" asked Jules, accelerating to fifty on the dirt road.

"No," said Caroline. "Not really."

"Oh, well. I'd have to agree with you today."

It was getting dark when Rancher Kirt led them to his treasure, which he kept on a shelf above his desk. Caroline shuddered, but Jules smiled and reached up to bring it down. A big, narrow head, high cheekbones, high forehead, as northern European as they came. There was evidence of a healed fracture from a year or so before death, just like the ankle on the island, thought Jules. A car accident, a riding accident. The jaw was gone, along with all the teeth, and the sharp edges of the upper jaw and brows had been ground down a bit by river gravel, but considering its fifty-some-mile journey the skull was in remarkable condition, and the circle centered just above the eyes was virtually perfect. It was also approximately the right size for the bullets they'd found in the island man's skeleton. Jules tilted the skull to peer through the hole under the overhead bulb, then touched the bleached porous spot on the top of the skull, about two inches across.

"Did you have this outside for a while, or did you always keep it inside, in the shade?"

"Shade," said Kirt. "I wouldn't want my place to look like some sort of demonic outfit."

Jules imagined the skull poking out into the sun on the island grave, a rounded white rock growing brittle in the elements. It was a wonder no one had stepped on it, crushed it before the river rose and carried it off. "I think this could be our boy." He handed the skull to Caroline. "The age is right."

"Do I get it back?" asked the rancher, looking forlorn.

"If the head matches most of the rest of what we find, I think we'll have to bury him."

"Just the same, I'd like a receipt. Things get lost."

Jules felt his pockets for paper. "Anything get lost the last time, when you first found it?"

"Two teeth with gold fillings," said Kirt, flipping through supply catalogs on his desk, finally tearing a corner from a back cover.

"And they told you he was a hundred-year-old Indian?" asked Jules in disbelief.

Kirt shrugged and handed him the scrap and a pen. "They didn't tell me anything."

Jules thought for a moment before he scribbled "Received on 11/4/94, from A. Kirt, Sheep Back Road: the skull of an unidentified man, lacking lower jaw, teeth or other attachments. J. C. Clement, Absaroka County Sheriff." He handed it over and watched Caroline, cradling the skull, delicately insert her pinkie into the bullet hole.

In the car she held it gingerly on her lap while she waved to Kirt through a cloud of dust.

"How can you be sure it's right?" she asked.

"I can't, but there's still some sediment in the crannies inside. We can compare the deepest layer to the island grave."

"That's a long shot," said Caroline flatly. "I don't see how we can get far without teeth."

"No," said Jules. "Though at least knowing he had two gold ones tells us he's not the usual forgotten guy."

"He could have been a rich Indian."

"No," said Jules, slowing slightly to touch the skull with one finger. "That suture between the cheek and the upper jaw is curved, and in an American Indian it would be almost straight. And the cheekbones recede."

Caroline absorbed this for a moment in silence. "Should we have a sketch done? Can you guess what he would've looked like?"

He peered down at the skull again. "It's hard without the jaw. It's not the sort of thing I learned. We always did the basics—age, height, state of health, and what it meant for how the person had lived. But we know this guy was a well-fed blond Anglo, money for medical treatment on his leg and mouth and head. He was probably handsome—high forehead, even brow, big eye sockets, nicely spaced upper teeth—but you never can tell about cartilage in the nose or ugly lips or ears, a receding chin or birthmarks or scarring. We'd have better luck trying to do a computer match with a sized photo, but it'll be hard matching the pose."

They were silent for several miles. It was dark enough now to only make out the silhouettes of mountains and trees. Jules was aware again of the closeness of the car, the lull of the engine and their quiet breathing, legs in identical ugly uniforms only eighteen inches apart.

"He saw it coming, didn't he?"

"Who?"

"Him." She pointed to the centered bullet hole in the skull on her lap. "He was shot twice in the stomach, and then someone walked right up to him and did this."

"He might have had his eyes shut."

"I doubt it."

She meant that the hole was too perfectly placed to be anything but the ultimate fuck-you gesture. "I doubt it, too," said Jules. "It came last."

"Where do I put him?" asked Caroline. "I don't want him on my lap anymore. I should have opened the trunk before we left."

Jules smiled. "Put him on the seat, between us."

JULES WAS IN the mood for some quiet, thorough self-pitying self-destruction that weekend, but he was scheduled to work both days. Jonathan had to go to a wedding in North Dakota, and Harvey needed to coach his kid's team in a soccer tournament in Miles City, and this meant a balancing act. He bought a bottle of whiskey and then began to methodically clean his house, so that he wouldn't touch the bottle constantly. By ten o'clock, when Edie knocked on his door, he'd drunk only a third and his upstairs was actually habitable.

"I'm sorry," said Edie. "I'm very, very sorry about how it all came out."

"No problem," said Jules. "Would you like your things?"

"I suppose I should sooner or later," said Edie, pushing past into the house. "But I wanted to say goodbye first."

In hindsight, Jules found this patronizing, and was embarrassed that he hadn't screamed or shut the door in her face. Instead he simply started drinking again when she left a few hours later.

WHEN HE GOT to the station Saturday morning, he plunked the skull on his desk as a goad and object lesson, then turned on his computer. He scanned in the best Polaroid of the skull as well as a half dozen photos from the old yearbooks of men who'd played basketball and lacked gravestones, and started chugging coffee.

It didn't work as well as he'd hoped. He needed a specialized program, point-by-point comparisons. Three of the men were all wrong. Of the rest, Atticus Rinkle's photo was too fuzzy, and Henry Whitsan's chin was tilted up, a hard angle to capture on a chinless skull. Another nominee, from the 1931 yearbook, was named Rolf Eiger and looked too heavyset for the long, thin leg bones Jules remembered.

All in all, Henry Whitsan's photo was closest. The forehead and cheekbones were about right, and the rest of him seemed long and straight enough. Jules rummaged through the drawer for a comparison photograph and came upon a good black-and-white of him and Patrick and Peter and Divvy that spring, after they'd returned from the first search-and-rescue of the year. The results were encouraging: nothing matched up with Peter's visage. Jules's face was proportionately closer; Divvy was off by almost an inch across the temples and cheekbones. Whitsan's photo had anomalies, too, but none that couldn't be explained by the angle of the shot; the man was invariably lounging.

Jules hadn't intended trying Patrick Ankeny, but he was enjoying himself so much he didn't mind studying his rival's lovely face. Ankeny's half-Crow background made the differences obvious, especially in the cheekbones, but the forehead and eye sockets were a virtual match, far closer than any of the other men in the modern photos, closer than anyone but Henry Whitsan. Jules stared at all the photos, not in the mood to be confused.

IT WASN'T AS if Jules didn't know when he should stop. At the grocery he bought oranges and grapefruit for some healthy, fresh-squeezed juice. He filled a bucket with cleaning supplies and attacked his basement with a clear head and a foul mood.

At eight o'clock he picked up Jetta and drove her to the bar in the Best Western on the outskirts of town, a place neither of them usually visited. He stuck to soda water for the first fifteen minutes of the conversation while they covered all the horrible things Jetta's sons were probably doing all the time.

Sobriety, as usual, made him impatient, and Jetta had an annoying way of savoring her martini olives. "So what did you want to talk to me about?"

Jetta flushed and literally wrung her hands. "Is there a statute of limitations on a bad land deal?"

"What do you mean?"

"It's this digging around for old names that's brought something up," said Jetta, looking weepy. "It's a rumor I've heard, a secret. You can't tell anyone I've asked you about this."

Jules signaled the waitress, pointed to Jetta's martini, and held up two fingers. Jetta buried her face in her hands.

"If some land was come by crookedly"—she waved her fingers without taking her hands away—"years ago, and this was discovered, would the land have to be given back?"

Jules frowned. "That depends on how it was taken. Seems like a question for Axel."

This was not what she wanted to hear. "You don't have a clue?"

"You haven't told me enough. You don't just steal land like you steal a car. And it might depend on how long ago it happened."

Jetta lowered her hands. They shook. "Fifty years ago, at least." She leaned forward, and the words poured out. "I found out that Dad won our ranch in a card game. I think he might have killed a man for it."

Jules socked back half his drink and shuddered with pleasure. "Huh," he said after a long moment. "Who told you this?"

"Flo. Nestor confessed to her, told her that's how he'd gotten his land, too. That's why she's so sure he committed suicide."

They looked at each other. Jules was dubious. There had to be more to the story; no one really bet thousands of acres.

"Did Joseph and Nestor win it, or did they kill the rightful owner? One's a bit worse than the other."

"Flo thinks maybe both. She says Nestor was really a mess about it and said that the ranch would be taken away."

"Who's the dead man?"

"I'm not supposed to say."

"If they won it, why would they have to kill someone for it?"

She shook her head, near tears, unable to split hairs about disaster.

"I think it's perfectly legal to win a ranch in a card game," insisted Jules, knowing he sounded like an idiot.

"If that's how it happened," Jetta said. "But maybe the man wouldn't sign the deed."

Jules finished his martini; he could already feel the vodka moving through his veins, too good for real comfort. "Henry Whitsan, right?"

She stared.

"Explain how this came up again."

"Nestor told Flo he might lose the ranch because someone else really owned it."

"When?"

"I don't know. Sometime before the party."

"Thursday night, when she brought him food?"

"I don't *know*."

Jules looked into space.

"Say something," said Jetta. "I don't trust Axel to not talk about it, and I trust you, because you love Joseph. I don't know what to look for, and if I go poking around in property records someone will tell Axel or Dad, or both."

"Have you asked Joseph about it?"

"Of course not," she said, appalled. "Anyway, Nestor said something to Flo about how the truth was going to come out, like it or not, and Flo got it in her head that there was something in the Whitsans' trunks—a deed, maybe. So we messed around Halloween, never got any farther than figuring out which trunks were which, and afterward it all seemed absurd."

"But?"

"But then the museum burned."

"I'm sure there's an explanation," said Jules feebly.

"Give me a for-instance," whispered Jetta.

Jules thought it over. "I'm not opening those trunks for you. Not on the sly. Where was Joseph two nights ago?"

"Whose side are you on?"

"It's a job," said Jules. "I have to think of it as a job. But I'll look into it, and I'll tell you first."

THEY STAYED ANOTHER two hours, something they hadn't done for fifteen years. When they finally left he drove with exaggerated care, and when he saw Caroline's patrol car downtown, a full two blocks away, he reached over and pushed Jetta down under the dashboard.

"What the hell are you *doing*?" she howled.

"It's Caroline," he said, trying to keep the panic out of his voice.

"So what?" said Jetta.

"I don't want her to see us. I don't want her to think I'm protecting my family."

"What's wrong with protecting your family? What's more important, your family or what Caroline thinks of you?" asked Jetta bitterly. But she stayed down. Jules waved to Caroline without slowing; Caroline waved back, startled.

"I'm not sure," said Jules, trying to make it sound like a joke.

Weekends didn't get much worse.

JULES WOKE EARLY Sunday despite his by-now-ingrained hangover, thought of his uncle, and lay staring at his ceiling with a full chest of dread.

At 8:00 a.m. he looked at the computer comparison of the skull and Henry Whitsan's photo again. He tried to tell himself that Henry Whitsan didn't look like a nice person. It still wouldn't make the land story any easier to face.

Jules roused the grumpy clerk and recorder to borrow her key. In a file drawer in the back of the office he found the records concerning the dozen small ranches on the Mission Creek drainage. By 1930 the area was already dominated by three large ranches: Amundsen, Ganter, and Whitsan. By 1940 the die-off among the small ranches had accelerated, with only five clinging to the periphery of the Amundsen and Ganter ranches. The Whitsans had left the map, and their five thousand acres—a mile of the creek and some of the nicest nooks and irrigated land on the drainage—had been divided neatly between two very young ranchers. Joseph Ganter had taken a thousand acres of bottomland and creek, and Nestor Amundsen, who'd had plenty of creek already, had taken four thousand acres of benchland.

Two hours later Jules had photocopied nine separate bills of sale, all with the same flowery signature, "Henry Orien Whitsan," giving away his sisters' Eden with big conscience-less loops, the signatures for "Joseph Clement Ganter" and "Nestor Karl Knut Amundsen" relatively cramped and pithy. Jules compared the signatures to that on Whitsan Senior's last will and testament, written in 1934; he compared the first signature, written on May 20, 1939, with the last, written on July 13 the same year, and he checked with a magnifying glass to see if the ink on the dates matched the ink on the signatures.

So far, so good, or at least as good as a bad thing could be; maybe Henry Whitsan had really pissed his own fortune away, rather than having it taken from him. Joseph couldn't come out of it smelling like a rose, but he probably didn't care anyway.

As an afterthought, Jules flipped through the town records, then turned to the grid on the wall. He wanted lots 420 and 421; after that it took only a moment to learn that Miles Athel Birdland, an orphaned cop in his early twenties, had bought his nifty house on the town's best street in August 1939.

That had apparently been a great year for almost everyone, but Jules had a horrible feeling that it had been very bad indeed for Henry Whitsan.

JONATHAN, CLEAN-LIVING HOPE of America, made it back from North Dakota at four. Jules drove home and started on the remnants of the whiskey and another cleaning binge, this one beginning in his bathroom. He loaded in five CDs at top volume to goose him along and cover the noise of the ringing phone, mostly poor white music for a poor white and the unspeakable base of his very own toilet. An hour later he'd moved on to his kitchen floor and was on his hands and knees, scrubbing and singing along to something truly embarrassing like "One Way Out," when he heard his name bellowed and turned to see Caroline Fair in the doorway, vibrating in sound waves.

"I tried knocking," she screamed.

Jules, crimson, rose creakily from his knees and dropped the sponge as if it were a gun.

Caroline yelled again. "We've got a domestic call and Jonathan's dealing with an accident."

Jules came to his senses and brushed past her to turn the music down. She bent to get the sponge, and the glimpse of a pearly, slender back and waist between her T-shirt and jeans made him suddenly feel like a character in a Victorian novel, a fettered, orgiastic mess.

"Are you okay?" asked Caroline, giving the whiskey bottle a sidelong glance. "I had a couple of glasses of wine with dinner myself, and I know neither of us were on call. The man's already left the house, so this might not be a huge rush—"

"I'm fine," said Jules. "I'd barely gotten started."

Caroline drove anyway. When she parked in front of a familiar blue frame house he sobered up in a big way. "Who called it in?"

Caroline looked down at her scribbled notes. "A lady named Ben Wingate. I think she works at the Baird."

Seeing Jules didn't make Ben happy; she had a warped enough worldview to not be able to put aside vanity even after a beating, which was possibly one of the reasons she and Jules had never gotten along that well outside of a bedroom. Jules made trips to the bathroom sink for cold washcloths while Caroline asked questions, and no one mentioned that he seemed to find his way there without asking directions.

"And then he left," said Ben, holding an ice pack on the side of her face. "After I called. He wouldn't leave the first ten times I asked."

"Do you know where he went?" asked Jules.

"He said he was going home, cool as a cucumber," said Ben.

"Do you want to press charges?"

"Of course I want to press goddamn charges. He broke my nose. But he only hit me once."

"Once is plenty," said Caroline.

"I know that," said Ben. "I mean I didn't give him a chance for a second."

"I don't think your nose is broken," said Caroline, "But we'd be happy to take you to the hospital. Did he bite you, too?"

Jules had been holding a second ice pack to the back of Ben's head, where she'd hit the ground, and pulled back to look.

Ben touched her neck. "Ever seen a hickey?"

"That's a pretty dramatic one," said Caroline.

Ben gave her a stony look. "I guess I don't recall Jules being into them. But I didn't dial nine-one-one about a hickey."

"What's the guy's name?" asked Caroline, not missing a beat.

"Neil Amundsen," said Ben. "I imagine now you won't want to do anything about it."

Jules froze.

"I think you imagine wrong," said Caroline calmly. "Can you tell me where he lives?"

They drove her to the station. "You've been seeing him for a while?" asked Jules.

"I have," said Ben defensively. "I knew he was an asshole, but I didn't have a clue he could lose his temper like this."

"Did you happen to go home with him after that anniversary party a couple of weeks ago?"

She looked at him suspiciously.

"I have a reason for asking," said Jules.

"No," Ben said. "I didn't go to his house. He went home with me."

Caroline, curious, watched the disappointment flicker over Jules's face.

BACK IN THE car, after they dropped Ben at the hospital, Caroline drove fast but still sounded calm. "I don't think you should be on this call."

"I don't think you should, either," he said harshly.

"What's that supposed to mean?" asked Caroline. "You've slept with that woman, right?"

"Yes, I did," said Jules. "Three years ago now, before I went out with Edie. It didn't last long."

"I didn't ask for details," said Caroline.

"Pardon me," said Jules. "Notice that I didn't ask about Neil."

"Ask *what* about Neil?"

"About how you two spent a long afternoon together the day Nestor died."

Caroline gaped. "I didn't go out with him that day," she said, outraged.

"But you went out earlier?"

"Never."

"Lunch that day?"

"Hell no," said Caroline, finally losing her temper. "He's horrible. Why would you think such a thing? Why didn't you just *ask* me?"

"He told me you did," yelled Jules. "Or he at least implied so. Grace thought so, too."

"Did *what*? Why were you even speaking to him?"

"It happens from time to time in the course of the working day," said Jules icily. "We're not talking spare time here. I was questioning him, and you were his alibi."

She looked panicked. "I don't think I've so much as talked to Neil Amundsen outside of the station."

Jules felt great relief, but embarrassment prevented him from expressing this sentiment. So he looked dubious, and Caroline slammed the dashboard with her open hand.

They were quiet for a mile or so. "Well," she said, still pissed off, "now that we've established that neither of us would get in bed with Neil Amundsen, can we agree that you aren't the person who should talk to him tonight?"

"Be my guest," said Jules.

NEIL LIVED IN the valley south of town, along the river. The house was a shabby A-frame but the land was probably worth tens of thousands; no one on a county salary would be able to afford the rent, let alone the purchase price.

Neil opened his door politely, all innocence, and invited them in. He wasn't quite as dapper as usual, but at first he tried to charm Caroline, who did the talking. It didn't work.

"I'll repeat myself," said Caroline. "You're under arrest."

"I think you're joking," said Neil. "Or very stupid."

Jules surveyed the room. The walls were cluttered with big game trophies: bighorn sheep and elk, mountain lion and bear, buffalo, antelope, moose. If it lived in the state and weighed more than fifty pounds it was on the wall. "What is this anyway?"

"My father was quite a hunter," said Neil.

"I see," said Jules. "Do you like to hunt?"

"Very much," Neil answered.

"You intending to hang Ben up here? If you stuffed her fast the bruises might not show up."

"Jules," snapped Caroline. "Please be quiet."

"Okay," said Jules, wandering over to the monolithic fireplace. Neil had a decanter and two glasses and a bowl of nuts on the hearth; it was so cheesy it made Jules's teeth ache.

"Not to be trite," said Caroline, "but are you going to come quietly?"

"Unless you enjoy cuffing people," said Neil, starting for the door.

"Shitsucker," muttered Jules. The mantel was covered by items—pictures of Neil (and no one else) as a child, trophies, a pocket watch inscribed with his graduation date, some fossils, a chunk of obsidian, and something that looked like a short elephant tusk.

"Jules," said Caroline. "We're going."

Jules opened his mouth to speak. Neil was already out the door.

"What?" asked Caroline, exasperated.

"I'm not sure," Jules said. "Never mind."

15 *The Tall Boy*

BLUE DEER BULLETIN
SHERIFF'S REPORT, WEEK OF OCTOBER 31–NOVEMBER 6

October 31—*Numerous incidents occurred Halloween night. Please note the article on the facing page.*

November 1—A possible prowler was reported near the old middle school. An officer investigated.

November 2—A report was received of teenagers throwing gophers at passing cars from the east side overpass. An officer talked to the teenagers.

November 3—Nothing to report.

November 4—A sixteen-year-old girl was reported for using a vehicle without permission. Officers are looking for the girl.

November 5—A concerned citizen reported a yard full of dogs without water or food. An officer found this was the case and took the dogs to the shelter.

November 6—Nothing to report.

WHEN HE GOT HOME THAT NIGHT, JULES, COUNTING on having Monday off, finished the bottle of whiskey, finished cleaning his house, and clung to the image of Neil in a cell.

At 7:00 a.m., when the call came, his eyes were so dry that the simple act of opening seemed to scrape them raw. Jules sat naked on the side of his bed, clutching one hand to the sorest eye, the weight of his hangover gradually sinking in as he listened to the telephone. "You're killing me, Grace."

"Wesley's dealing with a car accident, and Ed's back is still out. Jonathan's sleeping and Harvey's still out of town. And Caroline had to go on a call late last night."

"I have to take a shower," said Jules.

"You'll do what you must, I'm sure," said Grace. "I haven't had quite enough coffee, either."

"What are these people doing up so early?"

"Being jerks, Jules. Why ask me? Aren't you curious about the call Caroline went out on?"

"No," said Jules. "I went with her. Is that piece of shit still downstairs?"

"His mom bailed him out at 4:00 a.m. Now, get hopping. The neighbor who called it in mentioned blows."

WHEN JULES ARRIVED they were all standing in Flo's front yard while Alice's and Peter's puppy bayed from the other side of the street. She did this whenever Alice and Peter argued; according to her owners, she was a very sensitive dog. Jules addressed her first.

"Shut the fuck up, Pearl."

Pearl sat and wagged her tale appreciatively. Flo and Alice and Neil and Peter all stopped making noise as well, and most of the early-rising bystanders took tentative steps back toward their porches. Peter was purple with rage and cold, stalking about in a T-shirt and sweatpants; Alice and Flo were in pajamas (flannel for Alice, something shiny for Flo). Neil was in the clothes he'd had on the night before, but the shirt was covered with blood, and his nose looked like a baby eggplant, one of the fancy new mauve varieties. He'd been sleeping on his mother's couch when an eighty-mile-an-hour gust brought the dog bowl sailing into the living room, bringing down the picture window in sheets of glass. Flo had considered this a deliberate human act; Neil, probably trying to avoid another conversation with the sheriff's department, had acknowledged that it had been an accident but suggested recompense. Several things happened then, in no particular order: Peter had told Neil to do funny things to himself, Neil had called Alice "some sloppy bitch," and Peter had struck Neil. Neil had then tried to strangle Peter, and neighbors had interceded.

"It's my mother's funeral today," screamed Flo. "This shouldn't be happening."

"No one threw a dog bowl through your window," said Jules politely.

"They should have an anchor for that thing," said Neil.

Jules looked down at the aerodynamic marvel—a large, shallow, dimpled metal mixing bowl that resembled a Martian Frisbee. It reminded him of the kind of bowl you'd keep by your bed if you thought you might have to throw up during the night due to stomach flu or possibly a hangover.

"Let's go over this again. What happened to your nose, Neil?"

Neil glared. "What happened to your eye, Jules?"

Jules regarded him for a moment. "I believe I popped a blood vessel, Neil. Should I repeat the question, or should I beat you to death?"

Everyone stared at him. "Sorry," said Jules. "That just slipped out. Who started the physical dimension of this argument?"

IN A TOWN the size of Blue Deer, weddings and funerals began to blur together by your third or fourth decade. The same people usually attended, wearing different-colored clothing but by and large the same expressions. Ruth Birdland's funeral was exceptionally blurry, even though Jules had managed another two hours in bed after the dog bowl incident. He sat ramrod straight in a black suit and a back pew, not ceding the aisle to anyone. His own sense of pickling blended unpleasantly with the mourners' perfumes and the profusion of lilies. His mother Olive, aghast at his lack of color, peered over every sixty seconds and resorted to handing him a piece of gum.

"What did you do to yourself?" she hissed.

"Nothing new," said Jules bleakly.

Olive had probably thought she could stop worrying about wretched excess when her son reached thirty-five and became sheriff. Then again, Jules didn't recall that his father, who'd died as a sheriff at thirty-seven, had been particularly well behaved.

Caroline Fair and Cicely came in just when Jules had determined that the chewing gum might make him ill, and they sat one pew ahead of him. Caroline was wearing a skirt, and the wonder of it nearly finished him off. He was transfixed by the sheer sweep of black stockings, the arch of her foot in a black suede pump, the fine modeling of her knees.

"Jules, try to shut your mouth and look alive," said Olive.

Jules slumped, and the organ music went up a decibel.

The service was Episcopalian rather than Lutheran, but otherwise there wasn't much difference from Nestor's funeral, ten days earlier. The same professional attendees, mostly businessmen and dour spouses; the same noteworthy absences. Ruth Birdland had been too sick to make Nestor's funeral, but Flo had been there, and Nina Amundsen was here, now, for Ruth's; Laura Ganter had come to both. Joseph had gone to neither, and Miles Birdland had been nowhere in sight for Nestor. Neil, who'd lost two grand-parents in two weeks, hadn't publicly mustered a tear for either.

Outside, Jules shook the judge's limp hand, took secret pleasure in Neil's nose, and talked to the dozens of people he saw once or twice a year at such events. Everyone who worked in the county building attended, and every one of them commented on Jules's blood-red eye and general air of decrepitude. Axel Scotti, who wasn't blind, gave him a hearty slap on the back, and Jules could feel the prosecutor's mixed feelings radiate through his nervous system.

"You look like you need a nap," said Axel.

"Huh," said Jules noncommittally. He hated it when Axel tried to act as if nothing had happened. Caroline was ten feet away with her back turned, tapping her high heels to keep warm. Jules was a sucker for high heels. He lifted his eyes hurriedly when she started to turn, and discovered that Merle Ott was watching him intently. Merle turned to look at Birdland, willing Jules to do the same, and Jules saw Joseph come up to the judge, touch him tentatively on the shoulder, whisper in his ear, and very gently hug him.

Jules turned back and Merle was gone; turned again and Joseph was walking away. Miles Birdland had tears running down his face, but Flo was watching Joseph leave with a look of absolute hatred.

"You sticking to short syllables today?" asked Scotti.

Jules nodded.

"Were you the person who got my wife drunk Saturday night, or should I be worried?"

Jules watched Caroline help Cicely down the church steps. "I'd be worried no matter what."

"Screw you," said Scotti. "I hear you harassed my deputy last night, and I hear you were a little partisan this morning during a dispute over a broken window."

"You know what Ben's face usually looks like," said Jules. "She's probably working lunch at the Baird. Why don't you check her out?"

"That's not how I heard the story."

"The asshole hit her and she called it in. The asshole has a rep for doing things like that. She's pressing charges."

"Nope," said Scotti. "She dropped them an hour ago."

It made Jules twitch. "Jesus Christ," he said. "How can you support that little puke?" They glared at each other, and the other mourners clustered on the far side of the steps, unable to hear the conversation but gathering its gist. "Do people like you stick together?" hissed Jules.

This was a low blow, an old shot: Scotti, drunk, had hit Jetta after their first Thanksgiving together at the Ganters', back when Jules had been a senior in high school. Jetta had called home; Joseph had dragged Jules along for the trip to town, and Jules had watched, dizzy from feast wine, as the older man had beaten the younger one to a pulp, breaking Scotti's nose and two ribs, turning his balls into melons, explaining all the while that the large ought never to prey upon the small. Jules had had the unenviable job of taking his new in-law to the hospital. They didn't talk about it often.

Jules walked back to the station alone.

JETTA CALLED AN hour later. He'd researched the deeds, Jules told her, and it looked like nothing; nothing, certainly,

worth killing someone for. If the Whitsans told him differ-
ently, he'd let her know.

He could tell Jetta was relieved, but she didn't say thank-
you. Which made him behave badly toward the end of the
conversation, when she wanted an absolute assurance. "I'm
not saying he didn't kill the man. I'm just saying I haven't
found a reason for him to do it, and I haven't found proof the
man is dead."

"What's wrong with you?" she asked. "I think you wanted
to find something."

"I thought you asked me to check because I loved him,"
said Jules snidely.

"Well," said Jetta, "you should love him, but who knows
if you actually do?"

Jules spent the next half hour reading Monday's paper,
studiously ignoring the ringing phone until Grace actually
yelled his name. He looked up to see her point and nod,
which meant it wouldn't be an animal complaint or the
newspaper.

It was the arson man. "You've got a pretty average problem in that building, with one or two weirdnesses."

Jules made a face into the phone. "Fill me in."

"It looked like an old-fashioned school experiment, basic
as they come. Guy used a bit of everything to get the utility room going—turpentine, old paint, furniture polish and
solvents he probably found right on the shelves. Soaked the
wick, set the old punch time clock and loaded it with graph-
ite, and put what looks like an old horsehair chair above the
can of turpentine the wick led to, and *wallaah*."

Caroline was on the phone, too, a few feet away, smiling and stretched out in her chair with one delicate black-
stockinged ankle crossed over the other. The image caused

an assortment of sensations, all of them too much for Jules's weakened body and soul. He tried to shake off an acute and specific fantasy and broke into another sweat.

"Voilà," he said weakly. How on earth was he to continue working under such conditions?

"Now, I did find some rags, too, just in a heap by the chair. Looked like the painters were being sloppy, but that didn't make sense because they'd left most of their stuff at the other end of the building. And when I pulled apart what was left of the rags they were tied together, and damned if I don't think they ran right up into the room above. And up there I found more of the stuff they were dipped in everywhere."

"We should have noticed that," said Jules.

"Would have, but it was regular furniture polish—Sunkote, to be exact. I found two empty cans behind a trunk upstairs, thought at first someone had just been trying to spiff up all that old wood. Then I found the stuff on the ceiling, and upstairs on the floor above, just soaked into some of the chests and crates in that room with the funny pictures on the wall. He was definitely trying to lead the fire up."

"Any specific crates?" asked Jules.

"I didn't check everything," said the man testily. "Seemed pretty random. The guy was pretty careful with prints."

"None at all?"

"Old ones, and almost all of them were dusty under the ash or half smeared. He wore gloves."

Jules, with Flo weighing heavily on his mind, was annoyed by the "he." "Something got you convinced it's a man?"

"Most of them are. Though the place is filled with long white and gray hair."

Jules explained about the building's current tenants. "This just seems incredibly stupid and complicated."

"Well, if it hadn't been for the windows being open, and the wall being down, and the night being so goddamn windy, it would have worked just fine. The whole building would have gone. Though it's possible the person was trying to localize damage. But I'll tell you what *was* incredibly stupid."

"What?" asked Jules.

"I think the guy set up the timer, went through all that trouble to have the thing start on its own, and then waited around to watch. I think he managed to burn himself, maybe because the wind made the fire unpredictable. I found a few strands of hair and a real small piece of light blue cotton, might have been a work shirt hem."

"What color was the hair?" asked Jules. He had a reddish blonde and a brunette in mind, Flo and her son; he felt he was about to become a happy man. Maybe Flo wasn't so scared of fire after all.

"White," said the expert. "You got an old one on your hands."

Jules wondered whether anyone would ever again tell him something he wanted to hear.

"Now, the Suburban you showed me, that was really interesting," said the man. "I've got to thank you for that. Sorry I was cranky at the time."

"That's okay," said Jules, his pen poised. "What's so interesting?"

"The person who lit that one was almost completely inept, a real idiot. Most people get in there, really toss something like gasoline around, but this person barely got the job done."

Jules perked up. This was more like it.

"Now, I should have gotten the autopsy from you after I checked the car out. Was there any lag time?"

"Lag?"

"Between death and burning?"

"Maybe," said Jules cautiously. "It was hard to tell, given the damage, but this is exactly what I was hoping you could tell me. I could fax you a copy of the report."

"Doesn't really matter," said the guy. "The point is there was some delay, according to what I saw, between the fire being set and taking hold. It could have smoldered for hours before it kicked in. The car was new, with a good seal, and it might have acted like a sealed room: lots of heat, oxygen gets depleted, you have one of your extra-strong local breezes and then *boom*. Not quite spontaneous combustion, but close."

Jules tried to imagine the scene in the gully, the car looking innocent enough but so hot it ticked under the swooping wind.

"Guy tossed gasoline on the back of the vehicle and closed the door, but got barely any inside, and must have taken off without making sure it worked."

"How many hours?" asked Jules.

"I don't know."

"Roughly."

"More than one, anyway. The flare-up would have only taken a half hour or so. Was the car cold when you got there?"

"Not quite," said Jules. "It was still steaming."

"You probably came on the scene at least an hour later, probably more like two or three."

"Any chance the same person started both fires?" asked Jules in a moment of wild hope.

"I doubt it. Sorry. I mean, neither was necessarily a pro. Just because people start fires, it doesn't mean they know how. Sometimes they think it out, sometimes they muddle through."

"The Suburban was a muddle?"

"Yep."

"And the museum was thought out?"

"More or less. Maybe too thought out for its own good."

The phone rang again immediately. Jules wrinkled his nose and picked it up.

The voice sounded Irish, male, and elderly. "I'm calling about that body you found on the island a few weeks ago."

"Two weeks ago," said Jules defensively.

"You identify the boy yet?"

"No. We've been narrowing it down."

"I think maybe you narrowed too far," said the man.

"You called before," said Jules suddenly. "You're the one who wanted me to think about the body being tall."

Silence and the sense the man on the other end was waiting. "Well, think of what it means. What kind of game does a boy play when he's tall?"

"I know that already," said Jules testily. "Every single idiot who ever played for Blue Deer's been accounted for."

"I believe you've been led astray," said the voice, sliding into a bad Scottish accent.

Jules thought of the scene on the church steps, the clutch of skinny, tall old men. "What do you really know, Merle?"

Click. Jules took off his tie, put his feet on his desk, and shut his eyes. He stayed like that until Caroline finished her conversation.

"Caroline."

"Yes?" She didn't look at him, and her voice was polite but cold.

"I've got to talk to you about a few things."

"Okay," she said with exaggerated patience.

"We'll do a couple of errands and then have lunch," said Jules.

"I'm not very hungry," said Caroline. "But thank you anyway."

"You can watch me eat then, and I'll talk between bites," said Jules, starting for the door. "Because I'm obviously near death, and even if you think I'm pond scum I hope you don't actually want me to die."

Caroline reddened. "I don't think you're pond scum."

"Well," said Jules, "that's a start."

CARL JUMP, WHO was having equipment problems, didn't seem any happier than Jules. "I do not have the goddamn proof sheets," he said. He was on his knees near some complicated metal while Serena slept peacefully in a corner. "And I can't develop another set for you until the repairman comes. Did you ask Mrs. Amundsen?"

"We just came from her mother's funeral," said Jules. "I'll have to ask later."

"Couldn't happen to a nicer family," snarled Jump. "Maybe I'll ask myself."

Jules tripped just outside the door, and Caroline took the keys from him. "You do need lunch," she said, parking next in the alley behind the Baird. "And maybe some hair of the dog."

She climbed out, and once again her legs threatened to bring him to tears. She looked back inside the car and caught him staring. "Come on," she said. "I'm sorry I said I wasn't hungry. You can have a big fat sandwich and some fries and a Bloody Mary and tell me whatever it is you want to tell me."

It wasn't that he wouldn't have told the others, but he might not have given the whole story so cleanly. Ed or Harvey would have preconceptions about people they'd known for a lifetime, just as Jules probably still did; Jonathan was too dense to be dented by any of it, Wesley too professional to have patience with such a Gothic account.

Jules told Caroline about the arson expert's news, and the newest anonymous call, and the land acquisitions of 1939. He told her for the first time about Joseph's variable driving abilities. And he told her what he thought he'd seen in Neil Amundsen's house.

Caroline ordered a huge sandwich and watched him critically while he dithered over the menu options. "So what's the big deal with the proof sheets?" she asked.

"Jump said Neil Amundsen was with Ben Wingate the night of the party, making trips to the basement."

"What's in the basement?"

Jules was foggy that day, but he wasn't going to be tricked into saying "A couch, very comfortable, with a convenient wine rack, where I've been with the same woman and other sundry Baird staff."

"I don't know. A laundry pile? We can look while we're here. I wanted to see the proofs to find a shot of him walking out the door to kill his grandfather."

"It doesn't seem like the pictures really matter anymore," said Caroline. "Flo probably didn't want anyone to see Ben fiddling with Neil and burned the lot. Are you trying too hard to make him fit Nestor?"

She'd given *fiddling* a touch of humorous emphasis, flaring her upper lip for the f. "I'm trying not to smash him in without benefit of evidence," said Jules morosely, trying to leave his imagination dormant.

"You can't just ask to go back in and poke around his house. And it's unlikely he'd invite you for a friendly visit."

"He might invite you," said Jules.

"Forget it," said Caroline. "This is only a job." Her sandwich arrived, and she added tomato and pickle and mustard with elaborate care. "So why did you care what Neil did after the party?"

"The rapes," Jules said simply, watching her try to insert the sandwich into her mouth. Most of his hamburger was already gone.

"Oh, come on," said Caroline, muttering into her napkin. "He can't be that far gone."

"He had a reputation for being rough before this," said Jules. "He came back to town at about the right time, and the research I've done either leaves him open or with bad alibis, like the one Ben's given him for Nestor."

"She doesn't have much of a reason to keep giving him one now, does she?"

"No," said Jules. "But the other thing is that three of the six women have had dealings with the county attorney's office since last spring, and another lives a block away from Flo. The fifth woman had a brother who's a cop in Missoula, and Missoula is where Neil went to law school."

"It's still circumstantial," said Caroline. "What else?"

"He's the right blood type," said Jules. "O positive."

"I don't want to ask how you got that," said Caroline. "Is there more?"

"A real cheap shot," said Jules.

"Go for it."

"The profile calls for the bad mother cliche. And most of the women look like Flo."

Caroline put down the rest of her sandwich. "Eww," she said, searching for another napkin.

"So you have a few things going here," she said, draining her beer. "You're worried that your uncle Joseph burned down the museum, you're worried that your uncle Joseph might have killed a man for his land, and you're hoping Neil Amundsen is either a serial rapist or murdered his grandfather."

"Right," said Jules bleakly. He was beginning to slump in the booth.

"This is as opposed to your uncle Joseph having murdered Neil's grandfather. You kinda want Neil to be your everything."

"In a perfect world."

"He was at that party when the car went up."

"Maybe his mother helped."

"She was at the party, too," Caroline pointed out. "And everyone got there late, not necessarily just Neil and Flo."

"Anyone could have lit that fire if it didn't kick in right away. My whole fucking family," said Jules quietly, turning away to stare out the window.

"It would be nice if you could know your uncle wasn't a murderer."

"Yes," said Jules. "It would."

"It might make me like my grandmother more, too," said Caroline.

Jules turned from the window to find her six inches away, leaning over his plate. She gave him a soft smile.

Jules lurched backward.

"I just wanted your last fries," said Caroline. "You sure you're okay? You act like you strained your neck, and your eye looks redder and redder."

THAT NIGHT HE was due for dinner at Peter and Alice's, and Alice called before he left and asked him to pick up Peter at the Baird; it seemed that it was the county bar association's biannual cocktail hour get-together, and Peter might need scooping up. The shindig had started three hours earlier, at four. It seemed like a bizarre way to start the work week.

When Jules walked into the Baird he found Scotti and Peter and Neil in a single booth, all of them actually getting along, if only because they could barely talk.

"Buy me a drink," said Scotti.

Neil was listing to one side, serene; Peter was suspiciously bright-eyed.

"Sit down," said Scotti. "Now I hear you've gone and questioned the judge."

"Was he upset about it?" asked Jules. Peter was alert enough to slide over and roll his eyes in a warning sort of fashion.

"No," said Axel. "But I am."

"Well, shit," said Jules. "That's a shame."

"Jules thinks one of your grandfathers killed the other one," said Scotti to Neil. "Or maybe that my father-in-law killed your grandfather. Any minute now I expect him to nominate his own mother."

"They all hated each other," said Neil happily, his voice thick. "I wouldn't put it past any of them."

"I don't think that at all," said Jules. "I think Neil killed that old man."

Neil, who was faster than Jules would ever have given him credit for, shot over the table from the far corner of the booth and grabbed Jules around the throat. They hit the floor, with Scotti and Peter trying to pull Neil off by the shoulder and forelock. Jules, sure his larynx was being crushed, brought his knee up hard.

"Jesus," said Scotti, after he led Neil to the bathroom.

"You wanted dissension, you got it," said Jules. He herded Peter out the door. They looked at each other for a long moment over the car hood.

"This is usually a really boring get-together," said Peter.

"Glad I could help."

"I'm glad I'm a defense attorney," said Peter. "You know what that shit Neil did this afternoon?"

"What?"

"Had Jonathan out there looking to arrest Carl Jump."

"Now what?" asked Jules.

"He took the dog again."

Jules didn't intend to tell anyone he'd seen the happy pair. "Tell Carl it's not worth getting into trouble over."

"I've tried," said Peter. "But I'm afraid he's going to scoot."

They found Caroline and Alice with a wine bottle and stacks of books on the lamp-lit table. Caroline actually glowed in Jules's direction, smiling and flushed with wine, which tricked him into looking directly at her.

"Look what we've found," she said. "Just look."

Jules held his ground by the door. She came toward him holding a photograph and pointed to the image of a man's groin, which worsened his sense of being hooked to a low-voltage electric collar. But when he took in the headline—WINNING TEAM—he looked down to the caption and up into the face of young Nestor Amundsen and the first good likeness he'd seen of Henry Orien Whitsan, whose gold teeth didn't show despite a wide and handsome smile, who was tall and blond and wore a belt buckle shaped like a horse's head, shinier than the one centered on Nestor's boyish hips.

Jules took the paper from Caroline's hand. "Well," he said.

"Blue Deer roping champs, July 5, 1938," said Caroline. "Is that what Nestor's missing belt looked like?"

Jules was staring at Henry Whitsan. The face was so close to what he'd imagined from the skull it almost seemed familiar.

"Did anyone actually say they'd seen him get on that train?" asked Alice.

"I went through my notes," said Caroline cautiously.

"I went through your notes, too," said Jules. He turned to Alice. "Only my uncle. Only Joseph."

16 *Picture This*

WHEN JULES WALKED INTO THE STATION TUESDAY morning, Amber Jump was waiting for him. "Now what are you going to do?" she asked.

Jules dialed the photo shop and got a machine, then tried the number for Jump's apartment above the store. "Your dispatcher says an officer has already checked there this morning," said Mrs. Jump. "You'll have to do better than that."

"You know," said Jules. "This is ugly and stupid, but it isn't necessarily criminal. It belongs in civil court."

"You've got something better to do with your time?"

"Yes, I do. How many times has this happened now?"

"We were fine until we moved here."

"How long have you been divorced?"

"Nine years, since Serena was one. Carl came here last spring, and I put my house up for sale the day I found out."

Serena would make it another five years, easy, unless the competitive feeding killed her. Jules managed to not sound sarcastic. "You followed him to Blue Deer because of Serena?"

"Of course," said Amber Jump.

Her eyes filled with tears; Jules handed her a tissue. "He won't take off with her," he said. "They've probably just gone hunting."

"You know Carl?"

"A bit," said Jules.

"You think he's a nice guy?"

"Seems to be."

"That's kind of the heart of the matter, isn't it?"

Jules worked on the incident report. "Has he abused Serena in any way?"

"No." Her eyes glittered. "He's nice to animals."

WHEN SHE FINALLY left, he caught Caroline and Grace eating Danish and chortling over one of Jonathan's DUI videos from the night before: a man had claimed he simply didn't know the alphabet and so couldn't recite it. Jonathan had asked the man to walk a straight line, and the man had said he couldn't, and Jonathan had insisted, and the man had fallen on his face and broken his nose.

Jules watched glumly from the doorway, anticipating a lawsuit. Caroline turned and smiled and waved. He waved back.

"How are you?" asked Caroline.

The question was clearly not as innocuous as usual. "I'm a new man," said Jules. "Or a new something. You try the Whitsans?"

"Indie and Ettie are with Venus in Helena until later this morning, according to Cicely. But I got a new photo from the high school. He's straight at the camera in this one."

Jules scanned the new photo and duplicated the angle in a fresh Polaroid of the skull. It matched—the same sharp cheekbones, the same spacing for the eyes, the same smooth, high forehead before the centered bullet hole. For an absolute identification he'd have to send the skull and all the bones north again to the Missoula lab, but this was good enough to go on.

Caroline was typing up a report, and he allowed himself the pleasure of staring at her neck while she finished a sentence. "What else you got on this guy?" he asked.

She reached under her chair for a file. Caroline's desk was possibly messier than his own. "I flagged all four high school years of yearbooks and got a few rodeo clips at the library this morning."

He paged through the brittle original newspapers. "You just paged through?"

"The guy's pretty easy to pick out from a crowd," said Caroline.

"I thought you didn't like blonds."

Caroline stared at him. "I don't," she said.

Jules retreated.

In a 1937 photo from a fancy quarterhorse cutting, he recognized Joseph with a start and panned the other two dozen tiny faces, all neatly marked with numerals to correspond with the alphabetized names in the margin. There was Birdland sitting on a fence, and Nestor with his arm around a skinny girl in a bob, identified as Ruth Greer. Ettie had been gorgeous, the feminine equivalent of her brother. Indie, plump and grinning, was on Merle Ott's lap.

Jules squinted. Henry O. Whitsan and Joseph flanked the group in identical poses, both of them lanky and bowlegged, but Whitsan was an inch or two taller, probably six-two, and his right ankle was in a cast. Maybe he'd gotten the skull fracture at the same time.

Jules looked again at the smiling, arrogant face and followed the dead eyes across the photo to an ethereal blond girl perched next to Nestor on a rail. "N. Nissen," soon to be Nina Amundsen. He drummed his fingers on the photo for a moment and sorted through the rest. In another group shot, some sort of picnic out at Mission Creek in what looked like midsummer, Nestor and Nina were at center; it was probably their engagement party, and virtually everyone was familiar: Miles Birdland's future wife, Ruth, leaning back against Henry Whitsan's shoulder more than fifty years before she'd offer flowers to his memory; Birdland himself, thin and shy, with dark sleek hair and smiling eyes. Jules could recognize the face, but the soul had been gutted. Joseph was handsome and sharp-planed, with an expression that said he certainly knew this. Nestor was a milk-fed son of Norway, beaming out at the world without curiosity.

Jules straightened the crumpled, brittle top of the paper and peered at the date. The ranch had been entirely signed away by early July, but there was Henry Whitsan, smiling for the cameras on July 20, 1939, still friends with the men who owned his land.

A CLOSED SIGN hung on Carl Jump's door; a smaller note told them he was in Yellowstone with a class until Friday. Jonathan had left his own illiterate message, letting the photographer know he was wanted by the law. Jules kicked the door while Caroline nervously watched cars go by.

They found the Whitsan girls in their backyard, out of earshot of their telephone; in truth, anything more than five feet from their phone was likely out of earshot. They were struggling with their storm windows, and Jules installed five in record time while Caroline crawled around in the grass picking up glass from number six.

"Our brother Henry most definitely left town," said Indie as she gave them water inside. "It's difficult for us to discuss even now."

"Why?" asked Jules.

"Why what?" asked Indie.

"Why did he leave and why is it difficult?" asked Caroline, a little snappish as she picked tiny shards from her palm.

"Henry was not a good person," said Indie.

"I'd like you to be more specific, please," said Jules.

Indie wrinkled her nose and drummed her fingers on a side table. She looked done in, and she had a bandaged arm, probably from the window Caroline had helped pick up. "Our brother lost all our money and our land and we had to leave this place."

Ettie broke in. "Oh, he did, he did. He was bad, was Henry."

Indie gestured to the window: gold aspens, a quiet street, mountains floating above small houses. "Though Seattle was wonderful, our departure was quite traumatic. We'd hoped for more from life. Therefore we do not enjoy talking about Henry."

"Where did he head and when did he leave? I can't remember." Caroline hadn't wanted to approach them this way, mislead them about the purpose of the visit, but now she was doing as he'd asked.

Indie shrugged, an ungeriatric gesture, and drummed her fingers on the table again. "New York," she said bitterly. "The summer of 1939."

Caroline pressed on. "Did he write?"

"Let me make it clear," said Indie. "We never heard from him again, which was fine because we never wanted to hear from him again. Would you write if you lost eight sections and about forty thousand dollars in prewar savings? If I saw him now, I'd still slap his pretty face."

"How old was he that summer?"

Ettie shut her eyes to concentrate, like a little kid. "Twenty-one."

"How exactly did he lose everything?" asked Jules.

"Why do you want to talk about this?" asked Indie. "You think he's the man out on the island, don't you?"

Jules opened a satchel. "Do you recognize any of these items?"

Indie didn't actually look at them. "No. Not that I'd recognize a thing so many years later."

"You wouldn't recognize a gold belt buckle?"

Ettie, peering fearfully at her sister, edged closer and closer. "Maybe you should look more carefully, Indabel. The buckle does look familiar, and that wallet's just like the one Daddy gave Henry for high school graduation."

Indie narrowed her eyes at her sister.

"Had he broken his ankle or his skull at any point?" asked Caroline. "Did he have gold teeth?"

Ettie nodded her head vigorously.

Jules asked a second time. "How did he lose everything?"

Indie sighed and looked at a point above his head. "Bad investments, the high life while he was away at Rutgers, gambling. He played cards, drunk, and lost what was left of the ranch and the house. Poker, over the course of that last summer."

"Did he play with a regular group?" asked Caroline.

Indie wrinkled her nose. "He'd been forced to leave school that spring after all sorts of trouble, and he was drinking like a fish. I believe in the beginning, when he tried to put up too much money, or the acreage, his friends let it go and tried to fix things for him with the other players. But he was simply on a run. If you'd known Henry, how objectionable he could be, you wouldn't blame the boys he was playing."

Ettie smiled gently. "Joseph especially did what he could to help Indie and me after Henry waltzed away from the mess."

This was the moment he'd been dreading. Jules sat still, his pulse thudding in his ears, feeling Caroline's eyes on him. "Who were the men he lost the property to?" he asked.

"Joseph Ganter and Nestor Amundsen. I believe the regular fourth was Miles Birdland, though he was just a police officer then and had no interest in ranching. Believe it or not, they all used to spend time with a bastard like Henry."

Ettie blushed at the word her sister had used, rather than the sentiment. "It was just one of those things," she said.

Jules chose his words carefully. "I have heard that Joseph took him to the train."

Ettie nodded. "Yes, he did."

"Actually," said Indie, "I think it was all three of them. I think they knew it was going to take all three of them to get Henry onto the thing. He'd been on a binge."

"But there he is on the island, and neither of you seems surprised." Nor did they seem heartbroken.

"I would have been surprised if he'd made it out of this town alive," said Indie with a glimmer of a smile. "I'm sorry if we've misled you at all, but we didn't know for sure and thought it best to not volunteer information. Obviously Miles and Joseph and Nestor didn't stay to see if he really got on, or possibly, being Henry, he got off again to spite them. He wasn't particularly happy to be run out of town."

"If you guessed he was out there, I imagine you might know who put him there," said Caroline.

"Imagine away," said Indie.

Caroline raised an eyebrow. Indie smiled.

"You have to do a lot to be run out of a town like this," said Jules. "There has to be a final straw. What did Henry do?"

"A lot," said Indie.

Ettie looked apologetic but wouldn't add a thing.

"What did Ettie teach?" he asked as they walked to the car.

"English," said Caroline.

"And Indie?"

"Science," said Caroline. "She was a chemistry teacher."

THAT WEEK'S POKER game was scheduled for eight at Merle's house. Patrick Ankeny had called in sick, and the players were Jules, Axel, Joseph, Peter, Merle, Divvy, and, of all people, Miles Birdland. Axel, who'd been smug about Jules's hangover the day before, now had to play on one himself. Jules stuck to water, which made everyone stare.

Jules waited until the third hand. "Let's keep this on the q.t. until it's confirmed," he said, "but I think we've finally pegged that body."

Scotti jumped as if a cattle prod had been taken to his genitalia. "This is recreational time," he hissed. "Why are you telling me something like this now?"

"You were out all afternoon, Axel," said Jules. "Some seminar. Jetta didn't know where to find you."

"Who?" asked Divvy, wide-eyed and as stoned as a monkey.

"Old neighbor of Joseph's named Henry Whitsan."

"No shit?" said Merle.

Jules shot him a dirty look.

"Ettie and Indie's dad?" asked Scotti.

"Brother."

Axel glared at him. "Jesus. The fucker's been under your nose all this time? Why the hell did this take you so long?"

"We were told he'd left town, that someone had actually put him on a train."

Axel lit a cigar. "See, this is the problem with you. You believe everybody, and you get screwed, and you waste time. Who the hell told you this?"

"About Whitsan leaving town? The person didn't actually tell me," said Jules. "He told people at the time, so I suppose all of this is hearsay."

"Who?"

Jules started to deal. "Joseph."

Axel opened and shut his mouth, then put his head down on the table.

"Miles and I and Nestor saw him pack," said Joseph quietly. "I drove him to the station. I didn't wait to see him climb aboard."

"But somehow Merle knew who was buried on the island. He actually called me, used a lot of funny voices." Jules didn't care if he was destroying a sixty-year-old friendship.

"It was a rumor," blurted Merle. "A very old rumor. And no one knows the full story."

"Oh, bullshit," snapped Joseph. "There is no full story. He was out of money. He was a drunk who'd pissed the whole town off. Even his sisters wanted to see his ass shrink in the distance."

"I didn't say he wasn't a prick," said Merle defensively. "He was a prick and a murderer, the way I heard it. Killed a guy when he was drunk."

Joseph was quiet; Miles Birdland was so agitated that he scooped up all the cards on the table before they could play the hand. "Who'd he kill?" asked Jules.

It seemed like a reasonable question, easier than the big one of who'd killed Whitsan, but it annoyed Merle. "How the hell should I know after all these years? I was mostly trying to keep my cows alive and wondering why I didn't stay out east with the money and the pretty girls. It was just a whisper, but most whispers are true. Henry was an asshole. No one liked him."

"Then why did you all play cards with him?"

There was a long silence. "You know," said Scotti, "I remember when we held these games to relax. This isn't relaxing."

"We weren't the only men he gambled with," said Joseph. "There were big games back then at the Bucket and the Mint."

"Who played in them?"

Joseph shrugged. "Traveling men. We didn't know the high rollers. We were just kids."

"Kids who played with ranches."

Silence again. Jules sipped his drink. "I've seen the goddamn deeds, and I've talked to Ettie and Indie. You got land, Nestor got land, the judge here maybe got some money for a down payment on a house, law school tuition." He looked at Birdland and Joseph. "Is that right?"

Birdland stared fixedly at the table, rubbing the edges of his cards into his forehead.

Joseph began to lose his temper. "You're missing the point. Henry was an evil fool, and somebody was going to take everything away from him sooner or later. Did Indie or Ettie say we'd treated them unfairly?"

"Not at all," said Jules, hating him.

"He'd made bad investments in a racetrack in Great Falls, in the stock market, lost high-rolling games with men who wanted to kill him. After a year of covering him we started giving him cash to bail him out and he'd give us land in trade—or in Miles's case, help him out with legal jams."

Miles Birdland bolted what was left of his drink.

"He just wouldn't stop," said Joseph. "And when it was all gone, he was gone."

"Is that illegal?" asked Scotti stridently. "Trading goods for services?"

"Not at all," said Jules, suddenly tired. "But it's the sort of thing I like to know about when two of the men involved die violently. Unless someone at this table wants to swear up and down that Nestor Amundsen's death is completely unrelated to Henry Whitsan's body being found."

Nobody said a word.

"Why don't you start the bidding, Jules," said Joseph.

THE PHONE RANG ten minutes after he walked through his door, Wesley wanting company for a domestic disturbance. "I think you need to be on this one," said Wesley. "It's Neil Amundsen again, and I don't want to be the one to screw up."

Most of the lights in the house were out. Neil took forever to answer his door, and when he did he was flushed and in a bathrobe, with a similarly attired blond girl hovering at his elbow. Jules, mesmerized by the play of emotions crossing Neil's face, let Wesley do most of the talking.

"What?!" screamed Neil. "Pigfuckers! Get off my property."

"I didn't *call*," said the girl for the third time, more to her lover than to Jules and Wesley.

"Aren't you going to invite me in?" asked Jules, looking longingly past the blonde.

"No," said Neil. "I'm going to file charges for harassment."

"The call came in. The call's on tape."

"Well, check the goddamn number, because it wasn't me or mine."

On the way out, blinded as they turned away from the bright doorway, Wesley and Jules nearly tripped over a trash can in the driveway.

"That's one way of making sure you don't forget garbage day," said Wesley.

Jules kept walking, then slowed, turned, and pointed his own flashlight at the old one sitting neatly on the inverted garbage can lid.

"You don't happen to see anything obvious on it, like blood, do you?"

"No," said Wesley in a stunned voice.

"We can't touch it," said Jules.

"No," said Wesley. "But we sure can stare at it."

Jules rubbed his head. Wesley scribbled down a rough description. "Are you going to talk to him about it?"

If Neil was the rapist, knowing they'd seen the flashlight meant he might destroy other evidence. But if Neil was the rapist, even such a stupid rapist as to leave a grisly tool on top of a garbage can, then perhaps Jules's acknowledging he'd seen it would keep Neil scared and quiet, and at least postpone another attack.

He walked back to the door, listened for a moment to the sound of angry voices, and knocked. The door crashed open and Neil loomed out, apoplectic.

"Are you getting rid of that flashlight?" asked Jules, shining his own onto the trash can. "Because if you are, I could use it. Flashlights like that never die."

"What the fuck are you talking about?"

Jules stared at him. Neil flapped his arms. "What are you doing, talking about flashlights at this hour of the night?

And why is my trash in the middle of the driveway? What are you doing to my trash?"

It made them sad, but as Jules and Wesley drove away they admitted Neil Amundsen had seemed surprised by their questions, the location of his garbage, and the dogged way Jules kept discussing flashlights. Neil didn't want to talk about where he'd been on July 2, August 18, October 16, October 21, October 27, or November 1, and the third time he refused to discuss his location on the dates of the rapes, he'd picked up the flashlight in a rage and hurled it through the night air. They heard it clatter on river rocks, but Jules, holding his breath, could make out no splash.

The riverbank was public land; maybe it was a good thing Neil had thrown the thing, assuming they could find it in daylight. When they looked up the call it proved not to have come from Neil's house but from a pay phone at the twenty-four-hour supermarket, and the dispatcher thought it had come from a man, not a woman.

At dawn, Jules crawled around for an hour on the riverbank, breaking the razor-sharp puddles of ice between the rocks with his knees. Neil came out to the deck and screamed down threats of lawsuits, but Jules was careful to stick to the public right-of-way, and eventually found the flashlight in a willow thicket.

After he handed it over to Harvey, drank a pot of coffee, and changed his pants, he decided to hurl the proverbial shit into the fan.

Caroline walked by trailing a printout and humming.

"Are you working on anything pressing?"

"Not really," she said. "That Clyde City shoplifter."

"I have to go make myself unpopular with several people," said Jules. "Maybe you could keep me in line."

THEY VISITED FLO at her office in the clinic, walking in just as she was ushering out a chastened-looking middle-aged man. Flo was in a flirtatious mood. "Alcoholic," she said, tilting her head toward the door the man had exited through. "And men like that wonder why they have trouble functioning."

Jules and Caroline stared. So much for confidentiality, thought Jules.

At least she was in a good mood. She'd spent the morning of the day Nestor died seeing patients—she wasn't even offended when Caroline took their names—and from lunch until three or so had helped Jetta at the Baird. Then she'd headed to her parents' house to relieve the hospice worker who'd been with her mother. At five thirty, when her father arrived, she'd headed home to change into her party dress.

"Did anyone happen to come by while you were at your mother's?" asked Jules.

"No," said Flo. "Most people know enough not to drop in."

"HOW'D SHE SEEM?" asked Jetta. She was sorting dozens of white gym socks.

"Remarkably sunny," said Jules. "Without somehow being any nicer."

"She went on antidepressants," said Jetta. "It's made my life fifty percent easier. Now, if I could just hook Axel up, get him a Prozac salt lick or something. Are you two ever going to get back to normal?"

Caroline looked curious, but nobody wanted to enlighten her. "I don't know," said Jules. "So what were you up to that day?"

"The party," she said. "All goddamn day until I left to fetch Dad. Who hasn't said thank you."

"Flo helped out?"

"In the early afternoon."

"Why'd she leave?"

"I think she got a call. It was time to help with her mom."

Jetta finished the socks and started on underpants. Two teenage sons and a husband made for quite a pile of briefs. Jules hoped she'd run away soon. "What was Joseph doing when you got to the ranch?"

"Getting dressed after a shower."

"What had he been doing?"

"He said something about getting things out of his system. I think he'd walked the dogs."

"He told me he'd been burning garbage in the gully."

"Whatever," said Jetta.

"Had he been burning garbage?" asked Caroline as they left.

"No," said Jules. "At least, I never found the place."

NEIL WAS IN court, and Scotti was on the phone. Caroline read the bad jokes on the bulletin board while Jules flipped through Neil's appointment calendar. He had a trip to Missoula down for the weekend of Mary McLinchey's rape, though he would have driven back by late that Sunday night for the 8:15 court date penciled in for Monday. Neil hadn't bothered to enter dates with women, so who knew what alibis he might claim after midnight.

Caroline turned to see what he was doing. "Jules!"

He shrugged. They waited five more minutes. "You sure you want to be around for this one?" asked Jules.

"You haven't exactly been ripping throats out," said Caroline, stretching in a chair. "I'd just as soon hear what the creep has to say."

Neil had obviously decided on a policy of calm, as if he and Jules hadn't seen each other on the last three successive nights, as if he hadn't hurled obscenities and threats from his deck that morning. Jules, in a similar spirit, didn't ask Neil how his balls felt, and he refrained from attacking for a full two minutes.

"Why'd you claim you were with Deputy Fair that Friday afternoon?"

Neil looked at Jules, then at Caroline. It was a loaded look, and Caroline started to flush. Neil turned back to Jules.

"I was just trying to make you squirm," he said.

Jules stiffened, and Caroline turned a shade darker. "I was actually with Ben Wingate," said Neil primly. "You can check at the restaurant. I picked her up, took her home, headed in for a fast hearing at three and ran back to her house for more fun. Everybody left early that Friday—half the attorneys in the state were at a meeting in Billings." He slammed his appointment diary shut and leaned back in his chair. "By the way, are you two in the habit of ignoring arrest warrants?"

"Which one?" asked Jules. "I've got a few."

"Carl Jump. Are you protecting him? I've heard you're acquaintances."

"No," said Jules. "I'm not. We've checked on his shop twice a day, and the word is that he's in the park photographing eagles."

"Have you checked to see if he's in possession of his ex-wife's property? He stole a silver tray, among other things."

"No."

Neil cocked his head sarcastically. "Do you know how to get a search warrant?"

"Sure do," said Jules. "I'll go talk to your grandpa just as soon as I can get away from you. Now, how about that night, after the party?"

"Ben again. She's quite something." Neil smiled; maybe he was on happy pills, too. "But why do you care about that? When is it you think my grandfather died?"

It didn't seem that he knew what he was being suspected of, and this depressed Jules. "Earlier," said Caroline.

"What's that supposed to mean?"

"It doesn't get much simpler," said Caroline, flipping through her notebook. "By the way, what happened with Ben the other night seems like it could be part of a pattern. My notes say that in 1984, when you were seventeen, you were charged with sexual assault and the charges were subsequently dropped." She looked up. "What you might call date rape these days. Do you have any comment?"

It happened just as it had two nights earlier, the huge welling of rage moving across Neil's features. Jules stood. "You can shove those notes up your ass," said Neil.

"Better than you getting anywhere near it," said Caroline. Oooh, Jules loved her.

THEY GOT TAKE-OUT slices of pizza on the way to see Ben. Jules wanted to be there before Neil could reach her, or before Neil could call his mother and Flo could reach her.

"I don't want to talk to you," Ben whispered.

They were standing in the cloakroom outside the Baird dining room. Inside, patrons craned their necks, fascinated with the squad car parked out front.

"Did you see him that afternoon?"

"Yes," she said bitterly. "He screwed my brains out at approximately three thirty or four o'clock, had a real energy attack. I should have known better then."

"What about earlier?" asked Jules.

"What about it?" Ben turned from Jules to Caroline. "Why do you care about earlier? I worked lunch until two thirty, then helped set up for dinner. He picked me up after his hearing."

"What about later?" asked Caroline.

"I told you we were together after the party. I *told* you."

"I meant in the afternoon. Did he stay?"

"I had to get back for the party," said Ben wearily. "He took off and I got ready. I was due in an hour before the thing began, whenever that was."

THEY VISITED THE florist next. The man immediately remembered his earlier conversation with Jules: people remembered talking to police better than police remembered talking to people. "Who was at the Birdlands' when you delivered the bouquet from the Ganters? That would have been late October."

"A Friday, late afternoon, yes." He thought. "No one."

"No one?"

"Well, Mrs. Birdland, in bed. She called down to me. It was a bit awkward. But no one watching her, which I thought quite sad, so I found a vase for her."

"That is sad," said Jules slowly. "Did you make sure someone would be there soon? What time was this anyway?"

"I do deliveries after four o'clock," said the man. "Around then. Of course, I asked. She said her daughter was due back from errands, probably just running behind. I asked twice, because the poor lady was obviously in a fix."

"How so?"

The florist blushed. "Her bed needed changing. I felt so

bad for her, a lady like that being seen that way. But of course she was mostly past caring."

Mostly. Jules saw a good deal of abuse of the elderly; running bedsores, bruises from impatient blows, malnutrition due entirely to halfhearted feedings. But he was willing to bet Flo hadn't been in the habit of letting her mother sit in her own mess, that only a truly pressing concern would have taken her away.

THIS TIME JULES had a search warrant in his hands when he pounded on Carl Jump's front door. No one answered, and he drove around to the alley, and pried the back lock open while Caroline watched.

"What are we looking for again?"

"A dog bed and a silver platter."

"Jesus."

"Keep an eye out for the Ganter party negatives."

The dog bed was cozy in one corner of the shop, and an envelope lay on the clean worktable: "J Clement: Got these back from Mrs. Amundsen this a.m. Looks like she pulled the sheet with Neil's thing hanging out. CJ"

It was dated Monday, probably right before Jump found out Neil had issued a warrant for his arrest.

Caroline read the note, shook her head, grinning, and started looking through the photos. "Is that you dancing?"

"Believe it or not," said Jules.

"So that must be Edie."

"Umm."

"And there's my favorite woman," she said, pointing to an open-mouthed Flo Amundsen.

"Right before she fell down the stairs," said Jules. "I had

to take her to the hospital before I checked on Amundsen that night. If I'd gotten there any earlier he might not have been charcoal."

"What's the point in second-guessing?" asked Caroline.

"I feel like it," said Jules bitterly. "If I'd gotten there earlier we might know more now. It's not as if I was having fun with Mrs. Amundsen Junior in the emergency room. She claimed she'd broken her ankle, and by the next day she was moving like a figure skater."

"I heard about the swan dive," said Caroline. "I heard she hit you at sixty miles an hour."

Jules looked up suspiciously and scanned the sheets, trying to remember enough to guess at the time each batch of images had been taken. No one seemed to be gone long enough to make a difference, and maybe none of it made a difference, now that he knew Nestor might have spontaneously combusted.

Caroline had found the silver tray in the bathroom and was swinging it on a finger as she flipped through a notebook.

"What are you looking at?" asked Jules, eyeing the police scanner he'd found on a shelf. It was a perfectly legal thing to own, but he hated seeing it; what sort of person spent his free time listening to trouble?

"This is a log of film to be developed. I found Joy Schwartz's name."

"The before pictures," said Jules, peering over her shoulder. "Someone else signed for them."

"It's that waitress she worked with, the one who found her," said Caroline, pointing to the next name under the same date. "No wonder Jump didn't remember a red-haired anorexic."

Jules wandered around. Pinned on the unpainted drywall

were an Ansel Adams calendar and dozens of prints of Yellowstone landmarks, all probably Jump's, none really that good. He continued to circle the larger storeroom while Caroline flipped impatiently through the log. On a worktable he found proofs taken at Scotti's Halloween party, including a shot of him and Edie arguing, and carefully replaced the pile with that sheet on the bottom.

"Jules."

"Uh-huh."

Caroline had the desk drawer open. "Look."

She'd opened a small album and turned the pages for his benefit. Some group shots, probably family; some touristy snaps from warmer and more urban locales. Throughout there were women, at least two on each spread.

"He didn't strike me as a Romeo," said Jules. "Is that what's surprised you?"

"Wait," said Caroline. She flipped through faster now, and he noticed she'd been using the sides of her fingers. "There," she said, pointing to Mary McLinchey, smiling on her front porch. "And there," a page later, nodding to a smiling, plump Joy Schwartz, posed next to her Christmas tree.

Jules felt his pulse slow. *What happened to you, you skinny bitch?* He thought of how skeletal Joy Schwartz looked now. Jump had thought she would still be the woman in the photo he'd developed, the plump woman who'd dropped off the film.

Caroline turned to some loose photos at the back of the book, all taken with different cameras, all different sizes and levels of quality. She sorted free an image of the Billings victim on all fours, spilling out of a pink teddy, cupping her breasts and smiling at the photographer.

They shared a moment of silence. "I bet if I go back I'll

find the cop's sister and the girl in the alley. They all look alike, except for Joy Schwartz after she lost weight."

Caroline flipped the Billings photo over with a pencil and they read an order number and a date. It corresponded with the lines in the log, and the log had a phone number and address. She turned to the other loose photos and spread them apart. Jules recognized one of the librarians and a bartender and the woman who ran the pet store in town. All of them were fair, blond or light-brown or red-haired, and ample.

"We need to contact these women," said Caroline.

Jules nodded.

"If he hears we've been in here, he'll never come back," she said.

"We'll watch, all the time," said Jules. "Try to make that album look like you never touched it."

"We'll watch the alley, and he'll come in through the front and take this," said Caroline. "Or vice versa. Then we'll have nothing."

"I thought you were a goddamn optimist," said Jules, scanning the room for flashlights. "Let's check his apartment."

JULES CALLED THE Yellowstone rangers, the Gardiner deputy; called Ed, called Harvey, called Jonathan; called the Highway Patrol, and gave all of them Jump's license plate, photo, and car model, an '89 Honda. He put traces on Jump's credit cards and got an answer from an Amoco in Gardiner, but that only meant Jump had been near the park the day before. A Honda could go far on a full tank.

The Yellowstone rangers hadn't so much as glimpsed him. It wasn't impossible that someone would go in and out without registering for the backcountry, but it was unlikely that he could have spent so many days there without someone noting his presence by tracks, a fire or tent, a parked car. Possibly Jump had waited to head south until after he'd left a flashlight on Neil Amundsen's trash and placed an anonymous call.

Deer Lodge would acknowledge only that Carl Jump had taught photography to inmates for several years but not how he'd come by this job. A year earlier, not having a glimmer of understanding would have bothered Jules tremendously; these days he only cared about Jump's psychology because of the insight it might give to the man's potential.

17 The Mummy

THURSDAY WAS JULES'S DAY OFF, AND WHEN HE showed up anyway, Wesley and Harvey and Ed and Caroline told him to go away and let them look for Carl Jump without interference. At about noon Jules and Divvy and Peter loaded up Divvy's setters and Pearl to look for birds up by Martinsdale. Jules suggested a short detour to the Amundsen ranch, and made Divvy and Peter wait in the yard.

Nina gave him a cup of coffee before he handed over the buckle. "Well, of course it's Nestor's," she said, turning it over in her hands. "Though it's more tarnished than I remember."

"It's not Nestor's."

She stared up at him and down at the gold in her hand. "I don't understand," she said. "Why are you trying to match Nestor's belt?"

"This buckle was found on a body we dug up on the island in town," said Jules. "We think it may have belonged to a man Nestor knew and used to rope with, a—"

Nina screamed and threw the buckle across the room. She kept on screaming until Ira Meidenhaft appeared from the back of the house and gave her a paralyzing hug.

Jules waited outside, not sure at all how to continue. Peter and Divvy watched, confused, from the car. Jules gestured for them to stay put.

Ira finally followed him out. "You got some sort of electrical device in there? She won't tell me what set her off."

Jules explained. Had Nestor ever discussed a missing friend, a tall blond man? Not in so many words; Nestor had discussed a lot of old friends, but not many of them still seemed to be around. This man had been a roping partner and a neighbor, said Jules, the owner of the ranch that had once lain between the Ganter and Amundsen ranches.

Ira blinked. "The Whitsan place?"

Jules nodded.

Ira shook his head. "The only mentions Nestor made of the Whitsans were land-related, as in the Whitsan sections, the Whitsan springs. And of course I've met the Misses Whitsan." He looked toward the house. "But from the reception you just got, I'd guess Nestor and Nina weren't in the habit of discussing the man, anyway."

THEY HAD A huge, gut bomb lunch in Martinsdale—a chicken-fried steak for Divvy, liver and onions for Jules, and a chopped sirloin submerged in gravy for Peter—then staggered around in the wind for four hours. Divvy got the only bird, a Hungarian partridge, by aiming into the wind a full foot to the left. By five o'clock they were trying to warm up at the Baird bar, and Divvy and Peter were doing most of the talking, trying to come up with women Jules might date. Jules, who thought of *date* as a noun describing a dried fruit, did not bring up his coworker.

"What about the librarian you used to stare at?" asked Divvy. "I saw her there just the other day and she was actually wearing a skirt."

This didn't happen too much after November 1 in Blue Deer. "Engaged," said Peter. "Go for the masseuse."

"The masseuse and I know each other already," said Jules. "I'd just as soon take the rest of the year off anyway."

"You're obviously bearing in mind that it's already November," said Divvy with a smile.

They drank.

"Egads," said Peter, looking over Jules's shoulder. "The horror. The horror."

Jules swiveled on his stool, and Divvy snickered helplessly.

"Jules," said Venus Meriwether. "Alice was just telling us how hard it's been to find you, and here you are, like a ray of light or a bolt of lightning."

Jules looked through the bar door into the lobby, and a half dozen Aches waved back. Venus had tottered in for a refill; Alice was moving toward them with an apologetic look on her face.

Venus buried her nails in his shoulder. "We need to get into our museum. Is there any reason on earth you can't make me a happy woman immediately?"

Jules looked past her again to buy time. Flo was talking to Jetta, and behind them Caroline stared at the floor. He finished his drink in one long gulp. "I can make you a happy woman, but you'll have to bear with me while I get the key."

"We'll meet you at the back door in ten minutes," said Venus.

"That's quite a shuffle."

"You have such nice skinny legs," said Venus. "Just like your uncle. This'll help keep them that way."

Peter dropped him at the station, where Grace tried to tell him the sorry tales of the day. Jules covered his ears and headed out the back door with the key for the museum padlock. In the dusk lighting the older women practically glowed, pinks and yellows and aquas and floral prints. The younger women, in jeans and muted parkas, were dull in comparison.

Inside they oohed and ahhed over the damage, and he found himself enjoying being a guide. The members fell to talking about new paint colors and carpeting and all the wonderful things they might do with the insurance money, and Jules started to slide toward the door.

"Not so fast," said Alice. "Remember the trunks I've mentioned four or five times now?"

"Alice, you can bust a lock as fast as I can," said Jules. "I'm not particularly handy."

"I've inspired lightbulb jokes," said Alice. "Don't move."

She shot into the old office and returned clutching a crowbar. "Upstairs," she ordered.

"Alice, leave the poor boy alone," said Flo Amundsen. "Surely we can find someone with less important things to do."

"I haven't done a thing to make his life miserable lately," said Alice. "And you're the one who first asked where they were and got Ettie wondering about them in the first place."

"Oh, my," said Ettie. "Was that how it began?"

By the time everyone else had made the climb upstairs, Jules was toeing the first well-oiled Whitsan memory box. They gathered around in a semicircle while he and Alice argued about how to get the trunks open with as little damage as possible.

Indie was helpful. "I don't care if you break them," she said. "I don't think we should be opening them to begin with."

"Well, Indie," said Alice, "what do you want to do?"

"Burn them," she said bleakly. "I want them to disappear."

Jules raised his eyebrows at Alice. Alice shrugged. He turned back to trunk one, wishing Caroline wasn't right behind him to grade his manly hardware-busting performance, and blew away a cloud of fingerprint powder.

"The metal will be ruined but I'll try not to chip the wood."

"Good," said Alice. "Because they're valuable."

They exchanged a meaningful look. Alice grinned, and Jules snapped the first trunk open with the crowbar in one fast movement. He won some appreciative *ooohs* for his pains.

Clothes, knickknacks, some books. "My dance dress," whooped Ettie, who looked as if she'd had time for at least two drinks at the Baird before the meeting moved down the street. The news of her brother's death hadn't caused any discernible grief; probably, thought Jules, because she'd gotten it a half century earlier.

Jules popped trunk number two, and they all stared down at china, a Tiffany-style lamp, and a stack of framed botanical engravings. "We bought them in Sienna," said Indie. "In 1935."

Jules sorted through the prints; they were worth a fortune. Someone touched his shoulder. "How are you going to deal with this one?"

It was Caroline, and she was pointing to the old Yale lock on trunk number three. "I don't have a clue," said Jules. "I'd like to shoot it, but then I'd have to carry it outside."

"Ettie, why on earth did you put that thing on?"

"I didn't," said Ettie, still clinging to her dress but staring fixedly at the last trunk. "That must be the silverware and rug trunk, and I wouldn't have put our silver in there if the regular lock hadn't worked."

"Don't rely too much on memory," said Venus.

"It doesn't matter," said Cicely as Jules struggled with the pry bar. "He'll get it."

Fine for you to say, lady, thought Jules. After a half century in a dry climate a Yale lock was as good as new; if he had money he'd buy stock. He gave a final wrench and the lower brace flew across the room, just missing his mother's head. He didn't feel like apologizing, and he threw open the lid with unnecessary energy.

For one long moment he thought he was stuck in a hallucinogenic memory from some North African dig a decade earlier. The face was aquiline and sunken, the skin smooth leather, the color of dark honey. Even the Persian carpet wrapped around the man's body seemed an apt shroud, the beautiful silver spoons piled at his feet an offering.

Jules sensed commotion behind him.

"If that doesn't stop my heart, nothing will," said Cicely.

"It's the climate, you know," said Venus Meriwether. "The poor man looks freeze-dried."

"You're absolutely right," said Olive, honorary archaeologist. "That's your basic mummy."

Not one of them had screamed. Jules looked around. Ettie had tears in her eyes, and Indie was gray. Alice looked as if she'd been hit on the head; Caroline was watching Flo and Jetta, both of whom looked honestly shocked and revolted.

"Anyone know anything about this?" Jules asked.

"Jules," said Venus sternly, "this is no one we'd know. Can't you see he's not white?"

Jules sat back on his haunches and stared at the man's long, dark hair. Finally, a dead Indian.

AT NINE THAT night Jules switched on Harvey's floodlight, but it seemed all wrong, and he found a set of old mission lamps with working bulbs. They gave the room the look of a nine-teenth-century deathbed scene. He sat in a chair next to the trunk and looked at the man, who still lay as he'd been found, though now surrounded by a fresh and glistening variety of fin-gerprint powder. Harvey had insisted on taking all prints, even from the exposed skin, rather than simply shuffling the whole job off to Missoula, and did so surrounded by textbooks. He was ready for more now, waiting for Jules to pull aside the rug.

The face was cherry-colored leather, smooth and high-cheekboned, but probably had only been slightly plumper in life; the hair black and satiny, longer than would have been the fashion and pulled back into a ponytail. Jules pulled on gloves and carefully lifted aside the loose silver and world tour knickknacks: a china Eiffel Tower, a tiny metal model of the Forum, a small wooden gondola. Then he lifted open the carpet and took stock. The rest of the man's body hadn't held up as well as his face. One or maybe two cavernous holes in the chest, with dull glints of splintered bone be-neath, remnants of a third wound in the lower abdomen. One hand lay clenched in the body cavity, as if it had gone there to squeeze pain.

"A shotgun?" asked Harvey.

"Looks like it," said Jules.

"Is that another gunshot?" asked Caroline, pointing to the stomach.

"I don't know," said Jules. "If he went in here in the sum-mer it's likely his belly simply blew."

He carefully scissored open the shirt. Underneath the man had worn a thin, beaded leather vest. Jules slipped two fingers into the beaded pocket and removed a slip of stained light green paper.

"It's an invoice," he said.

29 July
Rcvd from Whitsan ranch: thirty yds of rein leather.
Provd: 180 lbs mollases oats.

The man had a ten-dollar bill and some change in his pants pocket, quite a bit of money for a killer to leave behind in 1939. Jules watched while Harvey dusted the man's belt and vest and took more photos.

Caroline was tucking each item into an evidence envelope. "When do you think the Whitsans will be up to talking?" asked Jules.

"Tomorrow morning at best. All they could say tonight is that they packed the trunks before they left for Seattle in the summer of 1939, and they hadn't seen inside them since."

"They knew," said Jules bitterly. "I saw Ettie's face before and after I opened that trunk. Has Cicely ever mentioned anything to you?"

"I would have told you," said Caroline.

"Help me lift him out," said Jules. "We'll try to keep him on the carpet so he doesn't fall apart."

The body was light, just a husk, and Jules could hear the old tissues give a papery rip when they lowered the pretty carpet to the floor. Underneath was more silver, some velvet-wrapped goblets, and a beautiful Purdy shotgun. Harvey flexed his fingers in glee.

"Do you think this is the dead Indian the ladies mentioned?"

"One of the stories I didn't want to hear. Yes." Jules was sure he was looking at Malcolm Gray Crane, even before he talked to Ankeny's grandmother, saw a photo, sent the man east or north to be spliced and tested. So many mentions of this person, and virtually none volunteered about the one on the island, dug up almost a month earlier. It wasn't hard to guess who'd been the finer human.

"Is it fair to assume the same person killed both of them? The dates look right."

"I guess we could assume it," said Jules. "Though why tuck one man in a trunk and the other in the ground? And one died from a shotgun, and Whitsan from a rifle."

"Maybe they shot each other."

"We should be so blessed," said Jules.

AT SEVEN THE next morning Jules moved the mummy to the hospital, where he carefully removed clothing and Horace took samples. By nine he'd cleared off his desk and made a list, fixed coffee, and read through the night's reports. And then there was no more putting it off.

He called Patrick Ankeny, once a pleasant act. "You know that guy you told me about, a guy named Malcolm who went missing?"

He listened to a long blank, Ankeny changing gears from whatever forestry crisis he faced that morning to his guilty love life to a month-old bar conversation. "Malcolm Gray Crane," he said finally. "My great-uncle."

"How old was he?"

"I don't know. Under thirty, over twenty."

"Did he wear his hair long or short?"

"I don't know. Why?"

"Do you have a photo of him?"

"The first time I remember hearing about the guy in years was a month ago," said Ankeny. "Call my grandmother. Her name is Lily White Button and she lives in Saint Xavier. Why the hell are you asking?"

Jules, who already had too many people to call, sighed deeply. "I think we found her brother's body. She drive?"

"Never learned. Where'd you turn him up?"

"She planning to visit soon?"

"Not for a couple of weeks."

Jules tried to remember what everyone was supposed to be doing that day. In his silence, Ankeny said, "I'm not going to get her today. I'm knee-deep in federal bullshit over here. I have a life."

"That's been made painfully clear to me."

"That's not what I mean."

"I know," said Jules. "I'm sorry. Maybe Wesley feels like a drive."

WESLEY PREFERRED SHUTTLING anyone's grandmother to a day spent mired in interstate rape statistics.

Lily White Button didn't pick up until the ninth ring because she'd been out putting plastic on her windows; she didn't seem a bit surprised by the idea that a brother missing for half a century might have turned up. "I talked to Patrick about Malcolm because it was time he was found," she said. As if Patrick had found the body, or anyone had deliberately sought it, except for possibly Flo or Jetta or whoever had set the place on fire.

After Jules hung up he stared at the phone for some time, nonplussed. He was even more mystified when he turned to see Harvey waiting patiently, an unprecedented vision; it was Harvey's day off, and not even payday.

"It bothered me all night," he said without preamble. "Two prints on that Indian's belt, on the back like someone had used it to help lift him. I knew I'd seen them before."

Jules stared. Four billion extant fingerprints in the world, and Harvey was sure of one set.

"Tented arches are quite rare," Harvey explained, running his hand through his corn silk hair. "Guess who they belonged to?"

"You matched them?" Jules was incredulous.

"I matched them. Not a shadow of a doubt. Found one on the shotgun stock, too, though nowhere near the trigger." Harvey was beaming, his pale skin pink with pleasure. "You'll need some coffee before this."

"Tell me."

Harvey grinned.

"Tell me," said Jules, wrapping one hand around the deputy's neck.

"Nestor Amundsen. Nestor Amundsen's prints on the leather belt and a fragment on that stock."

Jules went blank.

"Can you beat it?" asked Harvey. "Can you fucking *believe* it?" He gave another crow of laughter and wiggled all over. "Fifty-five-year-old fingerprints, and both guys as dead as they come."

A HALF HOUR later, Jules, made surly by confusion, was wondering what fucking good it did them; this revelation was right up there with figuring out that the likeliest man to want to kill Nestor himself—Henry Whitsan—had been dead for half a century.

Neil walked into the station, and Jules's mood worsened.

"Are you bothering to look for that rapist?"

"No," said Jules, signing off on the week's paperwork without looking up or really reading what he was sorting.

"I've just been sitting around, picking my nose, waiting for you to remind me about my reason for living."

"I went home at lunch and discovered that someone had tried to force open my back door."

Jules finally looked at Neil. "We'd be happy to keep an eye on the place if you'd stop screaming about harassment charges. I actually think you're in some danger."

"Why?" asked Neil, his face impassive.

"A pissed-off guy with a knife whose life has blown apart. We never would have suspected Jump if you hadn't pressed the doggy custody thing. I thank you, but I bet he doesn't."

"He wouldn't dare come near my house."

"He already did," said Jules. "Who the hell do you think left that flashlight on your trash? Me?"

Neil stared into space, uncharacteristically at a loss.

"You know what we just found?" asked Jules.

"No," said Neil, snapping back to life. "Was this something you actually left your chair to look for?"

"Hell no," said Jules. "It practically fell on my head. We found your grandpa's fingerprints all over a dead man's belt."

Neil turned gray.

"Go figure," said Jules.

"Have you told him yet?" asked Neil softly.

Jules smiled. "Well, no, I haven't. I was talking about Nestor, but you're assuming Miles Birdland. That's kind of interesting."

EVERY SO OFTEN Jules succumbed to vindictiveness. The mayor was usually the victim of such a mood, though Jonathan had also suffered. This morning Axel Scotti saw him coming, and would have slammed the door in Jules's face if he'd been agile enough.

"I see that look," Axel said. "I don't want to know about it. Why would you want to ruin my day?"

"I'm not trying to ruin your day," said Jules mildly.

"I know you're here to burn me," said Scotti. "I just know it. Is this about the man on the island?"

"Maybe," said Jules. "I think things are clearing up."

Axel squinted at him, wary.

"Whatcha got there on your tie?" asked Jules.

"Egg, you asshole. So what did you find last night?"

"Another body," said Jules, savoring the moment.

"Fuck you!" screamed Scotti.

It took him five minutes to fully recover. "Instead of wanting to know why Nestor might have killed someone in 1939, why not ask who killed Nestor in the here and now?" Scotti raised his eyebrows and wiggled them sarcastically. "I, too, would like to avoid even thinking about this decade, but—"

"You're ignoring a few other problems. For starters, your wife was observed moving crates about in a room that someone subsequently attempted to torch, and in which we subsequently found a body. She had an explanation, but at this point everyone has an explanation."

"Coincidence. She's a member. She had a reason to be there."

"On top of the coincidence that all those old shits grew up together, gambled together, *slept* together, for Christ's sake. C'mon, Axel. The guy in the trunk worked for Whitsan, and someone murdered Whitsan, and Joseph and Nestor profited. How can we pretend that people we know have nothing to do with it?"

Scotti gave him a bitter look. "You're making it sound really bad."

"Jesus!" shrieked Jules. "It *is* really bad. The only way it's going to get worse is if someone we love out-and-out confesses." Jules rubbed his head. "Everyone's lying, Axel. Jetta, Joseph, Flo, your nasty deputy, the guy who swears everyone in, every day."

"You always get paranoid."

Jules snorted. "There's always been a reason for it."

Scotti stared bleakly out his window at more snowflakes. "Is this by way of telling me we'll need an inquest for Nestor?"

Jules could only stare.

"Just find the fucking rapist and we'll come out of this alive. Maybe my wife will even talk to me again."

"Axel, there's more."

WESLEY ARRIVED WITH Mrs. White Button at noon. Her brother Malcolm had been twenty-six, and wore his hair long, and worked for a family named Whitsan with fancy horses. He'd disappeared at the end of July; she had no idea why or how.

"Really?" asked Jules. "No idea at all? I know it was a long time ago, but—"

"Really," said Lily White Button firmly.

Buffaloed once again by the Metamucil generation. She knew he didn't believe her, and Jules recognized she didn't give a shit for his opinion. "How'd you happen to mention him to Patrick just a few weeks ago? He said he'd never heard of him before."

"Patrick told me you'd found a body. I said maybe it's your great-uncle Malcolm. One body makes you think of another."

It certainly did. "Two men disappear in 1939, it's natural to think they might have been killed by the same individual," said Jules. "Or that one man might have killed the other, and then Lord knows what happened next. We think we've identified the body on the island as Henry Whitsan, who was also last seen that summer. Your brother worked for him. Were they friends, involved in some business together?"

"No," said Lily White Button.

Just no, without elaboration. "Were they enemies?"

"Not really. Malcolm didn't kill him, if that's what you're wondering."

Jules could have sworn she was smiling. He let it drop for the time being. She'd brought a photo; it was stunning how much the man in the trunk still resembled himself alive, albeit blurred and in black and white. The eyes snapped out, alert and large and amused by the photographer; no wonder he hadn't easily been forgotten.

"He looked like your grandson Patrick," said Jules.

She smiled, pleased, not having a clue what any praise cost him. Theirs had been a small family, just the two of them, so yes, she'd probably recognize Malcolm's clothing. She asked politely how Jules had known so quickly that he was dealing with an American Indian; Jules explained carefully about the body's state of preservation.

"Well," said Mrs. White Button. "Why don't we see if I can recognize him, then?"

In the hospital basement she stared at the body in silence for a full five minutes, sighed, and said that it was strange seeing Malcolm look so wizened but so young. Then she became businesslike. If Jules wanted to be sure, Malcolm had had two scars, one half circle on his shoulder from some youthful foolishness with a knife, and one on his shin from wire.

She watched intently, not at all squeamish, while he searched for and found raised scars on the leathery skin in both places.

"I wondered if we could take him back. Patrick has a pickup."

Patrick would probably be thrilled to hear how she intended to use it. "In a few days," said Jules. "Early next week."

"I'll just stay until we can, then. Don't cut him in pieces."

"We won't." He'd intended to send the man to Missoula, but now he saw no point. They'd identified him, knew when he'd been shot and what, if not who, had killed him. "Now, why do you think this happened?"

Lily White Button raised an eyebrow dramatically. "What would be the point to wondering, so many years later?"

There was a point, he was sure of it, but all the ways of phrasing seemed glib and stupid. He decided to be direct. "Was he killed by a man named Nestor Amundsen?"

Her eyes widened, thoughtful. "Nestor Amundsen," she said thoughtfully. The name didn't seem to surprise her. "No, no. He wouldn't have given Malcolm the time of day." She smiled. "No. He wasn't the man who killed Malcolm."

"You know that for a fact?"

"Yes."

"Then who killed him?"

She smiled. "Let me think it over for a while."

Jules rubbed his head with both hands so vigorously that when he was finished most of his hair had found a new angle. "Do you know why he was killed?"

"How could I tell you what someone had in their soul?"

"Do you know some of why?"

"Some of why was me. He was trying to help me."

She was finally crying as she walked toward the door. Wesley looked at Jules in confusion, pointed to himself, and followed her out.

"Now, that was some real aggressive questioning," said Caroline.

"I was being polite," Jules answered testily, knowing he sounded inane. "I'll talk to her again. She wants us to work for it." He wasn't eager to arrest an eighty-year-old woman for obstruction of justice, at least not that particular eighty-year-old woman. There were so many other candidates.

THE WHITSAN GIRLS, for example, out raking their lawn on a fine fall day. Ettie's eyes were bloodshot, her smile empty. Indie looked angry, but she'd also lost her liveliness. Neither had much to volunteer. They'd packed and locked the trunks in late July or early August 1939, right before they'd left for Seattle.

"They stayed at your farmhouse or—"

"Cicely's mother stored them soon after."

"You've never even once looked in them since? Has the lock been broken all this time?"

"I don't know how that lock was broken or who added the new one," said Indie. "We left, and when we moved back we couldn't find the keys, and really it would only have made us sad to see those belongings. They had no place in our life in Seattle, and no place in a small house like this."

He would have bet money that they hadn't looked in those trunks for fifty-five years because they were afraid of finding exactly what had been found. "Did your brother have a set of keys?"

"We certainly hoped not at the time. Part of the point

was to save things from him." Indie was sarcastic, still bitter. "He pawned my sewing machine. And Ettie's violin."

Ettie sighed. "Poor Henry. It was just one of those things."

Jules stared at her, startled. "You called me weeks ago about the body on the island."

"Never," said Ettie, smiling blandly.

"Ettie has trouble with numbers," said Indie indulgently. "She's not one for phone calls anymore."

"I have a photo here of the man in the trunk," said Jules. "Last night, did either of you happen to see him?"

Yes, they had seen the body, but just briefly; Indie supposed she could inspect the pictures. "I'll look. It will upset my sister."

"I *want* to look," said Ettie.

Jules had been careful to choose the least macabre photo possible, an almost sleeping profile shot. Ettie still burst into tears and handed the photo over to Indie, who peered at it through bottle-thick glasses from only two inches away, then lowered it, face grim. She patted her sister on the back, wiped Ettie's face and dabbed her own eyes with the same handkerchief.

"Do you know him?" asked Caroline gently.

Ettie looked at the photo again and dissolved anew.

"It's Malcolm," said Indie, dabbing cloudy blue eyes. "Malcolm Gray Crane, the sweetest, prettiest man you could ask for—except, of course, for his color."

Jules nodded. "His sister identified him this morning, too."

"Lily?" asked Ettie, sniffling.

"She worked for us, too, sometimes," said Indie. "It's nice to know she's still kicking."

"Malcolm worked for you that summer?"

"Malcolm worked for us for several years. We owed him a great deal."

"Do either of you have any idea how he ended up in there?"

They were quiet. "Any idea?" echoed Caroline.

"I've no doubt our brother killed him," said Indie. Her voice was shaking, and Ettie gave another great sob.

Jules flexed his fingers and met Caroline's eyes. "Why?" she asked.

"We'd rather not say," said Indie with great dignity.

"I'm sorry," said Jules. "But I'm sick of answers like that."

Indie looked as if he'd slapped her. "Well, you might want to buy yourself some aspirin, Jules. Because it's the kind of story a lady won't tell."

Jules and Indie watched each other. Inside the tiny, polite living room a clock ticked loudly; outside the wind was building again. Caroline gathered Ettie's soggy tissues and walked into the kitchen, where Jules could hear her opening cupboards, searching for the wastebasket. A minute later she stood in the door holding an old-fashioned can labeled "Sunkote."

"I haven't seen that stuff for years, since I was a kid and Cicely used it," said Caroline. "It's on sale again?"

"Indie found some in the basement," said Ettie happily. "It just turned up, and I've been polishing *everything*."

Jules and Caroline turned to Indie. She looked calm enough, but her fingers were denting the upholstery on the chair arms.

"Was that a cut or a burn on your arm, Indabel?" Jules asked gently.

CAROLINE SEEMED SHAKEN as they climbed into the car. "Are you going to charge her?"

"I don't know. I'd at least like to know why she tried to burn the place down," said Jules. "Obviously to keep us from finding the body—which I think we would have found anyway—or to keep us from identifying it."

Caroline nodded.

"But since she's just admitted her brother murdered Malcolm Crane, it seems we need to know why before we'll know why Indie started the fire. Can you think of anything from the meetings?"

"No," said Caroline. "But I'll try asking Cicely some yes-or-no questions."

AT FIVE O'CLOCK Miles Birdland found Jules chugging a glass of water in the station kitchen. "Do you have a moment?"

Jules wiped water from his chin. "Of course."

"What's all the ruckus about my grandchild?" asked Birdland stiffly.

"Our second visit inquiring about domestic violence happened in response to a prank call," said Jules.

"Any chance it was someone in your department?"

"Not much," said Jules. "I'm fairly sure it was Carl Jump."

"And the first?"

"Open and shut, or it would have been if the girl had pressed charges."

"What did he do to her?"

"Hit her in the face and knocked her down, kicked her when she started to get up."

Miles Birdland blinked and reached for one of Grace's

stale cookies. "I'm quite sure my daughter paid the girl to drop charges," he said finally.

"I expect you're right." Jules turned away and started piling dirty coffee cups in the sink.

"I saw your uncle at lunch," said Birdland. "We talked for quite a while, quite frankly, and he convinced me to tell you some of what we discussed."

Some. Jules started to turn. "I'd prefer you not look at me while I talk," said the judge. "Somehow I'd find that easier. Do you suspect Neil of killing Nestor?"

"Yes," said Jules. "Though I have no evidence." He filled the sink with soap and water. "Do you?"

"Maybe."

JETTA CALLED THAT NIGHT AT EIGHT. "COULD you do me a huge favor?"

Given recent events, such a blanket request seemed unfair. "Depends," said Jules, midway through creating a hash of leftovers, looking for parsley in the refrigerator.

"Flo was supposed to be out here an hour ago for dinner, and she's not answering her phone. I wondered if you'd check."

He slammed the refrigerator door. "Where's 'out here'?"

"Mom and Dad's."

Jules recalled the days when he'd been a regular dinner guest. "What's to worry you?"

"She's never late, and she's been a little shaky since Nestor died—"

"That's an understatement guaranteed to make me want to hold her hand."

"Think of it all," said Jetta. "Her mother, the body in the trunk, Neil supposedly hitting that girl—"

"Take my word for it," said Jules. "He hit the girl."

Jetta had always been good at ignoring the unpleasant, and now she moved past it without a pause. "I've never, ever known her to miss dinner. Never. Something's wrong."

Jules looked at his chopped chicken and garlic and

potatoes and onion, then threw the bunch of parsley across the room. He felt like the poor relation: good for errands, no reward necessary. He *was* the poor relation.

"I'll call back in a bit," he said. "Leave a message on my machine if she shows up."

THERE WAS NO car in Flo's driveway, but the garage was locked, as were all the house doors. Jules couldn't see a thing through the blinds. The kitchen windows were locked but uncurtained, and he saw no sign of either distress or current occupation. No one answered his knock or the doorbell, and the backyard was empty. It was raining and under forty, which meant the rain would turn solid by midnight.

He called back. "No one's home. Did she show up?"

"I would have called you," Jetta snapped.

"I thought maybe you were too busy eating." He wished his dinner was ready. "Maybe something came up with Neil."

"Neil was seeing some girl in Bozeman tonight," said Jetta.

Jules indulged in a brief fantasy of breaking and entering. "Maybe Flo's having an affair. Maybe she has a life you don't know about."

"No," said Jetta. "Though I wish she did. Was her car there?"

"I couldn't see into the garage. Would she use the garage?"

"Sure. She's scared of her shadow. She doesn't like being outside in the dark."

"Jesus," said Jules. "I hope she stops counseling."

He walked back and stood twenty feet from Flo's house, watching and listening as the snow started. On the other side of the street, Alice moved across her bedroom light holding a pile of laundry; Peter was probably already in bed with a cookbook. From somewhere in the neighborhood

Jules smelled wood smoke; in just a few more minutes of such heavy snow, the faint scent would be hard to pick out.

Flo's kitchen light snapped on and off, and Jules heard a crash and a simultaneous yell. He ran to the front door but it was locked; ran around to the backyard and was reaching for the screen door when it came open with a vengeance into his face and sent him flying onto his back in the cold, muddy yard. He had a vague sense of being trampled and quickly rolled onto his side for protection. From this position and through the pain in his face he was just able to make out the running, limping shape in the alley. A minute later he heard a car engine.

Jules staggered onto his feet and climbed back up the stoop and into the dark kitchen. He ran his hand along the wall until he felt a light switch, flipped it up and lurched backward in the sudden light, out of the way of the screaming woman with the butcher knife.

"You fucking asshole!" screamed Flo, bloody and naked from the waist down, swinging the knife.

"Stop!" yelled Jules. "He's gone! Drop it!" Flo didn't show any sign of having heard him, and he brought his hand down on her arm so that the knife fell to the floor, then put her in a headlock and kept her there, talking, until she recognized him.

CAROLINE, BEING THE only female officer, was on call for such situations, and it was a measure of Flo's trauma that she didn't mind seeing either of them.

"You sure you don't want an ambulance, Flo?" Jules asked. He'd turned the heat on in Caroline's patrol car so that it would be warm for the drive to the hospital; Flo was in shock.

She shook her head. Caroline was digging through the drawers.

"We could just take you in this blanket," said Jules.

"I want some panties," said Flo.

"And you'll have some," said Caroline. "Don't worry." She helped Flo slip her feet through the holes. "See those bites?" she asked. "The bruise on her face is from being kicked."

Jules had seen them, red nips up and down Flo's plump white legs. He rummaged through the closet with one hand while he mopped blood from his nose with the other and came up with some sweatpants and woolly slippers. Jules turned to put them near Flo's feet just as Flo pulled up her underpants, and found himself staring at an ugly purple contusion with half-healed stitches on an expanse of upper thigh. "What the hell is that?" he asked.

Caroline, who had a different view, looked as if she wanted to slap him. Jules made his voice gentle. "Is that a bite, too?"

Flo pulled the blanket over her legs. "An old one," she whispered. "A dog." She looked in the other direction, blinking at a steady rate of speed, tears dripping off her face. "Do you think I killed this man?"

"He left behind a lot of blood, but Jules says he was running," said Caroline. "So probably not."

"He'll come and find me," said Flo.

"No," said Jules. It was his fault; he should have anticipated something like this. "You'll be safe at the hospital. We'll make sure."

"I didn't recognize him until he started asking about photos," said Flo. "He said I'd ruined his life, that if I hadn't held on to the photos with Neil and that bitch you never would have come to his store. I just didn't want Jetta or Laura to see that picture."

"No," said Jules. "I would have had to go there anyway. He did this because he was angry with Neil."

"*It's not his fault!*" screamed Flo.

"I didn't say it was," said Jules.

"*None of it's his fault!*" she screamed again.

THAT NIGHT THEY had the biggest snowfall for that date since the twenties, when the weather had conspired with the economy to send people packing. By the next morning the world was puffy and white and peaceful-looking, and Jules tried not to feel immediately at odds with it. The snow at least made things quiet, and it was easier to think when it was quiet.

They'd taken his pickup to make it through the streets to the hospital, so that Jonathan could have the county's single four-wheel-drive vehicle for patrol. Caroline toed the six months of accumulated junk food trash on the floor of the cab. Jules's nose was taped and one eye had gone black. This was the third break of his lifetime; he noticed they didn't feel better as they went along. "Did the blood sample match the rape specimens?"

"Yeah. O positive. The other tests will take longer."

"Anyone willing to guess how badly she got him with the knife?"

"No."

No one with a stab wound had come to Blue Deer Hospital yet, nor had anyone visited the hospitals in Bozeman or Big Timber. Jules had Wesley check all the hospitals within a five- or six-hour radius and not one incident matched up; that morning they'd widened the search to an eight-hour circumference with no success.

"I can't really question Flo today," said Caroline. "Today it doesn't matter what she might have done a few weeks ago."

"There's not much point anyway," said Jules. "Not, as far as her lie about that day, now that we have the florist and Miles."

"He's her father. It's hard to believe."

"He did the right thing," said Jules.

At the hospital, Caroline headed down the hall to check on Flo again, but Jules loitered by the nurse's station until he saw Renee, an old acquaintance.

"Can I see Flo Amundsen's chart?"

"Of course not." She slapped his hand.

Olive liked working weekend mornings because they were quiet, and she wasn't much of a churchgoer, and after thirty years of working Monday through Friday for the Forest Service an irregular schedule was still a thrill. It didn't bother Jules in the least to lie to her. "Flo's got an old injury on her leg and she can't remember when she got it. Can you look it up for me?"

She peered at him over her glasses and put her mystery down with a sigh. Jules noticed that she tapped the computer keyboard with unnecessary force.

"About how long ago?" Olive asked.

"A few weeks anyway."

"October twenty-first."

"No," said Jules. "That would have been the night she fell on top of me at the anniversary party. That was her ankle."

"Yes," said Olive acidly. "There is a mention of a possibly sprained ankle, but she was also treated for some sort of laceration. Six stitches and some antibiotics."

Jules tried to remember if Flo had been limping before she fell. He'd walked her in to the hospital that night, even though he'd wanted to drop her in the gutter—nothing had happened between the tumble down the stairs and the emergency room. "A laceration? I didn't see a cut when she was flying through the air toward me."

"L-A-C-E-R—"

He peered over the counter. "Would you mind reading all that fine print, or do I have to sit on your lap?"

Olive tilted her head back slightly. "Here it is. Dog bite."

"You sure about that?"

"What is it with you tonight? It says here 'dog bite.' We don't get so many human bites. I think they would have mentioned it."

A dog bite, after almost a full month, had still been a god-awful-looking thing. Flo was so fond of grievances he was astounded she hadn't reported the owner, called for the mutt to be deballed or possibly beheaded for a rabies test. Maybe it had been warm enough a month earlier for Flo to be out jogging; maybe she'd never known who the owner was. But really it hadn't been warm: a month earlier he'd been postponing his camping trip with Wayne Contway, driving about on a thaw night looking for Nestor.

And Nestor's dog.

Jules smiled. "Does it say if the bite was fresh?"

Olive raised an eyebrow. "Of course it doesn't."

"Will you look?"

"Jules."

"Please look."

She gritted her teeth, hit a few keys and read from the computer screen. "Nothing up here suggests an old bite or an infection. It's all completely standard. Antibiotics as a precaution, no IV, no cauterization. What does it matter anyway?"

Jules stared straight ahead, lost in thought.

"Jules, she was bitten by a dog. We get a hundred people a year like that. What does it matter?"

"I dealt with a dog that night," said Jules slowly. "Though it was dead by the time I saw it."

"Oh," said Olive slowly. "I'd forgotten the rest of what happened that night."

"Don't tell anyone," said Jules, heading toward Flo's room. He'd wait in the hall; he couldn't look her in the eye just yet.

"I won't," said his mother.

He told Caroline when they were back in the truck. "Has Neil been with her all morning?"

"I don't know. He wasn't being very sympathetic."

"How so?"

"Didn't want her taking anything like Valium, told her to toughen up. Birdland asked him to be quiet two or three times." She sipped at a go-cup of bad hospital coffee. "It's hard to imagine someone so antidrug he wouldn't want his mother to dull the edges the morning after a rape."

"Neil's not antidrug," said Jules. "He's just afraid she'll talk."

AMBER JUMP CALLED at noon. Serena was back, fatter than ever; she'd materialized at Amber's front door at ten o'clock the night before.

Jules gritted his teeth. "Why didn't you call sooner?"

"We've been so happy," she said. "I couldn't think straight."

"Why didn't you tell us about Carl?"

"I didn't know he was a rapist. A shit, yes. He was under-age when the first thing happened."

He rocked forward in his chair. "What first thing?"

Amber Jump sounded smug. "Like I said, I don't know if he raped anyone, but he sure did kill his mother."

"You had a perfectly normal marriage?" asked Jules acidly after a moment of stunned silence.

"I told you it only lasted a year," she said. "Carl had problems." It was the first time she'd uttered an understatement.

BY THE TIME Jules called Joseph it was dark. "You still have snow on the ground up there?"

"Yes, and I don't find it amusing."

"Miles Birdland told me to call."

"That's good," said Joseph. "That's a tremendous relief. Did he tell you about his grandson wanting to swap cars that Friday afternoon, bringing the Olds back with muddy tires?"

"Yes." Jules was at home, folding three weeks' worth of wrinkled but clean laundry.

"I saw the little shit that day on the way to the ranch, thought it was Miles. It's worried me. And then there was the question of whether he'd want to protect the kid. Spoiled prick, trying to frame his own grandfather."

"I gather he doesn't care to protect him."

"No."

"When did you see Neil? Where were you?"

"It was after four. I was on the old road, the high one, on my way home from town." Joseph paused. "Neither of us were wanting to be seen."

"This would have been when you said you were burning trash," said Jules.

"Excuse me?" asked Joseph, startled.

"You lied," said Jules.

The quiet lasted several seconds. "Yes, I did. In truth, I

drove to town, paid a visit. And now you'll want to know who I saw, and whatever shred of respect you still feel for me will disappear."

Fred the cat, starved for company, knocked over a pile of towels. Jules suddenly understood. "I see," he said.

"She gets sad," said Joseph. "We've known each other since kindergarten, seventy-some years, and we have no anniversary."

Jules no longer had the energy, let alone the currency, to be moralistic. "But you were at Nestor's at some point that day yourself. I saw your tires."

"I visited him at lunchtime."

"Why?"

"I wanted to talk him out of something he intended to do. I can't tell more. I gave a promise."

"Might this be the same secret Miles has mentioned?"

"It might."

Jules threw a half dozen old socks into the garbage. "Flo told Jetta that Nestor had worried the land might be taken away."

"Flo said that? Who would have told her that?" asked Joseph.

Jules was sure it was a real surprise. "Nestor."

"No. Nestor would never have said that. The land was his to do with as he liked."

This statement was not particularly illuminating. "Is that the crux?"

"Maybe."

"How long did you stay at Nestor's?"

"I left at one. Nestor didn't feel so good; the beer had gone to his head, and he was going to lie down. Neil had called to say he was coming out."

"But you didn't see Neil until after four?"

"No. And it had been Nestor's impression he was coming immediately."

"Do you think it was Neil who took the shot at you?"

Joseph laughed. "Neil would have plugged me between the eyes. Look for Mother Bear on that one. I have a feeling she's still fixing his problems."

"Just a feeling?"

"There was another car behind Neil's that day."

A REAL BLANKET of snow meant the beginning of snow-mobile decapitation season, barbed wire playing a big role again in some motorized cowboys' lives. If it weren't his job to pick the pieces out of the snow, he'd cheer them on. As it was, the year's first incident happened just over the border in Yellowstone, and he and the park rangers argued jurisdiction queasily and good-naturedly ("Oh, no, we couldn't possibly take him. You enjoy him.") while waiting for the ambulance on Sunday morning.

Jules dealt with the machines again that afternoon. Late-season elk hunting had begun, and this last batch of snow had opened up more terrain, including one rich flat high above Blue Deer. A hunter had called to report an un-conscious man lying in the snow next to his rifle; when reas-sured of anonymous status (Jules pointed out that if he didn't say his name they'd likely never know it), he told the whole tawdry tale as witnessed through binoculars. Jules found the culprit's pickup at the Blue Bat, complete with an elk cow in the bed.

Bud Mazorski had been a year ahead of Jules in school, and seeing him still gave Jules a pit in his stomach. Bud was nobby all over, with a suave black Prince Valiant cut and an extra hundred pounds since the days when he'd landed on Jules and Divvy during each and every soccer practice. Jules bought the hunter a beer and allowed that the visit was official, albeit (hopefully) relaxed.

Bud liked telling stories. "So there I am, out on the flat, and I shoot this cow elk right through the neck, see her stagger. *Kapow*."

"Kapow," said Jules obediently.

"I haul my large ass over there, have to go down in a coulee and then up again, through the aspen, so I don't see the cow in the meantime. Takes me a good ten minutes to find her."

Jules nodded. He could almost hear Bud moving through the bracken, blowing steam like a bull into the cold morning.

"So I finally get up onto the goddamn flat again, and here's this tiny redheaded asshole gutting my elk, his tag on her."

"Uh-huh," said Jules.

"I say, "What the fuck are you doing?' The guy says, 'I took a shot, too, and I got here first.' Funny accent." Bud smiled and took a dainty sip of beer. "So I watch him for a while and he works away, hauling her guts out. He's doing pretty well for an asshole. I give him a few minutes and I say, 'Are you joking?' And he says, 'Fuck you.'"

Jules sighed.

"I tell you," said Bud Mazorski, "it gave me the giggles."

"I imagine it did," said Jules.

Bud shifted in his chair and lit another cigarette. Jules bought two more boilermakers. "So I figured there was no hurry, let him finish up, and then I popped him, and I tied the cow to his snowmobile, drove it to my truck, got her loaded, and left. End of story."

The hunter from Kansas City had gone down flat on his back, hunting knife still in one hand, cigar in the other. By the time his buddies had found him, the cigar had gone out and the blood on the knife had frozen. "Leaving the Arctic Cat running was a tad spiteful, Bud."

"I figured that dumb shit wouldn't be able to start it on his own when he woke up."

"Let alone walk," said Jules.

"It was an unfortunate occurrence," said Bud.

"Unfortunately, he wants to bring charges."

"It's not like I'm the only man to ever borrow a snow-mobile."

"That a fact?" asked Jules.

"Are you getting sarcastic on me?"

Who was running the interview? thought Jules. The answer was obviously Bud. "Yes, I guess I am," he said.

"Someone took Nuggie Reed's machine from outside of the Rosehip cabin. He trailed that thing five miles, found it all the way over to Mill Creek. When he came back with it he took the distributor cap off the guy's Honda."

"Honda?" said Jules.

"Honda, Toyota, something like that. It's still sitting out there, but Nuggie's got his Ski-Doo back. You might want to tow that piece of shit out before the snow gets any deeper."

"I might," said Jules. "Or I could just send someone in with a distributor cap."

"Nuggie flattened the tires, too." Bud sighed at such mindless violence. "Maybe I should just talk it over with the guy in the hospital, mano a mano."

Jules's eyebrows went up in disbelief. He shook his head slowly. "I'd appreciate you avoiding the hospital. Why don't you just get that animal packed away and we'll see what gives tomorrow."

THE CAR WITH the knifed tires at the Rosehip Creek trailhead was indeed Jump's, and the seat inside was soaked with old blood. After the tow truck headed off, Jules walked down the road, out of the trees and onto the open hillside a few hundred yards from where the coyotes had been playing with Nestor's prosthesis. He was two thousand feet higher than the river and only three miles away; after a few moments he could make out Neil Amundsen's roof.

Jules gave the car to Harvey, and Harvey worried it like a baby on a teething biscuit. He found microfibers from Mary McLinchey's rug, a wineglass with underlying fingerprints belonging to the woman from Billings, and a curly hair that matched those still attached to Flo Amundsen's head. The tires matched the prints from Flo's alley.

Jules was sick of tread prints, fingerprints, all of it. "Did you ever figure out who those other muddy tires belonged to?"

Harvey checked his notes. "Nope."

"Ask the tire store owner if he remembers Neil trading in the tires on that new truck of his."

"He's really sick of us," said Harvey.

"Tough."

SUNDAY NIGHT WAS quiet at the restaurants in town. When Jules showed up at the Baird at nine, Ben had only one table left. "Can I buy you a drink when you're through?" he asked.

She drummed her fingers angrily on her tray. "Why would I want you to buy me a drink?"

Jules smiled. "Well, it's probably more pleasant than heading to the station for an interview."

He walked through the lobby to the bar to wait for her, and managed not to startle when he saw Edie behind the desk.

"How are you?"

"Fine," she said. "Just fine."

"Things okay with Patrick?"

"Actually, they're great," said Edie. "Are you seeing Ben again?"

"No," said Jules.

A dubious expression crossed Edie's face, a look he knew well. He walked into the bar.

Ben wanted a Kahlua and vodka; Jules made a face and had a beer. "What's the point?" she asked.

"Did Neil ever give you anything?"

"Herpes?" she asked wryly. "Chlamydia? Something like that?"

"A gift."

She pulled on her straw and studied him. "You have anything particular in mind?"

"Something small and valuable that might have belonged to someone else," said Jules.

"Meaning I'd have to give it back?"

"Meaning if you have it, and lie, and keep it, you could be an accessory to murder."

She coughed and put down her drink. "Christ, Jules."

He shrugged. "No point in beating around the bush."

Ben studied him. "That's what started that fight," she said. "He wanted me to give this thing back, and when I called him a sack of shit and wouldn't turn it over he hit me."

"Do you still have it?"

She opened her purse and handed him a silk bag. Jules let Nestor's gold coin drop into his hand. "I kept it with me so he wouldn't try to grab it while I was working," said Ben. "Just make sure that prick doesn't come looking for me."

JULES COULD SEE it all, but there wasn't a thing he could do but hold his breath and hope Neil, the trophy collector, didn't clean house. He could imagine the rage, the pillow, probably a frenzy after a pull on the beer when he realized that the old man was still breathing. He'd driven the whale tooth into Nestor's head, then panicked. After the call for help to his mother at the Baird (2:31 p.m., according to the phone company), Neil had thrown Nestor into the wood bin before driving back to town for his hearing, and Flo had returned with him an hour or so later, leaving her mother alone. Together, neither of them icy thinkers, they'd tried to rig a suicide: shoot Nestor in the wound, shoot the dog after he bit Flo, probably while she was helping Neil tug the old man back out of the wood bin and into the Suburban. Neil would have bolted and left his mother with the problem of actually lighting the fire, and her nerve had finally failed. Flo had seen the merest wisp of smoke and run, and the fire had ignited despite her.

It was one thing to have no motive but a weapon, another to have no weapon, no motive, a single phone call, a fingerprint on a beer, a coin that could have been a gift, a lot of muddy tires, and a luxuriant imagination. On Monday morning Jules tried Nina Amundsen, and the answering machine told him that she and Ira had driven to Lincoln to see Nina's sister. They wouldn't be back until Friday, and they didn't leave a number; it would have been easy to call around town and find someone who had it, but Jules forced himself to be patient. Anything Nina had to say would need to be given in person.

JULES SET HIS hopes on Carl Jump, and Carl Jump came through. On Monday morning Neil marched into the station; someone had left a dead gopher on his car hood, and Neil took this as a kind of western Mafia warning. Jules agreed that the gesture seemed malignant and said he'd have everyone keep an eye on the place, drive by a few times a day. If Neil liked, one of the deputies could even escort him home and check the house at the end of the day.

Neil didn't want that much company. Harvey headed down the valley with a duck blind and set up a pleasant camp while Neil was in a hearing. He had the good shift, the sunny one, and didn't see a thing. Jules and Wesley split Monday night; at 2:00 a.m., when they switched, the temperature was only twenty-three. There'd been nothing to see again: no girls, no mayhem, no murderous photographers. A somewhat scary friend of Ed's, an ex-cop from L.A., had contributed nighttime goggles, and a few hours of staring through them put Jules into an unbearable state of paranoia.

Caroline was on the next morning, and when Jules visited she was sunning her face in Harvey's director's chair—the world had warmed up again. She pointed to the mountain above them, where the Rosehip Trail road was visible. "I saw a man walking down that road, and I think he was limping. I saw him twice. Is there any place up there to hide?"

Jules looked through the binoculars and counted a half dozen barns and sheds, not counting the hunting shacks probably hidden by the tree line. "I'll drive up there."

"Do you think that might scare him away?"

"I think it's likelier to push him down here. He had a chance to run away, and it looks like he'd rather have Neil."

He drove around on the driveways and two-tracks off Rosehip for the next hour. At five, he and Wesley settled down by the river together and watched Neil arrive, lugging charcoal and a bag of groceries. At a quarter of six, when it was almost dark, Jules saw some dogwood bushes just below the deck sway, and Wesley made out a solid dark blotch. At six, with the temperature still a balmy fifty, an obviously annoyed Neil came out to start charcoal in the chimney, left one of the French doors to the deck ajar, and climbed back into his car.

Jules and Wesley could still hear the engine when the dark blob started up the hill, and they followed suit. Moving meant they lost sight of the man, and they came around the house from opposite directions for safety's sake.

When Jules peered around the corner to the deck he saw Carl Jump picking at the raw hamburger Neil had left next to the grill, his face illuminated by the glowing briquettes. His left leg was wrapped with an old sheet and he had a large serrated knife in his right hand.

Jules stepped out and aimed. "Put the knife down, Carl."

Jump lurched, startled, and went into a half crouch, dropping the hamburger but not the knife.

Wesley came around the other side of the building.

"Did you see him come out of the house?" asked Jules.

"No," said Wesley, nervous and confused.

"Goddamnit," Jules said, enraged. Jump's face was gray, and his hand was shaking. Jules smelled something bad, and wondered if it was the man's leg. "Goddamnit to hell. Put the fucking knife down, Carl. You're under arrest."

Carl Jump, his eye on Jules's gun, started to lower the knife.

"Wait," said Jules suddenly. "Don't put it down. Throw it in there, through the open door."

Jump froze, completely unnerved, and stared at Wesley; Wesley stared at Jules.

"Carl, I promise your life will be happier if you throw the fucking knife into the house," said Jules, trying to sound reasonable. "Either way you have to get rid of it."

"If I act like I'm throwing it you'll shoot me," said Carl Jump, his voice cracking. "You're looking for an excuse."

"No," said Jules. "You have a knife and I have a gun. I'm not worried about your knife, and I'm not going to shoot you. Throw it through the door."

Carl Jump threw the knife and missed. "Pick it up and try again," said Jules.

"What's going on?" asked Wesley.

"Do it!" yelled Jules.

This time Jump managed. Jules's gun hand began to shake in relief, and the sweat on his forehead cooled in the breeze. He walked forward and cuffed Carl Jump. "Wesley, you better go into the cabin and retrieve the knife, and see if you notice any signs of Mr. Jump having broken in."

"But," said Jump, "I haven't—"

"Don't even talk to me, you horrifying piece of shit," snarled Jules, leading him halfway down the hill and cuffing him again, this time to a tree. "I thought you were human. I hope you never see your dog again."

Wesley was standing by the door, acting as if it was electrified. "What's going on?" he asked again.

"We're retrieving the rapist's weapon," said Jules.

The knife had gone behind some wood stacked by the

fireplace. Above the fireplace, as before, were Neil's and his father's trophies; this time Jules walked closer to the one he found particularly interesting.

"That's a sperm whale tooth," he said matter-of-factly. "I looked one up in a book just last week."

Wesley approached the tooth and raised his hand. "Don't touch it," said Jules. "Nestor owned one, and his happens to be missing, and this seems like it would be about right for the hole someone put in his head. Isn't that a coincidence?"

"Yes," said Wesley, peering at the ivory.

"I think we'll need to test it. And I think we should get a warrant and search this place. Don't you?"

"Yes," said Wesley slowly, "I guess we'll need to do that. But maybe not quite yet."

They heard tires crunch on the gravel outside; Neil pulled into the driveway with the blond girl right behind him. "You could have called," he yelled at her. "I just drove all the way to town for goddamn tonic."

She said "Sorry" without sounding particularly contrite. Neil was still intent upon her as he opened his front door, and he was inside before he noticed Jules and Wesley just a few feet away.

"What are you doing?"

Jules smiled at Neil. "It's a long story. I suppose your grandfather gave you that tooth out of the kindness of his heart?"

Neil looked at the mantel, then the other men. He started to speak, stopped himself, swung the bottle of tonic onto Wesley's head and was gone.

For some reason he headed away from the river, through the prairie grass, not reasoning out the fact that the grass ran more up than down for five miles before it hit a meaningful tree that might serve as a hiding place. Jules yelled and followed, his feet almost soundless on the damp soft clay soil.

Neil was ten years younger, and it was just possible that his conservatism had dictated a healthier lifestyle than Jules's. But Jules ran on hatred and longer legs, and he had the advantage of being able to see the other runner.

"Stop!" he screamed for the second time when he was only ten feet away.

Neil kept going. Jules didn't want to shoot him; he wanted to feel smug and beyond blame when he hauled the shit in. They were approaching a dry irrigation ditch, and Neil slowed. Jules accelerated and jumped, wrapping one arm around the other man's throat before they even landed. Neil brought his elbow up into Jules's broken nose; Jules screamed, pinned and flipped Neil, and hit him twice on the side of the head. Then he simply sat for a minute and tried to breathe.

Wesley panted up, and Jules rolled off, feeling his face. Wesley was cuffing Neil with blood running into his eyes from the cut in his scalp.

Jules stood shakily. Smugness had lost part of its appeal, and he kicked Neil in the ribs.

"DON'T LET HIM make a call," he said for the third time. "Just slow it all down."

"Carl Jump?" Archie was a mess; two men in one hour in an overcrowded jail, one of them the judge's grandson.

"Carl Jump doesn't have anyone to call. You can give him the phone for the night."

Caroline and Ed had both come to help, and she was trying to talk Jules into having his nose reset sooner rather than later. "If you don't go in right away you'll look even funnier."

"Thanks," said Jules. "Thanks a lot."

"I didn't mean it that way," she said, stricken. "I meant since the last break."

Jules made a snorting sound that proved quite painful. "As opposed to the first?"

Ed brought him another cold washcloth.

Flo wasn't home, and Jules called Jetta. "She's staying with her father. Why?"

"I'll tell you later," said Jules.

But Miles Birdland opened his own door and led them to the back of the house. "She went to the grocery. She's making apple butter and she ran out of lids or jars or some such."

The kitchen was dark and smelled of burned sugar; pots and pans were piled on the counters. Birdland rocked on his feet. "I generally avoid this room. Flo seems to live here these days. Have you come to get her?"

Caroline looked down, overwhelmed. "Yes," said Jules. "We have. Neil's down at the station, too."

"I suppose I'll have to visit then." He turned off a burner under a pot of water.

"Did she leave for the store long ago?" asked Caroline.

"It takes her a very great time to do simple things," said Miles Birdland. "I prefer that you arrest her there. I can't help her anymore, and I can't bear to look at her."

When Jules turned the car off in the supermarket parking lot neither of them moved for a minute. When they first saw Flo she was moving along the dairy aisle, then looping past the deli and down along the meat. When she headed for the vegetables Caroline got goose bumps and blamed it on the refrigeration.

"Bullshit," muttered Jules as they finished the first leg of the second loop. "Is the refrigeration making me dizzy?"

They waited for her to circle back to produce, then approached slowly as she finally paused in front of the canning lids. They were ten feet away when she focused on them.

"Are you here to buy wine?"

"No," said Jules. "We're not."

"Birth control?" She smiled.

Jules shook his head.

"I bet you can be fired for fraternizing. I'll check."

Jules took a step closer. "Flo, we're here to arrest you as an accessory to murder."

She flinched and reached toward the stack of canning lids. "Who am I accessorizing?"

"Your son."

Flo lifted her head. "I did it myself. I did it all myself."

"I'm afraid that we have proof that Neil at least started things. He's at the station now."

That was when she started to scream.

BLUE DEER BULLETIN
SHERIFF'S REPORT, WEEK OF NOVEMBER 7–13

November 7—A woman called to report loud meowings from behind her house in the early morning hours. She was concerned it might be a bobcat or mountain lion. An officer responded and found no evidence of such.

Numerous petty incidents were reported.

November 8—A report was received of an airplane attempting to land on US 89 near Clyde City in heavy wind.

November 9—A caller reported a dead rabbit on the sidewalk in front of his home. He was concerned that his children would see the animal and be upset. An officer advised him to put the rabbit in the trash.

November 10—A caller reported the theft of a Weed Eater and a stroller from her yard.

A possible DUI was reported on Hinchkrieg Road. An individual with a car phone followed the erratic Suburban until a deputy could catch up.

November 11—No incidents were reported.

November 12—A woman reported that her dog started to bark in the middle of the night, and she discovered her kitchen window had been opened. An officer is investigating.

November 13—A person called from Orlando, Florida, to see if his car was parked in his driveway. The vehicle was not on the premises.

An individual reported seeing a deranged man walking down a street with an ax. An officer talked to the man.

HE HAD THEM IN JAIL, FINALLY, THOUGH STILL with only the vaguest knowledge of what had spurred Neil to murder his grandfather. It was clear Flo didn't have a clue, either; she kept trying to say that she'd killed Nestor, but it was patently obvious she didn't know what she was talking about, didn't even know that the old man had been smothered first, or what had made the hole in his head, or that the gold coin and the belt buckle had been taken.

THE ACHES WERE due for a real treat Wednesday night, though of course for thrills nothing could compare to the arrest of a member as an accessory to murder, or to finding a body the previous week. Dr. Hans Craitson, the ever-charming obstetrician/gynecologist, would be talking about how the practices they were all familiar with had changed over the years. Laura and Jetta had donated a case of wine left over from the anniversary party, Ella's nephew had shipped some Dungeness crab out from Seattle, and Alice had put together some tea sandwiches and mixed one hell of a punch.

Alice and Caroline and Cicely set things up in the newly painted music room, where one corner, an exhibit of sewing machines, already looked like a museum. Nothing was too good for Hans, Cicely told them. Half of them had slept with him, and the other half adored him in a platonic, reverential way.

"And which are you?" asked Caroline. She'd gotten a bit snippy since she'd questioned her grandmother. Cicely had admitted to knowing Joseph and had explained nothing.

"Maybe you should start having your own fun," said Cicely.

By eight o'clock, when Hans Craitson began his speech proper, Alice and Caroline were mildly looped and had monopolized the crab salad to an embarrassing degree.

"I will admit to having recommended hysterectomies as a blanket solution to all sorts of problems in the past, but for a long time it really was the safest action. Ovarian cancer, cervical cancer, all of them had a horrible survival rate. Still do. So, beginning in the mid-thirties, we just started jerking the works."

Craitson smiled, they smiled. Alice leaned toward Caroline. "I'd love to see him try that line in a room of New Yorkers."

"Everyone would be lacking a sense of humor."

"Kinda a western concept anyway, 'the works.'"

Caroline started to giggle, her third glass of wine heating her cheeks.

"But it would be a mistake to think a doctor in my position only dealt with illness and babies. A good part of my job involved counseling women who'd been abused, especially in the days before they considered calling the police on their own. So I would call the police, apprise them of the situation and possibly ask their help in arranging a graceful exit for a woman. Which we did on several occasions."

"I can imagine how they handled the husbands," whispered Alice.

"This was, of course, in the days when a judicious use of police brutality came in handy," said Craitson.

The ladies laughed, then glanced at Caroline, who smiled nervously. It was all slightly surreal.

"And then there were the rapes."

"It's just as well Flo isn't here," said Angelina.

"The worst thing that can happen to a woman," said Mabel, shaking her head.

"I always thought it would be to have her child die," said Angelina.

"Well, of course," snapped Mabel. "That's not what I meant."

Craitson ignored them. "People think of rape as a modern crime. We all know it's not."

It was the sort of thing they loved to whisper about, then drop like a hot potato. Alice covered another cracker with crab. "Sometimes propriety is harmful, and sometimes the safeguards of a small town fail. I'm sure many of you remember the unfortunate occurrences we had in the late thirties. I saw five women over the course of two or three summers, and though they would not name the man who attacked them, I had suspicions and passed them on to the police."

Alice, surprised, dropped some precious shellfish in her lap. "The police knew? I never saw a thing about it in the papers," she blurted out. "You still won't talk about it."

"Of course you didn't read about it," said Venus. "It never has been worth discussing."

"If we'd discussed it then there'd be some happier women today," said Craitson sweetly.

"Some of the bravery of the younger generation was lacking then, understandably, and the situation was, anyway, very different," said Venus.

"How so?" asked Caroline.

"We all knew the man, or some of us did," said Venus. "But none of us really knew how far it had gone. Mabel knew about the poor girl in town, for instance, and Cicely knew about the maid."

Indabel Whitsan stood and left the room.

"Now that Indie's and Ettie's brother has been identified anyway, why be quiet about it?" asked Craitson softly. "Surely the Whitsan girls aren't to blame for their brother."

"No one did us a kindness by staying quiet, even at the time," said Ettie. Her vagueness had almost entirely disappeared in the last week.

"Henry Whitsan raped some women and no one reported him?" asked Alice, offended by the idea that she'd wasted sympathy and effort on such a man. "He's the one you've talked about before?"

"He had a problem with anger, and he felt above the law," said Venus.

"And he was right," said Caroline, turning to her grandmother. "You're just telling me this now?"

"We thought he'd left and the problem was solved," said Mabel. "It was a very difficult situation."

"I wish someone had put him out of his misery," said Ettie.

"Someone did," said Cicely dryly. "They just didn't do it soon enough."

CAROLINE DIDN'T GET around to telling Jules about what had been said at the meeting until the next day at lunch.

"Were they talking about it as if it was a rumor or fact?"

"More than a rumor, and only less than a fact because none of them wanted to own up to really knowing. For obvious reasons." She was watching the coffee machine drip again, very tired. "I suppose I should pin my grandmother down."

"I can, if it makes you uncomfortable. Where is she?"

"Right now?"

"After we have more coffee," said Jules.

CICELY WAS ORGANIZING Craitson's equipment with Alice, the two of them making bad jokes about turn-of-the-century forceps and gynecological umbrellas. Jules didn't want to hear about it, and they got off to a bad beginning. Cicely was annoyed, as if Caroline had committed a trespass by mentioning the previous night's conversation.

"It doesn't matter how long he's been dead," said Jules. "It's still my business to find out why and who."

"Did you ever read *Murder on the Orient Express*?" she asked acidly.

"I've already been told there might have been several volunteers," said Jules with a nasty grin. "But I'd like to hear what you have to say, especially if you took a turn with the gun."

Cicely opened a box and lifted out some old glass hypodermics.

"Who did he rape?" asked Jules.

"Why ask?" The question was sharp.

"We've been over that. Think of the question as official."

Cicely raised an eyebrow and shook out an old hospital gown. "He beat his mother's maid, a Finnish girl, but word had it that he did not actually rape her. He did rape another girl the next spring, a cousin of his visiting from Massachusetts. There was a silly girl he was seeing in town, the one who nearly burned down the Memphis when she killed herself; who knows what happened there. He raped another maid, an Indian girl who'd always lived on the ranch, and the same summer he was rumored to have raped a Norwegian girl."

No one said anything. "Don't look at me like that," said Cicely to Caroline.

"None of his friends did anything?"

Cicely wrinkled her nose in disgust. "It wasn't as if Henry paid for an advertisement in the paper. It took everyone months to realize how bad it was. After the cousin, I know that Joseph and Miles gave him what for."

"What's 'what for'?"

"Beat him. Actually threw him down a hotel staircase, managed to break his ankle, crack his pretty head." She opened another box and looked at Jules sternly. "Don't think your uncle or any of us thought lightly of it."

"But no police?"

She shrugged. "Miles was a deputy then. They knew. There wasn't enough to go on."

"What was the Norwegian girl's name?" Jules asked softly.

"I see no reason to be specific after all these years."

"I see no reason not to."

"Nina Nissen."

"Nina Amundsen?"

"Yes."

"'Norwegian girl,'" said Jules sarcastically. "You knew Nina. I've seen photos of you together, with Nestor and Joseph and Miles and Ruth Birdland at cuttings, along with all three Whitsans. Was the Indian girl Lily Gray Crane?"

She opened another box. "The name Lily rings a bell."

"Did you know her brother, Malcolm?"

Cicely looked at him coldly. "I don't recall meeting any-one by that name."

"I guess no one would have introduced you," said Jules sarcastically. "But maybe Lily served you lemonade, and you sure as hell knew who that man in the trunk was within a second after we flipped the lid."

Cicely pursed her lips.

"So what happened?" asked Jules.

No reaction.

"I can ask Nina."

"That'll make her day," said Cicely dryly. "Henry left. That was the end of the matter. Nina was engaged to marry Nestor, and they went ahead with it."

"Did everyone see him off at the train?" asked Jules. "Or did everyone take turns shooting him?"

"Spare me your irony."

"Was Joseph covering for himself, or Nestor, or Miles, or someone else?"

"He never whispered that particular secret in my ear," said Cicely.

THAT AFTERNOON JULES forced himself to clean his desk, and while he wallowed through forgotten problems he thought of Malcolm Gray Crane, dying for his sister; no wonder, half a century later, people remembered him more fondly than the other murdered man. Jules left a message with Patrick Ankeny to tell Lily White Button that she could have her brother's body, then called Indie and Ettie and told them Henry was theirs if they wanted him. He looked at the photos again as he tucked them into the files, thinking of how familar dead men could become: Malcolm Gray Crane had looked a good deal like his great-nephew

Patrick, without the added white blood; Henry Whitsan's young face and skull echoed still in Ettie Whitsan's high smooth forehead and pale blue eyes, eyes that happened to be the same color as Ankeny's.

The living and the dead were rolling together in a great snarled ball. Ankeny's eyes brought him to Edie, Edie brought him to Caroline, who was humming on the far side of the room, reading that day's paper. On the front page, facing Jules, was a huge photo of Neil Amundsen at his arraignment. He looked oblivious, arrogant, above it all; he looked as if he expected the world to shine his shoes for free. His eyes seemed paler in the black-and-white photo than they were in real life. Neil was fond of boasting about his "baby blues." His eyes were the same color as Patrick Ankeny's, but Neil was washed out, insipid in comparison.

Jules looked again at Henry Whitsan's skull and photograph, then turned back in confusion to his report, the final tucking away of a tall, blue-eyed blond who'd been rumored to rape a number of women, including a Native American maid and a local Norwegian girl. Lily Gray Crane and Nina Nissen Amundsen had lived on that same drainage during the same year, and they'd each ended up with tall grandsons who had pale blue eyes. Jules turned from the page to Neil to the skull with the centered bullet hole holding down paperwork on his desk. He slid open his drawer, rummaged through his search-and-rescue file, and found a photo taken of all of them for the paper that summer, Ankeny grinning in the aftermath of some stupid joke Peter had told. Neil and Patrick, two entirely dissimilar men; he'd thought they reminded him of each other solely because of jealousy, but now he saw the same forehead, the same height, the same eyes. Their grandfather, a rapist and wastrel, sitting jawless on his desk.

Across the room, Caroline folded the paper and met his eyes, puzzled enough by his expression to turn to see if he was actually looking at something behind her. Flo had told Jetta that Nestor might lose the ranch because someone else really owned it. Maybe what Nestor had said was that someone else deserved to own it, that he wanted the ranch to go to the boy he'd put through college, the boy he actually liked, the boy whose real grandfather had owned the land. Neither Ankeny nor Neil was his blood, anyway, and Neil, with his patent selfishness and way of treating women, must have reminded Nestor of someone he'd hated and quite likely killed.

Jules finally understood why Neil had murdered Nestor Amundsen, even though Flo, who'd helped her son clean up the mess, hadn't known why. Maybe Neil hadn't trusted her with the final secret; maybe he didn't actually know who the other grandson was.

"Are you okay?" asked Caroline.

JULES WALKED DOWN to the jail. Neil was reading that day's sports page.

"Do you know why Nestor decided not to give you the ranch?"

Neil didn't look up. "I don't know what you're talking about."

"Yes you do. Did he just say he wasn't giving it to you, or that he'd found someone else who made more sense?"

"I am my grandfather's heir."

"It's not like you needed the money," said Jules. "Do you just not take rejection well?"

Neil turned the page.

"I know who's going to get the ranch," said Jules. "But I

don't think Nestor actually told you, because if he had you would have killed this man, too."

Neil turned, annoyed, and brushed a pretty lock from his high, severe forehead, his deep-set light blue eyes glaring. "I'm going to see you unemployed. I'm going to see you in the gutter."

"Anyone ever tell you look like Nestor?" asked Jules.

"Never," said Neil.

"I didn't think so." He smiled. "You know, I've got you now."

"FIFTY-FIFTY HE'LL GET off," said Peter.

"We'll get more," said Jules. "Don't forget Flo's natural urge to discuss everything. Counselors think confession is good for the soul."

They were waiting outside Miles Birdland's house. Birdland had asked Peter for a ride out to Joseph's, where the poker game was being held that night. Peter had barely survived the shock of the request.

The porch light came on and all the interior lights flicked off. Birdland's tall, skinny frame moved slowly toward them down the sidewalk through the snowflakes, and for the first time Jules thought of him as a widower, alone in a house after a half century of company.

"So," said Birdland, folding himself into the passenger seat. "Law and order, off for a spot of gambling. Here's hoping none of your people pull us over on the way home."

"Here's hoping," said Jules. Jonathan was on duty that night.

THERE WAS BETTER food than usual at Joseph's: Laura had boiled shrimp and made mozzarella toasts and savory onion tarts. Joseph opened a bottle of burgundy and hauled out his humidor. It was a big table—Merle and Divvy and Axel and Ankeny were there, too—and everyone seemed relieved; Jules knew he should be happy, too.

A few weeks earlier, Jules would never have used Patrick Ankeny to get what he wanted to know, or he would at least have warned him first. But Ankeny would survive; he was the eventual winner in all ways.

The question came apropos of nothing, when Joseph had begun to relax.

"Who was your grandmother's husband?"

Ankeny peered at Jules over his cards. "Ned White Button."

"I remember him," said Merle. "A goofy little guy?"

Ankeny smiled. "Yeah."

"Your dad was Tom Ankeny?"

Ankeny began to look confused. "Right. Still is."

"So where did you get the blue eyes?" asked Jules.

The table stiffened, and Patrick stared. "What the hell has gotten into you?"

"I've got a reason for asking," said Jules. "I really do. And I think some of the people at this table know that." He looked at Joseph; Joseph raised his eyebrows and sorted his hand. Merle, who'd never cared for stress, looked suddenly miserable.

Ankeny glared at Jules for a long moment. "My mother was born before Lily married Ned. I don't know who the guy was. I don't think my mother ever did, either."

They played a hand; Jules won with three of a kind. He gathered up the cards and started shuffling. "What's your mom's birthday?"

Ankeny gritted his teeth, determined to be polite. "May second."

"What year?"

"Here we go again," said Axel, slamming down his hand. "It's mental fucking illness."

Ankeny was finally enraged. "Is this about Edie?"

"I'll talk to Lily myself, if you want," said Jules.

"It was 1940. May 2, 1940."

"You don't know why I'm asking?"

"No!" shouted Ankeny.

Jules believed him. He met Joseph's eyes again. "When you met Nestor the week before he died, did he tell you he wanted to give his ranch and the old Whitsan ranch to someone who really deserved it?"

"Enough," said Joseph. He put his hand down carefully and studied Jules. "It's a grand thing, seeing your education pay off. Miles and I told him we thought he was doing the right thing."

Birdland gave Jules a half smile. "Giving Neil things never did work. He had plenty of money, anyway, through Ruth."

Taking things away hadn't worked very well, either. "Does Nina know what Nestor wanted?"

"Nina just needed some time to think it over. She called Laura last night, and she and Ira will be back tomorrow."

Jules looked at Patrick. "See," he said. "Everybody knows everything, except for you and me. Nina Amundsen talk to you lately?"

"She called this morning. I'm going there for dinner Saturday," whispered Ankeny. "What's this all about?"

"In the summer of 1939, a man raped your grandmother," said Jules. "And I think that man, a guy named Henry Whitsan, also shot your great-uncle when he tried to protect her. He then raped Nina Amundsen, and Nestor—I think it was

Nestor"—Jules looked inquiringly at Miles and Joseph, who stared back without expression—"Nestor shot Henry Whitsan. Who was, I believe, your real grandfather."

"Someone raped my grandmother?" asked Ankeny, at sea.

"It wasn't quite like that," said Miles Birdland heavily. "There was a week or two in between. I knew all about it, and I did nothing."

"Stop worrying the thing to death," said Joseph sharply. "You must start enjoying life, Miles. You're about to run out of time."

Axel Scotti, looking rapidly from face to face, covered his ears. "I don't want to know," he said, in real anguish. "I think I'm going to be sick. I shouldn't be told things like this."

"Then shut your ears," said Joseph. "We're not telling you, we're telling Jules. And Patrick, my new neighbor."

A.C.H.S. SPECIAL MEETING
A TALK WITH SHERIFF JULES CLEMENT

. . . But what's interesting to me, in the end, is the way we tend to misjudge people according to their age. We assume people outgrow the more hormonal passions and angers, and while it's possible people incur fewer new obsessions past a certain age, it's also true that a hatred that was once young can stay young.

Of course all of this seems to apply to men more than to women. Women are more pragmatic. A woman would have said "Put the man on a train," or maybe "Chop the man into small bits and feed him to the grizzlies in the park." Either way I doubt anyone would have found the body, as we found Henry Whitsan's. During that poker game I learned that one of you actually disposed of Whitsan's luggage, and I certainly don't expect to find it.

For those of you not privy to the suitcase disposal, this was the way I heard the rest of the story, some of which is quite earthy:

Henry Whitsan truly was an awful human. He got worse as he got older, and he'd been booted from school over some sort of "woman trouble," the kind he was always asking friends—one of whom was a deputy—to help him with. He grew more violent as the summer wore on.

One night his friends were looking over a list for a horse sale when Henry showed up, drunk, and sat down looking pleased with himself. One of the friends asked if he'd been with a girl—it was that kind of look—and Whitsan said, "Why yes I have, but I got caught." He looked smug, and finally he added, "Don't worry, the bastard's dead."

These friends, who'd protected him for months, now had to face the fact that they were to blame for another man—Malcolm Gray Crane, who you all saw in the trunk—being murdered while trying to save his sister. It's hard to feel sympathy for the friends: they'd looked the other way, and in doing so allowed several women to go through great pain. This time, too, they avoided coming clean: They decided that Henry Whitsan should truly pay for their silence by deeding over the remainder of his property and by promising to leave town. Two of them got land, and the third got enough money to go to school, get married, put money down on the place in town. They provided for the dead man's sisters, and everyone else who guessed the truth looked the other way. One friend tucked away the body without telling the location to the others, and that was that.

As I said, Henry Whitsan was supposed to leave town. But he kept bingeing, and the friends kept missing their chance to ship him out in between. The situation lost its urgency over the next couple of weeks; they were drinking quite a bit themselves, and the friend who'd been closest to the dead man humiliated Whitsan whenever possible, which was often. He caught him in a back hall of a bar with a girl and hauled him out to the street with his pants around his ankles, told everyone Henry had lost his money, told everyone he'd been kicked out of school. This man, Nestor Amundsen, always minded that he'd not gone to college.

At any rate, Whitsan hit a relatively sober point, when the friends weren't paying attention, and he decided on a last stop before he left town. He raped and beat the girl Nestor Amundsen loved.

Nestor told his friends later that when he came back to the ranch he didn't shoot Henry Whitsan right away, but hauled him up onto the flat, beating him. Henry Whitsan wouldn't apologize, wouldn't stop laughing. Nestor told them he felt dizzy up there on the hill, and finally, he shot Whitsan. One of the friends buried him, and that was the end of the story for fifty-five years, until the body was discovered and Nestor Amundsen decided to come clean and give the ranch to Malcolm Gray Crane's great-nephew, Patrick Ankeny.

THANKSGIVING WAS AT JOSEPH AND LAURA'S THAT year. Jules tried to talk his way out of going in favor of Peter and Alice's, but Olive wouldn't hear of it, actually began to cry, and he capitulated.

Everyone tried to act normal, but there were no easygoing arguments, no snitting about someone's picking at the turkey or someone else's not knowing how to set the table.

Jules spent the early part of the afternoon hiding out in the barn with Jetta and Axel's boys, shooting hoops and throwing darts in the partially heated stable. Later he sat in the sunroom with Miles Birdland, another guest who was not quite at ease, and they talked about the judge's days on the CCC in Glacier Park and about how there really had still been wolves up there in the summer of 1936. When Joseph and Laura started to argue in the kitchen, Jules bribed one of Jetta's sons to bring them a nice Barolo and two glasses, and they sipped it in the weak afternoon sun.

Since they had never been in the habit of being social, Jules hadn't realized that Birdland tended to get emotional when he drank. Of course, his wife was dead, his daughter and grandson in jail—he had plenty of excuses. Birdland said he was sick of it all, sick of dealing with ugly people, sick of trying to make unreasonable people happy and never feeling that way himself. He was going to retire, and travel to the beautiful places in Europe—Ruth would never go anywhere—and maybe come back and write a local history or two. Or maybe just garden.

And then he wanted to talk about Nestor. "What bothered him, when I saw him that night before he died, was nothing about how our mutual grandson or Florence might feel about being disinherited. He'd started having dreams again once you found the body, and he couldn't get the sounds Henry made out of his mind. He couldn't believe he'd gutshot a man and left him to die."

"Well, he didn't," said Jules.

"Oh, yes he did," said Miles Birdland. "Twice in the stomach. Maybe that part floated down the river so you couldn't tell. He died on the way to town."

"Well," said Jules sarcastically, "that shot in the head helped."

Birdland took a minute to speak. "In the head."

"Yes sir," said Jules. "We found two bullets in the pelvis, just as you say, but there's also a hole in this skull, right above and between the eyes. Close range, very deliberate."

"Perhaps after the fact."

Jules stared at him, astonished by this queasiness in a hanging judge's sensibilities. "Maybe, but not by much," he said slowly. "It's something you can tell, even all these years later. Someone put him out of his misery."

"Ah, God." Miles Birdland began to cry.

"Come out and help me get the extra chairs," said Joseph from the doorway.

Birdland covered his face with his hands.

A nice holiday, thought Jules, following obediently. Maybe he should subscribe to the Birdland retirement-travel plan, start digging up pottery shards again. Neither of them had a compelling reason to stay in Blue Deer. A small town's memory had a longer, deadlier half-life than uranium; some things that happened could never be left behind. "Out of the past" might be a romantic way of putting it, but a simpler statement would be that bad things didn't usually go away. They popped up years later like a congenital heart problem, or a lie told in the first year of marriage that eventually destroyed the silver wedding anniversary, or shrapnel working its way into a lung. The flaw, the lie, the sliver needn't be compounded to destroy.

Jules and Joseph walked in silence across the mucky barnyard to the shed where Laura kept the extra chairs. The old gray cat, Max, followed just behind them. The dogs were crazed with boredom, and the yearlings in the fenced barnyard were skittish in the falling temperature and the beginning snow. The animals feinted with one another, the dogs nipping at Max and then the horses, the colts coming closer and closer to the men with each pass.

"It's good to see the mess put to rest," said Joseph in the shed, handing out chairs. "It's good to have things back to normal."

"We'll do fine as long as you don't try to pretend it never happened," said Jules.

"If that's how you want to be," said Joseph.

"It's not a question of want," said Jules. "Short of a lobotomy, I can't pretend. You always advised against it."

Outside the shed, the youngest setter began to bark at the cat, and the horses started kicking and farting and carrying on.

"I don't want to second-guess you," said Jules. "I don't necessarily want to ever bring it up again. But why the hell didn't you just tell me the truth?"

"Jules, I know it was wrong," said Joseph. "The point is that I don't care. I never have. And I don't believe in hell, either."

He started across the barnyard with two chairs, Jules with three, both of them sliding in the cold, slippery mud and snow already covering their shoulders. Jules took away one of Joseph's chairs without comment when the older man staggered again.

"Ask the puppy to lay off Max, okay? They're too goddamn near the horses."

"The puppy's fine, except for the barking," said Joseph. "Couldn't take her for a walk this morning. I was too busy helping Laura clean up for this shit show. She could have been yours, you know. That's twice you haven't taken me up on the offer."

"I don't deserve a dog right now," said Jules. "Too much

work. But call her off. Max's sick; he can't walk straight. Have you taken him in?"

"I can't walk straight, either. Max's old. That's what they'll tell me.

"You pay a fortune for the dogs and horses at the vet's."

Joseph paused to rest, snowflakes powdering his white hair. "He's fourteen, Jules. I paid a fortune for him when he was five and some asshole filled him with buckshot. I had him neutered, got his shots every year, got him shaved when he tried to kill a porcupine." He swung the chair weakly at the barking dog. "Shut the fuck up, Zilly. I've got one of those headaches."

"What does Horace say about them?" Jules tried to cut between the prancing horses and the crazed puppy and the maddened, arthritic cat, but Max kept wavering between.

"Horace says I need to learn to handle stress." Joseph started to laugh, a throaty, exhausted rattle. Max darted for the fence, hit a tree stump and veered off. The puppy charged in, not truly daring to touch the cat but close enough for Max to summon up enough energy to sprint directly under a bay colt's feet.

Jules heard the sound before his eyes could take it in. "Goddamnit," he yelled, running, swinging a chair at the horses. "I told you. I told you." The hoof had pushed the cat halfway into the mud. Jules knelt down and touched him, and the cat looked back.

Joseph came up behind them. "That tears it," he said.

Zilly started to bay. "Shut the fuck up," screamed Joseph, heading for the barn. When Jules looked up again from the calm, dying cat his uncle was on his way toward them with his Colt.

"No," said Jules. "Let's take him inside. He's not feeling anything. This isn't the way to do it."

"What, put him on the feast table? Get out of my way," said Joseph.

The cat looked up at the man and the gun and started to yowl. This time Joseph screamed at Jules. "I said get the fuck out of my way!"

"No," said Jules, still crouched next to Max.

Joseph clipped him with the chair and knocked him over into the mud. Jules watched the old man lean down until the gun was six inches from the cat and pull the trigger without turning away. And suddenly, sliding and scrabbling to his feet, he saw it all.

"You murdering son of a bitch! You get headaches back then when something was shot, when something made noise?"

Joseph turned to him, blue eyes still chilly but tears running down his face, then picked up his chair and started walking toward the house.

"I remember now," said Jules, following. "With Merle that day you talked about somebody putting Henry Whitsan out of his misery, and I remember thinking it was an odd choice of words. He wasn't miserable, he *caused* misery. But you meant it literally."

Joseph kept walking, knuckles white around the chair back, the Colt in his pocket.

"You never meant to take Henry Whitsan to the doctor. He didn't die on the way to town."

"Henry Whitsan was the scum of the earth."

"You shot him between the eyes," said Jules. "Someone you grew up with. How dare you call anyone else the scum of the earth? Was he screaming like that? It wasn't Nestor the noise bothered, it was you. Nestor gutshot him in a rage, but you finished him off because you knew best."

Joseph wheeled and swung the chair again, hitting Jules on the side of the head. Jules rocked on his feet, shoved Joseph down into the mud, and fell on his knees with his head bleeding. They watched each other, the puddles icing up, snow watering the blood and turning pink.

"You break my heart," said Jules. He stood and pulled Joseph to his feet. They were all watching from the steps, Laura approaching hesitantly, not sure if she should help Joseph or stay away. When Joseph walked inside she and Jetta followed, and Olive finally spoke.

"Jules, what's happened?"

He shook his head.

"Well, come in and wash up, then, and bring those chairs. Dinner's almost on."

He shut his eyes.

"Jules," she said softly. "Don't walk away from it. Come sit down for dinner."

Jules opened his eyes and studied his mother's sad, worn, intelligent face. "I will," he said.

He buried the cat first.

Acknowledgments

I'd like to thank everyone whose help made it possible for me to work during the last two years, including Stacy Sandler, Grace Johnston, Geri Lester, Kathleen and Dan Kaul, Marnie Gannon, Anna Harrison, and Steve and Will Potenberg. I'd also like to thank Cindy Murphy and Jan Kimmel for their way with words.

© John Potenberg

JAMIE HARRISON has lived in Montana for more than thirty years. She is the author of the Jules Clement novels as well as the novels *The Center of Everything* and *The Widow Nash*, the winner of a Reading the West Book Award and a finalist for the High Plains Book Award. Find out more at jamieharrisonbooks.com.